FAREWELL, MAMA ODESSA

FAREWELL, MAMA ODESSA

A NOVEL

EMIL DRAITSER

Northwestern University Press
Evanston, Illinois

Northwestern University Press
www.nupress.northwestern.edu

Excerpts of this book appeared, in somewhat different form, in the *Los Angeles Times*, *Jewish Literary Journal*, and *New Press Literary Quarterly*.

The characters in this book are fictitious; any resemblance to actual persons is wholly accidental and unintentional.

Printed in the United States of America

10   9   8   7   6   5   4   3   2   1

Library of Congress Cataloging-in-Publication Data

Names: Draitser, Emil, 1937– author.
Title: Farewell, Mama Odessa : a novel / Emil Draitser.
Description: Evanston : Northwestern University Press, 2020.
Identifiers: LCCN 2019027255 | ISBN 9780810141087 (trade
    paperback) | ISBN 9780810141094 (ebook)
Subjects: LCSH: Jews—Soviet Union—Emigration and immigration—
    Fiction. | Jewish refugees—United States—Fiction. | Jewish
    refugees—Italy—Rome—Fiction. | Soviet Union—Emigration and
    immigration—Fiction. | United States—Emigration and immigration—
    Fiction. | LCGFT: Biographical fiction.
Classification: LCC PS3554.R187 F37 2020 | DDC 813.54—dc23
LC record available at https://lccn.loc.gov/2019027255

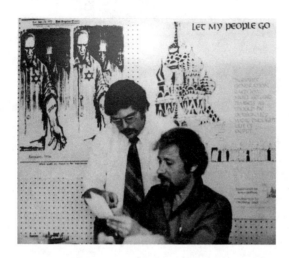

To Si Frumkin and Zev Yaroslavsky and, through them,
to all people of goodwill, Americans and people of other nationalities,
who took part in the protest movement on behalf of Soviet Jewry

CONTENTS

FROM THE AUTHOR

In 1967, after the Six-Day War between Israel and Arab countries, the Soviet Union, which supported the Arabs, broke diplomatic relations with Israel. While the Israeli victory became a source of pride for Soviet Jews, it caused the Soviet government to launch an anti-Zionist (read: antisemitic) campaign inside the country. This development came on top of a double whammy for Soviet Jews. Like all Soviet citizens, they led the hopeless lives of disenfranchised people, while also being subjected to official discrimination, regulated by secret instructions, in getting higher education and employment.

Pressured by human rights campaigns on a global scale, especially in America, to allow Jewish emigration, and dependent on trade with the West and Western technology to sustain their stagnant economy, the Soviet powers-that-be raised the Iron Curtain a bit. To save the Soviet system's ideological face ("no one in their right mind wants to leave the best country in the world!"), the government used the facade of "family reunification." Soviet Jews could receive invitations from nonexistent relatives in Israel, which made them eligible to apply for emigration.

Suddenly, it became advantageous to be a Jew in a country that had long practiced discrimination of its Jewish minority. Some Soviet citizens searched their genealogical tree in hope to find some Jewish branch or at least a leaf. A black market of bogus marriages to Jews flourished.

To pretend any Jew who wants to emigrate would be given permission and, at the same time, to slow down the avalanche of applications, the Soviet government created artificial barriers. It met all those who dared to submit emigration papers with state-sponsored ostracism and reinforced bureaucratic red tape, bringing about unwarranted scrutiny. To make it hard to receive such permission, a prospective applicant had to submit a character reference from his place of employment. Often, their bosses subjected them to public humiliation. They called an employees' general meeting where the coworkers shamed them for betrayal of the great Soviet Motherland.

To make granting permission to leave the country unpredictable, they turned the applicants down by citing state security reasons. Thus, a vocal community of refuseniks came into being.

Starting in 1970, the émigrés lucky enough to receive permission headed for Vienna. Those who lived in Moscow or Leningrad could fly there; all others traveled by train to the border station Chop (pronounced to rhyme with "hope"). After going through customs, they took a train to Vienna with a transfer in Bratislava (then Czechoslovakia). Upon arriving in Vienna, all émigrés had a choice. They could proceed to Israel or, if they chose another country, such as the United States, Canada, Australia, New Zealand, or South Africa, they boarded a train to Rome. They stayed in Rome and its vicinities until the entry visas to the country of their choice were processed. Nearly one million Jews emigrated before the fall of the Soviet Union in 1991.

For us, Soviet Jews, the question of where we were going was not the main issue. We didn't care so much where we were going—to Israel, Canada, Australia, the United States. We only cared about whether we were leaving—our main concern was getting out.

It was a risky venture. None of us had any idea what the future had in store. After being stripped of our Soviet citizenship, we couldn't go back. There was no sign the system would ever change. The Soviet Union seemed impregnable, and destined to last forever. We were out on our own, with our skills, our wits, and our terrible inadequacies. And no money.

On behalf of the American government, two nongovernmental organizations, the Hebrew Immigrant Aid Society (HIAS) and the American Jewish Joint Distribution Committee (the Joint), supported us on our way out of the Soviet Union.

The Soviet emigration had a significant impact on the USA, bringing to its shores the progenitors of future talents: gifted scientists, world-class mathematicians, brilliant movie and TV stars, virtuoso musicians, the future inventors of Google, PayPal, and WhatsApp, scores of young

Russian-American writers, and, at one time, the entire US Olympic Chess Team.

This book is my attempt to create a collective portrait of those who took the risk of jumping into the abyss of the unknown, and fled the Soviet Union. It addresses the formidable problem of assimilating to a world so different from the one they had known all their lives. They all faced this new world—full of different cultural assumptions, a distinct economic structure, and an unfamiliar political life based on democratic, not totalitarian, principles.

There was another problem, unforeseen, a question of self-identification. In the Soviet Union, a person was considered to be a Jew based on his or her ethnicity rather than religion. Soviet internal passports included a line (the so-called "fifth item") which identified its holder's ethnicity, e.g., Russian, Ukrainian, Armenian, Jewish, etc. It served the same purpose as the Star of David patch in Nazi Germany—it facilitated singling out Jews. At the same time, several generations of official atheism in the Soviet Union had resulted in an atheistic population, creating a society of non-believers. It led to confusion when Jewish émigrés arrived in the West, especially in the United States, where people are identified as Jews by their religion.

In this collective portrait of Jewish emigration from the USSR, I also try to tell my story. I talk about what drove me to make that fateful decision, what I experienced amid filling out forms, packing my bags, and saying farewell to people and places I had known all my life. When the idea to write about all these things came, over four decades had passed since my emigration. I could write about myself in the autobiographical style, using the first person, but this time it didn't feel right. The young man who left Russia back in 1974 is not the man I am today by any stretch of the imagination. So, I did something different. I wrote about myself in the third person and as two separate characters, the first, Boris Shuster, a young man going through the life-changing upheaval of emigration, the second, his older cousin Ilya, who emigrated to America a few years before Boris and is more settled. Both characters have the same childhood experiences, which mirror my own.

Only three people appear in these pages under their real names. One is my hometown friend, the Odessan poet Leonid Mak; the two others are the American human rights activists Si Frumkin (now deceased) and Zev

Yaroslavsky (now a professor at UCLA's Luskin School of Public Affairs). Many Russian Jewish émigrés, myself included, are forever indebted to these two men for their tireless efforts on our behalf.

The issues facing today's refugees have caused me to reflect on the years of my emigration. Although leaving your native land forever is a tragic event in any human's life, in my case, it's a tragedy that took place more than forty years ago. Often, drama becomes comedy with time. This is why some émigré stories I've included have a lighter tone to them. This assessment comes from the later-day awareness that, unlike the biblical exodus, the passage to the modern-day Promised Land took not forty years, but hardly more than a few months. Unlike their ancestors, the new arrivals weren't born free while roaming over the biblical desert. They still bore the brand of their totalitarian upbringing, and thought and acted accordingly. Climbing out from under the Iron Curtain, they jumped into the abyss of the unknown for the sake of their children and grandchildren, for the sake of giving them a chance to grow up in the Land of the Free.

I'd like to express my gratitude to Adrian Wanner of Pennsylvania State University, Konstantin Kustanovich of Vanderbilt University, and Gavriel Shapiro of Cornell University for their thoughtful reading of my manuscript, valuable feedback, and support of my work. Of course, any factual mistakes in this work are due to my own oversight.

On the writing stage, I received a lot of help from my friends and colleagues. Jennie Redling and Dr. Gary Kern read portions of the manuscript and gave me their valuable feedback. Emily Corvi worked on making sure my native-speaker Russian accent didn't obscure the narrative. Martin Weiss helped to make some Russian cultural tropes comprehensible to American readers. The last, not the least, my brother, Vladimir, was irreplaceable when it came to fighting computer glitches, which always tend to occur in most critical moments. To all my helpers, I'd like to express here, as they say it in Odessa, a "great Russian *merci*" (*bol'shoe russkoe merci.*)

FAREWELL, MAMA ODESSA

PROLOGUE

At the end of the eighteenth century, to secure access to the warm waters of the Black Sea, which made possible year-round navigation, Catherine the Great founded the port of Odessa. Not unlike New York, from its outset it turned into a melting pot of many nationalities. No wonder that when Mark Twain visited it back in 1867, he made a startling discovery. "I have not felt so much at home for a long time as I did when I . . . stood in Odessa for the first time," Twain writes in his *Innocents Abroad*. "It looked just like an American city . . . Look up the street or down the street, this way or that way, we saw only America! There was not one thing to remind us that we were in Russia."

French aristocrats on the run from their revolution planned, erected, and lent their names to Odessa—the duc de Richelieu, Alexandre-Louis de Langeron, Frantz de Volan, and many others. French city rulers, military leaders, architects, engineers, and other masters of trades lived here with their servants and retinue for long stretches of time. Affectionate, they filled the city with many descendants. The easygoing Gallic attitude toward life, the French wit, and a cheerful nature have poured over from their blood into the city itself. Laughter splashes about in Odessans' throats like a young wine in the throats of the inhabitants of a Provencal village.

Thus, Odessans are the French of Ukraine. They are also the Ukrainians, simple-hearted and a bit sly at the same time. And the industrious Bulgarians. And the business-like Armenians. And the stately Greeks. The Italians paved Pushkinskaya Street, one of the most beautiful of them all, shaded by the plane trees and chestnut trees. They lived on it for a long time; it was called Italianskaya Street.

As the city evolved, Catherine the Great invited Jews from all over the Pale of Settlement, where they were prescribed to live, to come over. She wanted them to help in trading grain to European countries. Jews flocked to Odessa en masse; they found their lives here a far cry from the stifling atmosphere of the shtetls where they used to live. It's hardly surprising that soon over a third of Odessans were Jews.

However, while enjoying life in this free-spirited city, they still had to be on guard against any knock on the door. And for a good reason. Time and again the knocks came not from a well-wishing neighbor who came over to borrow a pinch of salt for his soup: Jewish pogroms took place in 1821, 1859, 1871, 1881, and 1905.

Eventually, Odessan Jews had enough. To escape the scourge of the tsar, they took to the city port, boarded ships, and headed overseas. Blessed and prosperous became the nations into which these people poured in an endless stream of close kin. Had they landed above the Arctic Circle, their hearts, beating passionately, thirsting to live their lives to the fullest, would have made the icebergs melt. Wherever they settled, skyscrapers popped up, bridgework steel rattled from rivet guns, the decks of pleasure steamers filled up, and newborn babies appeared, one after another. As soon as those babies could pierce a meatball with a fork, they were handed a violin. Bash it out! Give us what you have! Reach for the stars! The Odessan genes gave America George Gershwin, Bob Dylan, and Steven Spielberg—to name a few . . .

Back then, not all Jews left Odessa. There were those who stayed, unable to tear themselves from the wondrous city. Though one could find grumblers among them, there was not a single whiner. Odessans have always known there are only two reasons for whining: bad weather and poor digestion. It is St. Petersburg where the gloomy breed. What do you expect from people living in a swamp? It is Moscow where sad faces abound. What other faces can people have who don't eat home-cooked broth from a freshly killed chicken, but feed themselves instead at the state-run eateries with pastries stuffed with the entrails of over-aged animals!

It's not surprising that, born in such a vibrant city, having absorbed its free spirit, and imbued with its inhabitants' vigor and cheerfulness, the great Russian Jewish writer, Isaac Babel, celebrated it in his *Odessa Tales*. It is only natural that from this bustling city Leonid Utyosov, the country's first jazzman, ascended to the all-Union glory. The mocking mode of the Odessa spirit, the propensity of Odessans to irony, inspired the best pages of the famous comedic novels the whole country read decades on end—Ilf and Petrov's *The Twelve Chairs* and *The Golden Calf*. On these streets, in the verbal duel between its citizens, the most side-splitting underground jokes took their shape and spread all over the vast country.

Several decades passed, and the time came to flee again from the new scourge called "Soviet power." There was nothing in the world worse than that power, or more repugnant to the free-spirited Odessans. Soviet life was a life filled with countless regulations, endless killjoy Party directives and warning signs of the No-Lying-on-the-Grass type. All this drove the Odessans nuts. What else is grass for, for God's sake, if not for lying on? That power, with its ubiquitous railway-type warnings—No Right Turn, No Left Turn—made their mouths taste like soot. Some demonic power dragged Odessans through a locomotive tunnel, filling their chests with the foul smell of burning fuel.

The day came when the Odessans said to themselves, "Enough! We love to live, and we want to live. Otherwise, we wouldn't have settled by the warm sea, at the edge of vast steppes with millennium-old wormwood overgrowing in the ravines. And the warm sea winds wouldn't wander all over our city like a giggling woman who had sipped young Moldovan wine and picked up a passerby by the armpits and dragged him along the city's streets, straight as a ship's masts."

That such a buoyant city had been part of such a cheerless country as the Soviet Union was a historical anomaly. From time to time, the state had paid for it through overturned police cars, cholera epidemics, and audacious comedy writers who couldn't be straightened out. People read their books in secret: youngsters under their school desks; white-collar city employees during their lunch breaks; train operators through dangerous transits, when they should have been looking at the signals, not in a book.

There is no such thing as a former Odessan. The place is forever in the veins of every person born and raised in that blessed city.

1
THE SACRED SOVIET BORDER

They were on their way to the city of Mukachevo in the Trans-Carpathian Mountains. Boris Shuster, a journalist from Moscow, originally from Odessa, was on assignment. Andrei, a journalist he had met at a local newspaper, was driving. It was warm; crickets were chirping, the air smelled of baked earth. Green slopes stretched away on the horizon. The evening was approaching, but the sky was still bright. Andrei suggested they look at those green slopes. He turned his blue "Muscovite" car onto a side road.

He pulled up to a foothill and stopped, but kept the motor running. Pointing out the window, he exclaimed: "There it is, my dear city slicker! The sacred border of our great nation. Have you ever seen it up close?"

Boris shook his head. A barbed wire fence, about ten feet high, closed off the territory at the base of the hill. Boris wasn't surprised. It was the way he had always imagined it. But seeing it was another story. In front of them was the "sacred Soviet border," as they called it in the press, the one the Americans and other Western foes dreamed of violating. Their dreams were in vain, because the border was impenetrable—"always under lock and key," again as they said in the press.

A wide strip of soil had been plowed up in front of the fence, and it ran off to the left and right into the mountains. It was clear that if any intruder, any spy, and not some careless little bird, were to jump down on this side of the fence, the soles of his heavy boots would leave behind imprints that read "Made in the USA." That's how cartoonists for *Pravda* pictured it.

Andrei started up again and drove along, pointing at the posts. Boris couldn't believe his eyes. The posts were topped with iron spikes, which were not slanted out—to keep foreigners from getting in—but pointed *in*, to prevent citizens from getting out. The plowed-up earth would show if any citizen tried. Now he saw what his friends often talked about. Their so-called freedom was a sham. In reality, they were all inmates. Only the size of their cell was vast; it was a colossal Gulag called the USSR, the Union of Soviet Socialist Republics.

The episode woke him up and made him think about leaving. He felt trapped. He said nothing to Andrei, and Andrei said nothing to him. He went off on his assignment in Mukachevo and filed his report, but the image of that fence, with its iron spikes and its plowed earth, stayed with him through the years.

As a freelance journalist for major Moscow newspapers, Boris had traveled the length and breadth of the land and had seen many things never reported in the papers he worked for. He visited collective farms deserted by peasants who lived in poverty and want. He saw the dejected faces of workers trudging into soot-covered factories, driven by their desperate need. He tasted the putrid lies that permeated everyday life. The thing worse than that was to know he purveyed them as a privileged functionary of the Soviet propaganda machine.

He recalled the time they sent him to cover the opening of a new naphthalene factory. An average person would not want to know about naphthalene, because if you read about it while eating breakfast, you'd lose your appetite for the rest of the day. Boris ruined his shoes in the muck hitchhiking to that factory. He had telephoned the day before. They assured him everything was ready for the opening—he could come. But when he arrived, he found not even a workshop, but only a flimsy awning that covered boxes of equipment sitting out in the rain. The locals took advantage of those unwatched boxes and scavenged them. Someone stole a bearing needed for a water pump; another grabbed a cable that could be used for wiring at home. Some others tore wooden panels off the boxes to fix their rabbit hutches. The factory may come into existence someday, but our poor animals need cages right now!

Stunned, Boris surveyed this bedlam of Russian life in its natural state: a state of grotesque disarray. He cursed his profession and his stupidity in choosing it and concluded it was the most disgusting job in the world. It was worse than guarding political dissidents in prison or arresting them at their homes. The next day, as soon as he reached the office and gulped down some lousy coffee from a thermos, he would pound out the standard hundred lines on his Olympia typewriter: "A modern miracle of technology has appeared in the Don Steppe, an area where until recently you could see only herds of wild horses." Really? Wild horses? When could you see them? Wasn't it in the Mesozoic Era?

No, he wouldn't have the stomach to write the naphthalene factory was functioning. That would be much too far for a man whose mother had told him lying was wrong. He'd do something worse: he'd find a shameful, perverted version of the truth. He'd write that "the builders of the gigantic construction still have a lot to do, but everyone is confident in the success of the Five-Year Plan." But who was everyone? Not Boris—he was not confident. Not the head of the information department, not the executive secretary, not the editor in chief—they were not confident in the success of the Five-Year Plan. No one was. So, everyone was no one. "Soon machinery will make all things possible. It will fill the country with the highest quality goods worthy of the builders of the great future of humanity." Bullshit.

Meanwhile, on the other side of the editorial office, pale women crammed the typing room, women drained of their blood by the grueling work they did to earn next to nothing. Their kindly neighbors watched their kids after school and tried to protect them from all kinds of trouble. Anger and despair filled these typists, and the gunfire of their keys, as if aimed at an invisible foe, pierced the paper.

Boris told himself for a long time that the world was imperfect, no matter on which side of the barricade you landed. This idea consoled him. At one time, he planned to take up a career much less emotionally taxing: to become a librarian. No need to state your politics here! "Do you want Engels's brochure on the origin of the family and private property? Here you are! Sign it out, please. Do you want to read *Queen Margot* by Alexandre Dumas? You are number three hundred and thirty-seven in line. Do you want a manual for the internal combustion engine? I'm more than happy to give it to you. Enjoy!"

However, librarians were paid miserably. Eighty rubles a month wasn't enough for a young man to live on. Besides, the quiet of the library might kill him—inactivity would cause that passionate Odessan blood of his to burst from his veins. In reality, he couldn't imagine leaving the world of journalism, as painful as the profession had proven to be. Nothing could compare to the joy he experienced when, after endless, painstaking rewrites, he would bring his work to the editor's desk and go home to anxiously await the call that let him know it had been accepted and sent to the typesetter. After that, he couldn't wait to go back to the editor's office and correct and sign the proofs still wet with ink. The magic of the printed word always held him captive.

But still, there was the problem of lying. For a while, it seemed Boris had found a solution: switch from reporting to satire. Although you couldn't criticize the state, you could write about "isolated shortcomings" that "slow down our relentless progress toward communism." They called the newspaper satirist to "fight the blemishes of capitalism in people's minds."

These blemishes were plentiful: greed, selfishness, careerism, corruption, boozing, red tape, all the sins. They were lesions and warts on the body politic that disgusted Boris, and he burned them out with "satire's fiery quill," as they called it. He was good at satire. He was born in Odessa, where the air is filled with sarcasm and where irony is the default mode of conversation. If you are in Odessa and hear, "I am beginning to like you," it means, "I am getting tired of you." Only in Odessa could you hear: "May all your teeth fall out, except for one! And may that one ache all the time!"

Odessa was the birthplace of many anti-Soviet jokes, such as:

"Good morning, Rifka Aronovna, how's life?"

"I'm surprised at you, Moisey. What question is that? What, do you live in a different country?"

No one would write anything like that in a newspaper. However, there were ways to vent your disgust toward dreary Soviet existence. Say some factory has produced a compote that causes the shoddy jars it's stored in to explode. Rather than rebuke the factory for its defective goods, which would be boring, you praise the factory for inventing an improved explosive for blasting rocks. If the café "Forget-Me-Not" serves terrible food and the waiters are rude, it's because the café manager protects his male customers' marriages. Because if a newlywed husband, having quarreled with his wife, comes in to eat at the café, he will learn to appreciate what he has at home and will run back to his woman like a puppy with its tail between its legs. The satirical article, also called the feuilleton, was the most readable newspaper genre. The advantage of its style was that the writer wasn't obligated to sing hallelujah to the Soviet authorities. It also spared him from mandatory citing of ideological bigwigs—Karl Marx and Friedrich Engels, Vladimir Lenin and Joseph Stalin, as was expected of a writer of serious articles. All a Soviet satirist had to do was to be amusing and express indignation on behalf of the powers-that-be.

But all too soon Boris realized he was deceiving himself. The kind of satire he produced was not the solution to the problem. To lie means not only to distort the facts but also to avoid telling the truth. Since he wasn't allowed to do it, willy-nilly he created the illusion that neither the dictatorship, inhumane and hypocritical, nor the economic system, helpless and clumsy as a cow on ice, was at fault for the ills of Soviet society—it was the fault of these "isolated shortcomings."

So, had he reached his limit in this genre as well? He did not understand how he could continue what he was doing without losing his soul. He asked the perennial Russian question, "What is to be done?" (*Chto delat'?*).

2

ONE SULTRY EVENING

Late one evening, amid a wild Odessan summer, Yury Bumshtein sat in his apartment on the third floor of a nondescript house on Theater Lane. Although he was thirty-five years old, people still called him by his teenage nickname of Yurik.

He sat in his black boxer shorts, wincing from the cloying fragrance of overripe jasmine wafting in from the street. He was wielding a hammer over a cobbler's last he held between his knees. A fancy lady's bootie, almost done, crowned the last.

"Lyubka, Lyubka, you Jezh-zhe-bel!" Yurik hissed through wooden pins clenched between his teeth. "You terror, you curse!" he went on, hammering pin after pin into the sole. "You'll be shin-ging a different sho-ng shoo-oon . . ."

Each wooden pin got three blows. The first blow pierced the rubber, the second forced the nail deep into the sole, and the third was to keep up the rhythm. The evening was sultry, the air—thick and savory. That overwhelming jasmine aroma made it seem as if each nail punctured his brain. But Yurik couldn't stop hammering; his work held him in a trance. Although it was stuffy in his room, the lace curtains were down, and the silky pink drapes were drawn.

With each stressed syllable, Yurik pounded the heel.

"Oh, you ter-ror, you curse!" he lamented. "Can you believe it? She orphaned her daughter, and the father's still living! Killing her would not be enough! Lyubka, you should be hanged and your body thrown to the dogs!"

Sweat blinded him, but in the heat of labor, he blinked the drops away. When they flooded his eyes, he stuck his face in the crook of his arm, wiped it, and went on working.

"Now you'll sing a different song!" he repeated. "You'll change your ways! We know what kind of woman you are! You don't care how good a man is. Honesty and decency are nothing to you. You're in it for the money. When a man is filthy rich—he's smart, he's handsome, he's great! But when he is just scraping by, you don't care about his thoughts or feelings!"

He pounded some more, mulling over his plan, and resumed:

"No-o-o, Lyubov Gershovna, I'm not someone you can push around. I can stand up for myself. When my father made me sit in his booth for hours watching him perfect his craft, I learned something. You think of yourself as Madama Butterfly, do you? You will stop your mockery soon! You'll stop making fun of me in no time! These boots will sell like hotcakes! They'll beat all the imports from Yugoslavia. Every single pair will sell, and women will keep wanting more. And I won't let them down, Madama Butterfly, or rather Mrs. Ratner, formerly known as Mrs. Bumshtein. You'll want to be Mrs. Bumshtein again, but I won't take you back—I have my pride! I won't live with a woman who cheated on me for fifteen years . . . and still does!"

He banged a pin into the sole of the boot with such force it went in at a slant. He pulled it out, swearing.

"You cheating bitch!" he yelled in a spasm of rage. But then he checked himself. You couldn't call a divorced woman a cheating bitch . . .

"Still," he sputtered, trying to recover his advantage, "a cheater is a cheater. Just look at who she found for herself. An accordionist Arkady! The Butterfly Polka, the Blue Danube Waltz! A miserable entertainment organizer! With permed hair, for God's sake! And a tan on his ugly mug! No wonder, since he's outside doing nothing all day. Entertaining the spa's patrons, they say. He waits for the evening, the sneaky bastard, to feel up other men's wives. He's got it coming!"

Yurik thought he should have told his neighbor Mitka about this guy Arkady the moment he first showed up. Mitka would have kicked his ass for Yurik.

No sooner had Yurik thought about Mitka than he heard a car screeching to a halt outside at the curb. A loud and unfamiliar voice shouted, "What do you grab the wheel for, you drunken lush?"

Speak of the devil, thought Yurik. It must be Mitka returning home from another night of drinking. Yurik stopped pounding the bootie and listened.

A car door slammed, then heavy feet stomped on the asphalt.

"One takes pity on you morons," the unfamiliar voice shouted again, "and this is the thanks he gets. I rescue you from the police, and you get me into an accident. What do you think you're doing, you fuck head, grabbing the steering wheel like that? Is this *your* taxi? Come on! Pay up! I've had it with you!"

Unintelligible gibberish from another man followed these words. After a long pause, Mitka's voice shouted in consternation, "Damn, it's got to be in my pockets! It's got to!" There was an audible sigh and the exclamation, "Oh, hell, I've done it again. I'm broke! I don't have a single kopeck!"

Dead silence. Yurik put down his hammer, got up and ran to the window. He parted the drapes. A cab driver stood there in shock as if a snake had just bitten him in the rear. The driver gaped at Mitka, standing there with a silly expression on his face, and took a swing at him. Mitka managed to pull back in time, and the two men sparred. Mitka was drunk and unsteady, and he took a couple of blows but started laughing.

"Stop tickling me, man! Ha-ha-ha! Believe me, it's all gone. I spent everything I had—on booze! But don't worry, boss. You'll get paid."

The two men were getting nowhere; they slowed down and stopped sparring. The driver was no athlete, and Mitka was so plastered he could hardly stand up. He came up and leaned on the cabbie.

"Please," he jabbered, "help me get over to the door. My woman will pay you. Tip you too, I swear! She always does, every time I tell her. I love you, boss, though you don't steer your boat very well. You change the tack without taking the wind into account."

"You slobbering sot!" yelled the driver in Mitka's face. "You're all a bunch of leeches, rats! Why do the cops keep pampering you in detox houses? They tuck you in at night. They should take you out and kill you! Each and every one. If you don't know how to drink, you should give it up!"

Here the cabbie grabbed Mitka by the throat and started slapping him on top of the head. Nothing sounds quite like a human head, except maybe a watermelon from Kherson when it's slapped to check its ripeness. But you slap a melon tenderly and lovingly like a newborn baby's tushie. A human head, on the other hand, has a higher register. The slapper doesn't care what music he's making.

The driver searched Mitka's pockets as Mitka slumped over his shoulder. Unaware of what was happening, Mitka raised up on his tiptoes, took a breath so deep his chest expanded all the way up to his throat and bawled, "Mashka-a-a-a-a!" While yelling, he slumped back down as the air went out of his lungs.

The front door clanked open, and Mitka's wife came out on the street. She wore a sundress with her broad shoulders exposed. Her face was covered with Nivea Crème for the night. Holding a cigarette in her right hand, shuffling in slippers, she approached Mitka, who had stumbled over to the cab and was leaning on the hood. While he tried to put on a casual smile, she shifted the cigarette to her left hand and punched him with her right one. Mitka whimpered and sagged to the ground. Mashka turned her gaze on the driver.

"So, you brought him back?" she asked.

"Yes, I did," said the driver, stepping up, "and I'd like to get paid."

"Here comes your pay," said Mashka. She raised her arm above her shoulder as if preparing to hammer a nail in the wall and hit him square in the side of the head with her fist. He went down.

Turning her heavy body around, she shuffled back into the house and slammed the door so hard it made the glass window shatter and fall like loose change on the ground.

An eerie silence fell on the street. Mitka was sprawled out on the sidewalk, unwilling to lift his head. The cab driver got up, rubbing his ear and weighing his options. Out of a second-story window, below Yurik, somebody called out to the cabbie below. "How much?"

"Five rubles and eighty-five kopeks," replied the driver, looking up toward the building.

But the person inquiring only cursed Mitka in choice words and slammed the window. However, someone else yelled from a higher floor. Then another. Coins tinkled on the ground. As on past occasions, the neighbors were helping Mitka. Yurik searched his pockets and found some change. He threw his contribution out the window.

Mitka, still lying in the street, raised his head.

"Hey, pal," he called to the driver in a scratchy voice, "did you get enough for the fare?"

"Yeah, I think so," the driver grumbled, picking up change with his right hand and rubbing his ear with his left.

"And that's how I pay up," concluded Mitka, and let his head fall back down on his arm.

The driver collected all the change, poured it into his pocket, surveyed the scene with contempt, and got back in his cab. The Volga started up with a roar and sped off into the night, its tires screeching.

Yurik shook his head and went back to working on the bootie.

"It's OK," he muttered under his breath, "there's still time. I'll show them what I'm worth. Soon . . ."

Nature had failed to make him tall and handsome, and the gorgeous Lyubka, this lush azalea bush in vigorous bloom, was way above him. Yet, he hoped to reconquer his ex-wife's heart. He imagined how, after having sold enough booties to fashion-conscious Odessans, he would go to the department store on Deribasovskaya Street and buy her a heap of dresses. However, on second thought, he recalled that Lyubka was an excellent seamstress and would never wear those ugly, state-manufactured dresses. He realized he had gotten carried away with his imagination and had gone down the wrong path. If he showed up at Lyubka's with those store-bought dresses, she would throw him out on his ear.

But the gears kept turning in Yurik's head. His imagination went back to the starting point and began all over again, springing forward as if in response to the crack of a pistol.

After getting rich from the sales of his booties, he would go not to a department store, but to the best consignment store in town, where sailors returning from trips abroad sell their foreign loot. That's where he would find a Parisian dress with peacock feathers across the bodice, something like the one in the movie *The Umbrellas of Cherbourg*. Buy that dress, and Lyubka would be his again.

And after that, he knew what to do. He would take her to Sochi during the high season. They would dine in a different restaurant every night. They would go to Aul of the Caucasus, the restaurant his pal Zhora talked about so much. Aul is what they call a mountain village, and they did it up that way. They designed the booths like *saklyas*, the native huts of the region, but they had a modern dance floor in the center, with a jazz band playing fiery dances from around the world: the rumba, the samba, the cha-cha-chá. After dancing, the couples would return to their *saklyas* and enjoy delicious shish-kebabs and lyule-kebabs. Waiters in national dress stood in the corners, ready at the first sign—of currency—to break into an enthusiastic dance.

And that's not all he would do. He would buy a baby-blue car, a Zhiguli, and find a leather bomber jacket with a dozen little zippers at some swap meet. He'd drive up to Lyubka's house and toss the car keys on a key chain with a mother-of-pearl fob into her outstretched hands. He imagined her won over by his tremendous success, pulling him to her bosom, hot and smooth as the sunbaked sand at the Luzanovka beach.

At that moment he heard a knock on the door.

"Who's there?" he yelled in vexation. He had one last stitch to pull through the sole, and the bootie would be done. There would only be some final detailing left to do. No one answered. He got up, cursing, and went to the door. He turned the key, but left the chain on, and cracked open the door. Pressing his eye to the crack like a chicken, he froze in amazement.

Out in the hall stood a young woman in a turquoise dress of crêpe-de-Chine with a fancy floral design. She had a bright gold epaulet on one shoulder and held a sparkling diamond-encrusted staff in her hand. She was a copper-haired beauty with green eyes and delicate pale-pink lips. Yurik was entranced.

"Who do you want?" he asked, staring.

"You," she said, putting her hand through the opening and caressing his cheek with a warm palm. A sweet wave of pleasure ran through his body. He discovered he was hungering for a loving touch.

"Who . . . who are you?" he stammered.

"My name is Promise, but my friends call me Maybee."

She smiled at Yurik, but he was in no hurry to undo the chain and throw open the door. Life had taught him to be wary of feminine charm. "Maybee" gave him a dazzling smile, took a step backward, and sunk into the blue wall, leaving Mitka in her place. Mitka's eyes popped from his head, and he bit his lips, trying to keep sober. By his side stood a short, portly man in a beige Shantung jacket and a polo with blue trim. He could have passed for a coach from the Dynamo sports association.

3
VICIOUS CIRCLE

Boris had figured out how he could make fun of the inefficiency of the Soviet system. It was allowed to satirize its "isolated shortcomings." So, one day, he wrote the following story:

The Wheel

I was about to become a grandmother. Any day my grandson or grand-daughter would appear in this beautiful world of ours. Everything had to be ready for the event. And a baby carriage came right after mother's milk in order of importance.

For two weeks I visited Detskiy Mir, a large store for children's products in our city: toys, clothes, furniture. However, every day the section where they sold carriages and strollers was as empty as a vacant lot. I wasn't surprised. Like all other Soviet citizens, I had seen the simplest things disappear from the stores. On any day, almost anything—socks, needles, matches, camera film, handkerchiefs, you name it—whoosh! Wiped off the face of the earth! So, I arrived every morning at five and gave my name to an ad hoc committee of other baby-carriage buyers who had already congregated there. When I asked them to put me on their waiting list, the committee gave me a number—617. They wrote it on the palm of my hand with an indelible pencil so I could show it to the cashier when the time came to pay—as proof I hadn't cut in line.

After a two-week wait, I entered the store one morning and found a big display of these beautiful contraptions, all new and smelling of oilcloth. But they weren't yet put on sale.

Everyone standing in line got upset. "Why are we suffering all this time," people moaned, "if we won't get our strollers?"

I pushed my way through the crowd to the manager's office and, looking him straight in the eye, asked:

"What's the matter, comrade? Why are you dragging your feet? Can't you see we've run out of patience? The baby carriages have arrived, we're ready to buy, so why aren't you selling them?"

The manager was unmoved. "So what if they arrived?" he said. "They have no wheels."

Dumbfounded, I looked back across the room at the rows of carriages. The man was right. Baskets, hoods, and handles, but no wheels.

"We have to pick up the wheels separately," he explained. "But the dispatch station has already assigned all its trucks for today, and we can't get any. Maybe if you took the initiative . . ."

He didn't have to continue. Like every Soviet citizen, I knew how to take such a hint.

"Okay," I called out to my fellow number-holders, "let's grab a truck and get those wheels ourselves. The babies won't wait to be born. And if we keep coming here every morning, we'll all lose our jobs. How many working days can you take off for a baby carriage?"

We chipped in a ruble each, flagged down a dump truck carrying girders to a construction site, paid the driver, and swooped down on the railroad freight yard.

Once there, we rushed straight to the boss and ordered:

"Hand over the wheels!"

"How can I?" he yelled back. "The boxcar carrying them hasn't arrived yet. The paperwork said the train was supposed to have thirteen cars, but only twelve showed up."

"What!? Where did the one with the wheels go?" we all asked in unison.

"What's wrong with you people? Did you fall off the moon or something? Don't you know there's a shortage of boxcars in this country?"

"Really?" we replied. "How come? Don't our Russian forests produce enough wood to make them?"

"Why don't you ask the railroad repairmen?" he snarled. "Ask them where the thirteenth car is!" And with that, he stopped talking and snubbed us.

"Don't you worry!" we told him. "We'll ask!"

I turned to my confederates and said, "Let's go to the repair shop and see what's cooking there."

We were at the site in a flash, but some meathead with a holster on his hip was standing at the entrance to the factory.

"Get out of here!" he growled. "There's secret stuff in there."

"Yeah, sure!" we shot back. "You're just putting putty on the boxcars."

"That's none of your business," he replied, puffing himself up. "And besides, it's a secret putty—the kind that doesn't fall off in the sun. I had trouble getting myself a can for home. Now get lost."

"No way!" we yelled. "You're just trying to putty up our brains! We need those boxcars to deliver those wheels so we can buy those strollers! Our daughters will give birth any minute. Putty up those boxcars with regular putty and get them running. There's not a moment to spare!"

"The boxcars aren't causing the delay," he countered. "We have plenty of boxcars. But there aren't any axles."

"Axles? What axles?"

"The ones on which the wheels spin."

"Why don't we have any?"

"Who knows? Every month the iron mill delivers fewer than we order."

We were growing more heated by the hour. We rushed over to the railroad iron mill, found the director, and grabbed him by his bureaucratic throat.

"Hand over the axles," we demanded, "or we'll make an axle out of you!"

"Comrades, please!" he whined, turning white with fear. "It's not my fault. We're having problems with our iron ore deliveries."

I was determined to see this business through to the end, even if I got into trouble at work. So we jumped back in our truck and headed to the mines.

We got there in a flash. "Hey, you!" we confronted the mine boss. "What's the problem? Is there a shortage of iron? Don't you have enough miners to drill the ore?"

"There is no shortage of iron," the mine boss snapped back. "Or miners. That's not the problem. We're having trouble with personnel. Katerina Petrovna takes care of all the forms. Without the forms, we can't process the deliveries, but she keeps taking trips to the city. She's hardly ever here."

"Why do you let her get away with skipping work?" I asked. "Get Katya back here! We'll make her pay for this! What does she do in the city, anyway? Visit her boyfriend?"

"What boyfriend?" the mill boss said. "Katya is over sixty years old! The fact is, her daughter just had a little girl, and she has one hell of a time hunting down a baby carriage."

Boris typed up his story and took it to an editor at a Moscow newspaper who had published his work before. The editor greeted Boris when he walked in and read it on the spot. When he finished, he chuckled, shook his head, and said in a low voice, glancing back at the door to make sure it was closed:

"Well, Boris, let's pretend I didn't read this, and you didn't write it."

He paused and added, his friendly tone vanishing:

"I mean if you'd still like to be published in this paper. Or in any other paper."

He looked at Boris as if he never saw him before. His face seemed to say, *Ahem, I thought I knew this young man. I thought he was a professional. Thought he was someone who knew what you could or you couldn't print in a Soviet paper!*

4
A LATE-NIGHT VISIT

The man at the door in the polo shirt was not a coach from the Dynamo sports association. He was another official and made no apology for knocking so late. Behind him in the hallway, Mitka shifted from one foot to another in confusion. He was there as a neighbor witness, a mainstay of Soviet legal practice. And a third man stood farther back, the mustachioed Zakharych, a police officer from the local precinct. He was there for the same reason. The official pulled a slip of paper out of a small briefcase known as a "Diplomat," checked it, and asked:

"Bumshtein, Yuri Aronovich?"

Yurik nodded. He didn't like the man, despite his cheerful smile, and his intuition did not fail him. The official opened his wallet and brought it up close to the crack in the door. Then he snapped it shut. The gold-embossed letters on its cover flashed in front of Yurik's eyes. It all happened so quickly that for a moment Yurik didn't realize what letters he saw.

The twentieth century is known as the century of density. We learned how to put an enormous amount of energy into a small vessel that could be dropped on a city and remove all resistance within it. So with the new semantic bombs. For the first time in history, you could make someone's heart stop by combining a few letters—SS, NKVD, KGB. Take your pick! The little letters on the intruder's ID, which seemed to emit a treacherous light, had the same effect: arrhythmic breathing and hyperventilation. There were not two, not three, but five of those letters, OBKhSS (Otdel Bor'by s Khishcheniem Sotsialiticheskoy Sobstvennosti), that is, the [Police] Department for Combating Theft of Socialist Property.

That meant the man was a finance inspector, come to remind a private cobbler of the law. He flicked two fingers up at the door, and Yurik took the chain off the hook. The door opened wide. Yurik's apartment was open for inspection, and that meant his plan for making money and winning back his wife was in jeopardy.

Yurik knew the law all too well. The Soviet Union is a socialist state, and that means you work for the collective, not for yourself. You cannot make shoes, sell them, and keep the money for yourself because you'll create competition with the state. If you and other citizens work on the side, you undermine the state's finances and, in turn, its military power. That is, when you work for yourself, you are bordering on treason. If you are so passionate about making shoes, make them at a state enterprise and collect your legal wages, minus income tax. And bachelor's tax, if you are still unmarried, still free as a bird.

That's the way Soviet law saw it, but not Yurik. He was not a parasite; he had a legitimate job. However, it was paper pushing, not a real job. All he was doing, day after day, was writing numbers. The only purpose of these numbers was to elicit a satisfied smile on the face of Igor Petrovich, the head of the planning department. They had no other use. That was why, day in and day out, Yurik moved back and forth between two points of terra firma, like a shoemaker's arched needle—from his desk to the desk of his boss.

His father, Aron Matveyevich, had repaired soles, added heel caps, and made boots. His work was meaningful. Yurik wanted the same for himself. However, at his current job, if he added on anything, it was just some piece of paper to some other piece of paper. Squeezing glue out of a bottle and onto his fingers, Yurik was angry at his parents, who worked so hard to get him into college, and yet made him miserable for the rest of his life. Instead of being a master cobbler, Yurik found himself with a diploma he didn't like and a job that bored him to death. But fortunately, his father had trained him in the craft.

Over time, Yurik spent his evenings making shoes. Shoemaking was his family trade, practiced by his Grandfather Matvey and his father. As a boy, Yurik spent hours watching his papa work. The long lessons had not gone to waste.

When Yurik took on a real man's trade, his old boring life fell by the wayside. At once, his new existence was more exciting, filled with hopes and problems. You try making shoes when the state doesn't sell leather to private dealers! A person could not own leather; as with any other raw material, it was state property.

Oh, that socialist property! Was there anything that wasn't socialist property? It seemed everything in the entire world was—that is, everything from the formerly German city of Königsberg to the once Japanese Kuril Islands. Yurik was uninterested in this world. He needed so little, just a few squares of good leather to make women's boots. He was desperate. All the rivers in the USSR flow into one big state-run sea, he reasoned. There must be streams that not only feed into the rivers but overflow into secluded lowlands during high tide. I need a small stream, he thought. A tiny rivulet will do. If I could catch some of that water in my hands!

Even before Lyubka had walked out on him and the desire to win her back had possessed him, he had looked for a secret supply of leather. He had to, his job was boring, and his miserable salary caused him anguish. By wanting more for their son than fixing people's shoes, his parents had doomed him to a hand-to-mouth existence. Because of his indigence, he needed their financial help; first some money for a vacation, then for a new suit.

Now he turned to them for help in getting leather. Or rather, he appealed to all of his many relatives. Upon receiving Yurik's request, his familial squadron sprang into action. They sent lookouts to the front, rear, and sides. All lines of communication were open and buzzing. They felt out every thread in their complex networks, including the people in their offices.

They could arrange everything for a dear relative, be it cans of Danish condensed milk or an imported windbreaker known as "The Canadian." But leather was not to be found, no matter how hard they searched. The defense industry used the quality leather. The state had imposed limits on its production, and it had cracked down on security at the plants.

Yurik was outraged. His schoolbooks had proclaimed shamelessly, "A human being is meant to be happy, as birds are meant to fly." But what happiness could there be, and what kind of bird are you, if, no matter how much you wave your arms in your black over-sleeves, you can't lift yourself off the ground! You may look like a falcon, but you are a chicken. All you can do is run around in your chicken coop with all the other fidgety chickens, flapping your wings and clucking. But you'll never leave the ground—you don't have what it takes. All you'll ever produce is a cloud of dust and a ball of feathers. If only he could make boots! Then, and only then, he could leave his coop behind him and soar.

Unexpectedly, Yurik found hope for soaring. His old college friend Zhora Koshtinsky had also tried to fly, but with much more success. Zhora had been soaring for a long time already. Both figuratively and literally:

he had been traveling on planes from Odessa to Moscow, and then to the Georgian town of Gagry. The first flight took him to the capital of culture, government, and business, the second—to the center of vacations, wine, and parties. It amazed Yurik. How had a person with the same education, the same miserable wages of an entry-level economist (a hundred and twenty rubles, which made you want to scream), gained flying power? Yurik asked him what his secret was. In response, Zhora gave him a brief lecture on the aerodynamics of a wing.

"Adverse wind flows over the top of the wing and pushes it toward the ground," Zhora said, flashing his Pierre Cardin cufflinks. "Favorable wind supports the wing from underneath and lifts it up and off of the ground. Got it?"

"Not really," muttered Yurik, trying to recall a page from his physics textbook with a diagram of air streams flowing around an airplane wing. "Is it possible to change the direction of the wind?"

"Of course not, Yurik," Zhora said. "The winds are out of my control. But it's long been known that we, the Soviet people, are masters of nature. If we want, we can make rivers flow the opposite way, or make a sea out of a desert, or vice versa. And if we want—we can reshape the political map of the world. So, got it, you silly goose? You've got to have a head on your shoulders, not a wind tunnel."

"Hm," Yurik nodded. "I've got it. Your office pays good bonuses, and it does it on a monthly basis. Not like my job—we get them once a year, and it's nothing to brag about."

"My kettle," Zhora said, tapping his temple, "cooks fine. And yours? Not so well. I make a bundle by gambling, you see . . . I play cards."

He pulled his college-mate's nose, made a train-whistle sound, jumped into his brand-new latte-colored Volga sedan, and drove away.

Yurik sighed, watching the shiny vehicle depart. Maybe if he had a car like that, he wouldn't have to worry about some damn accordion player?

Yurik was amazed when Zhora showed up the next time. They were not close; they met occasionally to catch up.

"Here," said Zhora, retrieving a package in thick brown paper from the breast pocket of his snazzy jacket. "Could you please keep it for me somewhere at your place?"

"What is it?" Yurik asked, still amazed by the visit.

"I got some money together, thanks to my being thrifty and cheap. Eighteen thousand rubles, give or take a few. You need not sign for it. I trust you."

Yurik looked in the bag and was shocked. "Why don't you put it in the savings bank?" he blurted. He had never seen that much money. He had seen figures of that order in his office papers but always thought of them as abstractions, imaginary units of higher mathematics that did not exist in reality. "You can earn some interest," he added.

"Well, you get not only interest from banks," Zhora chuckled. "You get some trouble too." He smiled, "I told you, I won big playing cards. It's clean money, but current legal thinking doesn't approve."

Yurik nodded, took the package, and put it under a pile of bed sheets in his wardrobe.

"Don't worry," he said. "It's safe with me."

He didn't like the restrictions of the law either, prohibiting playing blackjack even for fun on the beach.

"Next thing you know, they'll ban Go Fish," he snorted, feeling he ought to sympathize with his friend. "They ban everything. Even if you want to fix the soles of your shoes, go find some good leather. And forget about making any boots!"

"I'll do what I can," Zhora said. "Quid pro quo."

Yurik couldn't believe it; good luck had found him. That didn't happen often. His hope was dim, like a thirty-watt light bulb in a communal bathroom, but he kept it burning. A month later Yurik's informants reported that, though the security of the leather-processing plants was sturdy, it was nothing that Napoleon French brandy couldn't handle. The plan was simple: some of his relatives would supply this liquor to some of his other relatives, and they would use it to disarm the security guarding the factory.

There was a hitch. They had shipped the entire stock of that brandy stored in Odessa to Moscow for the Special Session of the Supreme Council of the USSR. It was understandable. How could you expect the distinguished delegates to consume some Soviet—not French—brandy after traveling to the capital from every corner of the multinational union? The fact that the French brandy was made in Armenia changed nothing.

So Yurik had to wait until the end of the Supreme Soviet. Meanwhile, he itched to work. He had to make do with replacing rubber heeltaps and patching holes in neighbors' shoes—worthless and low-paying jobs.

Then luck struck again! One beautiful evening, Zhora brought a large stack of excellent quality leather. It had an oily sheen and was soft like silk. Such unexpected good fortune made Yurik sweat all over. He ran into the kitchen, looked into his empty fridge, rummaged through his stale-smelling kitchen shelves, and set the table.

Zhora raised his eyebrows at the sight of canned sardines in tomato sauce, a staple of bachelor cuisine, which Yurik, overjoyed, opened. Zhora also looked at the half-empty bottle of vodka known as the "Crankshaft," with jagged lettering on the label, and he slapped Yurik on the back. It's not worth the trouble, he explained—instead, they should go to the restaurant at the Red Hotel to celebrate the beginning of Yurik's new life.

They stayed at the restaurant until closing time. Having once been smitten by his beautiful wife, Yurik became anxious when the young waitresses, one by one, joined them at their table. They all knew Zhora by name. Their large laughing mouths mesmerized Yurik. In those days, purple lipstick was in, and Yurik imagined purple butterflies, their little wings trembling, had landed on the girls' lips. No matter how much he tried, he couldn't bring himself to relax, and he got drunk faster than usual. The butterflies fluttered by his face, and one landed on his cheek for a moment. A long-forgotten kiss: wet, heart-stopping, teasing him with a vague promise. Without warning him to buckle his seatbelt, his life had taken off. He got dizzy. For the first time in his life, he overslept and was late for work. Now that night and Zhora were a distant memory.

Suddenly the finance inspector standing in the hall was talking about Zhora, citing his given name, patronymic, and surname: Georgy Adamovich Koshtinsky. He asked if he, Yuri Aronovich, knew the man.

"Actually, I . . ." Yurik wanted to say "know him" but stopped himself short. Who in his right mind ever tells the truth to the Soviet authorities? ". . . don't know him," Yurik concluded, trying to reverse his false start. He told himself it was the truth. Did he really know Zhora? A few get-togethers outside college. So they went to a restaurant one night, big deal! Accidental drinking buddies.

However, it was too late.

5
THE LAST STRAW

Boris's failed attempt to publish "The Wheel" was the tipping point in his thinking about whether to emigrate. He finally accepted what his parents had been saying for a long time. He felt what many young people in the country were feeling, not just the Jews. The Soviet Union had no future, and neither did he so long as he lived there. He was not yet thirty years old, healthy and full of energy. He yearned to live life to the fullest, but his energy had no outlet in his homeland. It depressed him.

Is this all there is for me here? he asked himself. Is there nothing ahead? I've already published all of my satire that could ever see the light of day. Am I going to be reduced to writing disgusting books about the builders of the Baikal-Amur Railway, pretending I don't know prisoners built it? They beat those workers for things as harmless as breaking a tool or looking too long at a guard.

Living his entire life in the USSR scared him. Wherever you turned, the doors were closed like the lid of a coffin. When he returned to Odessa for his vacation, his father agreed with him and tried to shame him for his hesitation in applying for an exit visa. It was too late for his father—he was too old to start life over again. He worked as an engineer for a construction design firm, while Boris's mother was an accountant at a tailor shop. Somehow, they made do. What else could they want at their age? However, their son had his whole life ahead of him. He needed to escape the country that had a stranglehold on him.

After seeing the so-called "sacred Soviet border," Boris felt he had to leave as soon as possible. It became a matter of life and death. And in fact, such were the stakes: those they let go had their Soviet citizenship stripped from them. There was no turning back. The very thought of it made him ill. It would be like skydiving into the unknown, crossing his fingers and praying his parachute opened in time, or at all.

He knew the time for action was now. Even a few years ago, who would have thought it would be possible for anyone, let alone Jews, to apply for emigration? As Boris had learned through the grapevine, head honchos at the Kremlin had decided to win over America through favors so they could receive trade privileges. Despite their ideological hostility, the Soviets couldn't do without those damn capitalist countries. Where else could you buy wheat, when, no matter how hard you try, you couldn't produce enough on your own? Where else could you get your hands on advanced technology and know-how? In return for trade privileges, Americans pressured the Soviets to ease the plight of Soviet Jews by allowing them the right to emigrate. Thus, a rare opportunity to get the hell out of the country arose. And Boris knew he had to act. Who knew how long this window of opportunity would remain open?

Applying for emigration was a risky move: the state might reject his application. Boris tried to understand the logic involved in slowing down the Jewish exodus, but it never made any sense. He could see why they would close the gates for Jewish scientists and engineers who worked in military laboratories—they knew state secrets. But the authorities turned down applications from Jewish actors, writers, and painters too. It was part of their Machiavellian scheme. The powers-that-be wanted to make it clear that no one who applied for an exit visa was guaranteed one. The risk of being turned down loomed over the head of every Jew who contemplated leaving. Boris knew, if they nixed his application, he would become a "triple pariah," like all the other refuseniks.

He was already used to being a "double pariah." When he became interested in journalism, he left his tedious engineering work and did freelance writing for Moscow newspapers and magazines. They paid him for piecework—that is, for each article he published. He nestled in a narrow little room in a communal apartment in one of the old houses on Crooked Knee Lane in downtown Moscow. The periodicals for which he wrote often had openings for staff writers, who received regular salaries, but they never encouraged him to apply.

Why? he asked himself. They often posted clippings of his work on the editorial bulletin board, calling it the best thing published that week, or sometimes even that month! But they never invited him to join their staff.

The department head who published his articles shrugged and always said the same thing, "C'mon, man, you know all too well why."

Indeed, Boris did know why he was not eligible for the position. First, he was not a Party member. Second, he was a Jew. A double pariah. With a double humiliation: he not only had to accept this injustice as normal, but thereby to approve it. If they now learned he filed for emigration, he would become a triple pariah, and they would stop publishing his work, despite the fact that he signed it with a pen name that seemed Russian. He fashioned it according to a long-established protocol perfected by other Jewish journalists in the country. He shortened his patronymic, "Markovich" and became "Boris Markov." It looked and sounded like a Russian name. Problem solved.

Well, if they won't let him leave the country, he'll have to find another job, perhaps as a boiler-room operator or night watchman in some Moscow high-rise. There were always openings for those low-paying positions. They called it full employment.

But still, Boris couldn't muster the courage to take the final step: to go to the Exit Visa Office. Eventually he found courage through an unpleasant incident. Later on, Boris realized how lucky he was that it happened—it was all because of his love of books.

Even as a teenager in Odessa, Boris couldn't resist the chance to browse a store that stocked rare books. Nothing pleased him as much as leafing through the yellowing pages of some ancient tome. Once, while visiting his classmate Eugene Brodsky's home, Boris saw shelves of books belonging to Eugene's father, an engineer with the Black Sea Shipping Company. Behind glass panels were specimens of a world that existed long before he and Eugene were born. Their very appearance evoked a time much more romantic than the present, a time that stirred his imagination. There were spines of calico binders embossed with gold and gilt-edged pages. The collection included books on the history of naval battles, art around the world, all eight volumes of *World Geography*, and publications from the late nineteenth and early twentieth centuries.

These volumes served as testaments of ancient worlds to new generations. Sometimes, with Eugene's permission, Boris would pull out a book and lift the liner, delicate as a bride's veil, and study the old lithographs and watercolor paintings.

Back in his high school years, he often visited the vast stationery store on Richelievskaya Street. Someone nicknamed it "Two Elephants" because, once you entered, two giant, almost-life-sized replicas of elephants, trunks lifted, welcomed visitors on either side of the main walkway. In the far left corner, there was the rare book section. The books spread out on the counter of this section were works of art compared to Soviet book productions, with their dull and lackluster covers like dirty potato skins.

The salesclerk who guarded these old and beautiful volumes was one with his wares: a tall, thin, stooped old man, with a slight tremble and the physiognomy of a scholar. His hair was always combed, and he wore an old-fashioned, somewhat battered, but clean, suit. Behind him sat books typeset in Old Church Slavonic and Old Russian alphabets, with all those *yats*, *izhitsas*, *fitas*, and *yers*, their pages yellowing, some even browning. Master artists had created their antique lithographs and folio covers. All these things, coupled with the silent salesclerk looking out from under bushy gray eyebrows, gave the rare book section the mysterious aura of a museum.

The old man hovered over volumes under glass that were particularly valuable, pressing his hands against the showcase. It was clear he loved every single book in his department not with fatherly love, but with a much more passionate, grandfatherly affection. No doubt he was torn by two conflicting emotions. On the one hand, he had to sell these books. On the other, he wanted to keep them from hands that might mishandle them, treat them without respect for their aging ink and binding. The old man cast a quick appraising look at anyone who approached his counter, especially youngsters. He faced the dilemma of whether to allow some young kid to touch his goods or to give him a stern look and a harrumph to let him know he was watched. He would wait and consider whether the hands of a potential buyer were worthy of his wares—he studied his or her every move, evaluating their reverence (or lack thereof) toward what they were about to touch.

Young Boris had the well-groomed appearance and good manners of a Jewish boy from an educated family. Still, when he extended his hand toward a volume, the old man saw Boris's baby-face and narrowed his eyes.

"Well, young man, are you sure that's what you're looking for?"

Now living in Moscow and leading the busy life of a metropolitan journalist, Boris often regretted not finding the time to stop in a store full of rare books. One day, while bouncing around the offices of different Moscow newspapers, Boris came across a book bazaar along the Moscow Arts Theatre Drive. The warm day was rare for springtime in Moscow. Some sellers opened lightweight aluminum tables. Others laid the volumes out on mats on the sidewalk. Boris could not resist—he felt like leafing through at least one book.

He barely had time to pick up one of the luxurious volumes of the *Brockhaus and Efron Encyclopedia* when, out of nowhere, a gang of young men with red armbands on their jackets pounced on him. They were a squad of volunteer police helpers, the so-called *druzhinniki*, who on the police's cue raided the illegal book traders. Without uttering a word, one turned over the tables, throwing the books on the ground. Others grabbed at the sleeves of some other book buyers.

Boris had just returned the book to the owner when somebody's hand gripped his shoulder. He wanted to throw it off, but they punched him in his ear, tied his hands, and dragged him to the police station on Petrovka Street. Boris was furious. Why on earth were they beating up people for trying to buy a book!

However, when they brought him to the precinct, the pale-faced officer on duty, a lieutenant in a uniform with a university badge on his lapel, wrote a report stating Boris had taken part in an unlawful book-trading operation and resisted arrest. He demanded that Boris sign the statement. Are you out of your mind? Boris wanted to say, but he knew it was futile. He had learned from his work as a journalist that the state was always right. He had gotten himself into a mess.

Then he did something he had rarely done, even in a difficult situation. It was something no ordinary Soviet citizen could do: he produced his press card. Despising himself for telling a white lie, he explained to the policeman on duty that he was at the book bazaar to collect material for a satirical column about the illegal book trade. Reluctantly, they let him go.

Boris could not overcome his self-loathing for a long time. This incident was the last straw. It gave him another opportunity to experience what he had already known for a long time: he lived in a police state, a country where everyone, save for a small elite, was at the mercy of the authorities.

Now, more than ever before, he had to escape the clutches of the Soviet regime. He had to do it once and for all, no matter how risky. Only now, the bitter truth of a joke he had heard reached him. At the border, the guards tell a Jew leaving the country that his favorite parrot cannot go with him. You may export a bird only if it's stuffed or stiff. The Jew begs the customs officer to let him take his beloved parrot he's had since childhood—he can't live without it! He's desperate. He does not know what to do. At this point, the parrot casts his vote. "Take my advice, Moshe," it says. "Stuffed or stiff, we've got to get the hell out of this country."

The next day, Boris was on his way to the Exit Visa Office.

6
ALL IS LOST!

Smiling and smacking his lips as though he had just enjoyed a delicious meal, the police inspector asked Yurik whether he knew Koshtinsky. As soon as Yurik uttered, "Generally, I don't," the inspector snapped, "Generally? What about in particular?"

"In particular . . ." he hesitated. His mind was racing. He grimaced. Denying his relationship with Zhora was stupid. The police inspector must have known he and Zhora were former classmates.

To say Yurik was scared would be an understatement. The world around him shape-shifted as if he were in some modern painting. Yurik's sight was altered; he had the vision of a bee. The world was geometric, broken into diamond-shaped bits of various sizes. The pitcher on the table; the curtains, his mother's gift to her divorced son; a stub of a red Jonathan apple sitting in a tea saucer—all of it! The fat policeman who came from the abbreviated agency also became a rhombus. To Yurik's horror, the man's face separated from his body and appeared to gaze at Yurik from each of the rhombus-shaped sections of his stocky physique.

This fragmented visitor now lowered himself onto a chair. On the other side of the room, next to Yurik's work stool, lay a fancy bootie almost finished. If the policeman didn't turn around, it would escape his notice. It was unlikely. Undoubtedly, someone snitched on Yurik, and now this paunchy man was here to search his apartment. He didn't appear at Yurik's door to have some tea with raspberry jam. Could Mitka, in one of his vodka-fueled hazes, have blabbed about Yurik's private business to his drinking buddies?

Now, however, the question of who gave him away to the authorities was purely academic. One thing was clear: Yurik would not be enjoying his freedom much longer.

A sound rattled in Yurik's ears. Somewhere in his brain, a phonograph needle was running through a worn-out record groove, playing the familiar lyrics of "The Space Travelers' March," a song beloved by the Soviet people: "Fourteen minutes left until we start . . ."

"The song is about me," he thought in despair. "Only it's not fourteen minutes to the start, but till the finish. It's all over for me! I can't believe I'm getting caught just as I'm making my first boot . . . But, wait! I know what I'll tell him! I'll say to them this is my first and my absolutely last boot. I'm very sorry, Comrade Inspector; I made a single boot out of sheer curiosity. Just to see if I could do it! Besides, how could I sell a single boot! You need a pair, or else it's useless, right? So, I did nothing wrong, right?! All my life I've dreamed of making shoes because it was my family's trade. But when I was a teenager, there was no shoemaking study group at the Palace of Young Pioneers. There were groups of young carpenters, young plumbers, young electricians, but young shoemakers—nothing for young shoemakers! So, I figured I should try my hand at making one, that's all. I've made one! And that's that! I proved it to myself! Case closed! May my hands wither away and fall off if I ever make one more, Citizen Chief!"

Yurik felt a sliver of hope. "Maybe he'll believe me . . . Maybe he'll let me go . . ."

However, instead of stating his defense, Yurik's throat produced a short, pitiful bark. He gazed up at the inspector from under his brows and heard what the man had been saying to him for some time already:

". . . and Georgy Adamovich also told us that, because of his illegal activities . . . you know, he got it into his head he was our Chase Manhattan Bank, an apostle of hard currency in our country. That's not nice of him. You know well he's not supposed to be playing with hard currency. It falls squarely under an article of the All-Union Criminal Code and the relevant Criminal Code of the Ukrainian Soviet Socialist Republic . . ."

Well, here it is, Yurik thought. So much for Zhora's trip to Moscow! So much for his Black Sea vacations! So much for all that talk of wind! It looks like Zhora has waved his arms too much, and now he has blisters in his armpits. Maybe that'll keep him from acting like such a big shot for a bit.

"Well," the portly man continued, "your friend Georgy Adamovich is not a bad person at heart. Oh, if only he could keep his eyes off the state's hard-currency reserves! Well, he thought of his friends. First, of you, Yuri Aronovich . . ."

"He thought of me? Why?" Yurik's foreboding turned his mumble into a nasty growl. "I'm neither kith nor kin to him."

"That's right," the government agent smiled, "no relation to you, but still, he mentioned you right away . . ." He hesitated and corrected himself. "Well, *almost* right away—he thought of you. And, I must say, he spoke about you warmly."

Yurik listened, bewildered by his late-night visitor's peaceful and friendly attitude. He found himself lost in conjectures, not knowing how to understand the man. Why on earth was this fat jerk in a sports shirt chatting so casually? You would think he wasn't a cop at all, just some next-door neighbor dropping in for a sip of seltzer—Odessa style, with jam, instead of syrup.

Gradually Yurik's distorted vision returned to normal, and it hit him that the visitor wasn't interested in him at all, but in something to do with Zhora. Relieved as he was, Yurik couldn't help but feel bad. Zhora trusted him and had helped him in difficult times. The inspector wanted Yurik to snitch on his friend. Why else was he talking in such an unctuous tone?

The image of Zhora's package appeared in Yurik's head at the same time the inspector asked him about it.

". . . eighteen thousand minus small change," Yurik heard. "He apologized for the inconvenience and asked you to hand the package over to us. Here's the prosecutor's sanction for the seizure of the monies. It is a mere formality," the inspector assured him, waving his hand and making a wry face. "Just get us the money. I'll give you a receipt for it. And that's that . . . Here's the attesting witness," the inspector motioned toward Mitka, who was leaning so heavily against the doorframe that he could barely stand up. "Your yard-keeper, Ignatiy, got sick. So, instead, a neighbor of yours, Dmitry . . . uh . . ." The inspector turned to the door. "What's your patronymic?"

"S-s-avelich," Mitka stuttered. Using both his face and body, he tried to tell his neighbor he was acting as a witness against his will. If his relations with Yurik turned sour, who would he borrow booze money from?

The inspector smiled again, eyeing Yurik. Is it possible this amateur shoemaker would do something stupid? He knew people who seemed easy to interrogate, like Yurik, sometimes acted up. They might pull a prank that a seasoned criminal would think twice before doing because it would only make things worse for him.

Yurik nodded. "Let me go get the package." A crazy idea flashed through his head. What if he were to assume the righteous indignation a Soviet citizen should adopt, having been accused of some shameful act? In a fit of rage, he could throw the visitor out of his apartment. In desperate moments, Soviet spy Shtirlitz of the TV show *The Seventeen Moments of Spring* did that to pushy Gestapo agents.

"Giving it back is no big deal for me," Yurik muttered, moving toward his wardrobe. "I had no plans for it, and I didn't expect to gain any interest on it. I didn't even know there was money in that package. Zhora asked me to hold on to the package, and so I did just that."

Yurik had barely pulled on the wardrobe door handle when he heard a light scraping sound. He paused. The scraping stopped. However, the moment he tugged the door handle again, it returned. At first, he didn't pay any mind to it, but with each inch the door opened, he realized with horror *what* the scratching sound was.

The warm air of the room, humid, saturated with the sweet smell of jasmine, had turned into the ghastliest February frost, causing his nostrils to stick together. His teeth ached, especially the upper one, which had a steel cap placed over it two days earlier. Although this was an inappropriate moment to worry about his tooth, Yurik couldn't help but to berate his dentist's sloppy work and curse that quack.

An instant later, a sensation of ice-like frigidity seized Yuri's jaw, paralyzing its muscles. His left hand, soldered to the door handle, stopped pulling the wardrobe door. By sheer willpower, he bent his frozen left arm at the elbow and thrust his right arm into the open edge of the door. The horrible sound ceased. For a moment.

Before deciding what to do next, Yurik shot a glance out of the corner of his eye to see if the stout man behind him was watching. Damn! Wary of Yurik's behavior, the night visitor had risen from his chair and was gazing in his direction, alert like a cat sensing a mouse beneath floorboards. The frost that had overwhelmed Yuri's body only moments before gave way to tropical heat. Sweat trickled down his steaming forehead and accumulated at the tip of his nose. It tickled mercilessly. Yuri thought he might die if he did not wipe off the sweat. However, how could he do such a simple thing when both hands were occupied in keeping the closet door from opening?

The itch at the tip of his nose grew unbearable. Yurik contemplated scratching it by means of an acrobatic maneuver, crossing his arms almost past their ability to bend. He went for it. With a spasmodic jerk of his body, his left hand still on the door of the wardrobe, he yanked free his right hand, which had been keeping his pile of leather sheets from falling onto the floor.

In that instant, gravity prevailed. The closet door yawned open. The dim light of Yurik's chandelier revealed brilliant saffron-yellow sheets of the highest quality, as they tumbled over each other in their haste to reach the floor.

A L L   I S   L O S T. The letters swam before Yurik's eyes like neon letters on the roof of the department store on Deribasovskaya Street. An eerie silence ensued. His head limp, Yurik looked down at the leather sheets piled on the floor. The sheets lay there, like a pile of tarot cards that revealed the events of his past life, where he is now and what is in store for him in the near future. He didn't have to be a fortune teller to know what was coming: one Jack of Clubs and his Queen of Hearts will part forever, and misfortune, many years long, awaits that hapless Jack. Just like that very moment, when he was that close to embracing Lyubka, she turned away from him again, this time forever.

In terror at the possibility the police inspector would spot his almost-completed bootie in the opposite corner of the room, he had forgotten that his leather was left where Zhora's package was!

The visitor pushed the creaking chair out of his way to the wardrobe. It was an ordinary creak, but Yurik heard it as sequential train cars ramming into one another and the shrill hiss of a train whistle. He saw the brownish-gray boxcars, flogged with rain, boxcars with "40 people, 8 horses" chalked on their sides. Farewell, dear Lyubka, farewell . . .

The metal plates on the bottom of the officer's shoes tapped on the parquet floor as he walked over to Yurik. *The son of a bitch takes care of his imported moccasins,* Yurik thought in frustration, as he picked up the leather in mortal anguish. He had the sudden urge to explain to this cop how these luxurious items had ended up in his wardrobe, but no matter how much he struggled, he couldn't think of anything. All that popped into his mind were random letters, letters that don't even have sound. There were also some dots, lots of them . . . Large and small . . . Some plump, some tiny . . . They were interspersed with colons and quotation marks.

The inspector grew bored waiting for Yurik to say something sensible.

"Hm," the fat man said. Gazing down at the figure of this hapless artisan gathering leather sheets from the floor, he could barely restrain himself from exploding into laughter. "I see you're *our* man as well."

With his unruly hands, Yurik could finally grab an armful of leather sheets and plop them down on the table. From under a pile of linen, he also brought out the package with Zhora's money.

A few moments later, he sat in the chair the inspector had pulled out for him and signed the paper certifying that at his apartment, the organs of Combating Theft of Socialist Property had seized and impounded twelve sheets of high-quality leather, two-and-a-half feet long by two feet wide. The inspector gave Yurik a receipt for handing over eighteen thousand rubles, in the hundred-ruble denomination, which, until the courts could confirm the identity of their original owner, were considered the property of citizen Bumshtein, Yu. A.

Yurik also signed the summons attesting he was to appear as a witness in the case of the State versus Citizen Koshtinsky, G.A.

The visit ended. Happy with his unexpected good fortune, the fat man told the dumbfounded Mitka, who was an audience of one for the entire ceremony, to go home. The policeman placed the stack of money into his "Diplomat" briefcase, tucked the leather sheets beneath his arm, and left.

Yurik remained seated at the table. He stared for a long time at the core of the Jonathan apple in the saucer. Now, no power in the entire world could save him from the troubles that lay ahead.

7
A LETTER FROM AMERICA

Boris knew well that, in the West, you couldn't live without a car. After filing his application for an exit visa, he took driving lessons from a stocky, blond driver recommended by his friends. Screaming over the motor and into Boris's ear, the driver yelled, "Easy, easy! Treat it like a lady!" Boris gripped the steering wheel. He jerked the gear knob while slamming on the gas pedal, and then the brakes. The old and rusty Muscovite jumped under his uneasy control, like an inflatable toy in a baby's hand.

He knew he would go to America, not Israel. His cousin Ilya, five years his senior, had been living in Los Angeles for a year now. Both were passionate about literature. They used to read and share books that fascinated them. They had also tried writing, showing first drafts to each other. Being older, Ilya often set the tone in their disputes about Hemingway, Steinbeck, or Fitzgerald, whose works the metropolitan magazine, *Foreign Literature (Inostrannaia Literatura)*, published.

Nevertheless, both became engineers. Ilya became a refrigeration expert, and Boris, an electricity expert. When they had graduated from high school, Jews weren't allowed in humanities departments around the country. After World War II, the Stalinist tradition of not letting the unreliable Jewish element into the ideologically sensitive sphere had already been entrenched.

After graduating, Boris was sent to work as an electrical engineer at a power plant in a Moscow suburb. Soon, he discovered his plant's employee newsletter needed writers, and Boris jumped at the opportunity to write articles. During visits to Moscow throughout the next year, he began contributing short pieces to the *Moscow Komsomol Member* (*Moskovskiy Komsomolets*) newspaper. They were short on staff and welcomed free-lancers. This turn in his life excited Boris so much that soon his writing interfered with his engineering job. He stopped writing for a while, but, without newspaper work, his life seemed dull and empty. One day, with his eyes closed, he made the leap. He quit his job at the plant and began to live on his freelance income. The pay was not great by any measure; he had to watch every kopeck to make ends meet. It was a difficult life, but it was still more satisfying than his previous work.

His cousin Ilya stayed in Odessa, where he worked in an engineering design office, wrote poetry, and contributed lyrical prose sketches for the regional Odessa paper, *The Banner of Communism* (*Znamia Kommunizma*), in its "Creativity of Our Readers" section. Two years ago, he had found a great-aunt on his mother's side living in California, applied for emigration on the grounds of "family reunification," and left the country. About half a year later, some American tourist from Los Angeles gave Boris a picture of Ilya taken in America. He was not by himself, but with his family: his wife Bella, whom he married shortly before his departure from the country, and their year-old son Maxim. In the picture, all three of them were sitting on the steps of the house they were renting. The architecture was of an Old Spanish era—the house's pediment was arched, with cypresses on both sides of the cropped lawn.

But the house was a secondary matter. Boris was taken aback by Ilya's appearance. Was it possible that this well-groomed gentleman, washed by daily American showers, was his close relative and old friend? Look what freedom does to a human being! It was amazing how, in a short period, the gloomy expression that rarely left Ilya's face had disappeared. Every movement of his former friend had been uncertain and wary; he often looked desperate. Boris understood that he must look the same way. He pulled out his Journalists' Union membership card. Every muscle in his face was tight. Compared to his now-American cousin, Boris looked like an inmate at a maximum-security prison. The only thing missing from this mug shot was a plate with a number on it.

Boris gave it some thought. Was that surprising? A face reflects the environment you live in, and it bears the emotional impression of every-one you speak to daily. If people smile at you, you smile back. If they look at you with disapproval, you frown too.

Ilya sent letters suggesting Boris shouldn't drag his feet. He should fol-low Ilya's example and emigrate while it was still possible. Ilya was the one who arranged for an official letter of invitation to go to Israel. The Exit Visa Office accepted applications only from those who could produce such a letter from a relative in Israel. The Soviet Union, like a small girl spotted with her hand in the cookie jar, tried to appear innocent. The authorities pretended the Jews were leaving the glorious Soviet state only because they were too family-oriented, all one big family.

While preparing for his journey, Boris tried to picture himself on the other side of the border, and it frightened him. "What am I going to do over there? I'll be a stranger there. Here I am a Jew, and they don't want me to forget it. Who am I going to be over there? I don't know the language, or history, or culture, or even the religion of the people that the fifth line, ethnicity, in my passport binds me to . . . but is it only a formality? After all, no matter how I tried to be like everyone else, it did not work. It seems, like other Jews, I'm made from some other substance. Being a Russian and being a Jew are *two very different things*. You cannot dissolve the oil in water. No matter how much you run them in a blender, they never mix."

In one of Ilya's first letters to Boris, he made it clear: if the authorities approved his visa, he would have much more to learn than how to start a car or make a U-turn . . .

Dear Boris! (Ilya's letter began),

You may find it amusing, but I had hardly stepped on American soil, when I ran into trouble with the law. Here is how the whole thing happened. Having just arrived in Los Angeles, I found myself looking squarely into the face of an unexpected dilemma: no automobile—no life. Public transportation in the city is so dismal you can live here without a car under one condition: you must condemn yourself to a vegetable existence. But I had to find work, and that meant traveling, not just by index finger through the want-ads, but in person through the streets of this endless city, vast as the Central Russian Plain.

In no time at all, with the help of Charlotte, my American aunt, a car turned up, a Dodge veteran, born in 1966, the color of a sea wave. It was a little dented on one side, and the paint was peeling on the other, but, when the dealer suggested I take it for a drive, I thought he was making a cruel joke.

"Thanks, I'm just looking," I said, not without dignity, hinting that I understood and appreciated the joke. You can trust me on this, Boris: even the Odessan head honcho, the First Secretary of the Regional Party Committee, would give an arm and a leg for such a beautiful automobile.

The dealer, however, insisted the car was already mine, Charlotte had already made the arrangements. Ahem, my aunt seems like a decent woman. How could she chisel the poor car dealer that way? To buy such a limousine for four hundred and some dollars, including the cost of registration?

Charlotte broke my reveries by nudging me toward the door. I opened it as if it were the gate to a crystal palace. Lord, how wide was the seat! You'd have to ride a bike to get to the other door!

Encouraged by the dealer, whom I'd avoided looking in the eye because I'd been feeling like a party to a con game, I turned the ignition key.

There wasn't a sound. I breathed easier. Now I understood everything.

"The engine doesn't work," I told Charlotte, gaining confidence. "It doesn't run. I wonder what the repairs will cost?"

"What's with you?" She pulled herself behind the wheel.

She turned the key—silence.

"What are you, crazy?" she said. "The engine works, you can't hear it."

I didn't believe it. I opened the hood. The fan was blowing. Holy cow! Boris, do you remember what a din there was when your parents' neighbor Victor, the sailor, invited us for a spin in his brand-new Muscovite? He turned the engine on—and we couldn't talk, we shouted into each other's ear.

Well, here I was now, behind the wheel of such an elegant car, cruising out of the lot. I went around the block, putting my right foot on the gas and the brake pedals, and trying to figure out what to do with my left leg. It was of no use with an automatic transmission. I'm sure a few more Five-Year Plans, and the Soviet-made cars will catch up.

When I pulled up to the manager's booth, my face already showed all the marks of belonging to that world which had been inaccessible to me, that of diplomats, tailcoats, and high-society receptions. Bella told me later she fell in love with me a second time at that moment.

We put the car in the backyard. Everything happened so suddenly; I couldn't get used to the idea I had become the owner of an automobile. Time and again, I looked out the front window and asked Bella:

"Listen, whose cruiser is that in the yard?"

I walked around the limousine, expecting a proprietary feeling to take root in me. After all, that car was all I had . . .

But no such feeling materialized. The car existed in its own world, and I lived in mine. I forced myself to wash it. I felt I was a cleaning man, putting the gloss on the ceremonial limousine of some Hollywood star or carousing Arabian sheik.

Now, having just passed the driving test, I drove to an employment agency. They gave me an address and told me which "freeway" to take and where to get off. I knew what a freeway was in theoretical terms. During my driving lessons, we had stayed close to home on surface streets where you have to put on the brakes and look both ways at every intersection. From the name, I understood that freeway meant a "free" way. There are no traffic lights or crosswalks.

"So much the better." I put away my Thomas Bros. map book. And so I drove with a light heart as I turned onto Highland Avenue. It was the street with the entrance to the Hollywood Freeway, which I was supposed to take.

Uneventfully, staying within the legal speed limit of 35 miles per hour, I drove under a bridge and found myself on that freeway. The Highland on-ramp led into the far-left lane—the only place I know of within the Greater Los Angeles area where this situation exists. I drove peacefully along, looking out to the side, to see what an American freeway was like. It was tremendously broad, and the cars flew by like crazy. Well, I'll be smarter than that. I let them fly by if they like. I've got time. I looked at my watch: at thirty-five miles per hour, I'll make it with time to spare. And yet, no one signals on the streets, but here they're tailgating me and honking their horns like freaks. Who knows! Maybe it's okay to do that on the freeway?

The weather was beautiful that day, and I felt elated. Here I was, going to my first interview in America; perhaps I would even get a job. The sun shone, and people waved as they drove by. I waved back at them. What good-hearted people Americans are! Though they all seemed to be in a rush, they still managed a greeting.

After a little while, not only ordinary drivers, but even the police pulled up to me, waved, and shouted something.

"What?" I looked at him, smiling. But all I heard was: "Right, right!"

Aha! I assumed the police officer was saying "All right."

"All right! All right!" I shouted back.

Still another police officer came cruising up, this one on a motorcycle. He was waving too. "All right!" I shouted at him.

A helicopter hung right above me in the sky and circled. I looked up: in the cockpit, another policeman was waving. Look at all the attention I'm getting! How do they know I'm a recent immigrant who welcomes moral support, especially today, on the day of my first interview? Ah, what remarkable people live in America! All nice folks, to the last man. Even the police . . .

Little by little, however, I realized something was wrong. The motorcyclist the closest to me looked angry and didn't wave his hand in hello, but thrashed the air.

At last, I understood he was inviting me to pull over to the right. I looked behind me—Oh Lord! How can I pull over to the right when cars are rushing past me at twice my speed?

"No thanks!" I shouted to the policeman. "Thanks for asking, but I'm fine here. I'll get there. I'm not in a hurry."

Meanwhile, the motorcyclist pulled up alongside me, and almost climbed in the window.

"GET RIGHT!" he shouted.

I didn't risk taking my eyes off the road, but with my peripheral vision, I could see he was getting mad. I looked around: Bah! There were police all around me! And they were signaling with everything they had—headlights, flashing lights, their hands, caps, helmets; they even turned on a howling siren. Why are they so upset with me? I'm not going over the speed limit—I entered the left lane at thirty-five miles per hour, and I'm still going the same speed . . .

Perhaps a little explanation is in order here, dear Boris. I passed my driving test without cheating. I studied by looking at sample tests with all the specific questions that appear on the test—all five versions. There was no question about how fast you should drive in the left lane of the freeway. Charlotte's grandson took me to the DMV to take the test—an easygoing, young airhead. When I asked him if everything I needed to know was on the cards I studied, he waved his hand:

"You know too much as it is. Here's my advice: once you pass the test, forget the rest. It only gets in the way."

. . . And so, goaded on by both the air and ground forces of the L. A. Police Department, I switched over into the right lane. The whole scene cried out for a film crew from the eyewitness news. I wound up on the shoulder and stopped the car. One by one, the police surrounded me. The motorcyclist came first; then two police cars came rushing up, with howling sirens and flashing lights. The helicopter pilot, seeing I had surrendered myself to the mercy of the authorities, circled once in farewell and flew away.

It struck me that the first thing the police officer did, as he removed his gloves, was to ask, "Is this your car?"

My God, flashed through my mind, even they can't believe it! Just a short time ago I also had doubts on that score. Later I understood that this phrase is a standard part of the traffic offender's interrogation.

The policeman stood, his legs spread apart, slim, even elegant in shining black leather boots and a shoulder belt, his freckled face gleaming and moist with sweat. At that moment, he reminded me of a movie cowboy, and I shuddered again, realizing I had entered that frame of the film, that I was in America. Stretching out beyond the policeman's shoulders was the vast city—an image which for me is the image of America.

"Is this your car?" he asked again, getting out his notepad.

He paused and gazed at me, trying to figure out what sort of strange bird I was. I guess he figured it out, because he said with soft affection in his voice, the way one talks to idiots, "The right lane is for children, do you understand?"

I just made a touchdown on American soil, after all, and, at the first instant, I thought, "Who knows, maybe American teenagers have a special lane set aside for car rides? So they ride back and forth along the freeway. But what's that got to do with me? I was in the far-left lane!"

"At the speed you were going," he said, seeing I was digesting the information with difficulty, "at the speed you were going you can only drive in the right lane, with the children. If you don't want to kill yourself or someone else."

It seemed he hadn't excluded that possibility. But wait a minute, let's assume I was going 38 miles per hour—that's the figure he wrote in the official report while we were talking—that's over 60 kilometers per hour. What does he want me to do, fly?

"What I want," he said, as if answering my question, "is to see you don't kill yourself."

I wouldn't have been surprised if he had said something like "life's beautiful," or "you're still young," or something else in that vein.

On that day, instead of an invitation to work, I brought home a summons to appear in court. I could have paid the fine, but there wasn't any money, and Charlotte proclaimed in a bellicose tone: "We'll fight it!"

In court she told my tale in grand style, emphasizing my poor English (so right!), and how I still hadn't recovered from the happiness of being in America, so I wasn't quite myself. She called me a big Russian poet (a gross overstatement), explaining that, at the moment when I should have gotten into the right lane, I was seeking a complex dactylic rhyme. She dragged out some of my hidden skeletons, all of which were news to me. From all that she portrayed a vivid image of an eccentric, unbalanced, and debilitated gentleman, whom even relatives were wary of dealing with.

When the sense of what she was saying filtered through to me, I became worried. What if the judge doubts my mental health and expands the question: How did this psycho slip into the United States? Won't he be a drain on society? You probably have to spoon-feed him.

However, everything worked out. After hearing out Charlotte, the judge banged his mallet and said:

"OK, that's enough, lady. He was going too slow, and he was in the wrong lane. But there were at least five lanes there!"

Glancing at me once again, the judge sighed and, looking up at the ceiling, mumbled something. All I could make out it seemed was, *Oh, America! How far can your generosity spread?!*

And he dismissed the ticket.

Hugs, Ilya

Everything in the letter puzzled Boris. Forget the grandeur of American cars, how was it possible Ilya could afford a car—the life-long dream of any Soviet citizen—with the small allowance given to him by the Jewish community? Maybe, if he could leave the country, he might also one day sit behind the wheel of his very own car. Such a thought still seemed like nonsense to him, like Khrushchev's assurances from the high podium that "the current generation of Soviet people," to which Boris belonged, "will live under communism." Then again, what about the gentle way the police officer took Ilya off the road? Boris, Ilya, and everyone else they knew here in the Soviet Union was always trying to keep their distance from police officers—just in case. Then, the softness of the judge's ruling. A vast and strange land was waiting over there, on the other side of the Atlantic Ocean. Boris braced himself to handle the peculiarities of American life.

8
WHO'S GOING TO SAVE ME?

The inspector left, but Mitka still loomed in the doorway. He spread his muscular, overworked paws in an apologetic gesture. His downcast appearance revealed that, although he did not understand what had just happened, he had a gut feeling his credit line with Yurik had been closed, at least temporarily. Now Yurik would have to worry about other things. Mitka shook his head dejectedly as if saying fate screws us all over in ways we're not prepared for. He wanted to say something, but, shuffling his feet a little more, waved his hand in defeat and left.

Yurik sank into a chair. They'll throw me in the can, he thought. They'll throw me in there for sure. Why wouldn't they? I guess this is the end of my young life. Next thing you know, I'll be ancient. I'll be an old man when I get out, somehow linger half a dozen years, and it'd be about time to kick the bucket. I'm worthless! I'm a victim of circumstance, no doubt about it!

"If, at nightfall, the Soviet authorities visit you, get ready for the big house." Yurik knew this Russian truism well. He was born in a family of simple folk who sank their heads into their shoulders when the terrible scythe of the Great Terror of 1937 cut down some of the country's brightest. Still, growing up, he learned the family rule: it's best to keep your distance from the monster that is the Soviet power, with its thousand eyes and gnarled fingers, calloused by a revolver's trigger, grinning with chapped lips and gleaming steel caps on its teeth.

It is amazing how misfortune clears your mind and frees your senses. As soon as Yurik realized he had fallen into the crocodile jaws of the law, the ex-husband of a beautiful woman gained the hearing of a dog and the sight of an owl. Right after being overwhelmed with despair, a rush of unjustified vigor shot through his body.

Stop whimpering! Yurik said to himself. *Do something!*

After putting on his best Sunday pants and a nylon short-sleeved shirt, he ran into the night.

"Trouble!" he muttered, swiftly moving along the street, trying not to gallop. The local on-duty policemen, smoking in a driveway in the dead of night, could have mistaken him for a cat burglar and followed him.

Oh, a thief is a thief. Well, maybe I'm not a thief, but I crossed the line. They didn't give me leather as a reward for heroic labor. There is a military quota for leather. Those idiots might as well accuse me of undermining the defense capability of the USSR. And Zhora can go to hell, too. Some idiot he is! Couldn't he have found a better place to safeguard his money?

A crucified man, crushed by destiny, lies plastered in a skillet, like some spring chicken, ready to be grilled. You barely endure the heat from the pan on your skin, and now some horrible weight is pressing you down onto the pan—and you cannot escape, no matter how hard you try.

Ah, Yurik, Yurik! The crowns of the sycamores along Pushkinskaya Street, which took in the fugitive, rustled from a sudden wind. The hapless man ran through the tight shawl of air, thick with violets. It was a hot, pitch-dark night. Through the darkness, he only saw the white summer dresses of passing Muscovites. These girls had come down to Odessa to swim in the warm sea and sunbathe on the beach. If luck would have it, they'd fall in love with some well-to-do man, one of those polar explorers from Norilsk who came to Odessa to catch some sun before returning to the long dark nights in the north. The scent of flowers and love saturated the air of the Odessan streets. On nights like this, one wants nothing more than love.

Yurik headed toward Lyubka's place, though he felt a lump in his throat at the thought of her not spending the night at home. Or, even worse, that she was at home in the arms of that damn accordionist with the dumb hair. That robber would put his filthy paws on her breast, a wonder of nature, the very sight of which had always made Yurik gasp, yearn. With his eyes closed, he would bring his lips to that rosy miracle of nature. Oh, what a deadly torment! Oh, the most bittersweet woman to love in the world! Oh, that laughing woman, scoffing with her big mouth and smoky blue eyes! I love you, damn you! I adore you and curse you. I want to see you every hour, on the hour, and am afraid of your spell. The very sound of your voice melts everything inside me as if I'm just a sugary mess. Love exhausts and gnaws at me, and that sweetness melts me down . . .

Yurik stopped for a moment. What could he do, in just one night? He decided, a lot! One must fight for his destiny.

He strutted down the sidewalk, trying to figure out en route what he would do if he found that damn entertainer at Lyubka's place. I'll kill him, he told himself, I have nothing to lose now. He placed his house keys between his fingers and squeezed his hand into a fist to create a makeshift weapon. He knew he had no chance against his ex-wife's lover: the man was taller than Yurik, and his shoulders wider. But fierce hatred overwhelmed Yurik to the point where it didn't matter who beat up whom. The fight needs to happen. He'll kill me—so be it! But I'll make him bleed. I'll scratch his brazen face raw. The main thing is I'll make sure he has a scar across his mug; a big scar that would scare the girls off. I'll disfigure him. After that, I don't care what happens.

The treetops cover Pushkinskaya Street like an awning; when walking, one only gets a glimpse of the streetlights every few steps. In the semi-darkness, along the most beautiful of Odessa streets, the trees resemble the legs of elephants, their trunks holding up bales of leaves.

As he reached the house on Trinity Street where Lyubka lived, Yurik stopped. Why was his ex-wife the first person he wanted to talk to about his misfortune? Why would she care? Whenever he visited his daughter, he would try to strike up a conversation with Lyubka, and she would repeat over and over, "Yurik, we are strangers now, with different surnames. Mine is Ratner; yours is Bumshtein."

For a while, he walked around near Lyubka's entrance hall, his hands deep in his trouser pockets, up to his elbow, as if somewhere in their seams he could find the key to the snare that had captured him, trapping him in such an embarrassing way. Yurik sighed deeply once or twice. In the middle of this terrible sweltering night and horrified by the oncoming nightmare, he was not ready for a fight. His fists unclenched. He looked at the windows of his former—now Lyubka's—apartment on the second floor, positioned right above the driveway. They were dark. Yurik hesitated at the entrance to the front hall of the building, but at the last minute decided not to go up and wandered away.

It was late, and there was no one to go to. There was not even a place where Yurik could go to drink it off. Everything closes at the same time kids go to bed; not just the grocery stores, but the restaurants too. What else are restaurants if not a haven for the tired and tormented soul, who, no matter how hard he tries, cannot fall asleep? Damn it, they've turned restaurants into some daytime canteens!

Anger at this life, putrid with the taste of castor oil, in which happiness is a stranger to the common man, but well known to big bosses and thieves, overtook him.

He walked away from his former home. Crossing the street back and forth, he walked, having no clue where fate was dragging him.

9
WATER FLOWING AND NOT FLOWING

Boris waited for the decision regarding his exit visa. He knew that whether they permitted him to leave or not, his life was bound to take a dramatic turn. Recalling the last Winter Olympics, held in the Austrian town of Innsbruck, Boris thought the way he felt now must be the way a luger feels. Lying on his back, he flew, feet first, on an unfamiliar track at an eye-bulging speed. He didn't know which way the route would turn and which side to put his weight on. Boris stopped reasoning altogether, submitting to whatever instinct overwhelmed him at the moment. It meant he was oblivious to his surroundings and the decisions others were making. He knew learning how to drive was a sensible thing to do, but it was also a distraction from the terror he felt.

Now Boris stood in a long line at the local traffic police office to take the exam for his driver's license. Although he had burned all his bridges, something was still gnawing at his heart. Maybe it was the empty feeling he had from throwing everything away. As if some giant tigers, their large claws curved like Turkish sabers, scratched at his heart. His whole being, not just his feet, grew cold. *What am I doing! Where am I going? A different world awaits me. A strange land . . .*

Like all Soviet lines, the line for taking driving exams crawled. Boris stood at the door leading to the corridor for a long time. First, you had to submit your papers to one clerk, then stand in the cashier's line to pay for your license. Squinting at the setting sun, Boris looked around in melancholy, saying good-bye to all familiar around him:

The low wooden fence, gray from aging and rain, in the precinct's courtyard. On the sidewalk across the street, an elderly woman was walking, her head bent. She stepped slowly, her gray woolen scarf wrapped around her head (although it was the end of March already, it was still cold). She carried two string bags, one with potatoes covered with old-age spots, the other with two heads of cabbage with a brown fringe of rot. The woman's face bore the expression of utter hopelessness, of mental numbness, as if she were dragging herself behind the coffin of a loved one.

Two men in unbuttoned long dark jackets, grunting and sweating, were dragging a brand-new kitchen cabinet to the nearest driveway. A young man walked the other way with his hands in the pockets of his light jacket, and a newspaper rolled under his arm. Judging from his puckered pinkish face, he had been drinking and could no longer feel the cold. A young woman in a beige coat with brown fur trim walked behind him, keeping a safe distance. Her pretty face must give her a lot of trouble; annoying attractive women on the street is a beloved pastime of Russian men. Her clenched lips lent her face the unmistakable expression of *Don't even think of coming close with that drunken mug of yours.*

"I have lived among these people all my life," Boris told himself, "but, no matter how hard I've tried, they remain strangers. What do I have in common with them? Their songs, groaning, filled with hopelessness and grief, don't speak to me. I want to live my life to the fullest, to do my best work, to see the world, to realize all my abilities. How can I appreciate the charm of drunken bravado? A Russian man, stupefied by vodka, breathing the smell of spirits into your face, asks you whether you respect him because he knows no one does. He knows it: because he has no respect for himself, others don't either. Isn't the reason his eyes light up at the sight of a bottle of vodka because he can stop feeling anything about himself? In that state, at last, he can love everyone. Except for Jews, of course."

Boris liked the Russian people. He appreciated their generosity of spirit, their spontaneity and wholesomeness. Nevertheless, he could not shake off the fact that so often thinly veiled hostility was hurled at him because he was a Jew. That happened even with the most cultured Russians. Sometimes it was a quick smirk. Perhaps he only imagined it. Because of his thin skin, he had the Jewish tendency to expect the worst. However, one might ask, why did expecting the worst feel natural to him? Was there a reason?

Boris recalled a recent evening of terrible loneliness. All his friends had left town to be with their families for May Day. He was a bachelor; his parents and other relatives lived in Odessa. He stood in his small rented room, at the window overlooking the alley. It was drizzling. The lights in the building on the other side of the lane shone brightly. In one of the apartments, the occupants set the table in the living room. In the kitchen, around the stove and the refrigerator, dressed-up women bustled. People kept trickling into the building, carrying shopping bags with bottles and food.

One woman, a pretty blonde, noticed Boris, and surmising from his motionless figure that he had nowhere to go, waved him an invitation.

Boris hesitated. Should he go to a home full of total strangers? It was already getting dark when he threw his jacket over his shoulders, pulled out a bottle of Georgian wine he was lucky to find in a store the day before, and crossed the street.

The party was already in full swing. Women's cheeks grew crimson and men's eyes gained a pink hue. Everybody tried to shout one another down and laughed. Boris felt the truth in the Russian saying "A sober man and a drunken one can't be pals." He also realized that, no matter how hard he might try, he could not catch up with the drunk guys, even if he wanted to.

There were not enough men in the company for every woman. Yet, despite intoxication, when Boris came in, the male guests frowned at the blonde woman who invited him. She had made a mistake. Boris had typical Jewish features: curly black hair, dark brown eyes, and a solid nose. The blonde woman shook her head, invited Boris to sit next to her, and put beet salad on his plate. A man on Boris's left gave him a long cold look, sat still for a moment, then reached for the bottle in the center of the table. He pursed his lips and, with a coldness incongruous with the general gaiety, said to Boris, "Should I pour you a drink or are you man enough to do it yourself, sir?"

Boris felt like getting up and, without a word, leaving the party. Everyone around the table was singing the "Moscow Nights." Forgetting about his existence, the man next to him swung his fork in the air, joining the chorus. When they sang the refrain, "The river is moving and not moving," Boris rose from the table, and without looking at anyone, and making no disturbance, walked out.

10
STROLLING ALONG THE BROAD

After leaving the building where Lyubka lived, Yurik roamed the streets. Finally, he stopped. With difficulty, he pulled himself together and headed toward the city center. He figured he might see one of his friends there, and maybe they'd give him some advice. He couldn't perish, just like that. He had to do something.

It was late May. The lilacs were in bloom, the air saturated with their smell. The air stopped moving, unwilling to cool the overheated bodies of the city dwellers. Impatient by nature, they cooled themselves, acting out the old Odessan joke, "If fanning your face tires your hand, move your head instead." It seemed all Odessans poured into the streets, taking part in the evening ritual known as "a stroll along the Broad."

Since he was a teenager, Yurik loved to go on these strolls—sometimes alone, sometimes with Zhora. The Broad (short for Broadway) was what Odessans nicknamed the central part of Deribasovskaya Street, the stretch between Preobrazhenskaya and Pushkinskaya Streets. No one even thought to peek at the part of Deribasovskaya Street south of the intersection, the part that went down to the seaport. If the Broad were the guts of the city, this area was its inflamed and sickly appendix. There they might rob you down to your underwear.

However, north of the intersection, in the well-lit part of Deribasovskaya Street, the Odessans felt like they were in the capital of the free world. Enthusiasm for a relaxing evening stroll along the Broad was much higher than for the May Day parades. The city poured into the Broad; some came on foot, others took a trolleybus or tram. If people were coming from the outskirts like Little Fontan Boulevard, they'd try to catch a taxi. It didn't matter if it was a sailor back from his long voyage or a vacationer sick of his health resort. They would fling their arms wide open, trying to catch the cab, and jump into the middle of the street. Stopping a taxi was never easy. The taxi drivers would sneak under a man's arm and rush to the airport. There, they preferred to pick up passengers that stepped off the plane, ecstatic to visit the city they'd heard so much about. Such a passenger was easy prey for the oldest trick in the Odessan taxi drivers' book—take the passenger to the Broad after making a short detour to the neighboring city of Kishinev, capital of the Moldovan Republic. In a quick, three-hour trip over the Dniester Steppes, the passenger could breathe in some fresh air.

Wherever Yurik entered the street, he slowed down to ensure he missed nothing the Broad had to offer. And it offered a lot. He could start his stroll at the big food store at the corner of Deribasovskaya and Preobrazhenskaya Streets. There, at a kiosk open to the street, he could drink a glass of the world's best seltzer, infused with fragrant strawberry or cherry syrup. You had to drink it slowly, or else you'd choke on your own happiness and prickly soda bubbles. However, if the evening was too stuffy and there were too many thirsty people on the streets, it was only fair that they would dilute the syrup until it tasted like a light manganese solution. The female vendors in starched white kerchiefs rinsed the glasses in a little fountain on the counter upholstered in zinc. When his turn came up, the customer would put his coins in a small seltzer puddle on the counter. From time to time, with the deft knack of a Monte Carlo dealer, the saleswoman raked the change into a little tin plate.

His stomach filled with little gassy nettles, the soles of his frivolous sandals à la some Roman senator from the history textbook slapping on the sidewalk, Yurik stepped under the arches of the Passage. In this marvel of European architecture, in the windows of its boutiques, local souvenirs were on display. Painted with aniline dyes, a little wooden sailor in his bell-bottom trousers on the deck of a sailboat, *Greetings from Odessa . . .* a desktop clock with a gilded colonnade, reminiscent of the local Prince Vorontsov's Palace, another marvel of European architecture . . . a plastic blonde in huge sunglasses, wearing a coquettish hat . . .

After window shopping, Yurik rolled over onto Deribasovskaya Street, along with the other strollers. Before reaching the Chronicle Movie Theater, he peeked through the slits of the cream-colored curtains that covered the windows of the diet diner. It was perhaps the most bizarre enterprise in the city. Can you believe there are people in this city who sleep on tattered mattresses and still eat like the President of the French Republic? In Odessa, they revere only the freshest produce, which the city housewives schlep home in shopping bags from the most prominent farmers' market of southern Russia, Privoz. Compared to it, the biggest Paris food market, nicknamed "The Belly of Paris," was only a train station in some remote region of Russia where the trains make three-minute stops. At such short stops, they sell things only the long-distance passenger would go for: a cracked boiled egg, a soggy pie filled with wild cranberries, and half-rotten pears, the kind picked up off the ground.

During the daytime, the health food diner's waiters roll their eyes up in disgust, serving a visiting cholecystitis patient steamed turnip cakes, which the locals would not touch even if you threatened to castrate them. These cakes were such an insult to their gourmet sensibilities it was impossible to appease them with anything, except maybe with a bloody steak.

In the evenings, with all the window curtains drawn, the diner hosted weddings and celebrated graduate students defending their dissertations. Toward the evening, the dull daytime smell of the health food diner dissipates. The food they're serving now brings mindless joy to the hearts of the partying people.

Flattened on baking sheets, the marinated chickens hiss. The sharp smell of onions infused with the subtle aroma of freshly picked tomatoes, still warm from the sun, floods your nostrils. The diners' teeth crunch on delicious radishes. Also on the tables are bottles of the young Moldavian wine Shabo, not to be confused with Chablis in other parts of the world. As you drink the former, you find that while their names sound similar, only Shabo makes your body melt with sweet tenderness.

The waiters might pour you something stronger, like *gorilka*, which is a Ukrainian vodka with a red pepper submerged in the bottle like a small submarine. There is also a bottle of Armenian brandy on every table. Walking home with your gaze toward the sky, you see the five-star rating of that brandy, now multiplied by thousands.

Having gawked at the banquet for a while, Yurik crossed the bridge and plunged into the City Garden with a rotunda in the middle. In it, the local naval cadets' brass band pressed the valves of tubes, horns, and helicons, blowing out dreamy waltzes, "On the Hills of Manchuria," "The Amur Waves," and others. Synchronous with the music, pebbles squeaked under the feet of people walking along the intricate sandy footpaths. Off to the side, in the sandbox, apple-cheeked Odessan children sat, watched over by their grandmas and nannies.

After walking through the garden, past the steps leading to the movie theater named after the brave prerevolutionary Odessan pilot Sergei Utochkin, Yurik returned to Deribasovskaya Street. Soon, he stopped at a huge fish store he liked to visit. There, two burly, net-wielding salesmen chased a big carp around the aquarium in the middle of the store. Distraught by the crowd of people and bright lighting, the carp splashed water all over the store.

Overwhelmed by the din of the crowd and the kids squealing, their noses glued to the glass, the carp twitched, opening its pink accordion-like gills and flapping its fins. Its mouth was open in bewilderment as if to say, "What's going on, fellow citizens? Have you lost your minds? Haven't you seen a live carp before?" The glittering of loose fish scales in the salesmen's curly heads made them look like jolly sea gods. Summoning all its strength, the carp jumped out from the aquarium and into the arms of some plump Odessan lady in a straw hat, buying fish for dinner on her way home from the beach. Trying to catch the carp, the fellows ran into the lady's arms, guffawing with delight.

Making his way out of the store, Yurik continued his walk until he reached the spacious "Ice-Cream Parlor." Odessans used to come here with the whole family. They savored the ice cream, sucking it off their spoons. From time to time, one could see melancholy in the gaze of the fathers. In the postwar time, this place had dazzled them. Café! The sound of that French word evoked daydreams about living a free life like the Europeans. Café! Anything could happen in a place with such a romantic name. An unexpected encounter . . . a pleasant acquaintance . . . they even served young Moldavian wine with ice cream. Who knows what unexpected twist of fate that wine could lead to!

In reality, nothing of that kind had, or ever could, happen in the Soviet food-serving outlets. It was the southern part of the USSR, not France. As if to honor the memory of those postwar times, at the ice-cream parlor, they played tape-recorded songs that made patrons feel daydreamy. "Marousen'ka!" Levantine singer Leonid Utyosov sang, "as soon as the war's over, you and I will sing and dance, my Marousen'ka!"

From the loudspeaker, you could hear sentimental prerevolutionary songs:

Mama's tormented heart
Barely beats in her chest.
One mama's tormented heart
Is seeking peace in the quiet:
"Don't call the doctors,
Just get me my son back
Oh, if I could be with him for just an hour!
It's so hard for me to go on living!"

He also mumbled exciting and mindless Georgian songs:

There's a mountain in the Caucasus,
The biggest of them all.
The Kura River's running underneath it,
Quite a turbid river it is!
If you climb up that mountain
And throw yourself down from it,
You have plenty of chances
To say good-bye to your life.

Love and affection
Are dear to us, the Caucasus people.
But, if the little woman's eyes deceive you,
May God have mercy on her soul!

These playful tunes, a far cry from the military marches and propaganda songs of the Five-Year Plans, were a sheer pleasure for the customers. The music made it enjoyable to eat the *plombières* and *crème brûlée*, produced on site. They scraped the ice cream out from long cylinders that resembled artillery shells lodged in crushed ice. Tall porters would come stomping in their rubber boots to deliver the ice in large burlap sacks. The ice porters with jute bags on their backs that covered their heads resembled overthrown Arab sheiks, forced to earn their daily bread with manual labor.

They placed fragile square wafers on the bottom of a rectangular mold, covered with solid chunks of sparkling ice cream, then pressed out the little briquette, covering it with another wafer. You couldn't get enough of it! With the ice cream, they served a carbonated drink with a splash of "a little cherry pit" (*vishnevaia kostochka*). It was a thick and aromatic domestic liqueur. Ah, all this had been a long time ago, in Yurik's childhood, when the Soviet authorities, still shell-shocked by World War II, had been only coming to their senses, letting underground business flourish in some provinces.

Yes, all these things had happened back then, long before his life turned upside down when he met Lyubka. But on this evening, he passed all the shops and restaurants and didn't bother strolling through the City Garden alleys. A sullen, homely man, hands deep in his pockets, he dragged himself along Deribasovskaya Street. He kept close to the buildings, away from the crowds. Trying to spot acquaintances, he peered into the faces of men passing by. The crowd shimmered with the mother-of-pearl colors of polyester leisure suits and colorful dresses. The Odessa-based whaling fleet Glory had just returned to town, and the city's fashionistas dressed up in fancy, foreign-made clothes.

Yurik saw no one he knew. He had no one to listen to his worries and calm him. Midnight was approaching. He found himself back on Pushkinskaya Street and stopped. Where should he go now? He was about to veer off to the left to go home to his native Theater Lane, but then he turned around and strode off in the opposite direction. For some time, he didn't realize where he was going, until he found himself standing on Zhukovsky Street at the building where his former in-law, Lyubka's cousin, Eugene Pozniak, lived. He was chief engineer of the Odessa Plumbing Factory, a smart man, and in the past, he was warm with Yurik. Maybe, for old times' sake, he'd be willing to listen to him and, perhaps, tell him how he could get out of his troubles.

11
THERE ARE ALL KINDS OF JEWS

Boris was lucky; he waited just over three months to get permission to leave the country. He sighed in relief. His fear of being stuck in his home country had vanished. But they let him go. Who would want to hold on to a satirist, let alone a Jewish one! The emigration stream of the late sixties, which began as a small trickle, had grown into a wave that had been swelling rapidly.

Boris threw a farewell party, inviting friends and acquaintances from his fraternity of journalists. A bunch of people crammed into his small room and drank that evening. The guests came up to Boris, one after another. Some tried to find out whether he knew something about living abroad that they did not. Others just made small talk; it seemed they had come to the party only to look at the daredevil who would skydive. What made him so sure his parachute would open in time, and he would safely descend into an unknown land? In the eyes of others, a glint of fear flashed, the fear people have when visiting a gravely ill relative. They forced a cheerful smile that only hid the dreadful thought: they, too, might one day be in their relative's place.

Long after midnight, the guests dispersed. As he said good-bye and shook hands with one, Boris hesitated for a moment. In reality, the right thing for him to do would be to slap the man in the face instead. However, the soft-mannered Boris couldn't bring himself to do it.

The man who deserved such a slap was Arik Weissman, a fellow journalist. On the eve of the party, Boris was leafing through a journal in which his writing had appeared in the past. He stumbled upon a satirical article with a byline carrying Arik's real surname, instead of his usual pen name, "A. Belenky."

The theme of the piece was hardly new. From time to time, such write-ups appeared in the Soviet press. Articles like the ones Weissman wrote were a tool of the Soviet state, used to halt the influx of exit visa applications.

In this piece by Weissman, as in other similar articles organized by the powers-that-be, a Jewish family from Riga appealed to the authorities to protect them from "the provocations of the Zionists" after receiving a letter from Israel. The letter tried to make them stray from the "righteous path of buiding communism in their Great Motherland" and lure them to move to their "historical homeland."

It was unclear to Boris whether such a letter existed or if the Propaganda Department of the Central Committee of the Communist Party had fabricated it in cahoots with the addressee. Whatever the case, Boris did not expect to see Weissman's name as the author of such an article.

"Why did you do it?" Boris asked.

"They made it clear if I refused, I should forget about publishing my book, or worse."

From time to time, the magazine that employed Weissman published small brochures. As with other Soviet publications, they paid well for them not because the reader couldn't get enough of them, but because those brochures promoted socialist ideology. Whether they sold well wasn't that important.

"Aren't you thinking of leaving yourself?" Boris asked, perplexed, referring to the article.

"It's all right," Arik replied with a chuckle. "Over there, they like the renegades, too."

No matter how hard Boris tried, he couldn't come up with any historical parallels. No renegade, apart from Karl Kautsky, the Marxist ideologist whom Lenin had scolded in one of his pamphlets, came to his mind. Well, why would anyone in the world like a renegade?

Boris learned some of the details of Arik's assignment. They had called him at night and told him to take the earliest train from Moscow to Riga.

"All I could do was write it as poorly as possible," Arik said in his defense.

However, Boris couldn't commend him for that. Arik didn't have to try hard to write poorly. Besides being a hack, he was also lazy. He wouldn't have such a cushy staff position at a major magazine if his daddy weren't an establishment writer with some ties to the KGB. Besides his run-of-the-mill journalism and his inborn laziness, he was also afraid of flying. If they sent him on a business trip somewhere in the Urals, he took five days to get there by train. In that amount of time, Boris had managed not only to fly to another city to research a complaint mentioned in some letter to the editor but also to compose a satirical piece and submit it to a journal's editor. Arik envied Boris; his many publications always evoked the same derogatory response behind his back, "Our urchin is quite a hustler" (*Nash postrel vezde pospel*).

With the help of his daddy, Weissman had found a profitable and not-too-cumbersome business for himself. His father introduced him to some rich Abkhazian, who, for the sake of local prestige, wanted to have a reputation as an author. To accomplish this, he hired Arik to ghostwrite for him. Arik had roamed around his large apartment, lay down on his father's leather sofa, cursed the fate that made him a literary day-laborer, and finally came up with a storyline for a novel in the spirit of socialist realism. Some Abkhazian collective farmer had learned a new way to tie the grapevines, which enhanced the harvest. Weissman jotted it down and, without even bothering to reread what he had written, he shipped the manuscript to his Abkhazian customer. Over there, the man hired someone to translate the piece from Russian into Abkhazian. When the translation was ready, the customer carried the manuscript to a local press, where they published it right away. There was always a shortage of literary works in the style of socialist realism. A roll of banknotes handed to the editor facilitated the publication. Inspired by the substantial addition to his meager salary, the man brought the tale up to acceptable literary standards.

After they published the novel in Abkhazia, Arik marched over to the Moscow-based journal *Peoples' Friendship (Druzhba narodov)*. Soon, his work had appeared in Russian under his customer's name. They marked it with the phrase "Translated from Abkhasian." Besides the money, the customer sent Arik a smoked leg of lamb and a small barrel of Caucasian grape vodka called *cha-cha*.

When Boris learned about this, he could only chuckle. His journalist brethren had been doing whatever they could to survive. But hunger did not threaten Arik. His teeth didn't fall out from scurvy. When he was about to take a stroll with a girl down Gorky Street, his dad gave him eighty rubles for pocket money, which was more than half of what Boris made during a good month. But to write a vile and false anti-Israeli article for his personal gain was just too much.

"I asked to sign with my pen name," Arik tried to justify himself, "but they almost laughed in my face. As I understood it, they were after my Jewish surname, to begin with."

"Of course, that's why they asked you to write it—why else would they?" Boris wanted to say. Was it that hard to guess why they had awoken a laggard and talentless journalist in the middle of the night with an urgent matter? It appeared they could not find another compliant Jewish journalist.

Although Arik knew what he did was unseemly, and that Boris was hardly amused by it, he attended the farewell party. Without batting an eyelash, he said he saw Boris as a trial balloon of sorts. If Boris survived under the conditions of "decaying capitalism" as the Soviet media branded it, Arik would make the same move and leave the country too. He said he would prepare a list of questions for Boris; he needed them to be answered before he made his final decision. Arik would send it to Boris as he moved along in the free world. Time was of the essence, and the letter with his questions might even reach Boris somewhere along his route.

Boris wondered why Weissman wanted to leave. Like everyone else in Boris's circle, Arik didn't give a rat's ass about the Soviet regime. He didn't believe a word printed in the papers even though he was a journalist—maybe *because* he was a journalist. But how would he survive on the other side of the Soviet border without his daddy's helping hand? One has to work hard over there; that much was clear to Boris.

However, Arik assumed living abroad would be just lovely and swell. He imagined a carefree lifestyle with long five o'clock tea parties and strolls along the Thames or the Seine arm-in-arm with dressed-up women. As for the source of his livelihood, for some reason, he was sure that, in the West, cultured people like him supported themselves like the characters in Balzac's nineteenth-century novels.

He had no idea such a system hadn't existed for many years. He did, however, think this would be the least of his problems. He'd have a much harder time deciding where to vacation for the summer. Where would he go for his sojourns—to Nice, Cannes, or Majorca?

Arik loved dressing up, which in the Soviet Union meant having your suits custom made by a tailor. Arik called the sewing process a "construction." First, he needed to find the right cloth for the suit and pick the perfect pattern from a foreign magazine. Then, he searched for perfect buttons in Moscow haberdasheries. And he made sure one of the best tailors serving the Writers' Union would make his suit.

Boris shrugged: How on earth could he ever serve as a testament as to whether Arik should emigrate? He had never even dreamed of taking the time and energy to make himself a custom blazer, let alone have a full suit made. Of course, Alexander Pushkin was right in saying it is possible to be a "serious person and still think about one's nails." But he was talking about a businesslike person, not an idler.

Boris had no time for further ruminations. He had to make the final travel arrangements and fly off to Odessa.

12

WE'RE GOING, GOING, GOING TO SOME DISTANT LANDS

The air was hot and thick on Zhukovsky Street. At the open window stood a drawing board, behind which sat Evgeny Arnoldovich Pozniak, a sanitation engineer. A seltzer bottle stood within reach of his hand. On a chair next to him, an oscillating fan, which Odessans called "little toady," blew over his sweating face. His wife Irina had long been in bed. There was a good reason why, at this late hour, the master of the house didn't feel like sleeping.

"So," Evgeny Arnoldovich Pozniak said to himself, looking over little notes spread out on the drawing board, "objectivity is most important. There should be accuracy and clarity in every detail of the project. There's no reason to just follow your gut. Let's face it: when it comes to the question of emigration, people jump on the bandwagon without thinking it through.

"To do something just because others are doing it is to submit to mob mentality. And this is nothing but a relinquishing of reason, a behavioral anomaly suited for the lower primates. The herd instinct is a powerful thing. But with a sober, scientific, and rational approach, you can be fairly free even under the conditions of totalitarianism. We are living during a time of great advances in the fields of science and technology. It demands that a gathering of data inform all critical decisions. We mustn't forget its motto, 'Objectivity, clear thinking, and rigorous mathematical analysis.'

"So, let us separate the wheat from the chaff. Let's not waste time straining the murky water of rumors, gossip, and idle fancies. Let's turn to the facts that have precipitated and solidified. The crucial question must be answered: Should you stay or should you go? And if the answer is to leave, then when? And in what direction?"

He looked again at the notes scattered over the drawing board.

"So, sir," he said in a guardedly cheerful tone, "we're looking at the widest spread of the initial data. Chaos, the Brownian motion, unpredictability. Out first bit of data is a man from Cincinnati," he muttered, unrolling a piece of paper that rested in the upper left corner of the board. "He's a specialist with work experience similar to mine, but his degree is from the prestigious Moscow Bauman Institute, mind you. They hired him as vice president of a company producing the Morning Dew washbasins. His salary is comparable to that of the Deputy Chairman of the Council of Ministers of the Soviet Socialist Republic of Tajikistan. The specialist bought himself a house, an Alfa Romeo car, and hid extra money in an oil developments tax shelter in New Mexico.

"Case number two comes from the city of Minneapolis," Evgeny Arnoldovich said, reaching for the note on the right edge of the drawing board. "A sanitation engineer, like me, but with a lot more experience than me, and on top of it, a Ph.D., works as a regular draftsman. He isn't famished, but he endured a substantial blow to his self-esteem due to his loss of social standing and, as a result, his wife left him.

"Case number three: A specialist with scores of scientific publications in industrial design could not find any work. Desperate, he used his unemployment benefits to open two dry cleaners, a slaughterhouse, and a nail salon for his wife. He limited his diet to asparagus with cottage cheese so he could save enough cash to buy one more business—a spaghetti factory. He cursed the day when he'd left his homeland, where he had no such concerns."

Pozniak's fourth and particularly outrageous fact was one he pulled from a letter his friend abroad had sent him. To get the letter, he had to ride thirteen kilometers on a dilapidated bus to the town of Kuyalnik. But it was worth the schlep. It was a highly unusual letter, which became critical in creating an overall picture of the West. It stated the cold hard facts. The message was from the Solomon Islands, where his friend's uncle wound up after leaving the country.

That uncle, a former merchandise expert at the book warehouse of the Odessan Board of Education, didn't find work where he could use his expertise on any of the thousand Solomon Islands. He became dejected. The whole day long, he was lying on the beach in the shade of a palm tree, and a bare-breasted native woman saw to it he did not run out of coconuts. She split them for him with a blow of a saber preserved on the island since the Spanish navigator, Álvaro de Mendaña de Neira, had landed there in the second half of the sixteenth century.

"Let's make use of Boolean algebra. Let's find the median and the average of this data set. The bell curve of surviving ex-Soviet citizens under capitalism has no uniform distribution. We need to make this data usable for things like logarithms, integration, and extrapolation. So, what do we have in my case?"

The green desk lamp on the windowsill reflected in the glass of the open window. It made the face of the apartment dweller aquarium-green. He resembled an alchemist who decides people's fate and creates terrifying formulas intended to save humanity.

Narrowing his eyes, he put points on the Whatman paper. With these points, he had to project the curve of the probability of surviving under capitalism (CPSC, as he abbreviated it for himself). He decided he had to choose New York, where he had the best prospects: it's the city with the largest number of bathrooms per capita. At that moment, someone's pale-green hand appeared on the windowsill. Then there was another one. Then, the third one turned up. However, before that, the first one was gone.

After a short while, against the background of the blue-black sky, the upper part of someone's face, distorted in a grimace, appeared; Pozniak couldn't identify the eyes right away. They were shut due to the strain caused by climbing to the second-floor window. The stranger breathed heavily, which made the wings of his nostrils on his thick nose, just above the windowsill, flare. Sweat flooded his forehead and his eyes, which was not surprising on such a sultry night. His face gleamed with a green light as if a thin plastic film had been pulled taut over his face.

"Fantômas!" a frivolous thought flashed in Pozniak's mind, recalling the recent French movie about that mastermind criminal, a man of a thousand faces. His initial fright passed since he realized he could throw the stranger down.

"Eu-gene . . ." Fantômas said in a strangled voice, "H-h-help!"

Pozniak recognized his former relative, the hapless husband of his cousin. He leaned over the windowsill, grabbed Yurik under his armpits—with his legs dangling; he had almost fallen while Pozniak dragged him into the room.

{67}

"What's with you, Yurik?" Pozniak said. "You scared me to death. You're pale, sweaty, and green. Have you turned into a zombie? Did you poison yourself because of your unhappy marriage and decide to visit former in-laws at night? Have you forgotten where the door is? Or do you zombies think it's okay to sneak into a house through a window?"

Yurik was snorting, his nostrils flaring, trying to calm down.

"I didn't want . . . to wake . . . your family . . ." he uttered. "Saw . . . the light . . . didn't want to bother . . . didn't want to shout from the street."

"Oh, what a delicate soul you are!" Evgeny Arnoldovich said. "I thought you were an economist, but it turns out you're a steeplejack. One more surprise like this, and you'd leave me tongue-tied. Trust me; I could do without it right now.

"Well," he said, pouring Yurik some soda water from the seltzer bottle, "What's happened, Mister Steeplejack? Don't try to convince me you've climbed into my window to say 'Good evening.'"

Yurik gulped seltzer, staring at the bubbles bouncing around in his glass. He pursed his closed lips, causing the tip of his nose to move.

"It happened," he sighed, "it finally happened. Cops got me."

Mumbling to find the right word, he told Pozniak what had taken place in his apartment just a few hours ago.

"They'll put me in the can," Yurik declared, sounding relieved that his not-so-distant-future was now set in stone. He would be spared tormenting thoughts about his future, about Lyubka. Everything was simple and clear for the next five to seven years, followed by five-year probation.

"Easy, easy, easy," Pozniak said. "The most important thing is not to panic. Once you yield to panic, you're bound to be a casualty for sure. You put yourself at the mercy of happenstance situations, which tend to kick a man when he's down. Well, there's only one solution. You must leave, and as soon as possible."

"Leave? Where to?" Yurik said.

"The issue isn't where to . . . It is where from."

"From where?" Yurik asked, his mind overcome with the image of permafrost-covered tundra, his new home.

"Huh, Yurik? Hello?!" Pozniak waved his hand in front of his guest's eyes. "It's me, Evgeny. Are you here?" he said gently. "Leave Odessa, my friend. Leave the country. Leave the Union of Soviet Socialist Republics."

Yurik stared at him. Was the man joking? He thought a bit and waved dissmissively.

"Ah, Gene, I'm not up to traveling abroad now. I'll be traveling soon, at the government's expense. And where I wind up is their decision. First, I have no money to travel on my own and there is no way they'd let me out of the country now. You know how it is. Before they let you travel abroad, provide them with a character reference from your job and win over the approval of the regional Party committee. Memorize the names of the secretaries in all the fraternal Communist parties in Bulgaria, Poland, Czechoslovakia, etcetera, etcetera, etcetera . . ."

"You don't get what I'm saying, do you?" Pozniak asked, looking into the eyes of his visitor. "Or are you just pretending?"

"Well, I understand, I understand," Yurik mumbled. "I should apply for approval to travel abroad, for some cruise along the Danube River to clear my mind. In the meantime . . ."

"Ah, Yurik, Yurik!" Pozniak said, "It looks like Lyubka knocked all sense out of your head. How could you, living in Odessa, not see what's going on around you! Do you see that building?" he said, turning his head toward the window. "The decision to leave or not to leave torments everyone in that building, whether they are awake or asleep. I think about it at least twice every five minutes! And you don't even have a clue. Don't you know half the city is already gone, and the other half is sitting on packed suit-cases, ready to leave? Yesterday, I even heard a joke about it. Two Jews are standing on the corner of Deribasovskaya and Richelievskaya Streets, talking. Another one is passing and says, 'I don't know what you two are talking about, but we must go.'"

"Go where?" Yurik asked, dumbfounded. He remembered Deri-basovskaya Street flooded with careless pedestrians. As far as he could see, on this sultry evening, the strollers cared only about having seltzer and ice cream.

"There you go again! I've told you the question isn't about where you're headed to, but where you're leaving from. To where is a private question, a personal one, even an intimate one. It's nobody else's business. Have you heard of the Human Rights Declaration? Freedom of one's conscience and the choice of one's country of residence?"

All this talk of a "free conscience" startled Yurik. What each of these words meant was clear, but their combination was new to him. What does that mean? Could one's conscience be free? Some contradiction takes place here. If they ask you, "Do you have a conscience?" it means you aren't free to do as you wish but should act in good conscience. And here, some free conscience?

Meanwhile, Pozniak informed Yurik that the world had recently been witnessing a mass migration of people pushed from their homelands. The UN calls these people refugees . . .

"Ha, well damn right they decided!" Yurik interrupted him in disbelief at his ability to be ironic at this moment.

"Oh, I see you are hellishly ignorant," Pozniak said, his arms folded. "You're telling me you don't know about anything, even the Jackson-Vanik Amendment?"

"Which Vanik?"

"The American Vanik, you dummy. The amendment introduced by Senator Jackson and Congressman Vanik. The seventh year of mass emigration is in full swing, and you're in the dark as if you don't live in this country. Now I see why Lyubka dumped you—you're dense. What, you have heard nothing about the plane hijackers either?"

In one Voice of America broadcast, when a Soviet plane took off from the Simferopol airport, some wise guy handed a flight attendant a note for the pilot. He instructed the pilot to fly the plane to Turkey instead of Odessa. If he didn't, he'd blow up the bomb in the shoebox on his lap. The flight returned to Simferopol, they arrested the wise guy, and in his shoebox, they found nothing but the wires that had been seen peeking out the top. The whole incident happened on April first—some April Fool's joke.

"You mean the flight to . . . Turkey?" Yurik asked.

"To Turkey!" Pozniak exclaimed. "You might as well have said to Saudi Arabia. To Israel, of course! Jesus, you 're like some naive virgin. It looks like I have to educate you a bit."

Pozniak briefed Yurik about the summer of 1970, which started the legal emigration of Jews from the USSR. He told him about the group of desperate refuseniks who broke through the Soviet border on a small biplane. They bought all the tickets on a plane making a domestic flight, pretending they were flying to a relative's wedding. But, at the last minute, they were busted. As they were about to board the plane, a regiment of KGB troops with German shepherds sprung on them. They made a big stink about protecting the borders of the socialist Motherland. They labeled the guys as hijackers and terrorists, and, after a speedy trial, gave all of them long prison terms. They even sentenced two to death.

Hearing all this, Yurik felt ill. Pozniak reassured him:

"The authorities mitigated the sentences. The trial caused such uproar worldwide. The world asked why the Soviet Union sealed its borders and allowed no one out of the country. No wonder these people were desperate! The failed hijackers suffered, but something good came out. They gradually let our people go. Well, only in dribs and drabs, perhaps, but it's still something!"

Yurik remembered talk of Israel, and about his mother's neighbors who had gone to Toronto. His mother's distant relative, a certain Uncle Oscar, had left for Australia. Later on, he sent two postcards from there, both with "Finally here!" written in huge letters across the back. On one, Uncle Oscar, bald as a knee, was riding an emu. On the other, he peered from a kangaroo's pouch, waving his straw hat. Yurik didn't know what to think of the photos.

His uncle was a big man, weighing at least two hundred pounds. His weight could break the back of any large bird, even the emu. Not to mention the fact, if his uncle were to fit in the kangaroo's pouch, the poor animal could hardly move. Forget about jumping. Lugging him back and forth, it would get a hernia. Upon closer inspection, his relative had a picture of him taken in some Australian bazaar, sticking his head into a local photographer's cardboard cutouts.

But none of this ever registered with him; he was always still occupied with Lyubka.

"To leave, to leave . . ." he mumbled. "But how can I leave? Just walk over to the authorities and say, 'Hello, I'll probably be in the can soon, mind if I go abroad?'"

"All right," Pozniak said, "stop talking nonsense. Let's get to the point. Do you have an invitation?"

"No," said Yurik, recalling all the things the police inspector had said and done in his apartment. "I don't think so. The inspector said he would invite me to the hearing of Zhora's case as a witness. But we all know already how they do it. 'Tell me, what do you know about the accused? Thank you. Now you can change seats and sit down over there, at the defendant's bench.'"

"No-o," said Pozniak gently, as if he was addressing a young girl. "I don't have that kind of invitation in mind. I mean, do you have an invitation from Israel?"

Yurik thought for a while and asked:

"Well, who could invite me from there? I have no one there. No relatives or friends, not even acquaintances."

"All right, dummy," Pozniak waved his hand. "You're such a weirdo, Yurik. Nowadays, every decent person—and, just between you and me, an indecent one as well—posseses an invitation from Israel. It doesn't matter if you have anyone over there. Some people would come up with such a believable backstory for you you'd believe it yourself. Well, nowadays it doesn't matter whether or not you want to leave the country. You must get hold of an invitation for yourself just in case. It's like when you're on a plane: landing on water is extremely rare, but they have a life jacket under each seat. If you don't have an invitation, it's not a big deal. You could still get one through the Dutch Embassy in Moscow. You think the authorities aren't aware of this trick? Don't be naive! They're well aware of it. They pretend they believe in fairy tales as if they are another genre of nonfiction. Why is that? Trust me there are serious considerations at play. They want everyone to believe the whole emigration business doesn't indict, as they claim, the 'best political system known to humanity,' but just a matter of family reunification. As you understand yourself, not a single Soviet man has left because he couldn't endure the pain of living far away from his second cousin, twice removed. So, don't worry too much about the details. Such is the political game two great superpowers play with each other nowadays."

Pozniak felt he had dragged on too long. It was time for him to go to bed. In the morning, the solitaire game of making the most critical decision of his life would play out clearer. The curve he was plotting on the drafting paper already had a certain skew. He had to give his subconscious some time to work on it.

"So," he clapped his hands, "don't worry about getting the invitation, Yurik. One of my friends is going to Moscow tomorrow. He'll visit the Dutch Embassy and, while there, he'll give your data to the embassy people. They'll pass it on further down the line. In two months, you'll get a business-size envelope from Israel. With an invitation in two languages, Russian and Hebrew, to join your family member."

"Two months!" Yurik said with a deep sigh. "In two months, my address will probably be different. And as far as I know, they don't forward mail to that address."

"Hmm, you might not have enough time," Pozniak said. "You have a situation, Mister Bumshtein. How can we get you out of this jam?" Lost in thought, he wound the hair on his forehead around his finger. "Okay, here's plan B. You need to join someone, some family that already has an invitation from Israel. Say the head of a family applies for emigration and includes you in his list of his family members. It's a bit too late to adopt you as an orphan. Well, then you've got to get married. Find a broad for yourself. Not any broad but one with the invitation in hand. And marry her quickly."

"Marr-r-ry?" Yurik droned in puzzlement. After he had been divorced, the idea of another marriage never crossed his mind. He had never paid any attention to other women, except for the waitresses in the Red Restaurant during his carousing with Zhora there. It was always Lyubka and only Lyubka on his mind. Now his feelings were all mixed up. He would alternate between wishing the worst upon her and imagining her begging to be his wife again. It seemed like he was hoping for a miracle. And, as is well known, there are no miracles in real life.

"Well, your situation has a positive aspect to it, if you look at it from the other side," Pozniak said, wanting to cheer up Yurik. "To some extent, I envy you."

Yurik stared at him in bewilderment. When he had still been married to Lyubka, Pozniak had patronized him. Was he mocking him now?

"What could you be envious of?" Yurik mumbled.

"Clarity! In our time of complete disarray, deciding how one should act is the toughest task at hand."

"Well, clarity is all I have," Yurik sighed. "What about it? I wouldn't wish such clarity upon anyone. Except for one man," he added, remembering that vile person, Lyubka's fancy man Arkady, with his disgusting hairdo and his accordion.

"Dear Yurik! I've messed my head up already, trying to answer the crucial question of my life. To leave or not to leave—that is the question. And if I should leave, then when and where to? Each variant has its 'pros' and 'cons.' It drives me crazy. And you have a clear-cut answer to that question. It's a no-brainer. You must leave the country! As soon as possible!"

Pozniak shook his head in conviction. It seemed he was head-butting an invisible enemy. He never understood why Lyubka married Yurik, to begin with. The man was timid, with no prospects of making money. His looks were also nothing worth writing home about. But Lyubka—she's a knockout! However, he hadn't told her anything about his assessment of Yurik's prospects. Not so much because he didn't like to interfere in the affairs of others, but because he didn't have the full picture of Lyubka's situation to evaluate it scientifically.

Hearing out Pozniak's suggestion to find himself a woman, Yurik thought, since his fate had been making such a sharp turn, maybe he should marry somebody after all? He recalled his mother talking about one Lily from the photo atelier on Richelievskaya Street.

13
TRAVELING COMPANION KISA

Before leaving the country, Boris flew to Odessa to visit his family, and then took a train to Chop. His family couldn't come to visit him in Moscow because his father's old war wound had reopened. Boris had a long journey ahead of him, a voyage into the unknown, and he could not leave without bidding farewell to his mother and father.

To prepare him for his long journey, Boris's mother fried a whole chicken and boiled half a dozen eggs, as was their custom. His father gave him a Parker pen. It was beautiful: burgundy in color with a mother-of-pearl inlay. The father never used the pen. He kept it as a memento; the pen was his only wartime trophy. His father was pleased that, after pondering for too long about emigration, his son finally acted like a man and faced the unknown future. However, his mother was restless. Secretly she often wiped tears from her eyes. Of course, as soon as Boris would settle on the other side of the world, he would send them an invitation to join him. But what if something unexpected happens? She might never see her only child again!

When Boris packed, he didn't know what to take besides the usual things he brought on business trips. He didn't know what awaited him on this journey, and anything besides the necessities might prove to be a burden. He remembered the recent Tutankhamun exhibition in Moscow. Like the ancient Egyptians, he would surround himself with familiar household items to ensure a smooth transition into his new life.

So, not to bother with a bigger suitcase, despite his mother's insistence, he settled on his usual one.

The fact that Boris was traveling all by himself worried his mother. Who would look after her little boy over there in a strange land? She was already used to her son being a bachelor in Moscow, although she wanted him to settle down and start a family. Aware of how independent today's youth wanted to be, she tried, from time to time, to take care of her son's fate. If she learned a sweet Odessan girl was about to go to Moscow, she asked her to take along a parcel for her little Boris. She packed all of his favorite comfort foods, and it reminded him of his childhood years—home-baked biscuits, strudel, and even a few garden-fresh Fontan tomatoes, which he could never find in Moscow. She hoped once the young people met in this way, they might fall for each other and get married. Boris saw through it and didn't fall for his mother's trap. He had affairs, but he hadn't been crazy enough about anyone to bind himself with them permanently.

But Boris also felt it would be good to have companionship during his long journey into the unknown. The solution came about naturally. Victor, a neighbor in his parents' communal apartment, had presented him with a fluffy, white Angora kitten. Victor served as a sailor on a merchant ship and was often dispatched to the Mediterranean Sea. During a visit to a Greek port, he'd found an emaciated kitten in some gateway. He put it under his peacoat and brought it on board his ship.

The extraordinary grace of the kitten and the beauty of its white fur struck Boris. One of the kitten's eyes was blue, the other the color of amber. It gave the kitten's cute little muzzle a mystic expression as if it was an ancient Egyptian soothsayer or magician reincarnated into an animal.

Despite its young age, just nine months old, the kitten was of an independent spirit. It allowed those it was familiar with to come close. At the sight of a stranger, the kitten curled into a tight ball and readied itself to combat any unfriendly gestures.

When Victor had given him the kitten, Boris lamented he couldn't take it to Moscow. Keeping a pet in a communal apartment would be problematic; he traveled frequently. Who'd take care of it in his absence? At first, contemplating his emigration, he thought of leaving the kitten to his parents but decided to take it along. He had read somewhere that, according to an ancient belief, an Angora cat brings good luck. Well then, let this little graceful, enigmatic beauty be not just his road companion, but also a talisman. He gave it a simple name—Kisa.

Boris went to the Odessan New Bazaar, bought a round wicker basket with a lid, and lined it with some soft cloth. It seemed now he was ready for his journey.

At the last minute, he also took along his trusty friend "Olympia," a typewriter he had bought on the black market a long time ago when he had begun his journalistic career. He did so although he knew it would barely come in handy. What use is a journalist in the West if he can only write in Russian? He kept pushing this thought from his mind, only for it to return over and over again. What was he doing? He was tearing himself away from the only language, culture, and environment he knew; the only one in which he found a use for his abilities. Now he was about to jump into the unknown. Setting off on his one-way trip into the unfamiliar world with all the things he considered part of himself, he could not leave his Olympia behind.

The day came when he packed up everything he wanted to take along. When he finished, he discovered, to his surprise, he felt joy—unmotivated joy coming from the simple fact that he was alive, moving around and breathing. But why? The future was full of uncertainties, and, most likely, the euphoria was a reaction to the painful fact that his life, as he knew it, would end.

The night before his departure, he couldn't fall asleep. Quietly, so as not to wake his father and mother, he got dressed and set out on foot for the sea. First, coming out of the gateway of their building on 21 Lastochkin Street, where he was born and raised, he headed for Deribasovskaya Street, which was empty at this point. He walked down to Pushkinskaya Street, slowly, as if to say good-bye to each yard of the central street, so familiar to him from his childhood years. There, he turned right and, upon reaching Greek Street, he moved up to Kanatnaya Street, from which, through a few back alleys, he came out onto Shevchenko Park. Walking down one of its trails, he passed by the main stadium that belonged to the city sports society Chernomorets ("The Black-Sea Man"). Early in his life, while still a schoolchild, he would visit it often with his friends. At last, the central passage of the park brought him to the seashore.

He was lucky. The night was moonlit and calm. He stood on a cliff for a long time, watching the waves roll across without hurry. Since light plumose clouds muted the moonlight, it appeared as if tin were melting in the lunar path. After some time, he saw a fishing boat. The lines of Lermontov's famous poem came to his mind, "What does the sail seek in distant countries? What has it forsaken in its native land?"

Though painful, the answer to the second question was clear. No longer could Boris live in the country where he was born and raised. And he had no clue what was awaiting him in the "distant country." The only thing he seemed to be sure of was that he had the natural desire of any young human being: space to move and grow.

14
HOW TO MARRY QUICKLY

His relatives had already been trying to marry off Yurik. He resisted, making all kinds of excuses. He was ashamed to admit the truth: he was still in love with his ex-wife. To hide his true feelings for Lyubka, he would scold her when his mother was present. His mother would often bemoan that her heart wept over the sight of his suffering. Lyubka outraged her. Although Lyubka was still a divorcée, Yurik's mother would say the woman behaved like the "worst *goyka*," a non-Jewish woman. A woman of that kind wouldn't think twice about dumping one husband to marry another, all while waiting for the third to come along. Although his mother's words left his heart aching, Yurik kept quiet. Despite his resentment, he couldn't bring himself to hate Lyubka, no matter how much he wanted to. He would've liked to remind his mother that her own closest friend, Celia Davydovna, while not a *goyka*, had been married three times, but Mama still adored her. All he ever heard was "little Celia this" and "little Celia that."

Yurik grew tired of his mother's pressure to start dating, and gave in. He went to meet one Raya, a cashier in the men's section at the department store on Deribasovskaya Street. Nothing good came out of this visit. Yurik visited the section "little Raya" worked in, picked out some cheap, plastic comb, red and foul-smelling. He approached the counter where she worked and, at the last moment, changed his mind about getting to know her. He paid for his purchase, told her "Thanks!" and left without ever introducing himself. He couldn't bring himself to talk to her. Saying his mother sent him over would be silly and humiliating. He had never learned how to pick up women. He didn't have the right character for that. He lacked the ease and bravado for such business. He also was in no denial about his appearance. He was short, big-nosed, and his ears were radar-like. It was a hopeless case.

It's not that he disliked Raya. She was full-figured and lively; she even resembled Lyubka. Still, she was not her. Also, he could not help but feel that approaching another woman with romantic intentions, he was cheating on Lyubka. He knew it was silly. He and Lyubka were divorced. She had gotten herself a lover a long time ago while they were still married. And Yurik knew he should have done the same. But he couldn't bring himself to do it. If he'd court some woman, he would betray Lyubka. He wouldn't be able to look at himself in the mirror.

So, the red comb in hand, he came home and told his mother he'd wanted to invite Raya to the movies, but she developed a sudden toothache, and he took her home so she could rest. Mama sighed; she understood what "a sudden toothache" meant. She pitied her son and searched for another suitable candidate.

Yurik couldn't marry just any woman. As Pozniak said, his bride should have in hand an official invitation to immigrate to Israel. And he had to act quickly.

"What do you mean, marry quickly?" Yurik asked, looking at his former in-law in bewilderment. "What if that woman doesn't like me?"

Pozniak never considered Yurik bright, but now it seemed like he had lost his marbles altogether. The man was probably going to prison, but that doesn't mean he should lose his capacity to use his brain.

"Oh, dear Yurik," he said gently, "who told you she has to like you? We're talking about a sham marriage. She only has to like the money you'll offer her."

"Hm," Yurik cleared his throat. He still couldn't see himself getting out of trouble. He had been in a good mood that morning. He had a hope of getting Lyubka back. And now? Look what happened just in a single day!

"And how much can she ask for?" he asked.

"In principle, as much as she wants. But, there's been a going rate. You can expect to pay anywhere from eight hundred to a thousand rubles. And, how on earth can a regular Soviet citizen pay an additional nine hundred rubles to renounce their citizenship? Think about it—you *are* the economist. The average salary in the country is a hundred twenty . . . well, a hundred and fifty rubles. How could a single person who's contemplating leaving the country get half a year's salary overnight?"

"What do you mean, 'pay to renounce it'? What happens if I don't renounce it?"

"You amuse me!" Pozniak said, slapping his knee in delight at Yurik's naïveté. "Why does it matter what you call it? Don't you understand that imposing such a huge fine, your dear state wishes to slow down the pace of emigration? And if it doesn't, at least they can rob you blind before you leave. Even a mangy sheep is good for a little wool."

"Where would I get that much money?" Yurik gasped.

"What are your relatives for, Yurik? You have plenty of them in this city. Visit them and do it fast. And in the meantime, I'll find a woman set to leave. But act fast. Otherwise, they may force you to go in the opposite direction, like in that famous wartime song, 'They ordered him to go west, and they sent her in the opposite direction.' Only, in your case, we have the exact opposite. She'll go west, and you'll be building the Trans-Siberian Railway."

When Pozniak talked about paying a bride who could get him out of the country, Yurik thought of Yefim Butko (or Fima, as they called him in the family), his uncle twice removed on his father's side. As many relatives as Yurik had, they were all insolvent. Some could barely feed their cats with their salaries as salesclerks and cashiers. Others worked as accountants in small tailoring shops and received bonuses with which they could buy a bunch of nothing. None of them had extra money. All hope was on Uncle Fima, whom the family nicknamed "The Baklava Man."

The next day, Yurik wandered to Peter the Great Street and entered the building where Fima lived in a two-bedroom apartment with his wife Tina Grigorievna, his teenage sons Filya and Milya, and his mother-in-law, Esther Mikhailovna. He also had a grown-up daughter, Larissa, who lived with her husband in a cooperative apartment in the outskirts of the city, in the Cheryomushki district.

Before entering the apartment, Yurik stopped. He wasn't a resolute man. Showing up unannounced at a relative's home was difficult; especially one he had always kept a respectful distance from, for their incomes were vastly different. He hesitated at the door for a while, wondering whether there was another way to solve his problem. Nothing good came to mind. Out of timidity, Yurik pressed the doorbell and immediately released it.

He had come at the wrong time. The atmosphere inside the apartment was so electrified that, uttering one wrong word, any of the family members could explode. A scandal broke out because the head of the family put on his new silk suit, his creamy brown, patent leather shoes, grabbed his moth-colored London Fog raincoat and said:

"I'm off to a soccer match."

The effect of this simple phrase was striking. Tina's whole body shook, the diamond icicles of her earrings swayed, and her thin hands clenched into little fists waved in the air to the beat of her stamping feet. It looked like something out of a silent film melodrama, until she screamed, thus supplying the picture with a soundtrack of unbearable grief.

Following her lead, her mother sucked air into her lungs and boomed like a howitzer. The sounds coming from her chest were arranged in a sophisticated way. It was some medley of groaning, coughing, and ritual wailing kept in the tragic, lower registers of an organ. However, there were two leading music themes here: the theme of empathy toward her daughter's emotional suffering and the theme of contempt toward her husband. The latter theme was expressed so powerfully it was clear she despised and hated not only him, but all men.

The moment they heard the opening chords of the family scandal, both of Fima's fat boys Filya and Milya grabbed the candies and apples left on the table after the family dinner, crammed them into their pockets, and slipped out onto the street, knowing no one would come looking for them until nightfall.

Beyond the innocent utterance about a soccer game, there had been a little family secret. Except "the family secret" was not exclusive to the family for quite some time. The heart of the matter was that for two decades, Fima had been maintaining an interesting relationship with his former accounting clerk at the produce warehouse. Her name was Mila Kabaker, and during the past twenty years, she had transformed from a delicate-looking little thing, with freckles around her sharp nose, into a well-rounded Odessan lady. Thanks to her liaison with Fima, she lived high on the hog. As the Russian saying goes, she "rolled as cheese in butter." In fact, as time went by, she grew round, not unlike some exhibition-quality wheel of cheese herself.

However, this transformation didn't change Fima's perception of her feminine attractiveness. Quite the contrary. "If you grab a woman, you should feel her in your hand" was a Ukrainian proverb he often repeated. According to his passport, he was Ukrainian—Yefim Butko.

His real name was Yefim Feigelson, which means "son of a little bird" in Yiddish. Yefim wouldn't mind having such a poetic name if it didn't point to him belonging to a people whose ancient lineage wasn't at all an attractive quality in the eyes of the local population.

Yefim had become the man he eventually became because, unlike the vast majority of people, he lived not for today, but for the days to come. This trait made him stand out from the gray mass of humanity, who followed their superiors as if they were the photographers guiding them where to point their noses for the next shot. When he had learned that, during the war, the archives of his native town of Kamenets-Podolsk burned down after being hit by a German artillery shell, he found he could turn his luck around. After losing his passport during the evacuation, he asked for his new document to be issued to Yefim Butko. For fifty rubles a pop, two witnesses testified they had known him since he was a child. His passport attested he was Ukrainian, which made him more employable than if he were Jewish.

Tina Grigorievna learned about the existence of Mila Kabaker: there was no shortage of people willing to tell what her husband and his cute account clerk were busy with during their lunch breaks. First, Tina raised hell. All motifs in the melodrama *A Deceived Wife* were present—she smashed inexpensive dishes, pulled at her hair, and stamped her feet. Then she rushed to pack her suitcase. She took long enough to give her husband an opportunity to stop her, which he whiled away suppressing his yawning. In tears, she begged Fima to leave that horrible woman, that viper that wanted him to make her children fatherless. Though he struggled to imagine the quiet accounting clerk as a poisonous reptile, he told his wife what she wanted to hear from him:

"Well, if you want me to do it, all right, I'll stop it."

He fired little Mila, setting her up at the nearby produce warehouse. But he didn't break up with her. He visited her on Saturdays, right after the citywide soccer game. At first, his wife asked him why he took so long to get back from the game, but, in response, she always heard the same explanation, "There was overtime." That overtime sometimes lasted until the next morning didn't need to be explained. Fima was a good family man: he gave his wife all a wife was supposed to get, but he asked Tina whether he had the right to have something for himself, too. And she could not disagree with him. In her heart, she was glad the most boring and unattractive part of her wifely duties was no longer her responsibility.

Knowing what the sacramental phrase "I'm off to the soccer game" meant, Tina Grigorievna reconciled with the fact of her husband's liaison. However, she would throw a tantrum from time to time. The theme of that day's dramatic act was "There's no limit to male deceitfulness." It was to remind her husband that, for the stability of his domestic life, it was time to make another payment. Her current Astrakhan fur coat was rapidly going out of fashion, and it was time to upgrade her other outfits.

Fima was happy to see Yurik. At least for today, Yurik's appearance rescued him from compulsory viewing of the next performance.

"Come in, Yurik," Tina Grigorievna said, wiping her tears. She felt grateful that Yurik appeared at the critical moment when the sincerity of her grief was subsiding. Sometimes, while playing her crying role, she would get so into the act she felt miserable and would really cry.

"Sit down," she said. "Are you hungry?"

Yurik hesitated at the door. He declined the offer. He said he had some business for Fima but would come another time since it was clear he was in a rush. Tina Grigorievna didn't know what she should do next. It would be awkward to keep crying with a stranger in the house. So the momentum was lost. It would be hard to make herself cry with her usual device—imagining herself and her two boys huddled together on the street during a blizzard. She had seen this picture as a child in a book by Dickens: blizzards are rare in Odessa. She knew she was way too far from falling that low in her life. However, this mental exercise helped her to shed her first tear, and then it was easier. As soon as Tina Grigorevna's eyes moistened, she sobbed: from feeling sorry for herself, a crying abandoned woman.

Fima, however, didn't fail to take advantage of the opportunity. He slapped Yurik on the back:

"Come to the soccer game with me, Yurik. Moscow's team Spartacus is in town. There's a good chance they'll give our Chernomorets a good beating. We'll talk on the way."

15
THERE'S MANY A SLIP BETWEEN THE CUP AND THE LIP

The train from Odessa had arrived at Chop, a railroad station on the border between the Soviet Union and Czechoslovakia. When Boris emerged from the train to go through customs and transfer to the train to Bratislava, there was a sea of emigrants from all over the country already waiting there. With the instinct of a reporter, he sensed the historical significance of what was going on. He was mentally recording everything he saw; he knew he witnessed history in the making. The scale of the events made him think of the Great Patriotic War as the Soviet media called the Russian World War II campaign. Only now, it was the war the Soviet Fatherland waged against its citizens. It was the farewell punch in the stomach to people who had already lost their stamina, who for many years had been fighting for their dignity.

Boris had been struggling to decide about emigration for a long time. He was leaving the country, but in the depths of his soul, he still wasn't sure if it was the right thing to do. While he was saying farewell to his friends, his doubts kept tormenting him.

However, like many others, he came to peace with emigration within a short time—within the twenty-four hours spent at the Chop station.

Studying English, he had come across the verb "to chop," and now marveled at the prophetic name of the Soviet border station. He knew he would never forget these last twenty-four hours spent in the Land of No Return. These hours would be burned into his memory until the last days of his life.

Boris stood with everyone else on the platform, waiting for the train to Bratislava. Slate-gray clouds hung above the station; it was about to pour any minute now. Boris still could not come to his senses after what he'd witnessed in customs where all the emigrants had their luggage examined. The customs officers dug into it with a disgusted and haughty expression frozen on their faces. Children cried, and the men clenched their jaws in humiliation and powerlessness. The officials rummaged through their trunks, puckering their noses, as if what was in front of them were not possessions people had to work hard for their entire lives, but some rotten straw. They stripped the cases from the pillows and cut them open. At the inspection tables, feathers from pillows floated in the air, as they did during the pogroms. Under the pretext of some instructions, nowhere to be seen, they pocketed whatever goods caught their fancy: antique watches, a silver-framed photograph of the deceased grandfather.

They delayed the train for a long time. The station personnel strolled back and forth along the platform with hands behind their backs, and their faces resembled those of blood-thirsty vampires, drunk on blood and looking for their next meal. In response to a question regarding which track the train was about to pull up on, they answered every time differently. "Track one," they'd tell one emigrant, "track five!" they'd advise another one. "Track seven!" they'd tell yet another. When asked where the head railroad car would be positioned, without turning their heads around, not caring enough to stop walking to answer the question, one vampire would throw his finger up in the air: "There!", as another one of them would point into the ground near him, "Here!"

This tactic was one more way to taunt the exhausted people. Confused, the emigrants would rush along the tracks, dragging their suitcases from one platform to another, running back and forth, only to run off in some other direction. It seemed the torture of uncertainty would never end.

The train arrived thirteen minutes before departure. Withered, their past lives now lost forever, the people rushed to the cars, dragging their bags and suitcases. There were many emigrants from Central Asia, who traveled with lots of children placed on their shoulders. The faces of the adults, fatigued and meek, bore expressions of resignation and misery.

With his suitcase in one hand, the Olympia typewriter under his arm, and a basket with Kisa in the other hand, Boris jumped onto the footboard. He moved along the corridor, trying not to breathe the thick smells of the Soviet railroad cars, the odors of yesterday's tea and sweat and settled dust he knew all too well from his many business trips. He pushed past the leathery-faced car conductor, whose eyes were half-closed and cunning.

The man positioned himself in the aisle, obstructing the path for those who were coming in. Making everybody even more nervous, he shouted that everyone was to occupy only the places printed on their tickets. The impudent grin didn't leave his face. Boris felt like screaming. The country he was born in wasn't Mother Russia, but the vindictive stepmother in fairy tales, who wasted no opportunity to torment her children.

Although the station clock showed there were still seven minutes left until departure, frequent locomotive whistles made everyone fear they would miss the train. Where would they sleep? People lost their minds. Another day of sitting on their suitcases near their torturers! They packed the car aisles right away, slowing down boarding even more.

Having stowed his suitcase, the basket with Kisa, and his Olympia onto the top berth, Boris made his way against traffic back to the car entrance. Upon reaching it, he positioned himself in such a way that he could reach the handle of the emergency brake. Guessing what Boris had in mind, two male passengers followed him, trying to stay close to him. Nodding, they signaled they'd help him if needed.

The conductor stood nearby, placing his hands into the pockets of his tunic and lasciviously observing the sweaty, rumpled people climb up the steps of the car.

"Move away from the emergency brake handle," he said to Boris, chewing on a toothpick.

"If even one man stays behind," Boris said, "I'll pull it."

"You have no right!" the conductor bellowed and moved toward Boris. "You'll pay for it."

Boris's two silent assistants moved closer to him. Boris tensed. Rabid hatred toward this last representative of the Soviet regime who stood in front of him boiled up in him, ready to spill at any moment. He knew, if it became necessary, he wouldn't fail to pull the emergency brake handle. Nothing would stop him even if the conductor pulled a gun on him. Waiting for the train boarding to end, he and the man froze, facing off, like cowboys in the American Westerns do before the shootout starts.

Finally, the train buffers clanked, rumbling from the locomotive to the caboose, as if checking whether all cars were coupled. The crowd rushed forward, pushing with their elbows. A child shrieked. Boris figured, if his bodyguards blocked him from the conductor's sight, it'd be easy for him to rip the seal from the red brake handle. If the emergency brake valve wouldn't yield to pulling, he'd hang on the handle with his legs tucked under him.

The train jerked again, this time with such force that Boris couldn't hold on to his spot; he was pushed out into the car vestibule. He looked at the platform for the last time. Two men with heavy suitcases in their hands tried to jump onto the car's footboard. Boris extended his hand to one. Out of the corner of his eye, he noticed that someone grabbed the other man by the elbow. Boris sighed in relief. Everything turned out all right.

After the train took off, it slowed down, and two border guards appeared in the aisles. They went through the car, examining documents, peeking under the lower berths, and inspecting the upper ones where the luggage lay. Spotting Boris's basket, one guard jumped on someone's trunk and thrust his hand into the basket, but he jerked it back right away. Kisa didn't like strangers and scratched him as hard as she could. The man recoiled, squeaking like a little boy. He asked Boris:

"What's in there?"

"A kitten."

"Do you have the documents? Inoculations?" the guard asked in a hurry, hiding his vexation at finding himself in a foolish situation. Here he was, a guard for a great country, scared stiff by some small domestic animal.

Boris put his hand into his pocket about to pull out the papers, but the border guard apparently decided not to dwell on the incident, waved his hand, and walked toward the rear, yelling "Documents!" left and right.

Soon, all the border guards jumped off the railroad car, and the train gained speed again. Boris looked out the window of his sleeping compartment. He wanted to see what he had been expecting for such a long time. A border post with the Soviet coat of arms on top swam by. It was brightly painted; wide bands, green and red, curled down over its whole body, almost like a Christmas tree.

Can it be? Is this really happening?

The night came. Boris found himself in a compartment with Georgian Jews. They unwrapped paper bags with food prepared for the road: some fried chicken, several hard-boiled eggs, a few tomatoes, and a piece of soft cheese. After the nightmarish train boarding, everyone wanted to relax. The men opened a big bottle of moonshine. Their children and wives waited for the tea to be served. They waited for a long while. The conductor finally opened the compartment door with his elbow and staggered in, holding glasses and sugar cubes in blue wrappers.

"One dollar! Get your tea here," he announced. "One dollar!"

The passengers exchanged anxious glances with each other before reaching for their money. The long voyage had just begun. Each of them had only a hundred dollars the Soviet authorities had given them in exchange for rubles. Boris felt his face flush again as if somebody had slapped him. Knowing there was no one they could complain to about the robbery—what Soviet official would want to talk to the "renegades" to begin with!—empowered by his position, underscored by his uniform, this cad robbed the emigrants.

When Boris's turn came, he reached for forty kopecks and extended the coins to the conductor. Seeing the next dollar was not coming into his hands, the man raised his eyes at Boris.

"I cannot take Soviet money," he said. "Dollars only!"

"Why not?" Boris said. "This is still your country. The official exchange rate of a dollar is forty kopecks."

"I won't take kopecks!" bellowed the conductor. "Dollars!"

"You'll take them," Boris said. "This is still your country and still your money, asshole."

From the corner of his eye, the conductor peeked at ten passengers, checking to see whether they heard. After assuring himself no one had overheard Boris's words, he took the coins and left clenching his teeth.

He got his revenge that night when the train reached Bratislava. He woke up Boris by jerking at his shoulder with such force that Boris almost fell out from his upper berth.

"Documents! Border control!"

Still groggy from sleep, Boris didn't realize what was going on. Saying nothing, he reached for his visa to show it to the Czechoslovakian border guards who entered the car. When they left, his neighbor in the sleeping compartment said to Boris:

"Well, he yanked you good, I'll tell you . . ."

Boris wanted to find the conductor, but the man locked himself in his sleeping compartment and disappeared.

The next stop was Vienna.

16
PLAY THE LUNAR RHAPSODY FOR ME

Lyubka had married Yurik out of pity. He rambled and clambered around her. He whined. Lyubka was already over twenty years old, and, though she was as gorgeous as Odessan women come, men walked right past her, not realizing what they were passing up. Besides, Lyubka was rarely alone; she always had a bunch of girlfriends around her. She was only alone when sewing dresses at home. However, her countless girlfriends would visit her, even if just to chat. Lyubka's machine did not stop moving, and neither did her mouth. Young women who came for a fitting shared all parts of their lives with her, even issues too intimate for their gynecologists. All these stories amused Lyubka. Listening to them, she would laugh so hard tears pooled in her eyes, dissolving the mascara. She would have to dry her eyes with a handkerchief so she could see the chalk marks on the fabric again.

Despite being married—or, perhaps, because of it—she remained indifferent toward sex for a long time. When she tied the knot with Yurik, she was not into it at all, nor was she interested in other aspects of marriage. She had to get married so that her mother would stop grilling her. Later, she would confide to her girlfriends why another man appeared in her life.

"He touches me," she used to say about Yurik, "and it's over before it even begins. And Arkady!" She would shut her eyes. "Oh, he knows how to make a woman happy! You'd be ready to give up everything in the world for this!"

Lyubka met Arkady on the dance floor of an Odessan resort. At first, it was not him, but the music that seduced her, tensing her body. Lyubka loved nothing more than dancing. She always wore bright and colorful dresses or dark-colored skirts with red blouses; they suited her black, chest-length hair well. Even if she wasn't dancing with the crowd, she was humming. She met Arkady at the vacation resort for people in the sewing industry; one day she went there with her friend, leaving her husband and daughter at home so she could relax. Arkady was in charge of entertainment there.

She also liked him at once because he was joking all the time. Yurik was always frowning—his sullen expression rarely left his face. She craved festivities. Laughter is a vacation, a brief vacation for the mind, and a birthday celebration for the heart. When she came onto the dance floor with an unexplainable excitement, Arkady was already in the center, arms stretched out, inviting her to dance.

His white shirt, unbuttoned to expose his chest, contrasted nicely with his suntanned face and body. Although he was in charge of vacationists' entertainment, the way he carried his head made him look like a seasoned sailor, or maybe even an Olympic athlete. He had a full head of curly hair. Because of the small scar on his upper lip, it seemed he was always grinning.

When Lyubka stepped onto the asphalt floor of the dance pavilion, a tango melody poured from a loudspeaker. She froze, restraining herself from the desire to move her body to the beat of the passionate tune:

Play me a lunar rhapsody,
With a nightingale's solo.
I want to live in hope,
That a nightingale
Will sing for us.

This song was out of place as there were hardly any nightingales in Odessa. And yet, on the dance floor, Arkady swooped in like a gentle bird and gallantly offered his hand to Lyubka. A bit mockingly, mimicking some court aristocrat whom he could have seen only in a movie, he bowed to her, and she came straight into his embrace.

He knew how to treat a lady. While dancing, he spoke to her about something, though with some humor, but without being too familiar, keeping a certain distance—he understood this was the key to seducing a decent woman. Young suitors make the mistake of trying to converse with a lady as if she was an old friend too soon. Arkady knew from experience:

once a woman accepts your friendship, you lose her as a potential lover. Only courtly behavior will make her pliable. One has to bring down her defenses, to that point where she would have no choice but to rationalize, "Well, he's a man, and I am only a weak woman."

Of all the dances, Arkady especially appreciated tango. It allowed him to gather intelligence by probing the front line of the defense, giving him the opportunity to discover any vulnerabilities hidden from the naked eye. Tango is a man's dance. It is full of drama and passion and, if executed correctly, should make a woman feel like her meeting him was a matter of fate. The distinct ritual of tango allowed Arkady to be in charge, to dismiss the scruples inherent to women who do not want to be touched. Did I press myself on her appropriately? In tango, there is no place for such a question. You are in the arms of destiny, from which there is no retreat. A woman should surrender in dance long before she surrenders physically.

That was Arkady's credo. The rest was a natural extension of what had happened during the passionate lockstep. Depending on who was in front of him, Arkady plotted his course for the evening. He noticed whether a young woman was sentimental or a chatty little hen. He'd find out whether she had a boyfriend or just looked for an adventure she could whisper about to her girlfriends, to make them jealous. He appreciated Luybka's dazzling beauty and relegated her to the category of sentimental souls suffering from indecisiveness and confusion. Such women welcome anything that makes their heart tremble. They go for an affair without thinking, like a carp swimming to the light of a lantern held close to the surface of a pond.

No matter how hard Pozniak tried, he couldn't find a "bride" suitable for Yurik. Jewish women appeared to be in great demand, exceeding the supply. Russian men, Ukrainian ones, and men of other nationalities also coveted outbound Jewish women. How else could one escape from the clutches of the Soviet regime? A joke of that time circulated: "A Jewish wife is not a luxury, but a means of transportation."

Yurik knew they could subpoena him soon. He couldn't sit around and wait for a Jewish bride, sitting on her suitcases, to turn up. He could arrange an invitation from Israel for himself, but it could take several months before he received it. He could not risk it. Desperate, he decided to do what he wouldn't usually have the guts to do. He would go to Lyubka and ask for help. He recalled that one of their common acquaintances mentioned that Lyubka had already received an invitation from Israel and was also thinking of leaving. Now he knew where to. Officially, they had parted just a year ago. What if he would throw himself at her feet and beg her to save him? They would remarry and submit their joint application for emigration. If he was lucky and they received the permission quickly, he would have a chance. While the Soviet judicial system churns, he would jump across the Soviet border.

Along with this idea came a little mischievous thought. It is not without reason people say bad things are sometimes a blessing in disguise. It might be just that! They would leave together, and once they were out of the country, God willing, he and Lyubka would get back together. They have a daughter, and Lyubka must care about her future.

He wondered when he should visit Lyubka. He went in the afternoon, hoping he wouldn't find her Casanova, Arkady, there.

He was lucky. Lyubka was home alone, and their daughter Faina was at her friend Zoya's place. Before knocking on the door, Yurik pressed his ear to it. He heard the sewing machine clicking and sighed in relief. He knew from experience that when Lyubka was sewing and talking to him, she was less likely to explode.

"Long time no see, ha," his ex-wife said, letting him in. "Well, what do you want? Tell me. Hurry. I have a lot of work to do. Why have you schlepped here, sir? Explain yourself."

Yurik muttered hello and sat on a chair in the corner of the living room where Lyubka worked. He did it, lowering himself on the edge of the chair so he wouldn't damage the dress patterns hanging on its back. He didn't know how to begin the conversation and sat with his eyes on the floor.

"Well," Lyubka said, setting her sewing machine in motion again.

Yurik was silent, unable to utter a word. Lyubka continued to work without raising her head.

After a while, she couldn't stand it any longer and stopped the wheel of the sewing machine with her hand.

"Well!"

Overcoming himself, Yurik uttered, still addressing the floor:

"Let's get married."

Lyubka didn't make out what he said. Propping up her full face with her hand, she stared at her ex-husband.

Yurik raised his head and stared, meeting Lyubka's glare. He could never overcome his timidity when she looked at him like that, straight in the face.

"We ought to get married, Lyubka," he blurted out and, emboldened, straightened up in his chair.

"What's with you?" Lyubka cried out, and Yurik swung back, realizing he blundered. He should have first talked on some neutral topic. "Have you lost it?" Lyubka said. "I've told you at least a thousand times—it's over! And you . . . Just look at yourself! Here you go again."

She even opened her mouth in astonishment.

"You know, Yurik, you have a hole in your head. Here you show up, and, out of the blue, say let's get married again! Are you nuts or what? Tell me, please, why on earth should I? I've already tasted being married to you, thank you very much. Enough is enough."

She was about to start her machine again, but Yurik blurted out in despair:

"What am I to do now? Just perish? Isn't it enough that you've taken my daughter away? Now you want to get rid of me forever?"

"No one took your daughter away," Lyubka said, without giving much importance to Yurik's mumbling. "Don't whine."

Yurik puffed up his cheeks, sighed, rubbed his thighs in agitation, and, mustering his spirit again, cried out:

"If you won't marry me, I'll go to jail."

"You . . . to jail?" Lyubka laughed. "What for? Jaywalking? What else can they put you in jail for? They don't jail jaywalkers, as far as I know."

"They'll find what to send me to jail for," Yurik said.

Lyubka burst with laughter again:

"Oh, Mommy dearest, I can't take it anymore! What kind of things have you come up with now? To win me over by pity? By hook or by crook? Oh, Yurik, you make me laugh. You make my sides split. Besides, how can I save you from going to jail by marrying you again? What, they don't imprison married men? Don't make me laugh!"

Yurik blushed from the rain of Lyubka's raillery and exploded:

"Would you shut up already! You don't understand a thing! We'll get married, and together we will apply for emigration. And we should do it quickly. The only hope is that we'd have time to cross the border before they open a criminal case against me."

Haltingly, he told Lyubka about the night visit of the police inspector.

Hearing Yurik out, Lyubka became anxious. She paced the room, biting her lips. She was in her curlers, in a housedress she buttoned up carelessly. It all made her unattractive to Yurik for the first time and, thus, more comfortable to talk to. Not a beauty and some average man, but two most ordinary people, in great trouble.

"*Shlimazel! Loser!*" Lyubka wailed, even whimpered like a child, out of resentment at her misfortune. "Well, why do I deserve such a punishment! People get divorced and go on their own way. And here, as if I don't have enough of my own things to worry about, he still surprises me with some more. *Schmuck! Klutz!* Who keeps things like that out in the open? Why didn't you hang your illegal leather out the window for everyone to see, you idiot! Now they'll put you in the can for sure."

Yurik squeezed himself into a ball, cowering, with his head down and his hands in front of his face.

"Save me, Lyubka!" he said in a choking voice.

"Mama dearest!" Lyubka said, clasping her hands. "The devil made me marry a *schlimazel*! If there were an international competition of *schlimazels*, you'd win second place."

"Second," Yurik mumbled under his breath. "Why second?"

"Because you're such a *schlimazel*!"

Yurik took a deep breath and could not exhale. Something stuck in his throat.

Lyubka paced around the room in agitation, cracking her knuckles, her gorgeous teeth biting her lips.

17
THE VIENNESE DIVERTISSEMENT

K isa jumped off the windowsill, stretched, and lifted her pretty little muzzle up to Boris. *Take me out for some fresh air, and do it fast,* her stare was telling Boris. *Otherwise, I don't care if I hurt you. You know how my Turkish blood riles me when I'm depressed.*

That morning, the train had pulled up under an arch of the Vienna train station. While the emigrants unloaded their luggage on the platform, representatives of the Jewish Agency for Israel took aside a small group of those headed for Israel to the Schoenau Castle, a transit center in the Vienna suburbs. HIAS people brought others, including Boris, to a minibus and drove them to the city. It was drizzling, but after the car took off, the sun came out for a short while, as though enticing the visitors from the other world. Vienna sparkled with the bright yellow, sky-blue, and scarlet red of its billboards, store signs, and streetcars.

Despite the uncertainty in the immediate future, Boris's heart beat with joy. He had returned to his childhood, to that time when you live using all five of your senses at once. Any object you lay your eyes on engrossed you by its mere existence, teased you, *Here I am!* He fell face down onto the Viennese ground, clean and refreshed with rain. As if to validate him, a boy next to him asked:

"Is it a holiday today?"

A family from Moscow, a married couple with a boy of about seven years, rode on the bus. All the passengers had their faces glued to the windows. The boy was trying to comprehend why there were so many bright colors around him.

The minibus stopped at a building in a curved and narrow street. There was a sign above the front door: *Hardtgasse, 32.* Once again, it became cloudy, and it rained.

At the boarding house being used to accommodate the Soviet emigrants, everything made Boris uneasy. It began with the elaborate Gothic font that proclaimed the house's name, *Bettina*, at the entrance. The font reminded him of many Soviet wartime movies. He knew that in this city Strauss's waltzes and Schubert's sonatas were born. Mozart, Beethoven, Haydn, and Mahler composed their symphonies here. But it was also the city where, a few decades ago, crowds roared and raised their arms to salute Hitler. Boris had seen it in a wartime newsreel played at the Chronicle, a movie theater in his hometown. They greeted their beloved Führer as he rode around in his Mercedes-Benz, while the women sobbed, overwhelmed with the joy of seeing the great man.

They put Boris up in a tiny room on the second floor, at the end of a dark corridor. The room was musty and poorly lit. A narrow little window opened on the courtyard paved with square bricks. Even before entering his room, he felt like turning around and heading outside. All the surroundings of his temporary shelter reminded him of the communal apartment in Moscow where he had lived for the past few years. Could this be an omen? *Could it be I haven't left my past behind me?*

Frau Bettina, the small, middle-aged woman who owned the boarding house, reminded him of some cheerless character in a gothic novel. It seemed she didn't have time for smiles. She never stopped fussing. She would climb into the closets where she stored mattresses and sheets, or up to the attic for cans of meat and condensed milk. Boris saw no other workers. It looked like, to save money, she hired no one and tried to do everything herself.

Unpacking, Boris freed Kisa from the basket. She stepped onto the dark waxed floor and sat down, crouching her head and looking around. She wiggled her whiskers as though grimacing in displeasure. Looking around the room, she arched her back as if to say, *Here you are! Was it worth it to jog along on the car-wagon berths for so many days and nights, only to wind up in such an unpleasant place?*

Wanting to cheer up his friend, Boris had picked her up from the floor and put her on the windowsill. The kitten looked down through the narrow window, first with the blue eye, then with the amber one. It didn't seem to make her feel any better. She remained ambivalent, refusing to rejoice. Her whole being still resisted the new reality. *Where's the sun gone? Where is my Odessa? Will I ever live long enough to see at least a piece of fresh Black Sea fish, straight from the fishermen? If I'm stuck here for a long time, I'm afraid I might become depressed.*

At this moment, Kisa jumped off the windowsill and pleaded with Boris to take her outdoors. Boris put his shirts and underwear into the drawers of the old mahogany dresser, took Kisa in his arms, and went for a walk. He spent the following days wandering the streets until nightfall.

In the alley where the room was housed, cars of every imaginable brand lined the sidewalks. The rest of the city was like this, too. The vehicles huddled together. The sight of the infinite chain of cars was disheartening. They were all tiny: Volkswagens, Citroens, Peugeots, Fiats. Their owners were not ministers and diplomats whose positions demanded they move around in limousines, but ordinary people.

The very thought of owning a car was frustrating. Boris tried not to think about the fact that, in his former life, he couldn't dream of having even a rusty little car. All that connected him to the world of automobiles was a small red-covered booklet titled "International Driving Permit," which the Moscow traffic police department had issued to him after he passed the driving test. Yes, he had the right to drive a car.

He and Kisa passed by a small shoe store. Although its shelves were crammed with merchandise, the store was empty. A bored, prim sales-clerk stood at the counter. Boris paused. In the shopping window was a textbook illustration of the "inherent contradictions of the capitalist sys-tem": its tendency to overproduce, thus leading to overstock. What would happen if a store like this had existed in Moscow? Customers would pack it to capacity. Unable to stand the flood of emotions triggered by the sight of foreign-made shoes, they would smash the place to pieces.

Boris sneered to himself. He was experiencing decompression sick-ness. When they pull the divers up from the ocean depths, they don't do it in one shot. To keep the divers safe, they place them in a hyperbaric chamber where they reduce the air pressure gradually. A funny thought crossed his mind: What if, to avoid traumatizing emigrants from social-ist countries, they were to transport them step by step, giving them time to adjust to the new lifestyle? They could be placed in some little town where the store shelves would be filled step by step. First, stores with food and staples, then other goods, like shoes and clothing.

He wandered through the streets of Vienna with his quiet Kisa. He was carrying the kitten by pressing her to his chest, protecting her from the drizzle with his Italian nylon raincoat called a "Bologna," named after the city in which it was produced. Kisa clung to him. She sensed her owner's life was changing dramatically, and as a result, so was hers. For Boris, who was abroad for the first time, his situation felt murky. He had entered a new world, and despite how attractive and dazzling it was, to him, it was a strange and impenetrable one. That was the way he had felt about the women on the cover of *Vogue*. Once, while visiting Odessa, his parents' neighbor gave him the magazine. He had bought it while overseas.

The fact that he only had a few shillings in his pocket, given to him by the Joint, intensified Boris's sense of alienation. He was a pauper in a world where everything came with a price tag. Nothing was free, save for air and the water shooting from the fountains in the square. He could only afford to glance at the myriad goods in the display windows of countless shops along the Kärtnerstrasse, the central street. Everything around him was wrapped in a transparent film because all these stores sealed their products in cellophane.

Everything in Vienna was different; alien to the eye, yet familiar. Pondering this, Boris realized he had already witnessed the scene in Soviet movie theaters. Like many other Soviet people who had never crossed the border, he followed the basic plot of foreign films only superficially, while examining the scene's background and all secondary in it. He wondered, what did the city streets look like in that parallel universe projected on the screen? What was it like inside the houses? How did people treat each other? What did they think and care about? What did they believe in? What made them happy?

Without thinking whether his little pocket money from what the Joint gave Soviet émigrés was adequate, determined to prove to himself that this was his current reality and he wasn't just living in some movie, Boris stepped into a café to have the famous Viennese coffee, with a no-less-famous Viennese pastry. He climbed onto the porch of a café with an illuminated sign, and he pulled the glass door open. The faded reflection of some sullen young man flashed in front of him; from under his Bologna raincoat, the little pink ear of a kitten peeped out. Boris grabbed a table and allowed Kisa to stretch her legs after having been cramped in his bosom for such a long time. At first, the kitten refused to move. Her unending adventures had exhausted her. After looking around, she circled the table like a model strutting down the runway. Whether out of fear of the new site or due to her innate pride, Kisa spread her bushy tail in an arc, as if to say, "Big deal, this much-vaunted Europe. Ha! I come from a civilization so ancient that, while bears and wolves still scoured about here, my ancestors would rest on the laps of the viziers, surrounded by unprecedented luxury."

Boris broke off his pastry and poured milk for the kitten. The saucer was decorated with a golden monogram, the initials of the café owners' names. Kisa lapped up milk right away, but, sniffing the pastry, didn't touch it. She cringed with displeasure because Boris didn't understand that his beautiful traveling companion didn't like the prospect of growing plump.

After some wandering, Boris and Kisa stumbled upon the Opera House and explored it. Boris knew that the Opera House in his native Odessa was second only to its Viennese counterpart. But, looking at the gable of the Viennese Opera, Boris had his doubts. The Odessan theater was smaller but much more elegant on the outside. Perhaps the interior decoration made the difference—the painting of the walls and ceilings, the design of the auditorium. But, alas, he was too broke to see a performance.

It was drizzling. Kisa peeked her head out from under his cloak to look around. Boris smiled. He stroked her strained velvety back, so pleasant to touch. They went to the Viennese Central Post Office. Boris didn't know German, but scraps of Yiddish (preserved in memory from when his parents said something not meant for children's ears) helped him find the Poste Restante window. As he hoped, a letter from Ilya was already waiting for him. Boris opened the envelope. He found several handwritten pages.

18

MORE RELIABLE THAN STOCK IN COCA-COLA

Yefim Butko made his first fortune in the early fifties. The city was recovering from the destruction of war, so many buildings had to be built or repainted. At Privoz, he opened a booth with a sign above it that read PAINTS AND LACQUERS, and people came looking to freshen up their apartments with joyous colors. However, neither paints nor lacquers inspired Yefim. The bluing, which these people loved for its ability to impart freshness to whitewashed ceilings, did not excite him either. A businessman with little imagination might slip fine sand into the bluing powder and rejoice at the smidge of extra profit. Fima was sharper than that. He focused on linseed oil, often referred to as *olifa*, a more profitable product.

It was a divine product. Not only did it dissolve any enamel paint, but one could dilute *olifa*, opening the possibility of another creative method— "re-grading." Yefim added cheaper, artificially derived linseed oil to the natural one produced from hemp or flax. This way, he could make two cans of olifa out of one. No instrument of the city trade inspection could detect this. The name of the product made him think of some Persian princess. *O-li-fa!* May your name be blessed now, forever and ever! He would also make his children do the same, and especially his wife. *Olifa* provided her with the marvelous little things she loved to look at when she was in a bad mood. She would look at some bracelet adorned with small gleaming diamonds, and they would cheer her up. (Alas, she could only admire these baubles in secret, so as not to evoke jealousy or ill-will from neighbors, who might write denunciations to the police. How can the wife of an ordinary salesman of some paints and lacquers store sparkle with diamonds like Farah Pahlavi, the wife of the Persian Shah?)

As for Fima, like many Odessan underground millionaires, he dressed modestly, wearing a padded military jacket, which had become fashionable again. That jacket served as a nostalgic reminder to veterans of the difficult years that bonded them together. Years ago, Yurik had seen underground millionaires being escorted out of a courtroom. That the millionaires wore regular padded jackets, perhaps of better quality, struck him. There were no cheviot suits or shoes embroidered with silver threads. Just boots, quilted jackets, and khaki breeches—to the entire world, they looked like civilian employees of the army.

He had imagined all millionaires looked like the American ones on Soviet posters. Cigars in their sparkling white teeth, gold cufflinks in their silk shirts with laces. They were puffed like whipped cream, and their plump pink chins sunk into them. Those chins were delicate, like the bottoms of newborns; they needed to be powdered with talcum so that they wouldn't perspire.

Fima wasn't like that. Six months before the planned raid, he boarded up his paint-and-lacquers booth and changed his playground: he became the manager of a produce warehouse. The state snatched up anyone who didn't have the talent to keep their underground business under its radar.

At the produce warehouse, Fima waited it out, considering future opportunities. He found a new field where he could apply his talent. He had to leave sales altogether. A Jew in sales was always under suspicion. The fact that his picture was always posted on the Best Salespeople display wasn't any help, either. Per the stereotype, a Jew who wasn't an exemplary salesman was not a Jew, but some strange creature. The formula was simple: a Jew in sales had to be at least three times better than a Russian. If you couldn't be a salesperson, be a scientist. Get involved in designing ultra-precise machinery or study nuclear physics. In those highly sophisticated fields, you only had to be twice as talented as your Russian colleagues.

Fima found his real joy where he had never expected it: in a Turkish dessert called *baklava*. For the past thirteen years, he had worked at the factory producing these exotic sweets. He had never been so happy. He was no longer a salesman, some hermit monk who sat in the dim little shop with no ventilation. Now, he was a machine-shop manager. He was among people, part of the collective. He managed his shop deftly. The factory's red challenge banner, given quarterly to the best shop, was always displayed on the wall above his desk. His shop was the first in the factory that earned the right to put the honorary "mark of excellence" on the packages of baklava. His business motto was "Always be first, and rise to new heights." Those who drift are crushed, and the people who are flying are left unharmed. During the last, frantic week at the end of the quarter, he worked around the clock to ensure that the red traveling banner remained in his office. He was precise in his orders, and he didn't hesitate to act when he had to.

"If necessary," he would tell his daughter and son-in-law during family gatherings, educating them on the way things had to be done, "I'll hop on the plane and fly at my expense to see our industry's deputy minister. I'm trying to get through to him, but they won't let me in. They say he's at a conference. 'What's the topic?' I ask his secretary. 'How to increase the production culture,' she responds. I drop a box of made-for-export baklava in the secretary's lap and, still filthy from my travels, I barge into the conference room. I raise my hand and, with all due respect, ask the speaker to stop. 'Before improving the culture of production, I ask you to weigh my current production problems. I'm officially informing you that I decline all responsibility for fulfilling the plan for the quarter if you don't give me the fifty-two trucks I need to ship my finished product.'

"Everybody is in shock! The Deputy Minister rushes to the phone and gives his instructions. Only when I'm flying back can I breathe a sigh of relief. Well, I use fifty trucks to ship our production, and two truckloads I sell on the side.

"Initiative has to be encouraged!" He finished his story on a sincere note.

One could only surmise where he sent those two cars of baklava on a quarterly basis. But Fima's fame as an excellent worker had never faded.

"What's the issue, Yurik?" Fima said when they got to the stadium, and the soccer game had started. One of the Chernomorets strikers rushed the ball into the penalty area.

"Fima," Yurik mumbled. "Well, would you . . . please . . . lend me some money?"

Fima half rose from the bench. Not in surprise: many people asked him for money, but because the Chernomorets striker tricked the Muscovite center half, dashed to the goal, and struck at it. He missed! The whole stadium jumped to its feet. *Are we going to beat these Moscow scoundrels?* The next moment, they moaned in disappointment. Fima lowered himself onto the bench along with everyone else in the stadium, except Yurik, who was still lingering in his grief.

Fima was silent, and Yurik thought, because of the noise the fans produced, his uncle didn't hear his request.

Yurik was about to start over. Fima interrupted him:

"Okay, you need help, I can see that. How much?"

"About three thousand," Yurik said, lowering his eyes in embarrassment. Besides paying his fictitious bride, he still had to pay for the renunciation of his citizenship and buy the train tickets. There were other expenses involved too, both large and small.

"Dollars," Fima said.

"Dollars?" Yurik asked. "I need rubles."

"And I need dollars," Fima said. "I'll give you rubles, and you give me back the same amount in dollars."

Yurik was flummoxed. How did Fima know he was planning to leave the country?

"How did you know?" he asked.

"Aren't *we* curious?" Fima said. "It's so difficult to figure it out. Well, why else would someone urgently need money these days, if not to leave this *wonderful* country?"

"How am I going to pay you back in dollars? I can't mail it to you."

"Well, you'll just do it," Fima said. "Their mail system is much more trustworthy than ours, isn't it?"

There was not even a trace of a smile on his uncle's face. It confused Yurik. Was his uncle making fun of him, or what? There was a pause, and Yurik could not come up with anything to say.

However, what was on Fima's mind wasn't a mystery. It was the same thing on the minds of many other Jews. He was already preparing himself for emigration, contemplating his next move. Because he was Ukrainian on paper, his chances of receiving an exit visa were low. For the first time in his life, it would be beneficial to show off his Jewish origins. He was preparing to lose his passport again, produce his "lost" birth certificate, and find two witnesses (and this time, he'd have to pay them a hundred rubles each).

Unlike most would-be emigrants, Fima did not care whether he knew Hebrew, English, or any other foreign language. Even with Russian, he only knew as much as he needed. He memorized a dozen of the Party slogans, never bothering to consider their meaning. He already knew they didn't matter much anyway. He accepted it. Advertising slogans trigger unconscious reflexes. They advertised communism; that's their personal business. Everyone picks the business they feel like doing.

He also knew two dozen curses in Yiddish. He had enough linguistic skills to get by. He knew, if he needed them in business, he could always find educated people. His experience taught him the more educated they were, the more often they turned to him for money so they could get by until their next payday. The blind thirst people have for knowledge that wasn't worth a damn thing always amazed him. They couldn't make a penny from their education.

Well, would he be able to send his daughter to college on his managerial salary? It did not matter that she had good grades in high school. In this antisemitic country, good grades were hardly enough for a Jew to be admitted into college. He would like to see where she and her husband, even though he was a capable design engineer, would live now. Where would they get the money to buy their co-op apartment? All these bright minds, all these scientists and super-scientists, have been and always would be paupers.

These people lived like this in the USSR, and he wasn't convinced they would do any better in a country with a free market. Fima both pitied and despised them because, despite their bright minds, they didn't see they were praying to the wrong God.

"What city are you going to settle in over there?" Fima said, still following the soccer game.

Yurik didn't think about these things. He had no clue what was awaiting him after he crossed the state border. There was only one thing clear to him: he will be saved. Moreover, Lyubka and their daughter would be at his side.

Glancing at Yurik's bewildered face, Fima patted him on the shoulder.

"Okay, don't sweat it, Yurik. We'll settle things between us once we're both over there."

Fima believed his purpose in life was to help people. It was challenging to enumerate everyone he helped get apartments by giving them money to bribe city officials. These people thanked him as much as they could. Typically, with money. They would do it on their own; he would never insist on receiving anything in return.

Yurik wasn't the first man to ask him for a loan. Over the years of being an underground businessman under the conditions of "developed socialism," Fima learned to sort people. He didn't care much about IOUs, relying on his intuition and knowledge of humanity. He rejected some emigrants, just from the looks on their faces. "When I arrive in America, even the FBI wouldn't be able to catch this guy for me," he would understand, looking at the shifty eyes of some supplicant.

His reason for trusting Yurik had nothing to do with them being relatives. Fima considered none of the others to be solvent, but Yurik was honest and belonged to that rare and dying breed of people who would return their debt, even if they'd have to starve for a while. Money lent to Yurik was no less a reliable investment than buying shares of Coca-Cola on Wall Street.

19
SURVIVOR'S GUILT

Boris found a quiet corner in the Viennese post office and read the letter from America:

Boris, hello!

So, you are in Vienna. Congratulations! You've finally crossed your Rubicon. I'm very happy for you, and I can't wait to give you a big hug at the first opportunity.

I have exciting news. Though my emotions are not on a par with your life-altering state of mind—been there, done that—I'm also overwhelmed with what's been going on lately here, in America. I want to share it with you because it concerns not only me but you too. All of us, Soviet Jews. I have so much to tell you. Luckily, it's Sunday, and Bella with our little Maxim went to her girlfriend's baby shower. It's a ladies-only party. So, I have some time on my hands to write you this letter, which promises to be rather lengthy . . .

Do you remember how we were both flabbergasted when Fima, your friend from Moscow who came down to Odessa on his vacation to swim in the Black Sea, whispered to us so nobody would have heard him? Back in Moscow, he ran into a group of American tourists from Chicago. They told him that in America, many Jews (and non-Jews!) sported bumper stickers on their cars that read SAVE SOVIET JEWS! We stared at each other. There were people on the other side of the globe who cared about us? I have to admit: I felt a lump in my throat. I couldn't believe total strangers on the other side of the globe not only thought of us but also fought for our freedom.

So, can you imagine, not only did I meet one of those incredible Americans, but I've become friends with him? His name is Si Frumkin. A tall, slender man in his late forties. Blond. Every time I look at his bushy mustache, it reminds me of the ears of our Ukrainian wheat. When he walks, he has a light, bouncy gait. Looking at him, you wouldn't ever guess how much horror he'd lived through in his life.

When I asked him what makes him care about what happens to us, the Soviet Jews, he looks up at me in astonishment as if he were saying, What kind of question is this? Isn't it obvious? Are you even asking me this?

The secret of his obsession is that he knows first-hand what happens when some people suffer, and others turn a blind eye. As the Russians say, he knows it on his own skin. Here, literally.

He was born Simas Frumkas in the city of Kaunas, Lithuania, in 1930. He came into the world at the wrong place at the wrong time. He was hardly ten when his family got in big trouble. Twice within a single year, mind you! It happened for the first time in 1940, less than a year after Hitler's and Stalin's henchmen, Molotov and Ribbentrop, signed their secret agreement dividing the whole of Europe into what they called "spheres of influence." Shortly after, Hitler pounced on Poland, and Soviet tanks rolled into Lithuania. They took away the Frumkases' car and motorcycle dealership, and the family lost any means of support.

Less than a year later, Hitler had a change of heart regarding his friendship with Stalin. When he attacked the Soviet Union, German tanks rolled into Lithuania, and the whole family, including Si, found themselves behind the city ghetto's barbed wire.

The Nazis evacuated the ghetto in 1944, breaking up the family. They sent Si and his father to the Dachau camp, and his mother to a camp in Poland.

"My dad," Si told me, shaking his head. "I survived thanks to him. When they unloaded us from the train at Dachau, they sorted us out like cattle. The Nazi officer asked me about my age, and my dad whispered, 'Tell him you're sixteen . . . you're sixteen.' I was hardly fourteen but he knew already that, when a new batch of prisoners arrived at the camps, the Nazis disposed of children right away. A troublesome nuisance, that's what children were for them. But the Nazis needed to replenish their workforce. I was tall for my age, and they thought I'd be valuable as a slave."

They sent Si and his father to the aircraft-hangar construction site.

"How the hell did I survive it!?" Si shrugged at the mystery of his own life. "I was a young boy. I schlepped metal rods on my back, I carried bags of cement, unloaded some damned brass fixtures."

Si's face grew pensive and sad. His father didn't survive the ordeal. He died about three weeks before the day the Americans liberated the Dachau prisoners in 1945. Can you fathom, Boris, what Si was going through?! He was just a kid!

Well, in 1949, after bouncing around the world for a few years, Si came to the States as a displaced person. He studied here. Earned a master's degree in history, a topic he had become a victim to in his childhood. He worked in the textile industry and soon ran his own business in downtown L.A. His company, Universal Drapery Fabrics, produces drapes and curtains of all kinds. He became a businessman. But survivor's guilt tormented him. "How come I lived, but my father and so many others perished?" he asked me repeatedly, looking into my eyes as if I had any wisdom about the whims of fate.

That's why as soon as he heard about the plight of the Soviet Jews, he invested so much of his time and energy into a business that promised him not big returns, but big trouble. It wasn't his first choice to get involved personally. He tried to engage the local Jewish Federation Council. But they told him not to rock the boat because the American government was seeking a rapprochement with the Soviet Union. That is, they tried to pacify the beast with some trade favors and small talk.

Being both a scholar and a victim of history, Si knew appeasing an aggressor never worked. His inspiration for getting personally involved in the fight came from one Jacob Birnbaum. Back in the spring of 1964, the man single-handedly launched a campaign on our behalf. I saw the man's picture in a paper. A tall guy in his late thirties, he sports a goatee. They photographed him wearing a Russian-style winter fur hat, the one with ear-flaps, you know . . . I guess he wore it on purpose—to make it clear who he was fighting against: the country abusing human rights.

Jacob is a German Jew. I read his biography in the paper. Shortly after the Nazis came to power, they attacked his father in the street. Then, a bunch of German boys caught six-year-old Jacob and stuffed his mouth with dirt. His family managed to leave the country before it was too late.

"I bet that's when it all started for him," Si shook his head when I asked him about Jacob. "How could someone forget such a thing! His childhood memories had made him swear to himself he'd never be silent regarding injustice."

After the war, Jacob's family migrated to America. He studied at the Yeshiva University in New York. One day, in the spring of 1964, he walked down the corridors of his dormitory and banged on the doors, urging his classmates to get into the streets to resist the treatment of Soviet Jews.

"Well," Si's eyes glistened with delight, "could you imagine, Ilya? In a few days, a thousand students gathered in front of the Soviet U.N. Mission. Jacob's office was his dormitory bedroom."

Soon, Si followed in Jacob's footsteps. First on his own, then together with his friend, Zev Yaroslavsky, a UCLA student who also had Russian roots. Zev had visited his relatives in the Soviet Union a year before and came back to the States horrified at what he learned during his visit.

These guys threw themselves into action. They hardly went unnoticed; they weren't small fries by any measure. If Si stood six-foot tall, Zev was a good five inches taller and a few pounds heavier. It wasn't their appearance that brought them to the attention of the police. Their provocative actions gave them a lot of headaches. Just between you and me, I bet they also kept busy the KGB spooks operating here in Southern California. Those poor fellows could hardly keep up with the pair.

First, Si and Zev got involved in run-of-the-mill demonstrations. They burned Soviet flags in public. They protested against travel agents that promoted trips to the USSR. They picketed Soviet athletes who came to L.A. for a field and track competition in the coliseum . . . When a Soviet freighter arrived in the Port of Los Angeles, the guys rented a motorboat and headed out to the ship. They planned to paint LET SOVIET JEWS GO! on the side of the vessel. But how could they stay in place when they cut the motorboat's engine? Si solved the problem by mooring their boat to the freighter with nothing other than a toilet plunger.

When the Bolshoi Ballet came to town, Si and Zev printed their own playbills and, at the theater entrance, handed them to the theatergoers. Below the ballet cast of *Sleeping Beauty*, they put a note. It called on the public not to ignore the fact that the country capable of producing such an enchanting spectacle was also capable of treating its Jews as second-rate citizens.

The police duly arrested the pair. But the judge let them go. He found their action an exercise of freedom of speech granted by the U.S. Constitution. Unlike back home, they take their Constitution seriously.

Si and Zev's first significant action took place in December 1969. With Hanukkah approaching, they organized a march with lit candles. Could you imagine it, Boris? Five thousand Americans from all walks of life,

Catholic nuns included, marched through downtown L.A., from the Music Center all the way to City Hall. The L.A. Mayor, Sam Yorty himself, joined them.

One important detail for you to know: in America, if the media doesn't cover a public protest, nobody would know and care about it. It's as if it had never taken place to begin with. So, Si gave a heads-up to the *L.A. Times* city desk, and Zev grabbed the attention of several celebrities, such as the big TV performer Steve Allen and newsman George Putnam. As a result, the L.A. candle-lit march received nationwide coverage . . .

(This is between you and me, Boris. When I learned about this story, I asked myself: Why have so many Americans troubled themselves on our behalf? Gradually, I learned that many people here feel guilty for not responding back in the late 1930s. German Jews, to escape the Nazis, came to these shores but were turned away. Americans didn't want to get involved in European affairs. Many here thought "the pond," as they call the Atlantic here, was big enough to protect them from European calamities.)

But back to Si. His next operation involved sending thousands of post-cards to his business clients, encouraging them to pass the cards along to everyone they knew, asking them to write SAVE SOVIET JEWS! and ship them to the Soviet Consulate in San Francisco.

Knowing well what the Consulate workers would do with the provoc-ative postcards (that is, throw them into the garbage can), Si and Zev, his partner in crime, brought a cardboard box filled with the cards to the Con-sulate doors. When, as expected, the Soviet officials refused to accept it, Si and Zev threw the box over the fence into the Consulate yard. The Sovi-ets didn't think of anything better than to throw the box back. Since Si saw it coming, he had alerted the press beforehand, and a midair shot of the rejected box with postcards thrown back from the Soviet Consulate appeared on the front pages of many American papers.

Their next publicity stunt took place at the L.A. Car Expo. Here, in the States, a car is so much more than a means of transportation. They treat their automobiles like beloved pets. Come Sunday, they clean and wash them, polish and shine them. Almost make love to them. So, the car shows rival beauty contests in popularity.

Some foreign countries send their vehicles to those American exhibits. A few years ago, the Soviets showcased a brand of sedan called the Lada. I bet you never heard of it back home because it was "Zhiguli." For West-ern markets, they scrapped the Zhiguli name, which sounds awfully close to "Gigolo." (Taking into consideration how feeble-powered the Soviet car is, it would offend all gigolos of the world. They'd feel the car brand name mocks their masculinity.)

So, for export, the Soviets christened that mouse of a car Lada, giving it a romantic twist. As you may recall, Lada is the name of the Old Slavonic goddess of love and beauty.

In America, more people pour in to the auto fairs than into the city zoos. The press covers it extensively. And TV reporters are also there. So, Si together with his buddy Zev got hold of some press cards, and, with photo cameras around their necks, arrived at the spot where they displayed the Soviet Lada. To advertise new cars, it's customary in America to hire beautiful girls. Scantily clad, they walk around the limousines, sit on their hoods, lifting their legs. I take it the point of these advertisements is this—if you fall in love with the girl, you fall in love with the car.

So, Si asked one of the good-looking girls sitting at the registration desk to place her pretty derriere on the hood of the Lada and give him a smile for the camera. Thrilled at the sudden chance to be in the papers, the girl obliged him. At the last moment, when she'd already made herself comfortable on the Lada, Si handed her a placard which he asked her to hold up for him above her head for a picture. Raising her hands upwards to display the banner, the girl had no idea what was written on it, until she saw she created quite a stir. The photo and TV reporters hurried toward her from all over the vast exhibition hall. The placard she held high above her head read SAVE SOVIET JEWS!

The more I learn about Si, the more he keeps amazing me. Consider this. Back in our homeland, from our cradles, they drilled it into our heads that all an American businessman, capitalist pig that he is, thinks about is how to line his pockets with money until they burst at the seams. And here, instead of fretting over every penny, businessman Si Frumkin doesn't spare any expense in throwing a monkey wrench into public indifference regarding the issues he cares so much about.

Here are a couple of examples for you, Boris. What they call football here, in America, has nothing to do with what we are used to seeing back in Russia. Here, contrary to the game's name, they play it with their hands. To give you an idea of what this game is all about, imagine a group of ultra-Orthodox rabbis trying to smuggle their most sacred book, the Torah, into the Soviet Union, where, as we all know, they don't welcome it. The rabbis are confronted by Soviet border guards armed to the teeth and ready to lay down their lives to prevent the dangerous book from penetrating Soviet territory.

It seems anything goes to win. The moment they tackle the ball-carrying player down to the ground, the opposing team jumps up and piles in a heap over him. Since the tackle often causes concussions, the players wear helmets, not unlike medieval knights for whom cracking their opponents' skulls was the ultimate pleasure.

The spectacle is exciting, like any bar brawl; as you know, violence is highly watchable. Once a year, on one of the Sundays, they play the final American championship game; they call it the Super Bowl here. It takes place at some huge stadium. The Sunday of the match is an unofficial national holiday. The streets are empty as if aliens invaded the country, declared martial law, and imposed a curfew.

The whole country stocks up on beer, chips, and popcorn and sits down in front of the TV sets. It is one of two days a year when Americans gain half of their excess weight. (The second day is Thanksgiving, when it's customary to fill yourself up with the meat of the most innocent bird on the American continent—turkey.)

Before the game begins and during halftime, the world's biggest pop stars perform—Michael Jackson, Paul McCartney, the Rolling Stones, you name it. The entire country, including newborns, even if their eyesight hasn't developed yet, watches this competition. For the amount of money the advertisers pay per TV minute, you can buy a house here in L.A. (by no means a cheap place to live) with a pool and a two-car garage. You could probably buy both those cars, too!

So, could you even imagine the pretty penny it cost Si to hire a helicopter to fly a banner that read SAVE SOVIET JEWS! in the skies over a packed stadium?

On another occasion, Si threw his money at the wind. Literally. If you recall, back in June 1973, the Soviet papers reported that "at his summer residence in San Clemente, California, President Nixon gave our dear Leonid Ilyich Brezhnev a royal reception." They also expressed their delight that the conversation between the two leaders took place in a "warm atmosphere of cooperation between the two superpowers."

What the papers failed to report was that while they celebrated and pampered the Soviet head honcho, the President's Secret Service found themselves in hot water, trying to avoid a potential public relations scandal. Si had paid for five thousand black balloons painted with the words LET MY PEOPLE GO!, which covered the skies over the Nixons' nest. What the hell could they do to prevent the Soviet guest of honor from peeking out the window and seeing these balloons? He was bound to be offended.

The bizarre spectacle disturbed not only the guards but all the neighborhood dogs too. As if the world was ending, they barked until they became hoarse.

However, not all of Si's and Zev's operations ran smoothly. Sometimes, an unforeseen detail made all their efforts go down the drain. After learning that the Soviet water polo team was about to play the Americans at the Long Beach Water Stadium, Si bought a bag of instant red paint, industrial strength. The night before the match, together with Zev, he made his way inside the stadium and poured the contents of the bag into the pool. In a few minutes, it seemed filled with blood. To make it clear what their symbolic action was all about, Si wrote SAVE SOVIET JEWS! in huge red letters on the pool's tiled wall. In the morning, the pool workers drained the red-tinged water and replaced it with untainted water. Wiping off Si's graffiti was a much easier task for them.

This setback didn't make Si skip even a beat in doing what he felt he must do. In 1973, fluent in Russian, he visited Moscow and secretly met with many refuseniks' families. He talked to them, took their pictures, and filmed them. He brought back tons of evidence of human rights abuse to America. National TV and the print media featured his video clips and photographs. Si had also started the "Adopt a Refusenik Family" campaign across the country.

But, the man's most daring operation was the one he carried out to discredit the Trojan horse of Soviet propaganda, General Dragunsky. You know, Boris, we must give some credit to the Ideological Department of the Soviet Central Party Committee. They know their onions when it comes to brainwashing the Western public. A few years ago, when the campaign for emigration rights began in the West, they sent a tour group to the States. To dispel the "myth" that they discriminate against Jews in the USSR, the eighteen-head delegation included Jewish and non-Jewish professors of law, historians, and scientists. As if to say, "Look, ladies and gentlemen, don't you see Soviet Jews are equal among equals in our country?"

The cherry on top was appointing Colonel General David Dragunsky, the highest ranking and most decorated Jewish officer in the Soviet Army as the delegation head. Dragunsky had gone on propaganda missions before. First, in Brussels, where he put together a meeting countering the World Jewish Conference on Soviet Jewry; it dealt with abuses of human rights in the Soviet Union. Then, he visited Latin America on a similar mission.

Now, he came to the States. After visiting New York, Washington, Kansas City, and San Francisco, Dragunsky brought his delegation to Los

Angeles. I'm getting ahead of myself, but I'll tell you that if he'd had known what Si had in store for him, I bet he'd skip the Los Angeles metropolis for his own good.

When news of the delegation's arrival in Los Angeles reached Si, he did something that would render Dragunsky unsuited for any future propaganda operations. When he learned they expected the General's visit at a Beverly Hills villa where he was to meet with the representatives of the Jewish community of the greater Los Angeles area, Si phoned the host of the gathering. He told him there was no need to wait for the General's appearance at the villa anytime soon. Comrade Dragunsky resolved not to return to the Soviet Union and, instead, to seek political asylum in America. Regarding his current whereabouts, the General prefers them to be undisclosed for obvious reasons given the circumstances.

Much agitation and commotion ensued. The host and his guests placed many calls. Soon the rumors took on a life of their own, and they even reached the *L.A. Times* journalists. I don't know what happened when Dragunsky showed up at the villa, or how he tried to deny the politically embarrassing rumors. Although upon his return to Moscow, the General beat his breast assuring his higher-ups he had been the victim of a bourgeois provocation—it didn't help. Believing there is no smoke without fire, the Party bigwigs removed him from his post. He could no longer travel abroad.

So, Boris, when you are finally here, you must meet Si and Zev. We should do whatever we can to express our gratitude for all they have done—and are still doing!—on our behalf.

Hugs, Ilya

20

YOU GO RIGHT, AND I GO LEFT

Like any normal Jewish person living under ripe socialism, Lyubka became excited when she learned about the opportunity to emigrate. She was still young, full of energy, and she wanted to start her life anew. She hardly knew what she would do on the other side of the Soviet border. However, her intuition told her that, although it was doubtful she'd be able to take over the market cut of Dior or Gucci, she could make a living in the business. If she could survive in the Soviet Union on her own and support her daughter, she would not die of hunger wherever fate would take her.

The only thing holding her back was the thought of losing Arkady forever. Their affair was tumultuous because he was married, but his wife didn't want to even hear about a divorce. After Lyubka informed him she would leave the country, he brought her enormous dahlias; they were purple, the color of her eyes. He said he wouldn't stay in the country for too long. He would settle some of his business, divorce his wife, and then he would find Lyubka in the West, where they would live together till death do them part. Lyubka prepared for a long journey, torn between believing him and not believing.

Lyubka didn't feel like tying herself down with her ex-husband again. Like a chick pecking through an eggshell, her hope for her future life with Arkady jumped up and down in her soul. Although it seemed Yurik wasn't aware that she could not take their daughter out of the country without his permission, it was only a matter of time before he found out. He would refuse to sign it, not only to spite her but also because he was attached to Faina. Now, when he had gotten in trouble, he had even more reason to make Lyubka take him with her. To make matters worse, Yurik probably still hoped to get her back, which would present another hurdle.

Lyubka paced around the room, not knowing what to do. Yurik sat in the chair, breathing hard. His whole destiny, his final hope of salvation was now in the hands of his ex-wife.

No matter how hard he tried, he could not control his breathing. He grabbed his ears and, bending over, exhaled. Together with the air that burst out of his lungs, a deep groan emerged from his chest.

Lyubka glanced at him out of the corner of her eye. She felt sorry for her ex-husband—although he was unlucky, he wasn't a terrible person. She paced around the room again, wringing her hands. What can you do under such circumstances? She ought to save Yurik. No matter how you look at it, he was the father of her daughter.

"All right, Yurik," she said. "Let me think about it."

Yurik stood up, went to the exit, hesitated a bit at the door, glanced at his ex-wife again, and left.

Lyubka couldn't keep her eyes closed the entire night. The next day, cursing, crying, and laughing at her crazy lot, she went along with Yurik to the marriage registrar's office.

The registrar official was a withered, homely woman, no longer young. From the look imprinted on her face, it was clear she never had a man, and not for lack of desire. She read their application and set a date for their marriage registration in a month's time.

As he was about to regain his hope, Yurik turned pale. Both forgot the registrar offices had been trying to improve their statistics by reducing the number of divorces due to hasty marriages. To get married, a bride and her groom had to wait a month after submitting their marriage application. For Yurik, staying an extra month in the country meant he had a great chance of leaving the city, not in a passenger car headed west, but in a boxcar going the other way.

"But we aren't some kids," Lyubka said to the registrar. "We've been married before. They introduced the new law for those who marry young, out of stupidity. We got divorced out of stupidity. Our daughter is fourteen years old already."

"I understand," the registrar said, proud for the socialist legality, which her duty called her to guard. "But I can't do anything. The law is the law!"

After a pause, Lyubka asked the registrar:

"Excuse me, what's your name?"

"Maria Petrovna." The fact that Lyubka addressed her not as an official, but as a human being, puzzled her.

"Do you mind if I call you Masha?"

Without waiting for an answer, she chattered:

"Here's the thing, Masha, I'm telling you this as a professional dress-maker. A burgundy crepe de chine dress with flowers on the chest should suit you. Believe me, when you wear it, men will barrage you with marriage proposals. There's only one thing I'd need—it's your measurements. Come over to my place this evening. I'd need just a few minutes of your time to take them."

It took a short time for the female registrar, who had already said farewell to her chance of feeling like a lady, to succumb to the temptation. The opportunity to sport a fashionable dress enticed her, and the silly Soviet law was pushed to the side. The woman pulled the first available form out of her desk and wrote Lyubka's address on the back.

"Just remember," Lyubka said to Yurik as soon as they took to the streets. "No tricks! Don't get any funny ideas in your head! Once we cross the border, you go right, and I go left."

21
ALL ROADS LEAD TO ROME

Ten days after arriving from Chop, together with the other ex-Soviet tenants of the boarding house, Boris headed back for the railway station. This time, he was going to Rome. Everyone took seats close to the windows. Nobody wanted to miss the opportunity to admire the views of the mountains, which they knew only from Vasily Surikov's famous painting, *General Suvorov Crossing the Alps*. Several Austrian soldiers brandishing Uzis passed through the aisle, proceeding to the open vestibule. There, they settled in, lit cigarettes, and exchanged short guttural phrases.

One emigrant, a middle-aged man with a short professorial beard, informed everyone that because, in the past, the Palestinians had attacked a train carrying a group of Soviet émigrés, the Austrian government had dispatched a security team as a measure of precaution.

The sight of the Austrian soldiers talking in German made Boris uneasy. Some other expats in the train car also flinched. It was the result of an ingrained reflex stimulated by the soldiers' uncanny resemblance to the Nazi soldiers in World War II films. They were also svelte and blonde. Some soldiers had the sleeves of their jackets rolled up. This detail seemed disturbing. It was the way Germans appeared in the newsreels, riding on their motorcycles over the fields during the first weeks of their invasion of the Soviet Union.

Standing in the vestibule, the Austrians spoke calmly. Their whole appearance seemed to say, *We're soldiers, we do what we're told. We have our orders to guard you, and we do it. It doesn't matter who you are.*

The train approached Rome early in the morning. It stopped on the outskirts of the city; as emigrants understood, it was done for their safety. They moved everyone along with their luggage onto the big, mastodon-like buses, which brought them to the "eternal city."

They placed Boris, along with others, in the hotel named Miramar. Now, they had to re-register with the Joint, pass the medical testing, and wait until the Joint could find sponsors for them in America and grant them their entry visas. Before Boris could finish unpacking his suitcase, there was a knock on the door. There stood a fidgety young man, an ex-Soviet who resold domestically produced items en route.

Although Soviet newspapers had claimed the ruble was the hardest currency in the world, the state reluctantly parted with American dollars. None of those who were about to depart had even an inkling of how long their journey would be. They weren't allowed to take any jewelry out of the country—not even a great-grandmother's wedding ring. Taking along something that had at least some value on the other side of the Soviet border was far from easy. Virtually all Soviet consumer goods were of poor quality. A half-decent joke circulated in the country at that time. At the end of a Japanese delegates' visit to the USSR, a group of Soviet reporters asked them what had made the greatest impression on them. The visitors nodded in unison: "The children! You have wonderful children!" "Children? That's it? Just the children?" the pressmen asked. "Nothing else?" "No, not really," the Japanese said. "Whatever you make with your hands is awful."

But there were exceptions. When fleeing from the Soviet land, people would stock up on resalable items. Among them were caviar in small glass jars with thick bottoms resembling spectacles for the near-sighted; lacquered wooden jewelry boxes from Palekh; clay figurines of the famous Gzhel artisans; Zenit cameras (no one could take along more than one of them); painted wooden spoons; linen sheets; Russian dolls for samovars; amber earrings and necklaces; and of course, Stolichnaya vodka.

The stranger who visited Boris's hotel room was one of the young people whom he had seen out in the streets of Odessa. They were blackmarketeers specializing in buying Western goods from foreign tourists and sailors and reselling them with high margin profits. Some black marketeers settled in Vienna and Rome and went on with their business. Only now they bought and resold Soviet-made goods to the local population—to the Austrians and Italians.

The stranger glanced at Boris's bachelor suitcase and the basket with a kitten. Kisa didn't like the uninvited guest's face. She picked herself up and bared her teeth, making it known to the rascal she wouldn't let him take her alive.

After learning that Boris had nothing but a bottle of vodka which he kept for a special occasion, the visitor turned his visit into a chance to chat with a fresh face in town. When Boris stepped out of the room to get fresh air with Kisa, the black marketeer followed him.

"I'll tell you," he said with an air of condescension, "this is all trifles. Those lacquered boxes, vodka, and caviar . . . my main business is cars. I buy from one guy and sell it to another. Drugs, this and that. Sometimes, I arrange a girl for a night for some foreign tourist. Making money is not a problem. The main problem is there's no spiritual life here. Back in Kiev, I could stop a girl on the street, charm her, chat her up, grab a bottle of vodka—and she was mine. And here?" he spat into the dark of the Roman night. "You don't know what you've gotten yourself into. Here, in the West, you cannot stop a woman on the street. You can't even count on befriending her. Here a woman is only for sale!" he growled. "And at a very, very high price!"

He sighed. Then, he waved his hand, instantly forgetting his anger. "All in all, you can live here . . . if you have money, of course."

He walked away, whistling and scanning passersby on the other side of the street.

Later, an old man paid a visit to Boris's room. The man was staid and moved slowly; his emanating dignity had no clear origin. Looking at Boris's shabby suitcase, he realized the young man had nothing for sale, but that didn't surprise him. He sat on a chair for a while, catching his breath. He told Boris he doesn't earn a lot on the émigrés' souvenirs. It's all child's play. The real thing was in America. Here, he was only doing it not to lose his entrepreneurial skills.

While Boris was waiting for an interview at the Joint office on Regina Margherita Street, he took long walks all over Rome. He often stopped, trying not just to sightsee but also to take in the millennia of European history etched in stone. However, the everyday life he observed on the streets interested him no less than the antiquity. He kept searching for familiarity, but everything seemed at least a bit different from his homeland. That was why he noticed everything. Every detail looked striking, whether it was the Roman trams, people's faces, or store windows. Being in Rome was like diving into a pool. A regular object, be it a tablespoon or a coffee mug, always appears a bit different when it's lying at the bottom of that pool. Even your fingers look paler; they don't feel like they are your own, even though they move when you want them to, albeit slower than you might expect. Here the sun broke through the water, and, looking up from the bottom, you see a swaying net of light, which resembles a moving fishing net made of shape-shifting light.

That's how Boris experienced Rome; it was a deep-dive snorkeling trip among the wonders of an ancient city. Only when he ran into a compatriot would his head emerge from the water. Although the emigrants talked about ordinary things—another site to see or where some bargains were to be found—this small talk sounded different, as if it were more important than usual. Each word uttered seemed three-dimensional, significant as if it had been calculated beforehand. The words seemed valuable in themselves, whether he was talking to a patron of the brasserie at the House of Journalists in Moscow on Suvorovsky Boulevard, or a furniture salesman from the store on Liteiny Prospect in Leningrad, or a news vendor on the corner of Richelievskaya and Deribasovskaya Streets in Odessa.

Great migration, Boris thought, wandering around Rome and bumping into his compatriots. It's like Noah's ark—all the animals being herded in pairs onto ships to an unknown land. Why is it you can instantly identify one of your brethren on the streets of Rome? You look to your left. You see a man of average height, and you immediately recognize him as a compatriot. He is slouching, and he seems unfriendly and frustrated. Even if he's dressed in a European suit, it sits on him awkwardly, as if he were wearing a square bathtub. His movements are uneasy, and his face expresses his self-inflated ego—he wants to look more experienced, more cultured, and wiser than he is. God, see how hard we're trying! What a pathetic sight! But what do I know? After all, I'm only an egghead Russian intellectual. Even back in Vienna, Boris noticed that Soviet emigrants disliked each other. Quickly, they grouped according to where they came from. Muscovites and Leningraders put on an aristocratic air. They preferred to communicate with their kind and shunned the plebeians—all those coming from provincial towns like Odessa or Kishinev. The members of the intelligentsia could not conceal their distaste for their fellow refugees who had been doing whatever they had to do to make a living. Even if it meant getting involved in the ubiquitous black market . . . Now, forced into close contact with these people, the ex-members of the Soviet intelligentsia, when they had to talk to them, barely moved their lips. In turn, the underground entrepreneurs from the provinces regarded those who lived on their miserly Soviet salaries as "office rats."

It would seem they were all brethren in fate. They all were burdened with the same concerns and had the same problems. They would have to get along—but somehow, they did not. Their suspicion of each other would not abate; it was like a rash they had developed and could not treat. They would still push people aside and cut in line at the registration table at the Joint and HIAS offices. A layer of lies, thick, like cigarette smoke in a pool hall, stupid and uninventive—not even lies, but sheer impudence—hung in the air. Boris suddenly felt that what was happening shouldn't surprise him. After all, in their home country, lying to the authorities was a way of survival.

However, he understood one lie. Newcomers, waiting to be fingerprinted, crowded the small reception room of HIAS, which was located on the top floor of a mansion on Regina Margherita Street. The procedure was hardly pleasant and somewhat degrading, so they approached the desk meekly. The scene reminded Boris of the way sheriffs in American movies, wearing wide-brimmed hats, their revolvers hanging cowboy-style, branded bandits in the pretrial detention centers. These people in the HIAS reception room were accustomed to standing in long lines. After all, they had spent the greater part of their lives in lines for Algerian dates, French bras, Czech boots, or a subscription to the multi-volume editions of Russian classics. They were used to being abused, usually with impunity, by the little people back in their country: by all those guards at the entrances to Soviet establishments, salesclerks in produce stores, shoving heads of rotten cabbage at them, or by butchers who forced them to buy bones for the price of meat.

However, until recently, they had been the citizens of a vast country. They had bosses, but many of them also had subordinates. Here they felt like cows about to be branded. A silent, middle-aged American man stood in his black suit, suppressing his annoyance toward the dumb emigrants, while he demonstrated how they should bend their ink-smeared fingers before pressing them on the paper.

Then came the paperwork. When asked about his skills, a Soviet emigrant was quick to say he was a sculptor, when in fact he had been a stonemason. He had no inkling that, if he told the truth, he would have earned the approval of Mary, the American social worker who was registering him. In the U.S., it's much easier to find a job as a stonemason than as an obscure Russian Michelangelo. Another emigrant, the manager of a small boat-house at the mouth of the Neva River, said: "I was practically in charge of the Gulf of Finland."

"The entire gulf?" simple-minded Mary asked.

"Yes. With all its tributaries."

Mary would roll her eyes. She couldn't understand these Russians. What a stubborn and incomprehensible bunch! The office was so packed there was no air to breathe. Look at this family from Dushanbe, the capital of Tajikistan. Five sweaty people: a husband, a wife, and their three children. All five of them were interviewed and dismissed, and yet, they sat down again in the reception room. The family is sitting huddled together. They are stuck to each other like bits of mud in a swallow's nest. To defuse the crowd, Mary screams to the Dushanbeans: "Please go! Why aren't you leaving?"

She's almost praying, trying to comprehend these strange people: "Oh, please. Please leave once your business here is over. There's no air to breathe over here!"

The family's silent; they only wheeze in response. Nobody moves a muscle. Finally, one can hear from the nest:

"We can't leave. We are waiting for Soloveichik."

"Why do you need Soloveichik?" Mary says in a panic. "Who's Soloveichik?"

"Soloveichik," the Dushanbe husband replies, "is our neighbor."

"Well, why are you sitting here? Wait for him downstairs."

"We agreed to wait for him here. We promised to show him where the cashier's office is."

"Well, I'll show it to him myself!" Mary pleads. "Go!"

"We can't," wiping sweat from his brow, the imperturbable Dushanbe man replies. "What if you forget?"

Mary desperately waved her hand and returned to her desk. *How can she understand?* Boris thought when watching this scene happen again and again, *that we cannot help but cling to each other? We used to feel that was the only way we could all survive.*

If you eavesdrop on their conversations, whom do most emigrants miss? Much more often than their relatives, they long for their friends. How can Mary understand what Russian friendship is! A byproduct of a sixty-year war between the state and its people, friendship in the Soviet Union is a blood brotherhood of war. Is there anything stronger than that?

{ *123* }

Try to survive on your own when the Soviet regime is charging toward you. The only thing that saves you is that you know you're not alone in enduring this trouble, that in a nearby foxhole, your brother-in-trouble also presses himself to the ground.

It was the year of the biggest wave of emigration. The stream of people who wanted to leave the country were from all walks of life. Next to ordinary white-collar folks, such as engineers, scientists, and teachers, there were many others seeking a better life—blue-collar workers offended by their superiors, fledgling scribblers, talentless actresses, and single women, both with and without children—all dreaming of finding happiness in America.

There were a few successful cinematographers, who, despite their fame and fortune in the Soviet Union, were birds trapped in a golden cage. In their midst were also underground entrepreneurs, who had decided that, if they had amassed some capital under totalitarian conditions, they could do much better for themselves in the world of free enterprise. Many of them argued, *We may not become Rockefellers: we are already aged, and we don't have enough capital to invest in big projects, but we're not done yet.*

One could spot some criminals among the emigrants, both amateur burglars and experienced armed robbers. To conceal their criminal pasts, they were let out of the country with families—some of their own, others hastily arranged. It wasn't hard to recognize them. Their angular gestures were the gestures of people unaccustomed to sitting around a family table. They were wary. Many of them had vulgar tattoos on their hands, which they tried to cover by pulling down the cuffs of their shirts. The Soviet authorities did their best to discredit the emigration. Don't you see, ladies and gentlemen, who is leaving our glorious socialist country? Scum. Good riddance to them!

Besides Jewish criminals, they released prison inmates of Russian, Ukrainian, and other origins. On the one hand, the state wanted to get rid of them, and on the other, it tried to do an ill turn to the West.

There were also some former film directors. Back in the USSR, wearing leather jackets and toting leather bags had been a sign of belonging to the country's artistic elite, and it set them apart from the rest. But here, in Rome, they were lost in the crowd of emigrants. While leather clothes were unattainable in the Soviet Union because of their cost, they were cheap in Italy. Even those who lived in Rome could afford it with their meager refugee allowance.

The former filmmakers (now émigrés like everyone else) moved around the city, making frequent stops, narrowing their eyes as if to arrange their lights and cameras. They couldn't accept that common fate made them not much different from other refugees. They convinced themselves they were in transit to Hollywood, destined for fortune and fame across the globe. There was just some slight mishap delaying them on their way to Hollywood. Over there, the actors had already taken their spots on the set, and the assistants already held pages of the script open for them, waiting for their director finally to cast the leather bag from his shoulder and take his place in the folding chair marked with the word DIRECTOR. In reality, like other refugees, the filmmaker was standing in line on the Roman street named after Regina Margherita, waiting for his handout from the Joint.

There were also the avowed dissidents. There were only a few. They wandered around Rome like boxers who couldn't fight for the next month due to a small scrape on their face. They were still full of athletic ardor, but there was no one they could wave their fists in front of any longer. Squinting from the Italian sun, they still caught their breath and mentally settled scores with Soviet power, not yet realizing the battle was over, and they would never rechallenge the hated system face-to-face. Now, they could only shake their fists at it from afar. They still wrote letters, first to the UN and UNESCO, then to Amnesty International and the Christian Union, and collected signatures for petitions. However, it was clear: the special place they had occupied in their society was lost to them forever. All of them, like the others, stood on the threshold of a new life which they could barely imagine.

In two weeks, Boris no longer was only visiting Rome. Walking up and down the Italian capital with Kisa in the basket, he understood he was now *living* in Rome. He was in limbo—something was different. He'd left one place but still had not arrived at his destination. He wished he could come somewhere permanently and begin the process of acclimating, which seemed impossible before it even started. He would entertain himself by studying English. He would walk along the streets of Rome, turning foreign words over in his head. They were pebbles. Odorless and tasteless, they evoked no associations in the way words in Russian did.

Only now did he realize the difficulty of mastering a foreign language. What could he, a journalist, do with that language? It was ridiculous. Words are not some bricks, which you can stack, one after another. In Russian, every word branched off into many semantic connections. The words were living creatures, not specimens in some herbarium. Sometimes, he would try to construct meaningful sentences by stringing together English phrases he had learned in high school. The results were terrible. It resembled a toddler's babbling: words without the ease of fluency, words lacking nuance.

The riddles of English grammar also overwhelmed him. Standing in line at the HIAS office, Boris befriended a nice fellow, a Ph.D. in biology from Leningrad, Mark Kholmsky. Boris discovered that the man was a luminary of sorts in his field, known for publishing lots of Russian abstracts of English scientific articles. When Boris asked him whether he could clarify the difference between the past indefinite and past perfect, Kholmsky replied without bothering to take his Marlboro cigarette out of his mouth:

"Four *mille*."

At first, Boris didn't understand what the man was referring to. He thought Kholmsky meant "miles." What did distance have to do with it? The distance from what to what? However, the deadpan expression on the man's face made it clear he was talking about four thousand (*mille*) of Italian *liras*, almost the daily allowance the Joint gave to the emigrants.

Boris was astonished at how quickly this Soviet emigrant adapted to the world of capitalism, turning casual relationships into commercial ventures. Oh, we will go far as a people! Who said that we'll perish under capitalism? It became clear that Russian friendship, much prided by the Russians themselves, was, in fact, only a means of survival in a totalitarian country.

Boris had no money to master the past perfect tense. He signed up for the free English courses offered to Soviet emigrants at the local branch of the World ORT School, the Jewish Association for the Promotion of Skilled Trades. The school was in a quiet alley near the Tiber River, which kept flowing, much like the Yauza River in Moscow.

It was reassuring that the teacher of those courses was an American; it was a chance to hear the language come alive, rather than regurgitating phrases from a textbook, like, "How do I get to the railroad station?" "It's simple. Turn around the corner and hail a taxi." It was British humor; but did the textbook's authors think Soviet emigrants were up for a laugh?

However, the lessons at school turned out to be of little use. The teacher was a middle-aged American on the chubby side, wearing an untucked, florid shirt. He sat at the edge of his desk, surveying the class, and slugishly talked about what America meant to him:

"She is like a wife to me. Sometimes I'm ready to throw her out the window. But it doesn't mean I don't love her. Well."

A long pause followed. The teacher was a volunteer, unencumbered by teaching skills. He had no idea how to fill his classroom time, besides citing personal anecdotes. He spent another half hour on a boring story about his ability to determine the origin of his fellow Americans by the way they pronounced the word "water." He repeated the word twenty times in different variations, uttering the first letter, his lips flapping. It was like he gargled that water.

Boris got on the bus for a tour of Venice with the other expats. Close to St. Mark's Square, at a kiosk where they offered glass trinkets, one Italian merchant, a tall and thin man, half-bent, his eyes narrow and bird-like, overheard the Russian tourists and pulled out a red booklet from his jacket. He tapped on the brochure with his crooked finger and spoke cheerfully.

"*Comunisti!* There are millions of us now! Soon, we'll take over all the power!" he added, bringing his claw to Boris's face and clenching it into a little fist.

"Well, your Communists will take away your little shop," Boris couldn't resist, picking up the phrase from his Russian-Italian phrase book in a yellowish cover, supplied by HIAS.

"That's right!" the merchant said jovially. "They'll take away my little shop, and they'll give me a department store."

"They'll take it away and won't give you a thing," Boris said in a muffled tone.

The merchant laughed, shaking his crooked finger at him.

"*No! Impossibile!* That can't be! They'll give me something. I voted for them! Uh-uh."

He shook his finger again.

"*Emigrante!* You abandoned Russia! It's bad!"

Boris shrugged. It had slipped his mind that Italy had lots of Communists reading their own *Unita* on all street corners.

One of his neighbors in the Hotel Miramar surprised many emigrants with his knowledge of local morals and manners. The man brought along a set of records of Vladimir Lenin's speeches to sell in Italy. His calculation was simple: such a collection would cross the border with ease because it was unlikely to be on the list of items prohibited to export. And no Soviet customs official would want to steal it. As a result, the set turned out to be the most profitable of all the items he had taken along to resell in Italy.

That the records with Lenin's speeches had found buyers at the Roman flea market named Americana caused cheerful bewilderment among the Soviet émigrés. Everybody still remembered the official hoopla over the hundredth anniversary of Lenin's birth and the mocking names of goods allegedly produced in the country to commemorate such a high holiday. A bar of soap branded "Around Lenin's Places" . . . A body powder called "Lenin's Ashes" . . . A bed for three named "Lenin Is Always with Us." And the nursery rhyme composed for the occasion:

> Who is that Bolshevik over there?
> The one who's climbing on the armored car?
> He wears a large cap,
> Mispronounces the letter r.
> A leader of all peoples and tribes,
> Guess who it is!

Boris soon found that the local Communists registered the presence of ex-Soviet citizens in the Italian capital. In one of the pastry shops he stopped in, on the counter, next to the coffee brewing machine, he found a small stack of leaflets printed in Russian:

> *Dear Soviet Tourists, beware!*
> *What you see in the shops of Rome shouldn't mislead you. The abundance of goods in these shops is the result of the ruthless exploitation of our Italian working class. We're continuing our struggle.*
> *—The Communist Party of Italy*

The text of the proclamation was baffling. It seems, in their ideological heat, the local Communists deceived themselves. Did they think these were tourists? When had it been possible for the Soviet people to take a train and come to Italy for sightseeing, and in such large numbers? If it were that easy, it's likely many of them would not have emigrated. As for the bit about the abundance of goods in Roman shops, it seemed the local Communists were not aware that a victory for communism would make the products disappear.

One afternoon, in an Ostia barbershop, Boris met another Italian Communist. He was young, hardly over twenty years old. His face resembled that of someone Raphael would have painted, with his slight goatee and large, sleepy brown eyes. Having parked his tiny Peugeot under the barbershop window, he entered the salon and sat down on the handle of an empty chair. Swinging his legs, he chatted with the barbers, who must have known him for a long time. It was the height of the working day, and he was blithely clanging a set of his keys; he was in no rush.

"You're from Russia?" he asked Boris. "Oh, I dream of going to Russia!"

"Why?" Boris said.

"Because I'm a Communist. I want communism to reign here in Italy like it does in Russia. It's quite a different spirit of life," he said passionately.

"Yes, different," Boris said and walked out of the barbershop.

22
BEATING THE SYSTEM

In response to Lyubka's reminder that she is only his wife on paper, Yurik shook his head and muttered under his breath that he would agree to whatever she demanded. But his secret hope to win her back, which was all but withered away, reignited within him. Yurik was so encouraged by her compassion that he became more determined than ever. He'd show Lyubka she had him wrong all along. Emigration is a complicated matter filled with unpredictable problems. A single woman with a teenager on her hands wouldn't be able to handle it on her own. It would be his chance to prove himself a real man, invaluable to her. He darted around the city on borrowed money from his relative, Yefim, buying everything needed for the journey: sturdy bags, canned meat, and goods to sell on the way.

To find all these things in a city even as enterprising as Odessa would be far from simple. The tide of Jewish emigration swelled up with each passing day. Those items that once only foreign tourists had sought moved from the store showcases to underneath the counter. The black market boomed with its suddenly enlarged list of scarce commodities. Yurik felt exhilarated whenever he obtained something he knew would be of value abroad, whether it was a Palekh box or a samovar doll, even if he overpaid for it. He would surprise Lyubka with the fact that they would depart in style. He had also wanted to spend Yefim's money on some nice clothing for them. You don't want to show up abroad looking like deadbeats! He was convinced that, on the other side of the Soviet border, the way you dressed was critical for the first impression, and any subsequent ones. Yurik went to the famous Odessan flea market where sailors' wives resold the foreign-made goods their husbands had brought back. There he bought a tweed jacket with leather elbow patches, similar to one some Cambridge professor wore in a British film he had seen, and a pair of elegant shoes made at the famous Czechoslovakian factory Batia. Yurik figured this jacket and these shoes would make him look respectable in the West. For Lyubka, he bought an astrakhan coat that he judged would flatter her. She would realize that, in his eyes, she was no less than a high-society beauty, an opera diva, or a billionaire's wife in a Hollywood movie.

However, he miscalculated. At first, Lyubka rejoiced at the expensive new piece of clothing. Standing in front of a mirror, she threw it over her shoulders. However, her practicality prevailed over her vanity.

"Yurik, are you crazy?" She threw up her hands. "How can you be such a fool! To drag such expensive goods across the border! You'd have to hire armed guards so that nobody would steal it! What have you done? Did you also buy a Kalashnikov rifle?"

Seeing how Yurik hung his head, Lyubka waved her hand and said she would sell the coat to her girlfriend.

There was one problem that wasn't that easy to solve. Every Odessan leaving the country as an emigrant had to do it through the Chop railway station. Aware of the Chop "meat grinder," which is what the émigrés called the long lines at customs clearance, Yurik opted to show his shrewdness and, in doing so, impress Lyubka. He'd show her the difference between a caring husband and some bastard with dumb hair preoccupied with perfecting his tan. If you are one of the first in line for the customs office in Chop, you will leave the country that same day. But how would he get to the station early enough?

Only one train ran daily from Odessa to Chop. It arrived a few hours before the transfer going through Bratislava to Vienna. With the massive influx of émigrés, there was a risk of not having enough time to get through customs before the Bratislava train departure, in which case, the travelers would have to spend the night sleeping on suitcases at the station. But what if there was a way to get to the station earlier than the train from Odessa?

Yurik opted to game the system; he figured if they took the train to Lvov, then took a taxi and rushed to Chop, they would get there ahead of the train from Odessa, overloaded with emigrants.

At first, everything went smoothly. Once the locomotive, still panting with smoke, dragged the coach to the platform of the Lvov station,

Yurik rushed to the station square. He negotiated a deal with a pickup driver who had brought potatoes to the city for sale. Then Yurik rushed to the station building and sought the conductor of the Vienna-bound train that would make a stop at the Chop station. Although Yurik had already bought tickets for this train, other passengers could grab their seats. For fifty rubles, the chief agreed not to give anyone else their places, so that when the train arrived in Chop, he would have no problems reclaiming them.

After a few hours of jolting around in the pickup, the Bumshteins arrived at Chop. Inspired by the successful course of events, Yurik cheered up. He jumped from the board of the truck and rushed to the luggage carts, which, as he had been warned, were hunted after by all departing passengers. He grabbed one before the other emigrants snatched them all up.

But here, his stock of good luck ran out. As if Fortuna had a limit to her blessings, it had all ended. It seemed as if the goddess of luck had suddenly realized she had gone too far in her generosity toward him. Enough is enough!

First, when they passed through the customs inspection, officials demanded to look into Yurik's wallet to make sure he wasn't taking more hard currency from the country than was allowed. Yurik handed his wallet over to some lanky, young officer whose face was cunning yet innocent, like a chicken thief in an Odessan market. Before the man could take it, another customs officer, a fat man with steel-rimmed glasses, tapped his shoulder from behind. He grabbed Yurik's waist and walked him through the door at the counter and into the inspection booth.

There, they strip-searched Yurik, invading all crevices of the human body. Blabbing on about the importance of the procedure and glancing at him with a poisonous grin—We know your kind, Jews! You've robbed our Mother Russia!—the customs thug ripped out the inside pockets of the professorial tweed jacket, which Yurik had paid good money for at the Odessa flea market.

Crying out *Aha!*, the ape stabbed the heels of Yurik's Batia shoes with an awl several times. Yurik was flummoxed. Did he look like an underground millionaire with money to burn? Throughout his life, he's never had money.

After getting ahold of Yurik's wallet, the young customs officer slipped it under the counter and pushed it into the bottom drawer. Sweaty, pale, and gutted, with his pockets dangling out of his jacket, Yurik returned to

Lyubka and their daughter. He asked the customs officer to give him his documents and money back. At this, the man's eyes grew bigger.

"What do you mean, a wallet? I gave you everything back."

"What are you talking about? They have pulled me aside and taken all my things."

"I saw no wallet."

The emigration process was already in full swing. Customs officers robbed émigrés left and right. However, Lyubka had seen where Yurik's wallet went, and, looking straight into the officer's eyes, she pointed to the drawer.

"His wallet is over there."

She stared at the customs officer with such determination that he realized the wife of his victim was a Jewish woman you should not mess with.

"Oh, yes, here it is!" he exclaimed in a voice filled with the surprise and joy of a boy who had found a ruble under his pillow, left there by the tooth fairy. He took the wallet out of the drawer and wondered aloud, "How the hell did it end up in here?"

It was time to board the train. Here, yet another unexpected glitch arose. It turned out that, in Lvov, when they replaced the locomotive, they also reversed the order of cars. The second car, in which Yurik had booked their seats, arrived in Chop next to last. Because Yurik was sure he was standing where his vehicle was to stop, he had already unloaded the luggage from the cart. The flock of emigrants seized the cart and rushed it away. Now, under Lyubka's contemptuous stare, Yurik, sweating, was forced to drag the heavy suitcases and trunks to the far end of the long train.

When he schlepped all their things to the car, the conductor blocked him. All the seats were already occupied. Perhaps, once he had received the bribe, the head of the Lvov train had forgotten his promise to Yurik, just as one discards an old tram ticket from his pocket. It was also possible the man didn't feel like keeping his word for a renegade leaving his great motherland. Another possibility was that he knew the sweaty little Jew couldn't file a complaint about him anywhere, except at the Israeli Knesset or the American State Department, and the chief of the train didn't give a damn about either. Regardless, the fact of the matter was that no matter how much Yurik fought, they wouldn't let him into the car.

First, he demanded their rightful places. Then he tried to persuade the conductor by shoving ten rubles into his pocket, which didn't help either. Though he was glad to earn the extra cash, the conductor couldn't do anything. Another emigrant family had already occupied Yurik's seats. These people were sitting there like boulders, and no force on earth could move them.

There were less than ten minutes before the train departed. Lyubka couldn't stand it anymore and demanded that Yurik find vacant seats before it was too late. Yurik ran along the platform, wiggling side to side like a rabbit avoiding the bullets of hunters. He jumped on the running board of one car and ran through it to make sure there were no available spaces and then jumped down to rush to the next one.

There were no seats anywhere. More people wanted to leave the country of "the world's most advanced political system" than there were seats on the train.

Yurik stumbled upon a conductor who told him, "Don't get underfoot. Get into the last car. It's empty."

Without asking himself why there was an empty car on a packed train, Yurik dragged the luggage to the end of the platform. Just as he, Lyubka, and their daughter shoved their suitcases under the seats, the train pulled off from the station.

Although it was already dark, they didn't switch the lights on in the car. Yurik was happy about it. He didn't dare to look at Lyubka, for he knew she was sitting next to him, turned away, with clenched teeth. If she'd look at him, it would only be to incinerate him with her stare. Meanwhile, sitting in the darkness, she sighed, hugging her daughter, telling her not to worry, everything would be fine. Her father may be off his rocker, but at least she has her mother to rely on.

Her daughter had a hard time going through this dramatic change in her life. Her whole appearance made it clear she considered what was happening to her violated her human rights. She was angry with both of her parents. What's so great about America! What the hell would she, Faina, get there that she didn't have in Odessa? They tore her away from her friends, from the beach in Otrada, from Dima Zolotarev, the only one of her male classmates who regarded her with adoration. Despite her hooked Jewish nose and the pimples on her cheek, he was too shy to approach her during recess. Where else on earth was there anyone like him? Were they in America? They destroyed her personal life in one fell swoop.

When the train crossed the border, the guards passed through the car, shining flashlights in their faces. The guards checked the visas, but they said nothing. Only when they finished checking did they swear at the "renegades" sitting in the unlit car.

23
THE ÉMIGRÉ *DECAMERON*

The stay at Miramar was about to end. Together with other expats, Boris had to find shelter in private homes while they processed the entry visas to the countries that accepted Soviet refugees. It was possible to rent an apartment in Rome, but it was expensive. The emigrants settled on the shores of the Tyrrhenian Sea, which was half an hour from the city by train. The town's name was Lido di Ostia, which the émigrés gave a Russian-sounding endearing twist. They called it *Lidochka*, or "Little Lida."

A sizable Russian-speaking community had formed there a few years earlier. The first thing they did was instruct Boris in the fine art of how to put Italians at ease when renting their property to Soviet refugees. Not that easy to get them to do it. The proprietors at first let the Russians in their summer residences and rejoiced over the sudden open emigration from the USSR. However, soon the newcomers made them wary. The new tenants had bizarre ideas regarding how many people could sleep in the same room and share a single toilet. When renting to them, the Italians had to be vigilant. "So," fellow travelers, who had been living in Ostia informed Boris, "if you have small children, it's better to keep quiet about them. Tell the Italians two people will live in the apartment, when, in fact, there will be three, and tell them three when there will be five. If possible, avoid *deposito*—cash collateral in the event something in the apartment breaks. Experience has shown that things break, or sometimes disappear. Never admit you are from Odessa." Few emigrants were surprised they turned the Odessans down.

When a Russian emigrant knocked on the door of an Ostia apartment to ask the owner whether he would rent it out, he heard in response: "*Odessa no.*" Although there was a linguistic misunderstanding—in Italian, *adesso no* means "not now"—the natives of the glorious Black Sea city earned the reputation of people who couldn't be trusted. It became known that the expatriates broke open the locks on the owner's rotary phone, and, in ecstasy, oblivious of the time, spoke to the whole wide world—New York, Toronto, Minsk, Kiev, Kharkov, and with Odessa, Odessa, Odessa . . .

One could understand why they would make these calls. Too great was the temptation to tell your Uncle Misha and Aunt Nellie back in Russia how you had made your way to a country you had known only from textbooks. Besides, how could you not answer their most urgent questions! How much do eggs and milk cost in Rome? Is the Tyrrhenian Sea warm? Is it warmer than the Black Sea? Can you swim in it? Are the Italian women as hot as they are in De Sica and Rossellini movies? Where are you thinking of going next, and has the sty on your nephew's, little Syoma's, eye subsided?

But why call places where you have no relatives, have never had relatives, and where they couldn't be? Places like Addis Ababa or Cape Town, for example. But a call placed to Rio de Janeiro was understandable—the city's name is so exotic! Perhaps they don't even talk in a human voice there; they chirp like birds of paradise! But why bother calling the Chancellery of Ceylon's Prime Minister to speak to Mrs. Sirimavo Bandaranaike? To seek political asylum? For heaven's sakes, there is nothing there on that island, except for tea leaves! Besides, read the papers. She was ousted from her office a few years ago.

All these antics, however, were only children's pranks. Much more dramatic things took place. The day before departing overseas, the former Odessans hired moving trucks and removed massive trunks, wardrobes, marble busts, and even the bedsheets. They took them to the enormous Roman flea market Americana. When visiting his apartment the next day, the Italian proprietor first thought he had gone crazy. Just that morning, he thought his health was stellar, but he had lost his memory and entered the wrong apartment. (Had it happened on the train, on his way to Ostia?) After opening the door with his key, stupefied, he examined whatever remained of his cozy place. He hadn't seen this much damage done to his property even during the last war, when the Wehrmacht soldiers were quartered in his Ostia apartment.

Out of habit, he hurried to close the door so that a draft wouldn't pull his cream-colored silk curtains into the window. But there was no need to worry. His three-room apartment was inviting and cozy like the Gobi Desert in the early morning hours. In place of his sofas and trunks, there were dust bunnies, wavering in the draft. In the corners of the living room were empty cartons of pasta, and along the walls empty bottles of Stolichnaya stood like hostages. (What was there to do? Here, in a foreign land, you could not redeem empty bottles for a deposit like back home!)

Boris headed for Ostia on a reconnaissance mission—he needed to find a place for himself. While there, he hoped to pick up a letter from Ilya, who assumed Boris would settle there, like most Soviet expats arriving in Rome. As he had promised them before leaving, Boris also wanted to write and send a letter off to his parents in Odessa.

The post office in Ostia was everything for the emigrants: a real estate agency, a point of exchange for valuable information, and a place where people bound by a common destiny met. Like the ancient Greek chorus, the post office commented on world events and on Soviet emigration in particular. Here, they exchanged rumors and gossip. Here, rumors turned to facts, the kind that had people swear "May I drop dead right here if it's not true!" Some brand-new swearings were born here as well: "If I'm lying, may I never reach New York!"

Boris recognized a crowd of compatriots from afar while standing in front of the glass facade of the post office. One could distinguish a Russian by their lack of the Italian's straight posture and neat hairstyle. Polished shoes among the Russians were the telltale sign that the wearer was a nerdy bachelor. Once you noticed a man's disheveled hair, wrinkled clothes, and dirty shoes, you could bet the man was Russian. His expression also bore a robust Russian imprint: a complex mixture of mistrust and the desire to look as important as possible.

Boris took a few steps toward the post office. A man of thirty with a shabby briefcase and the mild manners of a pickpocket departed from the crowd. Taking a step toward Boris, the young man examined him. When Boris caught up with him, the young man asked, "Need an apartment?" with a typical Odessan accent, rising until the last syllable, making it sound more like an ironic exclamation than a question.

A new profession for Soviet émigrés was born: the apartment broker. How do you find a place to stay in a foreign country when you don't know the local language? Young people with professorial briefcases materialized among the newcomers. They charged a small sum for their services.

Some of them undermined the trust of their customers. There was one young man who was known by his appearance to all the local emigrants. The man's salt-and-pepper bushy hair, eyebrows, and eyelashes made it seem like the person looking at you was not a human being, but some bat. This bat would bring customer after customer to the same apartment. After praising the apartment, he took a deposit from each of them to secure living space for the lucky one. Then, the bat would fly away for a few days, letting natural selection decide who would get access to the promised housing. After checking out of a Roman hotel, and driving up to their new apartment, the future settler discovered a brawl at the apartment door. Cheated tenants wheezed before the locked door, pushing each other away from it, like hockey players at the goals.

Boris kept walking toward the post office. The young man trotted next to him, explaining the complexity of the rental market. There was deterioration of housing due to social unrest in the country, the fall of the lira compared to the dollar, and an unprecedented influx of migrants from the USSR.

"The cheapest apartments are in the Communist district," the broker explained on the go, clutching a flimsy briefcase under his arm (even though he had nothing of value in there, just some crumpled paper and a number two pencil). He kept these items in case of a cautious client who'd demand a receipt for the broker fee, which was to be paid after an agreement was made. The client was not aware of the fact that, regardless of how things went, he would never see the money again.

Boris thought he had misheard at first. A Communist district? But then he remembered seeing hammer and sickle signs on lampposts when he was walking from the station. A portrait of Lenin was on some of them. *Was the escape from one Communist place worth it, if he wound up in another?*

"In the Communist district, the apartments are cheaper but worse," the broker said, falling into a professorial tone; it was hard to avoid when you told the neophytes about the nuances of their strange new Western life. "They're not safe either. In the fascist district, things are quieter. The apartments are bigger and cleaner, but more expensive."

Boris entered the post office and headed for the Poste Restante window. However, it was impossible to get to. The Soviet émigrés crowded all openings to the window. They opened the envelopes and read letters from their relatives in the Soviet Union and those lucky few that had already settled in other countries: in Israel, America, Canada, and Australia. They gossiped about the contents of their letters. Here they argued, chatted, and sighed about the relatives and friends they had left behind. Everyone was eager to explain why they'd left the country, and they didn't care who was listening. Perhaps they were reminding themselves what they were doing. They rambled on about what pushed them over the edge and made them leave the country. Why were they in limbo—neither in hell, nor in heaven, but in a strange Italian purgatory? Tell us, please, Signore Dante, what ring are we in now? If possible, can you let us know what awaits us in the next one? How many rings are there left?

At the post office, people would talk to you for no reason at all. This modern Decameron didn't observe British manners. They talked over each other, vying for the attention of expats with a directness that only ex-Soviets, accustomed to standing in line for hours on end, were capable of.

"Oh, how comfortable we were!" a tall woman in an orange dress sighed. "I was a project manager. My husband was the department head of our research institute. We lived in a condominium. We were treated with honor. We had respect."

She spoke with sorrow, bewildered why she was not sitting in her office, behind her polished dark-wood desk, but was standing in a crowd with all sorts of people. What does she have in common with them? Not much in the past, but there was one thing she shared with them right now—an unknown future, the x's, y's and z's in the mathematics of a life to come.

She languished somewhat, finding herself face-to-face with compatriots from all walks of life. If not for emigration, she would hardly ever encounter all these people standing around her now. Neither in the halls of her research institute, nor on all-union symposiums, nor at vacation centers for scientists, nor at the Scientists Club where semi-forbidden poets appeared reading their still unpublished work. But, what can you do! You have to approach your life dialectically. Look past the bad to see where you're going.

"God is my witness! We were so comfortable!" She shook her head in amazement at how blessed her past life had been. "We had no problems. The only blemish in our lives was our son, Tolik! Eighteen years old. An athlete. A bodybuilder. He went nuts! His muscles took control of him. He'd enter a tram, a bus, or a subway car and perk up his ears. Once he heard an antisemitic remark, he, without uttering a word, pounded that person's face. Over the past six months, this has happened seven times.

"No matter how much my husband and I tried to talk him out, to no effect. We told him, 'Tolik, maybe you misheard them? Just ignore them, don't give them any attention. Rise above that!' He only hissed at us, 'You don't understand what self-respect is!' He flew off his hinges. It's a great misfortune when your only child is sick. My husband and I realized if he acted up anymore, they'd throw him in jail. What was there to do? No one wants to give their baby to the wolves! We were forced to leave for our son's sake." She sighed again.

"I've never wanted to live in Russia," said a tall and thin man in an elegant double-breasted suit, smoking cigarette after cigarette. "This is a bizarre idea—to live in Russia. You can live in England, in France. In Finland, worse comes to worst. But in Russia? You could be born there if you have had bad luck. But to live there?"

"No, just listen to this," a young woman in a gray traveling suit said, holding an opened envelope in her hands. "My girlfriend writes from San Bernardino in Southern California. A few days ago, as she was sitting on the terrace of her house, drinking tea, two hummingbirds flew into her hair. She has long hair, down to her waist. Mind you, it happened just like that, while she was drinking tea. Wow, it's been just a year since she arrived from another world, and here she writes about hummingbirds like they're bees or flies."

"Why did I leave?" A burly man in a leather jacket shrugged, sucking on his empty cigarette holder. "Who the hell knows! I've never thought about the question. My boss, Aron Abramovich, had left. So, right after him, I also filed my documents. Don't laugh," he said, though no one even smiled. "I'd worked under him for twenty years. The fact they'd appoint someone else in his place terrified me. I got so accustomed to him. I wasn't even that accustomed to my wife!"

"Ask me," a broad-faced man next to him said, his protruding belly revealing his love for a hearty meal, "why I left, and I'd tell you I didn't do it. My wife exported me, like a piece of furniture. She didn't ask me. She ran around and arranged all the paperwork. When it was time to go to the railway station, she told me: 'Put on your raincoat. I've put your overcoat into the suitcase already.' So, I put on my raincoat. I'm not even Jewish."

"Why!" his energetic-looking wife said in a singsong voice, her eyes wide in surprise. "It's my father who is Russian. And you're a full-fledged Jew! Your mother's Jewish, and so is your father."

"Well, so what? They may be Jews, but I am not. I'm Russian, in body and soul. As Russian poet Lermontov once said, 'I love Russia, but with a strange love.'"

"It's the Russian broads you love, not Russia. Now you'll stop spending nights tomcatting around God knows where."

"Why, at the buffet at the Ufa Pedagogical College, no one knew I was a Jew," said a stout young woman with a thick mess of black hair. "Only when I've applied for emigration, they found it out, and they were all surprised. The personnel department knew but I've experienced no discrimination. Who cares! It's a buffet, for God's sake! They spit at what your passport says as long as you maintain your monthly sales quota.

"And how can you do it at a college where the students don't have a dime to their names? They walk around like underfed chicks. Well, what can you do in such a situation? They deliver say, a churn of sour cream from their warehouse. A little note from Maria Alekseevna, the warehouse manager, is pasted up on the can cap: 'Manya, don't add water to the sour cream. I've already done it.' What does it mean, you may ask. It's simple. It means, whether or not you like it, part of the proceeds from the sour cream goes to her. Otherwise, you won't keep your job. If you want to live honestly, you'll be a pauper. If you don't share your profit with them, they'll force you. If you resist, they'll fire you. Well, I came to the end of my rope with all that stuff, that constant tension! What if a trade inspector appears at the door, and my boss forgets to give him an envelope with cash on time? Enough! I'll find myself some buffet in America. People everywhere want to eat."

"I left Russia because it scared me," someone's sad voice uttered. "I was born and lived in a room in a communal apartment on Myasoedovskaya Street, 18, in Odessa. In that room, my father had lived and died. He lived and died in the same room where my grandfather had lived and died. And my son would also live in it his entire life until he dies. And the same will happen to my grandchildren, great-grandchildren, and great-great-grandchildren, down to the last generation. I was living in a coffin."

In search of suitable listeners, a short, red-haired emigrant with the curious eyes of a young cockerel came up to Boris. He was so eager to speak he did it before Boris even looked at him. His feelings were too strong. It was clear his brain and his heart were burning with some unsolved life mystery.

"Why?" he asked, without introducing himself. "Well, why, I must ask you?"

Boris was dumbfounded.

"Well, why," there was fire in the eyes of the inquisitor, "why don't our automatic incubators work the way the American ones do! Murder me, cut me into pieces, but I don't get it! By order of the ministry, they appointed me as head of the project of producing broiler incubators. I set up a commission on mutual exchange of experience with the Americans.

We made three trips to the States, to the state of Iowa. All members of the commission got every secret they could get out of the Americans about their machines. Whatever information they couldn't worm out, they stole. The blueprints, the specifications—everything.

"They brought it to Zagorsk, near Moscow, to our ministry's experimental base. I got the best specialists in the country on that project. They made our little incubator exactly like an American one. And what do you think happened? Four times fewer chickens came out than from the American one! It baffled the government. We had squandered that many American dollars, yet the results were laughable! They called me upstairs. 'What's the matter, Zalmanovich?' What was I supposed to say?"

He shrugged so intensely his shoulders reached his ears.

"I rushed with my team to Zagorsk again. We took that damn incubator apart. We checked every pin on the U.S. spec. We reassembled it. The same story! It produced so few eggs that stupid machine would only be worth it if the eggs came out golden. What the hell was going on here?"

"What, they fired you because of those chickens?" Boris said, careful not to damage the ego, delicate like an eggshell, of the failed godfather of Soviet-American chickens.

"What are you talking about!" The man was offended. He raised his chin. "The Ministry gave me a bonus for advancing new technology. But productivity! I left for a different reason, a personal one. It had nothing to do with the incubators. But, tell me please, why that kept happening! It's not like we got one or two chickens less, but *four times less!* I swear, or my name isn't Zalmanovich, the first thing I'm doing when I get to the States is heading to Iowa to see what's the problem."

His empty gaze made it clear that, once again, he was mentally disassembling that unfortunate incubator, a cog at a time, one little screw after another, so he could get at the bottom of the mystery that tormented him.

A married couple, both dental technicians from Moscow, stocky and beaver-cheeked, told their story. Excited, they kept interrupting each other, like Gogol's characters Bobchinsky and Dobchinsky in *The Inspector General*.

"I'll tell you, we had everything," she said.

"Well, just about everything!" he repeated.

"Tell us what your little heart has desired all your life," she continued, "and we had two sets of each. Gold watches, diamond bracelets, Finnish furniture . . . Well, just about everything! But we trembled with fear! We were afraid day and night!"

Hunching their shoulders and looking around, they showed how scared they were in their Soviet lives, their beaver cheeks quivering.

Looking through the crowd, Boris spotted a familiar face. It was a full-figured woman with a pretty and intelligent face. He had seen her in Moscow, at the local Exit Visa Office. At that time she had exclaimed, "I'm so glad I can leave this terrible country," and Boris winced at hearing such a bold statement. His life was changing dramatically. Look at that! In the center of the Soviet capital, this woman was blurting out the truth, and she couldn't care less. He even glanced around to see whether other people heard these words.

"God, I'm so glad!" the woman repeated. "What a terrible country!" She said it as if she'd lived in many other, decent, countries, but this one was not quite to her liking. Later, while talking to her, Boris realized he was wrong. She had left the country only once: for two weeks in the Bulgarian city of Varna, for a vacation at the Golden Sands resort. "Well, that's all right, all right. Once I get out of here, things will be different. Over there, things are different."

Back then she had said nothing more; she only nodded in satisfaction at the prospect of leaving, no matter where her fate would take her. Over there, on the other side of the Soviet border, a great and bright life was awaiting her. As if continuing that speech she'd made back at the Exit Visa Office, now, at the Ostia post office, she said:

"Oh, I'm going to the West with a single mission—to spread the truth about the Soviet regime."

She patted the cover of a book she pressed under her arm. "I'm so thankful to my Moscow neighbor, an old Bolshevik . . . Before the October Revolution, he had been in the underground resistance fighting the tsarist regime. He mentored me on how to smuggle my anti-Soviet novel across the border without carrying the manuscript. And I made it! As he suggested, I took this book along. It's beyond any suspicion. Everyone knows *How the Steel Was Tempered*, this Soviet propaganda staple by Nikolai Ostrovsky. But, as the old Bolshevik had done in his time, on the book pages, I marked the letters of my novel, one after another, pricking them with a needle in sequence. When I get to the States, I'll type the whole thing out on a typewriter. It will shake the world!"

Her eyes shone in triumph over the fools in Soviet customs.

Away from the crowd, leaning on the corner counter, stood a pale-faced man of thirty-five years old, in a shabby black suit and white shirt, peeking out from under his bushy beard. He glanced at the crowd with little interest. His eyes closed on their own from time to time. The carelessness of the man's clothes contrasted with the appearance of the other Russians, dressed up to look their best in Europe. The man muttered something into his beard. When the buzz in the room quieted down for a short time, Boris could hear the man's mumbling.

"My name's Moshe Yehuda Faybelzon. I'm tired . . . I'm a hundred and eighty years old. I'm the son of a rabbi who'd lived all his life in White Krynitsa, in Ukraine. My grandfather, my great-grandfather, and my great-great-grandfather were also rabbis. And God had spoken: 'Only free people have a place in the Promised Land. Those who were born in captivity must wander for forty years in the wilderness until the shameful habits of servility withered away.'"

However, soon the excited voices of the emigrants drowned out his words again.

"Yesterday, we were touring Rome and passed by the Colosseum," a middle-aged woman exclaimed. "I almost missed it. Why was there no sign saying we were by the Colosseum? In socialist countries, historical landmarks are all taken care of. What's with them here? Why haven't they fixed it up after so many years? And why is the Colosseum in such bad shape to begin with?"

"Mount Vesuvius did a number on it," someone said.

"When will we get an interview with the American consul?" sighed a young woman in a tracksuit next to Boris. "I can hardly wait for it."

"Why can't the consul come to our place?" an elderly woman, apparently her mother, addressed her. "What's with him? He is conceited, it seems."

Finally, it was Boris's turn to step up to the Poste Restante window.

24
THE BRATISLAVA TROUBLES

The train was running through the territory of the Czechoslovak Social-ist Republic toward Bratislava. The Bumshteins would have to wait five hours there to make their final transfer to Vienna. When Yurik began dozing off, the train suddenly stopped. Outside the window of their com-partment, the night, biblical in its magnitude, was pitch black, save for the North Star. It was as if God himself was squinting, looking curiously at the train of Jews fleeing from the country of Red Pharaohs.

Yurik lowered the window, leaned out, and found that their car had been uncoupled from the train. Maybe that's why nobody got on the last car.

In the distance, some lights flashed—it was probably the train stop-ping at some way station. Sighing deeply, Lyubka felt she had had enough. She would no longer rely on Yurik. It was no surprise to her. She left him because he wasn't good for anything. She yelled at him not to get in her way and exited the car. After a short time, she brought two workers from the way station; they had been fixing the rails by the light of lamps. They helped carry their belongings to the station, and Lyubka paid them with a bottle of vodka which she had brought for sale abroad.

On the platform, several people were sitting half-asleep, under the canopy, waiting for a train. Lyubka talked to them in Ukrainian, the only non-Russian language she knew. Odessa was a multilingual city; it had not only Russians, Ukrainians, and Jews, but Armenians, Greeks, and Bul-garians. However, in secondary schools, only Russian and Ukrainian were obligatory.

To Lyubka's surprise, they understood her. Czechs and Ukrainians are both Slavs. They explained that the train to Bratislava would stop here at six in the morning. Lyubka cursed herself for being a softie. That's what got her into this stupid mess; she was stuck in the middle of nowhere with her teenage daughter and useless ex-husband, with all their belongings stuffed into a few suitcases. She knew nothing about the country she was in, besides that they made good shoes, Pilsner, and tasty little sausages called *shpekachki*. She looked around for a place where she could at least put her head down and get some sleep.

Some man came up to them and pointed to the neighboring platform. The Bratislava train was about to arrive there. It stops for only one minute. Lyubka shook Yurik, who was falling asleep. They grabbed their belongings and rushed across the rails a few minutes before the train pulled up to the station. Some people helped them throw their bags into the car at the last second, as the train began to move.

Toward morning, a controller walked through the car and, looking at their tickets, muttered something in Czech, which sounded like "You're going the wrong way." Lyubka didn't pay attention to his words and dozed off again. Then, when they approached Bratislava, the controller again muttered, "Wrong way."

It turned out they were, indeed, going the wrong way. Even though the train was going to Bratislava, it was headed for the Bratislava-Nova Station, where only the suburban trains stopped. They should have been going to the Bratislava Main, the station where they were supposed to catch a train to Vienna.

Lyubka and Yurik ran out of money. Some sympathetic Czech passengers walked through the train and gathered cash for them, one Czech koruna at a time, like alms for the poor, so they could get a taxi in Bratislava. Also, they warned them they would have to schlep all their luggage from the third floor to the first by stairs to get to the taxi stand. The elevator in the lobby was only for station cargo. No one would permit them to use it.

As Lyubka said farewell to the passengers, one Czech woman, who had figured out they were Jews, shook her head and advised Lyubka to tell everybody they were Ukrainians going to Canada. It turned out being a Jew outside the Soviet Union wasn't great either.

But there was no turning back. Frustrated, Lyubka elbowed Yurik aside as they were unloading their luggage. She found the station master, and, using her charm, persuaded him to permit them to take the freight elevator.

Outside the station, she hailed a small pickup. When they came upon the passenger station and schlepped their luggage onto the platform, the train to Vienna was already leaving. The people who were seeing off the passengers still waved their handkerchiefs. The pickup driver offered to get them to its next stop, at the border with Austria, but he charged a hundred dollars for that. The Bumshteins had no choice but to sit on their belongings for the whole six hours until the departure of the next Vienna train.

25
STILL AT THE POST OFFICE

At the Poste Restante, they gave Boris three letters. One of them was from Odessa, from his parents. The letter was full of worries about his well-being (as expected), asking him to write back as soon as possible. There was also an elongated American envelope, which he knew meant a letter from Ilya:

Hello, Boris!

So, you're already in Ostia, congratulations! Where do you stay? Hope you've found a suitable apartment, without troublesome neighbors. Bella insists I pass along her tips to you. While in Rome, buy yourself some clothes made of suede or leather. They cost too much in America. And see as much of Italy as you can. You won't be back there anytime soon. Unless you write a best seller. Americans visit Italy (and travel abroad) mostly after they retire. I hope you'll get to revisit it earlier than that, but, in the meantime, see as much of it as you can. I'm sending you a check for two hundred dollars. I recall how, upon arriving in Italy, I wanted to go everywhere but was discouraged by how empty my pockets were. What I'm sending you isn't enough to see the whole former Roman Empire, but I hope it'll help you out . . .

Now that you are already on this side of the Iron Curtain, I want to share with you the discovery that struck me.

Though intrigued, Boris realized that reading the entire letter here at the post office, amid the noise and din, wouldn't be possible. Boris placed Ilya's letter back in his pocket and took out the third one, from Arik.

They had resolved in each letter to share any updates on their mutual friends. "Eugene joined the staff at the same office that Vladimir had worked at" meant that Eugene's emigration application had been rejected. Later on in the letter, Arik was asking Boris questions about his emigration experience, just like he said he would at his farewell party. Arik wrote that he understood that Boris was en route to America and could not answer most of the questions yet. However, Arik wanted him to know of the issues so that when he gets to experience America, they'll be on his mind and he'll be able to answer them.

The questions filled three pages of dense handwriting, which was difficult to make out. For a moment, Boris wondered why Arik hadn't used a typewriter. He guessed Arik counted on his writing to be illegible. He knew nothing the Soviet authorities enjoy so much as reading private letters sent abroad. Perusing personal correspondence was an old Russian tradition the Soviet power upheld with diligence. Arik's handwriting was his way of keeping the authorities unaware of his desire to emigrate. It seemed Arik had hoped the official would curse his chicken scratch, put his letter aside, and read another one that was much more legible. Like any other Soviet institution, the KGB charged its employees with maintaining a productivity quota, a certain number of letters to be read per day.

Although many issues concerned Arik, the most pressing one was the question of financial support: How much does an émigré receive, and for how long? He wanted to know what would happen if one did not find work in the allotted time. Would they deport you, or, without even providing you with a courtesy phone call to your mother, throw you into the Atlantic?

The next set of questions must have come to Arik after watching American movies. In these films, American directors exposed all imaginable and unimaginable evils of capitalism without realizing they were feeding the Soviet propaganda machine. Arik asked Boris to let him know whether terrorism by "Negroes" is as acute as it is in the movies. If it is, is it possible to buy a weapon for self-defense? Are bulletproof vests available for sale or can you get them only through connections? What role does string-pulling play in the States and is it possible to get by without it? If so, how can one work around it? Arik also requested that Boris outline any difference in how people interact in the U.S. He wanted to know whether Americans had any clue what friendship is, or whether they care only about themselves and are incapable of inconveniencing themselves for a friend's sake. Would an American, say, be able to phone a friend in the middle of the night because he needs a drink and all the liquor stores are closed already? Would the friend wake up and, with no resentment, pull a bottle of vodka out of the freezer, that he had set aside for such an occasion, and drink it with him?

Arik also asked practical questions. Is the high-handedness of employers that rampant in the United States, or are the Soviet newspapers making a big deal out of it? Can a business owner throw a worker into the streets just like that—because his wife left him, or the bad weather put him in a bad mood? When they interview you for a job, does the way you dress increase your chances of getting a job or does your appearance not matter at all? If it does matter, Arik asked whether the hosting Jewish community takes into consideration this expenditure when they decide on the allowance for the new arrivals. If this isn't the case, should he take his blazer along?

That blazer, which he had added to his wardrobe by hiring a private tailor before Boris's departure, was a feast for the eyes. Arik had been working on gathering materials for it for a long time. It took forever to find its gilt buttons, fit for an admiral's uniform.

The postscript consisted of a request, accompanied by many qualifications, such as "I understand you're a refugee and short on cash, but still, if you'd happen upon the chance" to buy and send a belt made of Italian leather by mail, even ground mail. The belt shouldn't be a narrow one; it should be at least three fingers wide. There was also a request to purchase a skirt for Arik's new girlfriend, as Boris understood. Although he has been married for a long time, Arik often appeared at the café of the Journalists' Club with some dressed-up beauty, usually another writer's daughter. The name of Arik's latest girlfriend was Olga, but, at the farewell party, he had warned Boris, if he mentioned her, he should call her Oleg. Boris wondered why, after leaving the country and turning his life upside down, he would care about the breezy girlfriends of his friend back in Moscow. It appears Arik had already been thinking about what stuff he could get from abroad to please his new flame.

Reflecting on the strange requests from Arik, Boris once again confirmed his observation: the supposedly classless Soviet society was divided into castes, similar to India. Especially when searching for a spouse in the elitist milieu. The army generals' daughters usually hang out with the writers' sons and the sons of academics with the daughters of movie stars. As a result, the Soviet elite bred, like the protozoans, via mitosis only.

During the parties, Arik would invite ladies to his dad's huge apartment at the Writers' Union housing next to the Airport subway station. Boris often grabbed the attention of women with his height, gray eyes, and an incredible head of hair. However, once the girls learned that Boris's father was a simple engineer, they'd lose all interest. Neither his hair, nor his eyes, nor his height helped. He didn't even get to reveal that he worked freelance and lived in a small room in a communal apartment.

Arik ordered the skirt for his girlfriend to the specification of its eventual owner. It ought to be made of "the thickest fabric possible, preferably denim." He also gave exact sizes: it should be 77 cm in the waist, no less than 66–70 cm long, and measure 100–102 cm in the hip area. Arik gave Boris free rein in choosing the style. "It can be buttoned," he wrote, "or it can have zippers." "It can be any other style," he added mercifully. However, Arik's clothing wish list didn't end. He assumed Boris would send everything else "as it becomes possible."

Boris was about to put the letter in his pocket when he saw a tall, stately man in a double-breasted gray suit and dark tie waiting for him to finish reading. He knew that Boris listened to the emigrants' stories, and he couldn't wait to tell his own. He was so set on having Boris hear his story he stood with his shoulder blocking the exit.

"I've emigrated honorably," the man said with dignity. "But not without misadventures. I approached the head of my science laboratory and told him, 'Kirill Petrovich, I don't want to cause you any problems. I'm planning to leave the country in you-know-what direction. If I file my documents now, you'd have to write me a character reference. They might drag you before the Party district committee and accuse you of having done poor political work in the collective. To avoid unnecessary headaches for you, Petrovich, I'm planning to check myself into a hospital for a month and take care of my kidneys. Then, I'll take another sick leave. Then, I'll quit my job. Then, I'll wait for a while, and only then I'll file for emigration.'

"And he tells me: 'Thank you, you're a good man. People have to be decent under any circumstances. But why can't you do it this way? First, you quit. We'll give you money for the unused vacation time. Then, you check into the hospital. Then, you apply for emigration. That way, the gap between your employment and applying for emigration will be longer. Maybe that way they'll spare me from writing your character reference altogether. You'll apply for emigration as a sick person, and there's nothing they can do to you as a patient.'

"I tell him, 'I know I'll disappoint you, but they might not certify my disability. Though my kidneys aren't in tip-top shape, they still work, and will probably delight my doctors, anyway. Let's meet halfway. First, I'll take a vacation, then I'll quit, and then I'll go to the hospital. And *then* I'll file for emigration. That is if I don't have acute kidney failure.'

"'In principle,' the head of the lab says, 'if you maintain your spirits, your body will respond and you could skip the hospital and cross the border. You'll get well on the other side of the border. Their medicine is better than ours is. So, quit first, and then you can do whatever you want.'

"So, I go to our HR office and Elizaveta Petrovna, the department head, demands I provide a note stating I have no classified material at my workplace or home. I wrote that statement and, out of our Soviet habit of not doing exactly what your boss demands, I didn't put the date on it. The HR head glanced at the paper, put it into a folder, and locked it in her steel cabinet.

"I go to all our departments and get all the signatures I need, come back to Elizaveta, and receive a certificate stating I quit my job and have no outstanding obligations to my former workplace.

"I come home and, as usual, tell my wife Inna about my day. And here, as I'm telling her about all the events, I feel my legs and hands shake. My wife screamed, 'What have you done!' just as I realized it myself.

"She holds in her hand the knife she used to stir onions in the frying pan, but the look on her face makes my immediate future flash before me: my blood drips from the tip of the knife instead of sunflower oil.

"'If you signed that,' my wife says, 'it means at some point you *had* access to classified material, even if you don't anymore. They won't let us go. We will stay here another twenty years; we'll grow old, and they'll send our son to Afghanistan to have some jihadist let his guts out.'

"She was right. They had denied lots of applicants on pretexts far less serious than that. What was there to do? I grabbed a taxi. I rushed to some alley in the Arbat quarters where, in some basement apartment, an underground lawyer who specializes in refusenik consultation lived. (If anyone needs him for a relative back in Russia, I still have his phone number.) The lawyer heard out my story about signing the clearance paper. Then, he rolled his eyes to the ceiling and said: 'It's not the clearance paper you've signed, dear man. You've signed your death sentence.' And he shook his head.

"I've noticed no criminal impulses in me, but, in my despair, that night I wanted to burn down our whole institute. I wished to start a fire that would turn the place (and my idiotic papers!) to ash before my former coworkers reached its steps the next morning. But that's easier said than done. Our institute is in the old Donskoi Monastery. Its walls are made of stone and are so thick even the Tatars, having their yoke on the neck of Russia for three hundred years, could not burn it down, no matter how hard they tried. Only I know what I lived through that night, and I will not tell you about it now. Imagine the pain, and double it, maybe you'll get an idea of what it was like.

"That night, my despair and hope, my protest and resignation, fought each other. And I still haven't decided what to do. An enticing option flashed through my mind: once I'm refused the exit visas, I'll find a job as an elevator operator. I'll read books on the job, sustaining myself on potatoes and onions.

"At eight in the morning, getting no sleep, I drank three cups of Turkish coffee, grabbed a taxi, and sped through the city, so I'd be first when our HR department opened.

"Elizaveta Petrovna stared at me:

"'Isaak Markovich? What're you doing here? Didn't you quit already?'

"I hear myself saying with vigor and even impudence:

"'I forgot to put the date on my clearance statement.'

"She pulled out my folder: 'Yes.'

"She handed me the document. I had signed it in blue, so I asked her for a blue pen. She turned away to look for it. I pulled out the clearance statement and put it in my pocket.

"The HR woman saw it and turned pale:

"'What're you doing?'

"'I have no classified material, and I'd never had any,' I reply with effrontery I never suspected in myself. 'The whole document makes no sense.'

"Her face grew pale out of hatred. Since the workday had only begun, she wasn't fully awake yet, but now she fixed her eyes on me as if she wanted to burn through me with her gaze:

"'You won't leave this place with this document. I'm calling the police. It's a classified document.'

"I don't know how I gained the composure of a cowboy, but right there, in front of her eyes, I yanked the paper out of my pocket, folded it in four, did it again, and tore the whole thing into small pieces. First, I tossed all the bits in the trash can, but then I changed my mind and put a handful into my pocket. They could glue the torn pieces of paper together, and it would still serve them as a pretext for keeping me in the country.

"I forgot to tell you that our HR head is a polite woman. In our institute, she is one of the few cultured people. There was even talk she comes from noble blood, from some surviving gentry family. She always keeps her fancy perfumed handkerchief in her jacket sleeve. She refers to everyone, even our young lab technicians, by their name and patronymic. Everyone marveled at how she'd wound up in HR when she could have been appointed the head of a research department. And she suddenly hissed at me: 'You'll answer for this, you dirty Jew.'

"I got upset when it came out of her. I assumed she was above it. But it's like my friend Misha Svirsky always says, 'Isaac, don't push anyone's buttons too hard. Eventually, they'll spew dreck.'

"Well, in the evening, my wife and I invited our friends over. We spread the damn document on the table, its missing squares left behind in the trash can—and drank a bottle of vodka. To our freedom. But look at me! I'm here, on the other side of the border already, and I'm telling you all this, but my hands and my legs still shake."

The man smiled at Boris and took a deep breath, reliving the horrific experience in his head.

When he finished, Boris wasn't the only person who had been listening. Some pale older man in a well-crafted dark suit of English wool had appeared from nowhere and stood by them. Judging by the slight smile on his face and his anguished look, it seemed he was traveling alone, and that something tormented him too. He had no one to talk to even for a quick chat. He spoke in a low voice but sputtered, sometimes swallowing his words, fearing they wouldn't hear him out to the end:

"I admit it's all my fault. There's no forgiveness for me! None! Well, what was there to do after becoming a Gogolian character, a dead soul! I never thought I'd be buried alive, even though I've looked death in the eyes many times. I'm from Tambov. I was an instructor of one of the district Party committees. Back in 1972, when the first emigrants left the country, I received a letter from Kiev, from my ex-wife, Marina.

"She wrote she wanted to go to Israel with our daughter Tina. She needed a paper from me, certifying that, well, I don't have any claims against her. What claims could I have? We'd broken up a long time ago. Our family, which we tried to save for our daughter's sake, fell apart. And now, my former wife was thinking of leaving for Israel. At that time, you know, for the Soviet émigrés, there was no America. Everyone was leaving for Israel. But I . . . Well, you know, as an instructor of a district Party committee . . . I'd joined the Party during the war. It happened in Kursk before that fateful battle. I believed in that stupid sign then: if I join the Party, I'll survive the war. Because the war had started, I dropped out of high school. After the war, it was difficult to make a living without a profession. My friends talked me into getting a Party job. As a war veteran, I was trusted.

"But then I faced a dilemma. I, a trusted Party official, had to approve of the unpatriotic move of my ex-wife. Marina pressured me to give her permission, to sign off on my daughter leaving for Israel. Well, to make it short, I chickened out. I'm telling it like it is: I chickened out. During the war, I'd been a paratrooper. I wasn't scared any of the times I jumped from a plane into the German's rear in the middle of the night. But with that permission situation, I chickened out and refused to sign my ex-wife's paper. If I signed it, they'd kick me out of the Party, and I would lose my job. What would I do then? . . . Later, Marina played a trick on me. She approached someone in Ovidiopol, which is where I was born. Well, she found someone, paid them off and got a false certificate for her daughter. The paper stated that her daughter's father had been dead for a long time. She left with our daughter for Israel. I knew nothing about it.

"Time went by. Seven years passed. And I realized what mattered. I had no one as close in my life as my daughter, whom I abandoned to save my skin. It wasn't easy, but I filed for emigration myself.

"Well, they kicked me out of the Party. I didn't care at all at that point. I realized, old fool, that, 'the honor and conscience of our era,' as the Party calls itself, isn't any damn party you join, but your family. And that's true not only for 'our era,' but for every other. Your family is the most important party you can be a part of. And where was my family? I was all alone. So, it turned out my daughter Tina in Ashkelon was my whole family. My daughter, who I betrayed! So, I filed my documents for emigration, and they tell me at the Exit Visa Office: 'We can't let you go, because we don't issue exit visas for dead people.' It took me more than a year to clean up that whole mess.

"Now, I'm heading for Ashkelon. No one is waiting for me there. But I still have hope. I'll ask Tina for forgiveness. I'll get on my knees. She should forgive me, eh? What do you think? After all, she's my daughter, right? We have the same blood . . . Will she forgive me? She should pardon me, right?"

And he walked away with his head down, not waiting for an answer.

26
MAYBE WE'LL PATCH IT UP?

The Bumshteins arrived in Vienna late in the evening. From the station, together with other emigrants, the representatives of HIAS took them to the city center, then down a quiet lane to their boarding house, Bettina. They placed Yurik, Lyubka, and Faina in a room with three beds.

On his first night, it became clear the hurdles of the long journey had damaged Yurik's mental capabilities. He lost his grasp of reality. After a long separation, chance brought him next to the woman of his dreams. As soon as the scent of her favorite perfume, Red Moscow, and her body, heated by her anxiety, reached his nostrils, Yurik lost his ability to think straight. He felt as if there had never been a bitter and prolonged rupture between them, and he wanted to get back together with her.

Yurik seized the moment. As soon as his daughter fell asleep, he slipped out of his bed, made a few quick steps over the cold floor, and got under Lyubka's blanket. He did so as if he had every right to do it, being her lawful husband.

He slipped under the covers and froze. His heart was pounding in his throat. He was next to his beloved again. He had already gathered the courage to embrace Luybka when he received a blow to his rib cage. Discovering an unwelcome guest next to her, without a word, working with her elbow, Lyubka pushed him off her bed. Her plans didn't include having a yoke put on her neck again, especially this one that was all too familiar to her. Trying not to wake her daughter, she hissed at Yurik:

"What's with you? Didn't we agree on things?"

"Well, you know," Yurik mumbled, turning his face away and grimacing at every one of Lyubka's jabs. "We have a daughter together . . . maybe we'll patch it up."

"Your face will be together with my fist, idiot," Lyubka whispered into the darkness. "What're you, stupid?"

After being pushed onto the floor, Yurik rubbed his side and ran back to his bed. He could not fall asleep for a long time. However, in the morning, as the first rays of the Austrian sun struck his eyes from under the edge of the curtains, he regained his hope. That's all right, he consoled himself. The journey into the unknown had only begun. He would still have many opportunities to win Lyubka back. He would prove himself a reliable person, the backbone of their family.

After breakfast, they went to an interview at the Israeli Sokhnut Agency. The official there, an elderly man with gray eyes and a sad face, tried to shame them by saying, "Look, you left your country with Israeli visas, and now you want to go to America." It was as if dealing with Soviet emigrants gave the man an ulcer. When his shaming wasn't working, the Sokhnut official repeated several times, "You won't find work in America," without bothering to ask about their professions.

After their visit to Sokhnut, it turned out they needed to buy food for their journey to Rome. They were to leave early Monday morning, and the stores were all closed on Sundays.

When the Bumshteins arrived at the market in the city center, it was Yurik's first encounter with everyday life in the West. Having lived all his life in his hometown, he remembered people saying, "If you want to know how 'rotting capitalism' smells, go to the London Hotel."

Only foreign tourists could stay in this hotel on the chic Primorsky Promenade, with a magnificent vista onto the sea and Odessa's port. Walking past this hotel, Yurik would notice unusual odors—of strong perfume, of moisturizers, and of deodorants emanating from cheerful old gents. They had their hair pomaded, combed, and parted. Their wives, despite their age, rouged their cheeks and powdered their noses.

Yurik knew nothing else about life on the other side of the Soviet border. At the market, he beheld pyramids of bananas; the best cuts of beef wrapped in cellophane; chicken parts: freshly gutted, boiled, pan-fried; piles of oranges, grapefruits, and some outlandish fruit he couldn't even name. Such a sight at an Odessan shop would cause people to smash the windows and leave the store in shambles.

This spectacle was enough to burst even a healthy man's blood vessels, never mind those of someone like Yurik, who had been going through horrible ordeals, one after another. Imagine: you've just crossed the border, and you get such a shock to your system. The sight of all the different eggs shocked Yurik. Pale yellow and blindingly white! Pinkish and the color of coffee with milk! They were nothing like what he used to see at Privoz. Instead of being smeared in chicken litter, they were washed, arranged in small boxes made of pressed paper or plastic. Six-packs, ten-packs, twelve-packs. Danish ones, French ones, German ones. It seemed like these eggs weren't for mere mortals, but for busy angels to refresh themselves between flights to their essential duties.

The folks that brought Yurik and Lyubka to the market, an elderly couple from Moscow, said they wanted to buy fish. There was a great variety for sale at the Viennese market, many species that even Yurik, who grew up in a seaside town, hadn't seen. Enormous carp swam in large aquariums, wagging their tails and assuming a dignified and independent air, as if to say, *Here we are, at the center of Europe, and it's no big deal to us.*

One carp reminded Yurik of a carp he had seen in the big fish store on Deribasovskaya Street. He even thought this carp winked at him. As if it were saying, *Don't you dare tell anyone about this, especially not the authorities! You'll blow my cover; I'm here on assignment.*

Yurik took a net and caught his fish acquaintance, even though he was apprehensive about it. When the seller stunned the carp by hitting it with a mallet, Yurik experienced a cascade of new feelings that had been accumulating in him the past few days. They came down on him with the crushing force of a sea wave crashing down on the head of an unwary swimmer. Yurik felt as if they had knocked him on his head and not the carp's. Yurik's ears rang, his head felt fuzzy, and he fell to the ground.

People caught him on his way down.

27
HOW TO GET EXILED WITHOUT REALLY TRYING

Boris had hardly stepped out of the post office when he heard someone call his name.

"Boris? Schuster?"

Some man of average height, but of powerful physique, came up to Boris and slapped him on his shoulder. He did it with so much emotion that, out of surprise and the man's sheer power, Boris was almost knocked over.

It was his compatriot, the poet and screenwriter Leonid Mak, with whom Boris had once attended the same Odessa High School No. 43. Both were happy they ran into each other. What are the odds! You pass two state borders on your way into the unknown, and you run into an old classmate!

Leonid pulled Boris into the nearest café to have a cup of the newly discovered Italian coffee drink called a cappuccino. And if possible, a shot of something stronger. God himself commanded it on such a happy occasion.

As they nursed a shot of cognac, Mak asked Boris how long he had stayed in Italy and if he lived in Rome or somewhere here, in Lido di Ostia. Then Mak told about the fateful circumstances that brought him to this small Italian resort town.

"I still don't know myself how it happened," he began. "Believe it or not, but last Wednesday I didn't have an inkling that in a few days I'd find myself here."

He looked around, squinting as if to make sure he wasn't dreaming he was sitting in this little café in the resort town on the outskirts of Rome.

"It all started one hardly beautiful morning back in Odessa," he said. "I was sipping my coffee, when Katya, the sister of Rosa Palatnik, a young woman I once dated, knocks on my door and says, 'Leonid, they've arrested Rosa. The trial starts tomorrow. You're the only one who can help. Only publicity can save her. The bastards won't let anyone into the courthouse. You must get in and tape the hearing. My friends will transcribe it later and pass the text to Voice of America and the BBC correspondents. You're a member of two Unions, the Soviet Journalists, and the Soviet Filmmakers. They won't stop you. They'll let you in the courthouse.'

"I tell her, 'Katya, what the hell are you talking about? What things do you expect me to do? I've recently graduated from the Screenwriting School. They hired me as a scriptwriter at Odessa Film Studio. Do you know how long I've dreamed of this to happen? They're thinking of letting me direct a film I scripted. If they catch me doing what you want me to do, can you imagine what they will do?'

" 'Well, tough luck, Leonid!' Katya says. 'You know it and I do that if you don't help, it'll be a kangaroo court. They'll lock her up for a long time.'

"She was right. I was in a bind. What else could I do under these circumstances! Rosa worked as a librarian on Little Arnaut Street. In her free time, she typed out all of Solzhenitsyn's novel, *The Cancer Ward*. They caught her. They compared imprints of her typewriter with those on a copy of the book they found in someone's apartment. All over the country, anyone who wasn't too lazy had already been retyping Solzhenitsyn's work. But Rosa was an Odessan. By punishing her, they wanted to spook all of Odessa's Jews, to stop them from bombarding the local Exit Visa Office with applications for permission to leave the country for good. These applications were an embarrassment to the authorities and provided fodder for the capitalist anti-Soviet propaganda machine.

"So, how could I say no to Katya's request? My romance with Rosa had been short-lived. Like the match for the world chess championship between Grandmasters Botvinnik and Bronstein, it ended in a draw, but she and I stayed friends. How could I let her perish in the Gulag without trying to save her?

"In the morning I headed to the courthouse. Naturally, only members of voluntary police squads were present. Of course, if you don't count the plainclothes local police and the KGB. There are also Rosa's parents who've arrived from the little town of Balta, a quiet provincial couple.

And here I enter the courthouse. I show them my press card. They twirled it in their hands, but let me into the hall. They thought one of the big papers, *Pravda* or *Izvestia*, sent me to do a write-up for the "From the Courts" crime chronicle column.

"To ensure I make as good a recording as possible, I take a seat in the first row. I have an enormous, old bulky Sony tape recorder attached to my belly. Neither Katya nor my friends, whom I called all evening, could find a smaller unit. To conceal it best they could, they fastened it onto my stomach by wrapping it with two towels around my waist. I borrowed a baggy jacket from our studio's cinematographer Zhora. I'm a large man, but he is even bigger than me. I ran the microphone wire through my jacket sleeve.

"When my friends and I were preparing for the action, it seemed we considered all eventualities. However, we failed to consider one thing— the horrendous phrasemongering of the Soviet court. Since the trial was only a sideshow, the court would blabber for a short while and convict Rosa at once. But, to prevent giving ammunition to the capitalist mud-slingers, the judge received instructions to observe all points of the Soviet legal procedure.

"Two whole hours pass, and my cassette runs out of tape. The damn microphone in my sleeve reacts to it with loud beeping. Loud enough for the damn judge to hear it and give me a dirty look. The whole hall stares at me. The policemen are ready to tear me into pieces. As soon as the judge announces a recess, they all throw themselves at me, pick me up under my elbows, and bring me into one of the side rooms: 'We're detaining you for disorderly conduct during a court hearing. What's that beeping of yours?'

"I'm buttoned up all the way. I point at my belly.

"'Please forgive me,' I say. 'I have a stomach problem. What can I do? I can't control it.'

"'All right, all right,' they say, 'stop bullshitting us! What do you have there?'

"They unbutton my jacket and find everything. Right there, on the spot, they pull the whole tape off the cassette and tear it into pieces. And they take away my press card.

"As expected, the court found Rosa guilty and sentenced her to two years in prison.

"All these things took place on Monday. The next morning, I go to my film studio, but the guard at the gates is already expecting me, just to let me know he cannot let me in.

"'You have no business here anymore,' he says. 'You no longer work here.'

"The studio director comes out and says:

"'God be my witness I've seen a lot of fools in my life. But I have to admit I'm encountering your kind of meathead for the first time. No, I take it back. You're not even some fool. You're a clinical idiot. We accepted your script and were about to invite you to direct your movie. Tell me, what's that on your shoulders? A human head or a cauliflower?'

"For a few months, no matter where I went, nobody wanted to employ me. They hired me as a hospital attendant in an ambulance crew that specialized in suicide victims. Nobody else wanted to work there. I stayed in that job for six months. From boredom, I made a documentary, *The Causes of Suicide*. My friends found me a movie camera that operated by winding, a military type, model K78. Every evening I filmed one of the poor souls.

I copied thirty-two suicide notes. I had an assistant. I gave our ambulance driver the whole supply of medicinal spirits, which was part of the onboard medical cabinet. In return, he found me strong lamps so I had enough light to film. He cut the ropes and pulled down the corpses, and I filmed all of this. I discovered some interesting patterns. They hang themselves on rainy or foggy days. Sometimes, they do it because of incurable disease. One young fellow's hip bone was broken in a hospital four times because they had put it together improperly. There were also cases of tragic love. Once, a boy and girl hanged themselves in the same noose because their parents wouldn't let them get married.

"I filmed for six months, but someone snitched on me to the authorities that I made an unauthorized film, and they kicked me off the ambulance for conducting 'anti-Soviet activities.' The KGB confiscated everything they found during the search: manuscripts of four hundred of my poems, a few plays and film scripts, and a novel. At the KGB headquarters, they have a pool table lined with tin. They put all of my work on this table and drenched it with gasoline. They wanted me to allow the burning, but I already knew how to act with them: if they ask you for something, it means you can turn them down. I didn't give them my permission, not that it mattered in the least. They burned everything without my sanction. I'm sure I was neither the first nor the last person who lost years of work on that damned pool table.

"Later on, they arrested me on other business. Someone had snitched on me, reporting that my verses were anti-Soviet. One morning, plainclothes police officers arrived at the communal apartment which I called home, handcuffed me, and drove me to 5 Bebel Street, the headquarters of the Odessa KGB. They brought me to the investigator, Major Vladimir Ilyich Linkov. Later, I wrote a poem about this episode. Here are some stanzas that give you an idea of what this room looked like:

> They painted the number 782 in pink paint
> > on a black bulky safe.
> The walls are pale-green.
> Cords of wires run above the wooden floor.
> The ceiling's white and high.
> A bulb is in the center of the ceiling.
> They covered the table with red wrapping paper.
> A phone, an inkwell, a fountain pen.
> An ashtray, a blotter, and a box of matches.
> There are tiny saliva bubbles in a white spittoon.
> And red stains on the parquet,
> > most likely, it is colored ink.
> And a sofa! How could I forget about it!

"An idiotic interrogation followed. They tried to find out about all my acquaintances. It turned out they knew quite a few.

> Room number five hundred sixty,
> Where they didn't torture me,
> Didn't spit in my face or stick a boot in my groin.
> They spoke loudly, pointedly, politely,
> As if accidentally pressing
> A sensitive button with a marble rocking blotter,
> Turning on a dictaphone.

"The investigator placed photocopies of ten of my poems on the table. They had them copied before burning. Just in case they needed them in subsequent interrogations.

"'Here's a piece of paper,' the Major says. 'You have six hours to write, in your own words, what each poem means and at whom each image hints. Here, for example, you write about rooks, and that every one of them flies away, but one, a white one, stays. Explain who or what you are referring to.'

They offered to explain why one fall evening,
When rooks shouted in black boughs, I was frightened
Hearing them screaming before flying away.
I stayed in the dead garden, looking around
In a crowd of sparrows and ravens, as I was growing white,
Clapping my white wings against my white hips.

"They left me alone in the interrogation room and locked the door behind me. For six hours, I slept on the sofa, my hands as a makeshift pillow. Out of boredom, I read the wall newspaper. It was a revelation for me. At the KGB headquarters, as in any Soviet establishment, they issue the "wall newspaper," that is, typewritten articles penned by the employees. I even found an article critical of the fact the employees of that esteemed establishment don't pay enough attention to practicing their shooting skills. As a commission discovered, many of them have forgotten how to shoot. I peeled off that article for myself as a memento of my stay at the KGB headquarters.

"Finally, they came for me. I told the investigator:

"'I see you are a cultured person. I'm also cultured. Therefore, we'll understand each other. I don't feel like incriminating myself. Nothing, except mocking remarks about what each image in my verses means, enters my mind. I sometimes don't know what these images mean. I don't feel like writing any nonsense. Why should I give you an excuse to lock me up in an insane asylum? It looks as if you like doing such things.'

"They let me go that day. But, for a few more months, once a month, they came for me at my home and drove me away for interrogation. On orders from central headquarters, they kept questioning me about my fellow students at the Screen Writing School in Moscow. My name turned up in the telephone books of some of them.

"Meanwhile, I had to make a living. By that time, I already understood I could only find employment in places where nobody else wanted to work. One day I learned the Odessa Rosa Luxemburg Confectionery Factory was looking for a loader. No one could hold on to that job over there more than two weeks. So, I went there. The factory had a cellar ten-foot deep with an iron slope. From above, from a truck body, they threw down a sack of sugar or cocoa beans weighing over two hundred pounds. You must catch this sack and get it on your back. If you don't catch it, the sack cracks open and the sugar or cocoa spills all over the place. No one could handle these bags. In fact, everyone who tried it before me ended up in the hospital. They placed a cushioned wheelbarrow at the spot where the sacks land, but the wheelbarrows cracked in a matter of days. So, they hired me to catch those packed sacks without a wheelbarrow.

"In my past, back in high school, I was the fattest boy. Everybody teased me and called me 'Fatso!' and 'Tub of lard!' Fed,up with the teasing, I picked up weightlifting. In two years, I became the youth champion of Ukraine in barbell lifting. I had a healthy back, and I knew, to take up a sack on my back, I had to use my leg muscles as shock absorbers. The moment the bag touches your back, you must bend your legs. You lower one shoulder and the sack rolls over your back sideways. Then you take it down the factory floor and put it down. Over there two other loaders pick it up.

"It's hard work. They adored me at the factory because I solved their technological problem. For lunch, they gave me liquid chocolate. I drank almost a liter of it and ate nothing else.

"One day, about eleven o'clock in the morning, the factory lunch break's coming up. I'm about to go to drink my chocolate as I've already become accustomed. And here the Head of Personnel, that brassy broad, runs to the basement and shouts at me for everyone to hear:

"'You've deceived our countr-r-ry! You've got two diplomas of higher education! Get out of our factory! Hit the road!'

"I shrug. What does the broad care about my two diplomas! Yes, it's true. First, I had completed the Odessa Polytechnic Institute and the Screen Writing School in Moscow. I don't understand why, but something in the pit of my stomach churned. And, by this stage of my life, I already knew for a fact the pit of your stomach never deceives you. It's too bad we don't always pay attention to it.

"Well then, the pit of my stomach churns. I leave the basement, and one loader hands me a copy of the *Evening Odessa* newspaper. He's already opened it to display for me a huge article spread over two pages. I take the paper and get on the trolleybus. I'm riding home to Gogol Street. The chocolate factory is near our Odessa-Main Railway Station, and the trolleybus route goes along our beautiful Pushkinskaya Street. That day I've been unloading sacks filled with cocoa beans since early morning, and I'm covered with the cocoa dust. So, here I'm sitting in the trolleybus and reading the article:

The father of this scoundrel, Leonid Mak, professor of the Odessa Polytechnic Institute, failed to bring up his son properly. He indulged all his whims. His son felt like entering one institute, and the father said to him, "Be my guest." His son felt like getting another education, and his father obliged him once again. We should ask a question: Can we entrust such a professor to educate our young people? We shall answer resolutely, "No!"

"I read all this and understand that I will not be able to look into my father's eyes anymore. With my own hands, I've destroyed his teaching career. His whole life's work. I told myself right there and then: *There's no way out, Leonid. Your place is now in jail.*

"As I say this to myself, they announce the next stop is Zhukovsky Street, which is right at the editorial offices of the *Evening Odessa*. So I decide my fate itself has led me to this stop.

"I get out of the trolley and go up to the fifth floor of the building, to the editor in chief's office. I come up to his secretary and tell her I must see the editor.

"'Where are you from?' she asks.

"'I'm from the Rosa Luxemburg Confectionery Factory.'

"'Ah, so that's why you smell so tasty! Take a seat. The editorial staff meeting's about to end.'

"I'm sitting and waiting for a long while. At last, the double door of the editor's office opens, and the editorial staff members leave one by one. Among them is one Simon, a journalist I knew. The man notices me and is about to return to the office to tell the editor he is in danger of getting his ass beaten, but I let Simon know with one look that, if he gives me away, it will be his own ass black and blue without delay.

"Finally, the secretary says: 'Please come in.'

"I enter the editor's office. At its farthest end, behind an enormous table, Victor Yanko, the paper's editor in chief, sits. I close the door behind me and turn the key, locking the door so that nobody can interfere with him and me.

"'Well,' I'm thinking, 'what should I do to him?' Since I will go to jail anyway, I might as well do something worthy of a jail sentence. They've been already after me for two years. For two years, everything has been headed toward getting me off the streets. So, at least I should do something worth their while. Maybe I'll throw the bastard out the window and let him go straight to hell. They'll put me in prison all the same.

"Meanwhile, Yanko finishes scribbling something. At last, he lifts his head.

"'Sit down. Why do you smell so tasty?'

"'I'm from the confectionery factory,' I say. 'I work as a loader over there.'"

"'Ah, a blue-collar worker! The body and soul of the proletariat! That vermin Mak works at your factory. Do you know him well?'

"I reply, 'Very well.'

"'How long have you known him?'

"'All my life.'

"When the man hears this, he makes a move to grab the phone, but I intercept his hand in midair. I bend over the table, take him by his belt and his shoulder, lift him up in the air, and carry him to the window. I place his back onto the windowsill and press him down with my whole body weight. The editor kicks and tries to get out from under me, but to no avail.

"'Vermin!' the editor shouts. 'You'll go to jail.'

"The windows are open, and it's still warm outside. It's September 5 and, as I look down, I am on the fifth floor. Look at that, I think to myself, what a coincidence! You, son of a bitch, are about to fly from the fifth floor of the building on the fifth day of the month.

"I push him out farther and farther so that his shoulder blades are already out of the window. The courtyard is paved with cobblestones.

"He screams, his voice hoarse, 'What are you doing?'

"'Who commissioned the article?' I shout, 'Who?'

"Yanko squeals: 'General Kouzin . . . General Kouzin.'

"By that time, I already knew that General Kouzin was the head of the Odessa KGB's Regional Directorate. Yanko himself, as my friends told me, had the rank of KGB Major.

"I push the bastard out of the window a little farther. The man sticks out from the window and cries out with his last breath.

"'What are you doing!' he shouts. 'What are you doing! They'll shoot you for this!'

"Here it comes to me. The scoundrel may have a point. If I throw him down from the fifth floor, they could bring in capital punishment. I've planned to go to jail, but not being shot . . .

"Still pressing down on the editor with my whole body, I spit in his face several times. This wasn't all that easy because my mouth was all dried up from all the excitement. Still, some nasty phlegm landed on his mean mug all the same.

"I let the scum go. The man slips down from the windowsill, planting his ass on the floor. I leave. Later they'd tell me Yanko let no one wipe off his face for half an hour. He waited for police to arrive and take my saliva off his mug for analysis to prove the identity of the man who attacked him while he was on duty.

"I leave the editorial quarters and walk up Deribasovskaya Street. I don't hide. I pass by the Wagner House. In Odessa, as you, Boris, know, the houses still carry the names of their prerevolutionary owners. From my childhood, I remember all of this neighborhood's hidden passages, but now I don't even think of using them. What for? All the same, I will inevitably go to jail. I turn onto Gavan Street and head home, waiting for a police car to drive up any minute and take me away.

"By the time I get home, they are already waiting for me at the entrance of my building on Gogol Street. A police lieutenant and another man in the raincoat with a small suitcase. As I pass by, the man in a raincoat opens his briefcase and takes out a glass fragment for specimen collecting, brings it to my face, and orders me, 'Spit!'

"I say, 'I won't.'

"'Spit, you bastard!'

"I tell him: 'You don't need my saliva because I admit I spat into that scoundrel Yanko's face. In fact, by doing so, I was spitting in the face of the entire Odessa KGB. Write it down.'

"'Don't be a fool,' the police lieutenant whispers to me. 'What are you saying such things for? You'll make it worse for yourself.'

"'No, no, don't worry,' I say to him. 'I defend myself this way. I know what I'm doing. Write it down, 'Especially in the face of General Kouzin.'

"I knew the only thing that could save me was publicity.

"For once, I was right. For starters, they jailed me for three days. I went on a hunger strike. They dragged me to the public prosecutor. The man told me:

'If you don't like our Soviet way of life, leave. Don't make waves. Don't spit in anyone's face anymore. Otherwise, they'll charge you with malicious hooliganism, and you get seven years in the can. And I assure you that you won't survive your term. The hard-core criminals will knife you to death . . . So, get your exit visa, and in three days get your ass out of the country! If you stay, blame yourself.'

"I can't believe I'm not there anymore, and that I'm here," Mak said. Smiling absentmindedly, he examined the faces of the café visitors around him. Is it possible his fate has changed so much?

He and Boris ordered another round of cappuccinos, still wondering how they could live in this world, without knowing such a fantastic drink exists.

They went to the railroad station. Mak was returning to Rome where he lived and waiting for an invitation from Israel. A translation job was waiting for him there. Saying good-bye, Mak gave Boris his Roman phone number.

"Keep in touch, man." Again, as at the beginning of their meeting, Mak clapped Boris on his shoulder.

As they passed the post office, from the open door came muttering, already familiar to Boris: "I'm old, I'm tired, I'm a hundred and eighty years old. And the Almighty made sure the fugitives wandered in the desert forty years."

28
ROME IS A DANGEROUS CITY

Whenn the Bumshteins reached Rome and settled in Miramar, Yurik became reclusive. He hid his dream of getting back with his wife as much as he could. After all the trouble he had caused his former family in Chop, Bratislava, and in Vienna, he didn't dare take the initiative in everyday affairs. He took hold of his pride and did everything Lyubka told him to do—as much as he could without snapping. He took solace there remained reasons for him to have hope. Lyubka's lover stayed far behind, beyond the Carpathian Mountains, beyond the nighttime clatter of the rails, along with his great hairdo—in Odessa. All that was necessary was patience, patience, and more patience. In the meantime, he would continue to throw sidelong glances and scrutinize every man approaching Lyubka, anticipating a new rival in each of them.

Yurik's attitude was not without reason. Despite the ordeals she endured while crossing several state borders, Lyubka's sex appeal remained intact. All kinds of men streamed to her in shoals and bit like hungry carps.

One day, somebody knocked on the Bumshteins' hotel room door while Yurik was absent. As per Lyubka's instructions, he was making rounds at the Roman pharmacies, armed with only a Russian-Italian phrase book from the Joint, in search of medicine for his grief-stricken daughter. It was not clear whether it was her nerves, or if it was the torturing thought she would never see her dear Dima Zolotarev again; either way, her hormones ran rampant, causing both of her cheeks to break out in acne.

The knock occurred while Lyubka was sitting in front of the bathroom mirror. She did her best to quickly perfect her face, but when she went to open the door, she had only applied her mascara to one eye, making her look like a surprised mime.

The expression turned out to be suitable for the occasion. The face she met in the doorway was an unfamiliar one. The visitor was an old man in an elegant beige raincoat with slightly tattered cuffs. He said hello, entered the room, and, without waiting for an invitation, lowered himself into a chair.

Lyubka has seen him the day before, in the lobby, when they were checking into the hotel. He rummaged through the export goods laid out by an émigré couple who would become Yurik and Lyubka's neighbors in the hotel. The old man was one of those second-hand dealers among his fellow countrymen who, after immigrating to Israel, went somewhere else. But by leaving Israel, he lost his refugee status, and with it the support of the Joint, so he made a living doing whatever he could in the Italian capital.

Lyubka apologized for having to leave her unexpected guest alone for a few minutes and went into the bathroom to finish her makeup. Passing by the old man, she judged by a single glance he hadn't come only to ask her the price of her souvenirs. The old man smiled that special restrained smile in the presence of a beautiful woman.

After fixing up her second set of eyelashes, Lyubka returned to the room and opened one of her suitcases. His elbows resting on his knees, the guest examined their contents. He did so with little enthusiasm but named high prices. It was not clear what profit he could make. He was a bit eccentric but honest, which was surprising because other hustlers tried to rip off their former compatriots. She had already considered selling her souvenirs to the old man so she wouldn't have to drag them along with her through Italy, but something held her back.

She wasn't mistaken. The old man glanced at her again and spoke somewhat cautiously:

"I see, Ms. Bumshtein, you're traveling alone with your daughter."

"How do you know?" Lyubka said. "Maybe I'm with my husband."

"I saw you yesterday at HIAS. I need little to understand a person. Maybe on paper, he is your husband, but I feel it won't affect what I will tell you now."

Lyubka also wanted to touch up her eyebrows. She went back to the bathroom, apologizing on the way:

"Excuse me a moment . . . But go on, I'm listening."

She stepped into the bathroom but left the door open.

"I have a suggestion, Ms. Bumshtein," the old man said, raising his voice so that Lyubka would hear him. "I have been living in Rome for eight months now. I have a small business; the income is small, but it's enough for me. It's enough for a couple if you know what I mean."

"Well, well," Lyubka laughed from the bathroom, "Are you proposing? Are you my bridegroom?"

The old man accepted Lyubka's laughter calmly.

"There's no need to formalize our relationship, Lyubov Gershovna. We're adults, aren't we? Let's wait and see. If we don't get along, well, it'll be a pity. We'll go our separate ways, and I will thank you for a pleasant acquaintance."

Lyubka wasn't surprised she was being pursued, but the courtship by the reseller flattered her. You could be a world-class beauty, and men, even old decrepit ones, still won't approach you with serious intentions. For such old men, all the fun is in sitting under the sun and warming their bones. Even though she had understood everything about him from her first glance, she still interrupted her cosmetic artistry for a moment, just to look at the daredevil once more.

"You know what," she said, coming out of the bathroom and slamming her little powder box, producing two fragrant puffs from its sides, "let me think about it. This is all too sudden. I've just arrived here."

"Oh, I know you'll have other attractive offers, Lyubov Gershovna," the old man said. "I'm aware my chances aren't too high. But, please take into consideration I was first."

"My God!" Lyubka laughed. "Listening to you, one would assume a line is already forming at my door. And you are the trailblazer!"

Lyubka was cunning. She wanted to hear more compliments. She loved listening to them. She compared the pleasure of hearing compliments to bathing with a bar of Le Blanc, a scented French soap she would buy at the Odessa flea market called *Americana*.

"Line or no line," the old man said, "there will be other propositions. It's like during the wartime evacuation: people become intimate with each other quickly. They lose contact with their roots—no need to ask your parents' permission. But everything falls apart just as quickly. It even happens to marriages that have survived many years. You wouldn't believe it, but your boarding card is not the only thing they rip in half at the border; they do the same to your soul, and, with some people, what remains of their decency. I had only one woman in my life: my wife. Such faithfulness is worth something these days, Lyubov Gershovna."

The old man raised himself from the chair quite gaily for his age (what only the presence of a beautiful young woman can do!), bowed, and headed for the door. "In short, I'm waiting with anticipation." He smiled before closing the door behind him.

Such a strange man, Lyubka thought. *He has a nice smile . . . well, let him wait. Who cares!*

Although Yurik knew nothing about this encounter, he wanted to move from Rome to Ostia, whatever the cost, and as soon as possible. Not only because the apartments in Ostia were cheaper than in Rome, but also because Rome was a dangerous place. That was because Lyubka liked all the young Roman men she met on the streets. They were all well-kept, combed their hair and styled it with gel. They all had these sexy mustaches. She imagined if she kissed someone with one of those mustaches, the sky would light up with fireworks.

"They're so cute," she told her female travel companions. "They have their hair done, unlike our men, who walk around like hobos."

And the young Roman men reciprocated her affection. They glued their eyes to her lush body. Since her heart belonged only to Arkady, the practical Odessan woman made use of the interest Italian men showed toward her. Lyubka hated public transportation; she had enough of commuting on the Odessan trams, stuffed like tobacco in pipes, where impudent men used the crowding as an excuse to press themselves against her breasts. She came up with her own way of getting around Rome. Since she had no money for a taxi, she would come to the crossroads and peer into cars waiting for the green light. Drivers invited her to get in. At the Round Market where Lyubka, like other emigrants, went to buy food, she asked to stop for a moment. She jumped out of the car and waved the driver farewell.

Once she came close to paying for the convenience of her form of transportation. She was unaware that in Rome, only streetwalkers peeked into the cars at the street intersections, soliciting business. She was mistaken for one of these women because of her Odessan style: her high heels, over-the-top hairdo, too much of both mascara and lipstick.

One day, by accident, she stopped the limo of an Italian man whom she had already fooled once.

She was embarrassed when he recognized her. She deduced from his angry facial expression and rude gestures that he promised to make her pay for her insolence. She hastily retreated.

However, this incident didn't stop her. She still bent over at the car windows, allowing the driver to take in the magnificent view. Only now she tried to remember the face of the car owner. She liked her way of moving around the city; it excited her and made her feel good about herself.

No, no, Yurik told himself when he learned about Lyubka's antics, *to Ostia, to Ostia, with no delays.*

29
YOU CAN'T TAKE THE COUNTRY OUT OF THE COUNTRY BOY

After parting with Mak, Boris walked to the sea. The skies were clear. The waves glittered in the sun like they did in his native town of Odessa. It was comforting. The sea is the sea, anywhere you go. He was not that far away from home . . .

It was the off-season, and the beach was lacking swimmers and sunbathers. Boris set himself down under one of the beach umbrellas and continued reading Ilya's letter, which he had perused at the post office and shoved in his pocket.

Now, dear Boris, when you are on this side of the Iron Curtain, I want to share with you a discovery that has struck me. It turns out that, although we'd fled the Soviet Union, we brought it along with us without realizing. This is how the first wave of immigrants brought all those cockroaches and bedbugs to the New World; they hid in the crevices of their old trunks and chests.

Alas, it was easy to get rid of the insects by throwing those trunks away, but what could be done with our crippled souls? As much as we would like to start over, it isn't so easy to get rid of the hidden junk that accumulated over our Soviet life.

However, it wasn't a discovery I had made myself. While on some business, I visited the offices of our local Jewish Family Service, an organization that helped resettle us, the newcomers. While walking down the corridor, I overheard one social worker speaking to another:

"Well, this is just between you and me, Isaac . . . Working with ex-Soviet immigrants made me come to a sad conclusion. You know the saying, 'You can take the boy out of the country, but not the country out of the boy?' So, recently I've realized: it's been much easier to take a Jew out of the Soviet Union than the Soviet Union out of that Jew . . ."

My first reaction, Boris, was, "What gibberish is he talking?" I'm both feet here, in America, and the USSR is in the opposite hemisphere, to begin with. I ran away because I hated the Soviet system with every fiber of my soul, with my whole being. It took so much effort to get out of that country. I took such a huge risk by even trying to leave the awful place I was born in by a whim of fate.

But, after giving it some thought, I came to the sad conclusion: that American man was damn right. When a mouse runs over to the other side of a room, it doesn't turn into a cat, does it?

True enough, I didn't discover it at once. It came to me gradually, although my Soviet past made itself present almost immediately. It snuck up on me during the first steps on the new land . . .

From the outset, we had to learn a new skill. We had to scan the local newspaper ads—while being not well-versed in English, mind you!—to find jobs. The fact we'd need to compose and send to potential employers a certificate called a *résumé* was a bizarre concept for us, aliens from another civilization.

Every aspect of writing it bewildered us. In this "résumé," we were supposed to highlight our abilities and talents. How could one be so brash as to state in black-and-white what a swell and able fellow he is? And the prospective employer was supposed to believe you?

When I first encountered this American custom, it dumbfounded me. All we had to do was to submit a piece of paper? How about that! What about a copy of your diploma? What about a certificate from your previous place of employment? And a reference letter? And here–wouldn't you know it!

It took some time to realize what I never gave a second thought. We all came from a culture in which they trusted no one. Your signature on any piece of paper had to be verified with a seal. Preferably, with a round one, although sometimes you could get away with an oval one and even a triangular one. The main thing was to have a seal . . .

Scholars still argue about whose bureaucratic system the Soviet Union had inherited. Was it from the time of the Golden Horde invasion and the Tatar-Mongol yoke, or was it borrowed from the Byzantine Empire? As if it matters that much . . . In my time, we all took for granted the truth of the saying, "Without a piece of paper, you're an insect." When my émigré friend, Grisha, applied for the postgraduate course in Russian studies here at UCLA, this ingrained understanding of the ultimate authority of a seal on any document caused him some embarrassment. He translated his Soviet diploma into English. One of his future professors looked it over, got rid of the errors, retyped the whole thing on his university stationery, signed it, and gave it back to him to take to the admissions office. Grisha was about to thank him, but after looking at the paper, he stopped short.

"Professor," he said. "What about some seal?"

The American glanced at him with sympathy, realizing that a Soviet Martian was standing in front of him. He explained kindly that, in this country, on such a document, his signature on the university stationery was sufficient.

So, to look for a job, compose a résumé . . . let your potential employer know about all of your successes and achievements. I have to admit it was one of the most difficult cultural hurdles I had to clear. We all have been raised in a culture in which lowliness bordering on self-abasement was expected of all of us. The centuries' old mentality of Russian peasant communes lingered. In English, the value of the individual is expressed graphically: "I" is always rendered as a capital letter. In Russian, not only is the word "I" (*ia*) always a lowercase letter (unless it starts a sentence), but, at every attempt to talk about what you take credit for doing, you're always in danger of being interrupted with, "Stop *iakat'*," that is, speaking too much about yourself. "Don't forget, man, 'I' [я] is the last letter of the alphabet." There's a whole heap of Russian proverbs and sayings meant to put people down, such as "What a one you are! You have a finger in every pie," "Don't get in someone else's sleigh," "Every cricket should know its hearth," and many others.

So, it's no wonder, dear Boris, that we all lived in the USSR guided by the saying, "Sit quiet and don't stick your neck out." And here, wouldn't you know it! In the American résumé, you're expected to tell a total stranger how swell and smart you are! In America, they're flabbergasted when you don't put your best foot forward. After a long job search, one of us Soviet émigrés was hired as a draftsman. In his opinion, with his poor English, that was the only job he could count on getting in America. From the cradle, being accustomed to modesty on the verge of self-abasement, he didn't disclose to his employer his real qualifications. So, one day, one of the company's engineers stopped by the newly hired draftsman's cubicle and showed him a volume he found on the bookshelf in his office. It was a manual on how to calculate submarine hulls, translated from the Russian.

"May I ask you?" the engineer said. "Is the author of this book your relative by any chance?"

"No, he isn't," the draftsman replied, glancing at the book, without interrupting his work.

"Wouldn't you know it! The same surname . . . oh, and the given name is the same as yours as well . . ." "No, it isn't my relative's book," said the newcomer, forcing himself to speak up. "It's my book. I wrote it."

The engineer carefully, so as not to offend him, peeked at the draftsman in disbelief. Is he pulling my leg? And, if he's telling the truth, is he right in his head? Why had he hidden his true worth during his job interview?

Well, the engineer reported his discovery to his higher-ups, and they made the draftsman a project manager and hired an interpreter for him.

At first, Americans' faith in anything they read in a résumé seemed to border on gullibility. You have to trust people, but to what extent!

(I'm getting ahead of myself, but I'll tell you, Boris, the truth: it took me a long, long while to realize Americans aren't as naive as they seemed to us, newcomers from another world. During one of my job interviews, I mentioned something I didn't include in my résumé. It felt like bragging. One time, while working as an engineer back in the USSR, I came up with a way of saving gas-pumping motors from overheating. They even published an article about this innovation of mine, complete with a diagram, in a technical journal. When my interviewer heard about it, it flummoxed her. Why didn't I include this in my résumé? When I blushed and explained to her my fear of being immodest, she told me not to worry about it. She took all résumé declarations with a grain of salt, anyway. To get closer to the true picture, as she explained it.)

Finding a job in America was hard also because of a lot of Soviet prejudices, which, unbeknownst to us, permeated our consciousness. Though we all were conscious opponents of communism and socialism, few of us considered getting into the field of trades and entrepreneurship in the capitalist country. A "huckster" (*torgash*), a "petty shopkeeper" (*lavochnik*), a "traveling salesman" (*kommivoyazher*), a "businessman"—all these terms were part of the anti-capitalist propaganda sneers. Communist ideology painted occupations of this kind with thick black paint. People engaged in trade in the capitalist world were all considered "parasites," "bloodsuckers," and "exploiters." It may sound like a joke, but the idea of a free market was so foreign to us, newly arrived Soviet immigrants, that one fellow who inherited a small stationery store from his American relative complained to his friends. He had a hard time running his business because the State Department failed to send customers his way . . .

There was another cultural barrier mighty hard to overcome—to learn on the go how to behave during a job interview. Here in America, there's a science to it, one unknown to us, ex-citizens of the country of victorious socialism.

First, know how to dress for the interview. To the American eye, we looked weird. During the long journey from the Soviet Union, many of us wore out our clothes. In Rome, many men bought cheap leather jackets, and women dressed up in leather skirts and trousers. I don't know what the Americans thought of us, seeing our infatuation with leather clothing. I guess we appeared to be petty mafia gangsters with poor English . . .

In other instances, having no idea how to present ourselves to the interviewers, we overdressed. We put on our best clothes as if we were heading to the opening night at the Bolshoi Theater—men in three-piece suits, women in ballroom dresses. American Al, the tall young man who here, in L.A., drove us to the interviews, looked at us like we were nuts. At one point, he couldn't hold it and told us that, for an interview, one has to dress the way one would when going to work at that place. A job interview, he said, isn't a charity ball for the benefit of homeless pets.

He also advised, when being interviewed, to project self-confidence. Self-confidence, my foot! You may have a hard time believing it, Boris, but some of our new arrivals came to the interview accompanied by their wives. They took them along for moral support. American employers felt that U.S. immigration officers had blown it. They let some weak-witted men from the Land of Soviets slip into the country. The interviewer was tempted to say in the most delicate form that the visitor made a mistake: the bureau for helping the mentally challenged was at a different address . . .

One of the most bizarre pieces of advice we got was to maintain eye contact with the interviewer at all times. How about that! Back in Russia, staring at a stranger means challenging him to a fistfight, and here, in America, the ability to maintain eye contact is a signifier of the interlocutor's honesty. For an American, you are a born liar if your eyes shifted during an interview . . .

You have to smile all the time! Over here, if a person can't produce a smile on cue, he has to see a psychotherapist. Or even a psychiatrist—to be treated for depression.

Now, how was an American interviewer to account for that fact that, where we come from, only an idiot smiles at strangers! We reserve our smiles for close friends, for loved ones alone. I bet that, for outsiders, the passersby on our Russian streets all seemed to have the dour facial expressions of Politburo members in their publicity pictures. When I now look at the Soviet ID cards I took along, I wince. In America, such a cheerless face you can find only in the mug shots of armed robbers. It looks like the only time they forget about smiling is when they're being booked and fingerprinted.

The cultural ban on a smile in a public place is so much a part of our self-awareness that, here, in America, some come to resist it. I heard on the Russian-language radio (an underground businessman from—where else!—our hometown, Odessa, has created it here, in L.A.) a discussion on this topic. The question argued was whether it's worth it to torture oneself to conform to the habits of the local population, which seems to smile nonstop for no reason. The talk-show hostess, a cultured former Muscovite, spoke with a sense of offended dignity, with indignation and defiance.

"What if I'm a serious person?" she said. "What if I don't feel like smiling right now? Why should I force myself?"

I also didn't have much reason to smile when I was looking for a job. At home, I had Bella and our year-and-a-half old Maxim, who needed an ample supply of diapers. Understandably, the Jewish community, which provided us with room and board when we arrived in America, pushed all of us to get a job as quickly as possible.

So, how do you smile under such circumstances? That a smile in America is a sign of courtesy and respect for strangers reaches our consciousness slowly. It's a novelty . . .

And, speaking of interview challenges, I don't even talk about the problem of our deficient English. The English in our school textbooks wasn't outdated; it was antediluvian. There is no surprise there, however. The authors of those volumes were hardly given a chance to visit an English-speaking country. So, the language of their instructions was that of the British aristocracy, that is, grandiloquent, lofty. For example, to show your confidence, instead of saying to the interviewer, "No problem. I'll learn how to do that," we uttered, "This is not an impediment. I shall accomplish the task of acquiring this knowledge in the future." In fact, since back in Soviet schools we listened to methodological recordings by some Brits, our pronunciation also was British.

Well, while many Americans find British talk sexy, when we, coming from a different linguistic realm, reproduce the British accent, we come across as being arrogant and irksome. We were instructed to pronounce the words through our noses, our jaws raised, as if we had water in our mouths. As a result, during our interviews, we spoke with the aplomb and arrogance of Shakespearean villains, the usurpers of the crown power.

The names of the simplest household items in English were absent in our vocabulary of pompous words. Forget about the idioms. I still remember how scandalous I was during my first year in America. One day, I called our local bank in Santa Monica and asked for Mr. Smith, the man in charge of auto loans. Whoever answered the phone told me: "Sorry, but Mr. Smith isn't available . . . He's passed away." I knew the verb "to pass." So, I asked: "And when is he coming back?"

Their answer was appropriate in this case: dead silence. How could I know that "to pass away" meant to leave for another world! Should I have known it, I wouldn't wait for the man's return. As you know, I don't believe in the resurrection of the dead.

On top of everything else, the first thing the interviewer required of me was to talk about my work experience in America. What experience could I have, having just arrived in America?

So, my situation was unenviable, and the search for my first job was an epic of countless trips from one end of the greater L.A. area to another. I kept making rounds in this vicious circle. Poor Al drove me from one potential employer to another, and his old bluish Impala panted like an asthmatic. (This all had taken place before I became the proud owner of my Dodge sedan, the one that, as I'd written to you about, I drove when I got my first traffic ticket.)

Over time, however, everything worked out. As I've written to you, a small company that manufactured connectors for computers hired me. They needed a draftsman. I never liked this part of my engineering education—the drafting. But, as the Russian saying goes, "The need makes you jump, makes you dance, makes you sing a song."

It took me a long while to get rid of many other hang-ups of my Soviet past. Having read lots of articles in the Soviet press about the inhumane essence of capitalism in general, and American capitalism in particular, after working for only a few months at the company that hired me (it has a cheerful name—A-OK Electronics), I feared they could fire me for no reason. I felt that way, even though Mr. Lesser, the company's chief engineer, a tall blond middle-aged German Jew, showed no dissatisfaction with the blueprints I produced. Or with my work ethic. Never late in the morning or after lunch. Yet, I still feared they could fire me for a small reason, on a whim.

Boris recalled the letter from Arik he had read in the post office. Arik also worried that American employers, bored idlers as they are, would fire their workers just for fun.

Boris returned to his cousin's letter:

But those weren't *all* of my paranoid fears. The company that employed me was small, about twenty people. The owners were two middle-aged Jews. They showed their goodwill responding to the call of the local Jewish community to help their newly arrived Soviet brethren to get on their feet.

Yet, came September, the day of Yom Kippur, and I reported to work. When I appeared at the door, Mary, our secretary, was surprised.

"Gee," she said, "I assumed you're Jewish . . ."

I showed up at my workplace not because I was an atheist, ignoring this Jewish high holiday. I grew up in a Jewish family. Although not observant, my parents always honored such a high holiday as Yom Kippur. I reported to work because, deep down, conditioned by my Soviet upbringing, I was still wary of the possibility of being fired for absenteeism in America.

But that was not all. After a while, I had some concerns about my health. During one winter night in Odessa, I had been foolish enough to stroll through the city wearing a light jacket. This led to some kidney issues. So, at one point, I needed to see a doctor. Yet, I didn't dare to ask for a day off for one and only reason: I was afraid to lose my job. What if my employers find me an unreliable employee—and fire me?

After learning about my situation, Charlotte, my American relative, insisted I stop this nonsense and make a doctor's appointment. If they fire me because of that, she said, my employer is a heartless beast. He doesn't deserve to have me work for him. It's okay for her, a retiree, to talk that way. I had a wife and a small child on my hands. What would we live on? We were in a new country with limited language skills. Every aspect of this new life was incomprehensible. Every little thing pounced on me from every corner, demanding I try to understand what was what.

However, not only was American life an enigma for us. We, Soviet immigrants, were also not so easy to crack.

"What the hell is going on?" my American friend Si Frumkin—I wrote to you about him already—told me the other day. "I don't get it."

His eyes wide open, he gave me his usual long, unblinking gaze:

"I wanted to help them. I gave them a job. And they . . ."

Si was our guardian angel, godfather, and midwife, all rolled into one. As I already informed you, he fought to set us free from Soviet bondage, and, once we arrived, he helped some to compose a résumé, others to find their distant American relatives.

So, now Si told me that, for the life of him, he couldn't understand why people whom he helped paid him back with such ingratitude. When he learned that a married couple among the new arrivals had a hard time finding a job—let's call them the Goldmans—he employed them in his small business, Universal Drapery. However, instead of doing their job in earnest like any other American, the Goldmans worked halfheartedly. They took smoke breaks all too often . . . they extended their lunchtime indefinitely . . .

Growing up in the West, Si didn't understand that the Goldmans had no idea they seemed ungrateful to their benefactor. The thought that they might annoy Si with their work ethic never crossed their minds. The reason for that misunderstanding isn't too complicated. As I've learned here, there is a deep cultural divide on what "helping" means. In the Russian consciousness, helping means giving someone money. In America, it is giving someone a job . . . Based on the premises of the Protestant work ethic, the American culture of self-respect assumes everyone prefers to earn his own living rather than being on the receiving end of handouts . . . Moreover, like most of us newcomers, the Goldmans brought along the only attitude toward work we had known in our Soviet lives. It was only in the Soviet posters that socialist labor was "a matter of honor, valor, and heroism." The real attitude to work was different. Without realizing it, we'd brought along the centuries-old Russian idea of work where labor had often been forced. An employee had rarely been interested in doing his best. Think of such old Russian folk sayings as, "Work isn't a wolf; it won't run away to the forest," "Even the horses croak from work," or "Eat until you sweat, and work until you chill." And the situation didn't change much in the Soviet era. "It doesn't matter where you work, as long as you can loaf about," people say, or give each other that jolly piece of advice, "If you feel like doing some work, lie down on a sofa, and it'll go away."

The reason for such a cavalier attitude toward work in Soviet times is expressed by the proverb, "They pretend to pay us, and we pretend to work." I'm sure you know firsthand that some office worker in Moscow (or Odessa) could come to work, take off his jacket, hang it on the back of his chair, and go about his private affairs for as long as he feels like. He could go to the store to stock up on scarce provisions, or on a date with his beloved, who also took time off from her workplace.

In this respect, the Soviet system is a victim of its own ideology. Since, by definition, there should be no unemployment in the country of "victorious socialism," the work force in many settings is bloated like a beer lover's belly. When I received my first paycheck in America, I couldn't believe my eyes. I brought it home and told Bella, to be on the safe side, we should wait before putting it into our bank account. It seemed the company's payroll department made a mistake. My check as a draftsman was not two, not three—that much I could still imagine!—but six times more than what I received for my last work at the engineering design office in Odessa.

Then, I realized, if something like my American company were to open in Odessa now, they would staff it with many more people. For example, in addition to drawing connectors, when it was needed, I stepped to the conveyor and worked as a quality control inspector. When some calibrator or another engineering device came in, they asked me to read instructions and teach others how to operate it . . .

The effect of Soviet propaganda that ran through our blood from childhood took even more dramatic form for my émigré friend Misha Zilberman. One day, he shared with me how he learned about the true nature of American capitalism. In practice, it turned out not to be as bloodthirsty as Soviet media depicted it.

Misha holds a Ph.D. in technical sciences from Odessa State University. He works for a company in Morristown, New Jersey. They hired him as a downsizing consultant. He's vacationed with his family in Los Angeles. (His wife Masha and daughter Alina couldn't wait to see the stars on the Hollywood sidewalks.)

"I don't get it," Misha shrugged. "Are they sharks of capitalism or what? I proposed a restructuring plan for the owner of my firm. I told him with excitement and enthusiasm that, if he follows my recommendations to streamline his production line, he'd be able to cut his payroll drastically. He could let go about 30 percent of his employees. My eyes sparkled with excitement, but his face turned pale as I talked. He stared at me with horror, as if I were a madman about to bite his head off. 'Well, Misha,' he said, 'is it possible to do some trimming of my staff, but not to let so many people go?' Here you are! I presumed all that any capitalist dreams about is to increase his profit by all means possible. And here you are . . . Well, as I found out in time, all that he, the company owner, cares about is how the New York Yankees, his favorite baseball team, played their most recent game, and how could he manage, under some pretext, to arrange a trip somewhere far away from his wife with Suzi, his twenty-one-year-old secretary . . . go figure!

"It also turned out that, although the company owner was proud of his success as a businessman, he was no less proud of creating hundreds of jobs for people in his town. Can you believe it! There wasn't a word about this side of an American businessman's psyche in the Soviet papers, mind you." Misha laughed.

Misha's boss surprised him in another way. One day, when Misha came to work by bus—his old Ford Escort was in a repair shop—the company owner, after learning about it, offered Misha a ride home. They didn't live far from each other. Moreover, he drove his Mercedes himself although he could easily afford a chauffeur.

"I worked for ten years at my engineering office in Odessa," Misha mused, telling me about it, "but my boss never *ever* invited me into his chauffeur-driven Volga, although he knew I didn't have a car. I only dreamt about it."

So much for the ideal classless society . . .

The amiability and gullibility of Americans amaze us. Here, they presume you are a good person, and you must do something awful to prove otherwise. While in our homeland, in our Russian consciousness, everyone is under suspicion, everyone is a bastard. You had to prove again and again you're a decent chap.

Also, American goodwill and readiness to help us, total strangers, was a complete surprise to us. Back in our home country, they told us day and night that, in the West, it is a dog-eat-dog world . . .

However, one thing about Americans rubbed us the wrong way in our first encounters with them. It is their reluctance to spill all the beans of their personal life to a stranger, the way we are accustomed to in Russia. It dumbfounded us. It looked like every man for himself here; a society of individualists . . . They mind their own business. No sense of the collective which we all have been conditioned in. It was so comforting to see on TV how, in time of any natural disaster, be it a flood or an earthquake, the whole American town was coming alive. They created a human chain passing sandbags. They stretched in line for blocks on end to donate blood. Well, Boris, we make many discoveries like that at every step of our new American life . . .

However, the saddest thing I discovered in America, the most upsetting thing, was that, with the cockroaches in our trunks, we brought our home-grown racism along. It's not a novelty here, in America. However, here they consider it the most painful and shameful consequence of the country's history. So, when I first heard from the lips of my former compatriots the words "black-assed" directed at African Americans, I nearly died from shame. How could they be that way! Hadn't every Jewish immigrant from the USSR who spewed these slurs experienced on their own skin what prejudice is? Hadn't they heard at least once in their Russian lives the pejorative "kike" being hurled at them?

Although in the Soviet Union they still pay lip service to internationalism and friendship among the peoples, in reality, as we all know, there are plenty of ethnic tensions. For example, between the Georgians and the Armenians. Do you remember, Boris, that joke everybody enjoyed telling?

They ask the Armenian Radio, "What's 'peoples' friendship'?"

The answer: "It's when a Russian takes the hand of a Ukrainian, who takes the hand of an Uzbek, who takes the hand of a Kazakh, who takes the hand of a Georgian, and they all together go to beat up the Armenians."

There were plenty of ethnic slurs to go around. In private, Russians would dismiss any Asian person coming from the Soviet republics—be it an Uzbek, a Kazakh, or a Turkman—as "*chuchmek*." Now, here, the other day I overheard two Russian Jews referring to Mexicans living and working in L.A. as "yellow-mouthed." It shocked me and made my blood boil. What the fuck! How could you, of all people, be racists toward people who did no wrong to you, to begin with? You, who know firsthand what rabid antisemitism is!

America isn't some paradise on Earth, populated by angels. Racial hatred is a sore spot in American history. A cold shiver ran down my spine when one day on TV I saw *Gentleman's Agreement*, an old American movie (made in 1947) with Gregory Peck in the lead role. He plays a journalist who's assigned to write an article about antisemitism in America during the first years after WWII. To understand how it feels to be discriminated against by prejudice, he pretends to be a Jew. He experiences the full impact of bigotry, both firsthand and through the anecdotes of his Jewish friend's life.

Well, it looks like Nazism was a plague, which, although Germany and its allies have been defeated, infected many people on both sides of the Atlantic. I'm a few years older than you, Boris, and I still remember how, after the war was over, while a boy standing with my mother in the lines for bread, I heard drunken voices in the Odessan crowd:

"Hitler didn't finish his job! He didn't crush all damn Jews to the end."

Then came the witch hunt camouflaged first as a campaign to eradicate the so-called Cosmopolitans. It was all too obvious it was a mere euphemism for "Jews." The campaign reached its apogee in the outrageous claims of the "Doctors' Plot." The luminaries of medical science, now called "murderers in white robes," made their way into the Kremlin to poison the country's glorious leaders . . . Only the death of Stalin, "Uncle Joe," as they call him here, in America, stopped the public execution in Red Square of the purported perpetrators of high crime. It was rumored to be followed by the mass exile of all Jews to the steppes of Kazakhstan and the Siberian taiga . . .

But was there any repentance or an apology on behalf of the Soviet government after the death of Stalin? Not a peep, while in America, they addressed the post-WWII antisemitism. They made that film I was talking about, which won an Oscar for best picture that year. However, was there even a hint of this shameful page of Soviet history in Soviet cinema? Or was it at least addressed in the newspaper pages? Heavens no!

After being overwhelmed by the film, I shared my impressions with the owner of my apartment, a Jewish old man. He shook his head and told me that, back in the fifties, you still could see warning signs on the fences of some public pools, such as "NO DOGS AND JEWS ALLOWED."

And that doesn't even compare to what African Americans experienced for many years. On our shortwave radios, from time to time, we caught and admired American jazz. We worshiped its biggest stars, Louis Armstrong and Ella Fitzgerald. To my disbelief, I've learned, while Louis was growing up, there still existed separate drinking fountains and bathrooms for white and colored people. Even when Armstrong became famous and traveled a lot, he sometimes didn't perform in some hotels because he couldn't stay there overnight. These hotels were for whites only . . .

About Ella . . . Even a decade or so ago, while the Los Angeles Times voted her one of nine Women of the Year, she couldn't live in the white-only neighborhood of Beverly Hills, the city where she was being honored.

However, this is in the American past. Although, alas, they haven't eliminated racism in the country in its entirety, by and large, America is remorseful about racial segregation. When I see my compatriots who have no reason to express contempt for people of another race, I'm tempted to say, "Damn it! You ought to be ashamed of yourself!"

The only explanation I can offer is that decades on end of relentless and overwhelming dehumanization have crushed their ability to empathize. They've become people with chewed-up hearts.

It's not unique, I guess. The male serf in old Russia was a misogynist. He used to beat up his wife regularly. Oppressed at the whim of his master's and his peasant commune's will all his life, he consoled himself only with the fact that God didn't make him a woman, the only being he had power over.

So, I wouldn't be surprised, when they get their citizenship and gain their right to vote, our former compatriots will cast their votes for some rabid racist running for high office . . .

Alas, Boris, I'm aware of the fact that all this garbage in our souls won't erode anytime soon. And I think I know why. I have to admit that before, it wasn't clear why, in the Book of Exodus, Moses made our ancestors wander in the desert for forty years before taking them to the Promised Land. Can you imagine it! Forty damn years! Only recently I dig Moses's wisdom. Forty years is the time for two new generations . . . I'm not some biblical expert or scholar by any stretch of the imagination. But I interpret Moses's story metaphorically. Do you remember the opening line of Pushkin's poem, "The Prophet"? It goes like this: "Parched with spiritual thirst, I dragged myself along in the dreary desert . . ." To me, the biblical "desert" is also a place void of spirituality. We, Jews running from the country of the Red Pharaohs, didn't have these forty years before stepping into the Land of the Free. The biblical desert is still in our souls; most of us still wander in it. Forty years! It means only our grandchildren will grow up free from the slavish mentality.

And with that, as they say, Amen.

Yours, Ilya

30
THE DANGEROUS COLONEL

Yurik still had a hard time, all because of Lyubka. It took so much to get her out of dangerous Rome and move into quiet Ostia, but soon enough new trouble came knocking. Damn it! He moved to keep Lyubka from the gaze of suave foreigners, only to see a former compatriot hitting on her. Lyubka, his former and future wife, the love of his life—Lyubka, whose breathing alone was enough to intoxicate his consciousness—became the object of adoration for a slick devil of a man. His cheeks were oily, his lips soft and girlish, and his bald spots extended all the way back to the crown of his head. His name was Basil (Basilisk!) Pavlovich, and he was a tender devil, not an ordinary emigrant of the ongoing wave, but a bizarre one—a former colonel of the Soviet Ministry of Internal Affairs . . .

His actual rank was that of lieutenant colonel. Since the émigrés had a habit of overstating their past achievements, he introduced himself as a colonel. They treated him with suspicion. Everybody knew that since the end of the Great Patriotic War, state departments, the Interior Ministry especially, had become sensitive to the ethnic composition of their staff and hadn't employed Jews. They tried to get rid of them by pushing them into retirement. Perhaps this "colonel" worked there, but not as an investigator. He could have been an assistant manager or an accountant. What Soviet institution didn't have a Jewish bookkeeper?

But that was also doubtful. The colonel insisted on his recent Interior Ministry past, and this caused all kind of speculation. At the post office in Ostia, where they discussed all the news, the émigrés first suggested he was a spy sent to the West with the stream of refugees. However, this theory was dismissed. If he was a spy, shouldn't he hide his past affiliation with the police? If he were a spy in his official records, he would be something like a store clerk, an accountant, or some other boring cover. A spy would be a quiet, unobtrusive person; he would walk around in a rumpled, shabby suit with shiny cuffs and ask to borrow a *mille lire* or two till the next Joint allowance. But this guy—one look at him and all you see is a colonel, even though he might have been only some border patrol agent.

The man sauntered around in a double-breasted American suit made of checkered cloth, the kind traveling salesmen wear in Hollywood movies. Elegant like a Rolls-Royce. And the bastard sported gold cuff links.

"That's how they plan it," said one wise man. "They count on reverse logic. It's obvious a spy wouldn't make his way to the West in his service dress. Thus, you'd dismiss the suspicion he is a spy."

"Well, this is how it goes," the wise guy said, waving his hands for emphasis. "He doesn't look like a spy, but in reality, he's a super spy!"

The colonel met Lyubka while looking for someone to help sell things. According to the rumors, using his former rank, he had taken nine suitcases out of the country, filled with bright Palekh lacquer boxes. He wasn't a fool, but to sell that many goods to the local Italians would take time. Because time was running out, he didn't mind having intermediaries. Lyubka could make friends with people regardless of their gender or age.

As soon as he met her, the colonel shifted from one foot to the other, sat down and got up. He offered to take her mushroom picking just outside Rome so they could talk business.

Despite his solid work experience in an agency that demands responsibility, the colonel couldn't think straight near a curvy woman from Odessa. The fact that mushrooms were growing near Rome as if it were a deep Russian province, like Ryazan or Kostroma, surprised Lyubka. She guessed what mushroom picking the colonel had in mind . . .

It baffled her even more that the colonel expressed his desire to collect mushrooms with a woman he'd just met, although he wasn't single. He headed for the West not only with his wife, a middle-aged Muscovite who walked around Ostia in bell-bottoms and a cigarette in a long cigarette holder, but with his mistress. That was what the post office crowd thought of the twenty-year-old strawberry blonde whom the colonel introduced as his niece. Watching him strolling along the promenade, with both women under his arms, the emigrant guardians of morality in Ostia noticed the colonel pressed the "niece" much closer to himself than he did his wife.

"As if it's not enough he's a spy," some people would say at the post office, "instead of having his hands free for his spying business, he drags along both his wife and his lover!"

"Well," the others said. "The man wanted to dismiss any suspicions. The broads are his cover. Would a spy cross the border with his ball and chains?"

"I don't understand," Lyubka said to Boris in the kitchen, making wide eyes. "He invites me to go out, meanwhile he already has not one, but two women at his disposal!"

Lyubka put off the mushroom foray any way she could. While the colonel was a groomed man and had money, Lyubka wasn't a dissolute woman; she was still faithful to her Arkady. In the prospective relations with the colonel, she was tormented not by passion, but by the opportunity to make a buck.

When Yurik learned about the colonel's attempts to get close to the treasure of his life, his heart sank. But soon, the situation resolved itself. The colonel received entry visas to America and had to leave, together with all his baggage—his unsold Palekh lacquer boxes, his wife, and his mistress.

One would think Yurik could breathe again, but in reality, the whole colonel episode proved that Lyubka would always torment him. His dreams were troubled and strange, and some of them were plain terrifying.

Once Yurik dreamed he was sleeping next to Lyubka on a bed as broad as Luzanovka Beach, one of Odessa's biggest. As always, he's tormented by his desire to embrace her, which she would never allow. And then some man shows up next to their bed. He's naked, with a large, turgid belly inflated like a soccer ball. The man is bald, tanned, and his peeling nose sprouts gray hair. A businessman, maybe the chairman of an underground cooperative that produces knitwear, one of those filthy rich dudes. And this potbellied man, if not an ace, at least a king of unknown suit, lifts the blanket on the other side of Lyubka, and prepares to slip in next to her.

Horror seizes Yurik, and he yells at the top of his lungs, "What do you think you're doing, idiot?" Trying to speak with the Moscow accent to pass for an intellectual, the fat man explains that he has the right to lie next to Lyubka because he's just married her. He suggests Yurik is the one who must get out of the bed. From now on, he explains, he would prefer not to have any hobos, schmendricks, getting comfortable next to his lawful wife. It doesn't matter if they are former husbands, relatives of her mother, or strangers with suspicious documents who have nowhere else to sleep.

{191}

"What nonsense!" Yurik exclaims, turning to Lyubka and asking her with his eyes if this is true. She responds with a silence that means, "Yes, it is true, he has the right to lie down next to me." *I'm dreaming*, Yurik realizes and tries to wake up. And he wakes up. But the potbelly doesn't disappear. The scoundrel is still there, pulling the edge of the blanket toward himself and yawning as if to say it's time to stop talking, he wants to rest.

"Damn it!" Yurik screams. "What about me? What about Faina, our daughter!"

In response, Lyubka says: "I don't care. I'm tired of living on a cot. I want three rooms. I want a convertible. I don't want to wait any longer. I want to live."

Yurik tries to wake up again, and he does, but again, nothing changes. The potbelly's still creeping into the bed.

Only before daybreak does Yurik open his eyes. His heart's heavy, pounding in his chest and in the back of his throat. In a cold sweat, with great relief, he sees Lyubka sleeping on the cot. She is there alone. Her plump hand flows down to the marble floor of their rented room, and part of her breast, seen from the side of her nightdress, is unbearably tender in the pale light of the dawn.

31
DEAR LIDIA, DEAR OSTIA

Boris finished reading Ilya's letter. He needed to absorb and think over many things in it. It would take not one day, perhaps not even one year of his future American life to do it. He agreed with Ilya on one thing: he still has to discover his inner self when living a different life, under different circumstances and a different moral climate.

He wandered along the beach, inhaling the salty seaside air. It smelled just like the Odessa beaches—the algae that had been cast away on the sand and heated by the sun emitted the odor of iodine.

Then he went into town and wandered at random, from street to street, sometimes peeping into the courtyards. Like in Odessa of his youth, living in the Italian village was ordinary. It was full of the usual everyday worries, which is the life people have in all corners of the world. No matter how interesting Rome was, he only wanted to spend his time waiting for an American entry visa here in Ostia.

Finding a room was far from easy here. The skills one gained in Soviet communal flats came in handy. The expensive apartments, which young couples from Northern Italy rented for the summer, now housed extended emigrant families, complete with grandmas and grandpas. There were not too many vacancies. Math professors were forced to live side-by-side with former managers of produce warehouses, and dentists shared rooms with tinsmiths from southern Russian farmers' markets.

Conflicts, however, arose not on cultural grounds, but around simple, everyday matters. Here, the unspoken cliquishness of Soviet society made itself known. A former professor became offended if he wound up in a smaller room than the former lathe operator's. Squabbles flared up due to other inequalities in real estate, whether it was the amount of sun per square foot a room received or how beautiful its view, or the level of noise from the street.

Two weeks later, with the help of a broker, Boris found a room on the second floor of a building on Vasco da Gama Street. The spacious apartment also accomodated two émigré families. Boris found himself in the middle of all the twists and turns in their lives—lives full of uncertainty and anxiety, the lives of all Soviet refugees.

In the room to the left of Boris lived Dr. Bromberg's family, which included his wife and their five-year-old son. Anxiety consumed the doctor; he had no idea what America had in store for him.

In this sense, he wasn't alone. The fear of the unknown, that ancient human fear, affected many emigrants. Each step in the unfamiliar world in which they found themselves caused tension. In Ostia, it had reached its peak. The final leg of the emigration process approached. To get a U.S. visa, they had to undergo a medical examination. Entry into the United States was banned for individuals with tuberculosis, sexually transmitted diseases, and mental health problems. Although these conditions were rare, many refugees still worried. What if the medical examination revealed they suffer from one of these ailments unbeknownst to them? Then what? They couldn't go back: the Soviet government had stripped their citizenship.

Because of the uncertain situation, many people developed hypochondria. Some young fellow, whom Boris met standing in line for his allowance at the Joint, interrupted their conversation and asked, pointing at his neck: "Don't you think it's swollen on this side?"

There were also those who extended their "Roman Holiday." They changed their papers, asking to be sent not to the States but to Canada, Australia, or New Zealand—to any other country that accepted Soviet Jews. Processing paperwork for these places took much longer than it did for America.

Dr. Bromberg struggled with a moral problem. He heard a rumor that, upon arrival in America, you must prove your Jewishness to the community that agreed to accept you. According to his Soviet internal passport, the doctor was a Jew. But he worried it wouldn't be enough proof for an American Jewish community. He was uncircumsized, that is, he hadn't been part of the sacred act that symbolized the sanctified, millennia-old, covenant with the Almighty. He was born to parents who believed the Soviet government had given freedom and equality to the Jewish people. They deemed religious rituals, including circumcision, antiquated; they never had the procedure done to him. Dr. Bromberg also considered religious circumcision an act of personal violence and was against it. But how would the Jewish community in America take it? Would they feel he'd cheated them; would they refuse to accept him? His young son, Yasha, had been circumcised in a Moscow hospital not for a religious reason, but for a medical reason—to reduce the risk of infection. Now this fact came in handy. But what about Dr. Bromberg's own private part?

He knew it was unlikely they would make him unzip his fly before the community would assist him and his family. But still, it meant he would violate the trust of those who would shelter him. He thought of correcting the problem by undergoing the procedure, which was easier said than done. Even if he procured a scalpel, it would hardly be proper to ask anyone to assist him. He could ask his wife to do it, but she was clumsy.

A family of Odessan Jews, the Bumshteins, occupied the room to the right of Boris. There was Lyubka, a vivacious and plump brunette, and her husband with the boyish name Yurik. Though he was a young man, Boris knew there was hardly a couple in the world that, from time to time, didn't have a strain in their relationship. Emigration proved to be a severe test of endurance for every family that went through it. The fact that the same Russian word, "brak," means both a "marriage" and a "defect" often amused Boris. Perhaps these things were not always that different.

Boris was dumbfounded that emigrant families in Rome were breaking up, bursting around him like soap bubbles. Soon, the reason for it became clear. A reflex developed during their struggle with the Soviet system kicked in. The motto of that reflex was simple; it was advice on how to survive under any circumstances, "If they beat you, run; if they give you something, take it." Take as much as possible. Some couples figured out that, if the head of the family or a single person gets a hundred mille lire and each dependent receives thirty-five, the moment you separate, you will get three times the allowance. The fight between temptation and morality was short, like a fight between a heavyweight and featherweight boxer.

Besides émigré families, there were also young, unmarried women waiting in Rome for their American visas. They dreamed of meeting their soul mates on American soil. But they were full of anxiety. What was waiting for them in America? They knew what Russian men were all about.

Wandering the Roman streets, they could see for themselves what Italian men were like; they imagined them to be the way they appear in Fellini's movies. Some single Russian women had Italian flings, only a handful of them longer than one-night stands. But the question of what American men were like as marriage material remained an utter mystery. This is why letters from America about marriage were already being passed around among the Russian women in Ostia, causing oohs and aahs.

The movies they had seen as teenagers informed the impression many women had of American men and American life. These films were part of the Red Army plunder after defeating Germany. For several years after the war was over, these films were screened in Soviet cinemas. Only a handful of them qualified as the spoils of war. Most of them were not German, but American. To avoid paying royalties for screening them in Russia, the authorities ran them without advertising in various clubs for sea sailors, railroad workers, or army officers. There was no need to advertise these movies. People packed the screening halls of the clubs to capacity. Most of the films were adventure flicks or thrillers, such as *Tarzan*, *Treasure Island*, and *Stagecoach*, or cowboy musicals starring Jeanette MacDonald and Nelson Eddy. Enthralled by Jeanette's charm and beauty, after attending the screening of a MacDonald and Eddy flick, teenage boys sang parodic ditties:

> Oh Rosemary, oh Mary,
> Open your doors wider.
> Your eyes are sky blue,
> In them, a cowboy finds his happiness.

But there were also films about everyday American life; through them, it was possible to glimpse into the enigmatic world on the other side of the globe. The interiors of American homes were the most astonishing. As if the spaciousness of the ground floor wasn't enough to stupefy spectators—you could play soccer in there!—there were also stairs leading to the second floor, to the bedrooms. In contrast, *if* there was a Soviet apartment with a flight of stairs, they led up to the attic, where they stored a sack of potatoes to be consumed during a long winter or empty suitcases waiting for the family's dream vacation . . .

Early life experiences often make the most profound impression on people's psyche. Deanna Durbin, Hollywood star and singer, held many girls spellbound. In her musicals, American millionaires appeared from time to time. They resembled their portrayals on Soviet posters: they were grossly obese, like dirigible balloons pumped to capacity, and they smoked big cigars.

In contrast to the bloodthirsty scowls on those posters, the millionaires in Durbin flicks were childishly innocent and good-natured. They moved around in long limousines driven by chauffeurs in uniforms, complete with a cap with a cockade.

Money was not on the movie millionaires' minds. All they thought about was how they could help talented but poor young artists. Some singer or a jazz composer . . . at the very least, a piano player. Deanna, a young beauty, handled those movie millionaires by placing an innocent kiss on their round cheeks. Right after the kiss, the millionaires' faces blossomed with sheer happiness, and the men reached for their checkbooks . . .

A letter that created excitement at the Lido di Ostia post office was from a former compatriot who fell victim to distant childhood impressions. In her past Soviet life, this compatriot—let's call her Clara—was a freelance journalist. She emigrated alone. She was pushing thirty and was unmarried. She left the country determined to actualize her long-lived fantasy: to marry a millionaire in America.

She was good-looking, and back home she had had a few lovers, mostly fellow journalists. But the moment she mentioned marriage, all of them reacted in the same manner: they slapped their pockets searching for a cigarette. Unable to find one, they asked her to wait for their reply while they make a quick run to the tobacco shop on the corner. It always seemed that, overnight, the shop moved to the Far North, beyond the Polar Circle, to Chukotka, along with her lover. Whenever she posed the question, she never saw the man again.

She had arrived in America a year earlier, and she immediately put her knack for investigative journalism to use. Soon, she found what she had moved to the other side of the globe for. As she expected, the millionaire wasn't handsome but, though past his prime, was in good shape. He smoked cigars, but only during rare breaks in his busy schedule. He had a car, but, alas, he drove it himself, so there was no use for a uniformed chauffeur like in the Durbin movies. That was a pity. In her dreams, Clara had imagined herself at the height of a governor's ball, walking onto a balcony to catch fresh air and calling to her chauffeur: "Georgie, darling, come over around eleven to pick us up. I'm devilishly tired already."

But he met her most important requirement: the American she found not only was a millionaire (he owned a small factory of electronic calculators) but was also single and had no children. She wasn't some gold digger. She wanted marriage the way it should be, complete with children.

Clara wasn't a naive woman. She made some realistic revisions to her plan. She understood she wouldn't get what she wanted with an innocent kiss on a millionaire's cheek. Clara invested what money she could raise into her operation. She borrowed from whomever she could and saved up the small allowance given to new immigrants. She did her hair. She curled her eyelashes. She applied lipstick of the latest fashion hue—the color of clotted blood.

The millionaire didn't put up much resistance. The young woman intrigued him. She was from a country which, in the past, had frightened every American. He still remembered how, during air-raid drills, at the sound of the siren, he, a schoolboy, would dive under his desk. Has there ever been a love spell more potent than curiosity?

Soon, everything Clara had wanted became hers, thanks to her careful planning. She became pregnant, and her millionaire proposed when she showed. He married her, and soon after she gave birth to a baby boy.

The millionaire couldn't see enough of his son. Not because the boy was incredibly handsome or anything (although you think that way about your own child). He looked the way most infants do, not much hair on his head yet—he resembled both Khrushchev and Eisenhower . . .

The man never had enough time with his son. In contrast to the Deanna Durbin films, it wasn't a radiant good-natured smile that occupied the millionaire's face at all times, but an expression of deep concern about his factory. He spent all of his waking hours there. Now, because the ultra-precise drilling device broke, the conveyor belt stopped . . . Because his manager had a toothache, the millionaire needed to step in. Sometimes bills weren't paid on time. Something else had come up, too. Clara seldom saw her husband. He came home late at night, exhausted as if he had been unloading steamships at the Long Beach port. He wasn't the American spouse she had pictured: a benevolent rich man bent on finding someone he could help by opening his purse.

To take care of the baby, they hired a nanny. As for Clara, she behaved the way she believed a millionaire's wife should. All day long, she loitered around the house, bundling herself in her robe and from time to time reading the latest issue of *Vogue* in one corner of the house, *Cosmopolitan* in another.

One hardly beautiful morning a few months later, after finishing his breakfast, but before throwing himself behind the wheel of his Mustang to rush off to his factory, her millionaire husband stopped at the door, gave Clara a pop-eyed look as if he saw her for the first time, and asked:

"What's with you?"

"What do you mean?"

"Why do you bum around the house all the time?"

While she tried to figure out what she had done to upset her husband, he told her before running out of the house:

"Here's the thing, my dear. One of two things needs to take place . . . Either we let the nanny go, and you take care of the baby . . . Or find something to do for yourself. I can't stand loafers."

Then he rushed to his Mustang.

Clara couldn't believe her ears. She hadn't seen it coming. His words set with her for the whole day, and when her American husband came home late at night, just in case, though she felt it would hardly help, she gave way to tears.

It didn't work. It seemed like the Russian proverb "Moscow doesn't believe in tears" was a global idea—they weren't given much credence on the other side of the Atlantic either. Wouldn't you know it! Work! Why must she be employed when there is no need for it? Was she a horse that needs to always be working?!

She explained to her husband that her only trade was journalism and, with her substandard English, there's no way she could be a journalist in America. Her husband replied, "Go and learn something else."

So, she applied to a grad school in the Russian department at the local university. In a letter sent to her old friend, now in Ostia, she lamented that although her idleness ceased to be an eyesore for her millionaire husband, she solved her problem only temporarily. The prospects of employment after graduation were quite grim. Not too many Americans were eager to study Russian.

But family dramas occurred in the immigrant households as well. Because he spent so much time in the Joint's waiting room, Boris inadvertently learned about one such drama. The story, which caused anxiety in men and evoked a devious glint in the eyes of women, was culled from a letter sent to an émigré in Rome by her former college classmate living in the U.S. They passed the letter from woman to woman until it became public domain. The gist of the story was that Nellie, the addresee's college friend, moved to Nebraska a few years ago from the city of Rybinsk on the Volga River. A chemical engineer by training, Nellie moved there with her husband, who used to work as a director of the local TV station.

Soon Nellie found a job at the laboratory of a large company producing superphosphate. It turned out the American women hadn't achieved full equality yet; hardly any of them were involved in producing quality maize fertilizers. For the company's image, it was useful to have a woman on staff, especially such a good-looking one. They gave her a salary commensurate with her education. Back in the Soviet Union, she never dreamed of making such money. All she had earned was a miserly 140 rubles a month at the IT department of a research institute.

However, her husband was out of work in Nebraska. It was a terrible blow to his self-esteem. He always considered himself a great artist of the small screen, but now he had no prospects, besides becoming a product photographer for a kitchenware company, taking pictures of pots and pans. Where were his former glory, the bouquets of flowers from his adoring female fans, the reverence for the artist, for his torments and his brilliant discoveries?

Nellie ended up with another child—a big, whimsical, and sullen child. Her exciting work and the regard of men (often her laboratory coworkers) made her feel like a woman: beautiful, complete, and self-reliant. She blossomed like a flower and smelled like one too; she bought renowned perfumes she had never even heard of back in her home country, like Chanel No. 5 and Yves Saint Laurent's Opium, designed to disrupt men's breathing.

Nellie became prettier and more cheerful by the day, and her American colleague, a good-looking fifty-year-old man, began courting her carefully. As the story goes, he dropped by her house (a two-story one with a swimming pool!) after work. During his first visits, his interest in her confused and dazzled Nellie. The man came by to talk to Nellie about the unusual properties of superphosphate, so delightful their regular working hours were hardly enough to discuss them all. Her ex-TV director husband went to the back of the house and got into the pool. He would lie down on the big frog-shaped pool toy and drift on it, staring at the quite regular Nebraskan sky.

It's hardly surprising that Nellie's colleague became a friend of the family. One day, while making love to him, a strange sensation made her tremble. At first, she thought something was wrong with her nerves. She went to see a neurologist. The doctor examined her and reassured her that everything was fine. In fact, she said she could only envy the strength of her patient's orgasm.

"Orga . . . what?" Nellie asked.

The doctor described to her the simple function of a small female organ called the "clitoris," which she had never even heard of in the Soviet Union. Her marriage to the TV director was her second. In both marriages, she would lie in bed as was appropriate for a respectable woman. That is, motionless. In her youth, her mother had explained to her that she must endure sex because it was the only way to have a baby. She shared her own sad experience. One day, early in her marriage, during sex something made her move. Nellie's father made a scene, asking where had she learned that. When he was growing up, it was assumed a woman who felt pleasure in bed was a fallen angel and had no right to bear children. What would she teach her children!

Nellie's intimate life had always been boring. However, this didn't stop her from being friends with both husbands.

After her visit to the doctor where she discovered the source of her happiness, Nellie's emotional floodgates flung open. In the arms of the "friend of the family," she felt like shouting for joy but bit her pillow instead. At work, she beamed and fluttered from one glass flask to another, like a butterfly.

She fluttered and fluttered until her actions caught up with her. Her life transformed, but the results pleased her. Once, at a party she threw at her home to which she invited her American colleagues and their wives, the guests talked about dieting and the benefits of moderation in lifestyle. Nellie could bear it no more and, overwhelmed with the joy her American life had been bringing her, exclaimed:

"Moderation's needed in everything, except sex!"

Everyone fell silent. A teenager, who came along with his parents, couldn't hold back his laughter. They shushed him. They glanced at Nellie's husband, the ex-TV man. He blushed to the roots of his hair and went to the fridge for a Budweiser.

Soon the couple separated.

But, the most surprising thing about this story for the Russian emigrants in Rome was that Nellie didn't rush into marrying this man. She just upgraded him from "friend of the family" to "boyfriend." The new arrangement seemed to please them both.

The reason for the domestic troubles in that story was as transparent to Boris as chicken broth for diabetics. However, he couldn't figure out for a long time why the Bumshteins' household was ablaze with raging fire. It didn't abate for even a minute, as if it were the furnace of a locomotive racing full speed ahead.

But then everything made sense. One day, Boris came out to the communal kitchen to make himself coffee and porridge for Kisa. He found Lyubka and Yurik chasing each other around the kitchen table. They were doing it with such intensity it was hard to see who was running from whom. Boris wanted to stop his neighbors. The sight frightened Kisa, and she clung to Boris's shin. Her bulging eyes of different colors seemed to say, *You bipedal ones, you're something else!*

First, Yurik and Lyubka ran after each other with their teeth clenched. He could hear only their angry breathing. Then, without interrupting their running, they exchanged quick insults, sharp like knives. Soon, it became clear what produced the fateful spark that made Yurik explode.

Before Yurik and Lyubka grew accustomed to their new living space, their suitcases not yet unpacked, they both rushed to the flea market with their first joint allowance. On the small tables near the Ostia railway station square, there were piles of all kind of clothes. Beach caps, sunglasses, sandals, women's blouses, and men's shirts—all of them Italian, of course. Back in the Soviet Union, everything was expensive given everyone's small salaries, but here hardly anything cost more than a few *milles*. Despite their tight budget, any emigrant could afford to buy something from this abundance of goods. Life glistened with the bright colors of Italian swimsuits and T-shirts.

Yurik was upset when he learned Lyubka had bought two pairs of tights with the family budget and sent them to Russia, but he bit his tongue. The tights were intended for Lyubka's former flatmate in her Odessa communal apartment. The woman was an alcoholic nicknamed "There-You-Go." Every time she entered the kitchen, she was wrecked on the strongest alcohol she could get her hands on, and would scream the same phrase at Lyubka (which explains her nickname): "There you go! Again, I'm living with Jews." She would shake her head, miserable over this sad fact. When Lyubka's girlfriends found out about it, they reproached her for encouraging antisemitism. She laughed and said, "I feel sorry for her."

Although she spent the family's liras on her former alcoholic neighbor, Yurik didn't condemn his ex-wife for doing it. He knew Lyubka felt good about it. She often extended her kindness to people who didn't deserve it. Another of Lyubka's acts, which soon became public knowledge, infuriated Yurik. She sent a shirt to her lover back in Odessa. Yurik pounced on her for it.

"What gall you have! Sending shirts to that bastard!" he shouted. "Twelve years, you cheated on me!"

Lyubka sighed, gasped, and laughed, running away from him. Through laughter, she kept repeating: "Not twelve, thirteen!"

When Yurik saw there was a stranger in the kitchen, ashamed, he left, slamming the door behind him. Lyubka sighed with relief and said to Boris:

"Oh, thank God for stopping me in time. He's such a weakling! Why did I even run from him? I could kill him, or at least maim him, but then I'd be in trouble."

It turned out Yurik hadn't left the apartment but was catching his breath behind the door. Upon hearing Lyubka's taunts, he again came into the kitchen and ran after her, growling:

"I am a weakling? I'll show you, weakling!"

They ran around the table again. Picking up Kisa, Boris hastened to retreat to his room.

32
A MOTHER'S GIFT

Next day, having settled in Ostia, Boris went back to Rome by a commuter train. The weather was hardly favorable for an outing. It drizzled. The gray felt of the clouds upholstered the skies all over. However, Boris remembered Ilya's advice—to see as much of Italy as possible while he was here. Who knew how his American life would turn out, or how soon he would be able to visit the beauties of Rome again? . . .

On the train, across from him, sat a short, lean, and brawny man in his early forties. He slouched a bit, clasping his knee with both hands, lost in reflection. When for a moment he switched his position, a tattoo in the shape of an anchor flashed on his wrist. He was the same émigré Boris had seen in the corridors of the Joint.

The man's name was Grigory, but his surname was unusual—Aus. It didn't seem Jewish. Unlike other émigrés, who adjusted slowly to living in an unfamiliar place and foreign everyday life, Aus handled the Italian life with surprising ease. And his supply of Italian words was richer than the minimal vocabulary of other émigrés. They used a limited number of words and phrases needed for survival. To that end, they consulted the pocket phrase-book with the canary yellow cover supplied by the Joint. To ask for directions or to inquire about some item cost: *Quanta costa?* Often, the international language of gestures sufficed to figure it out.

It soon became clear that Aus was also a resident of Odessa, a ship mechanic who had traveled abroad for several years in his past. He used to visit Italy and other countries. Such a colorful background . . . For an ordinary Soviet person, a trip even to socialist Bulgaria was a rare luxury. And here, look at him! A wandering Jew at government expense . . . Many émigrés wanted to talk to him under some pretext. Was he a real person or some fancy pants who had invented such a romantic biography for himself?

In response to pestering inquiries, Aus had just shrugged and said there was nothing special about his biography. And in general, he wouldn't have seen any foreign land if the Russian people weren't so bent on getting plastered . . . Boris hadn't had a chance to find out what he had in mind. What did alcohol consumption by unknown Russian people have to do with it? How was a Soviet Jew able to cross many state borders in the pre-emigration time?

Now, seeing this man in the car of the commuter train, Boris sat next to him—luckily, because of bad weather, the carriage was half empty. Boris introduced himself and admitted he was curious to learn more about something Aus had said. Namely, what did the Russian love for drinking have to do with his career as an overseas sailor?

Aus looked out the carriage window. It still drizzled. He sighed and nodded, signaling he was ready to satisfy the inquisitiveness of the former Moscow journalist. It was a long story, but if the young man was so eager to find out . . . Aus spoke with little enthusiasm. It seemed he was telling his story not for the first time.

"My mother was Estonian," he said. "I have her last name. I believe some surnames point to a person's dominant character trait. This is the case with mine. In Estonian, *Aus* means 'honest.' As you know, in the country we've left, it also means "being out of one's mind," or, as they have it in Odessa, "one's marbles got scattered all over," *shariki za roliki zaekhali*. It's true: Who, in his right mind, would ever tell the truth and nothing but the truth to Soviet authorities?

"But, thank God, here it's only rain behind the window, not the Soviet power. I'll come clean. I'll tell you as it is." He lit a cigarette and took a deep draw on it. "I'll start with the fact that I didn't have a father . . . Of course, he existed: my mother wasn't the Virgin Mary."

Looking around and, not finding an ashtray, Aus shook the ashes of his cigarette into his own palm.

"I was born on the wrong side of the blanket, so to speak. An illegitimate child. In my birth certificate, instead of my father's name, there was a dash . . . And I don't remember my mother. I was a baby when, after the Red Army tanks rolled into Estonia, the NKVD, the secret police, arrested her and my grandmother and took them away. They exiled them to Siberia . . .

"I hope you don't ask what for. Otherwise, I would suspect you're a foreign spy who had been poorly educated about what the Bolsheviks did after they secured that infamous Molotov-Ribbentrop Non-Aggression Pact . . . Like the Nazis, when capturing a new territory, the Soviets went after Estonian intellectuals, no matter how modest their position in the country was. As far as I know, both my mother and my grandmother were schoolteachers. For the occupants, it was a practical matter. Any possible dissent complicates their rule. Once you remove a nation's brain, it's so much easier to handle the rest of the population . . .

"So, the NKVD stuck both my mother and grandmother with the notorious Article 58 of the Soviet Criminal Code—anti-Soviet propaganda and agitation. They wanted to put me in an orphanage, but my aunt, my mother's sister, won me back somehow. She raised me. She later married another Estonian man who lived in Odessa and moved there.

"Well, then . . . Neither my mother nor grandmother returned from Siberia. They perished there. Later on, when Khrushchev's rehabilitation campaign of people wrongly accused in Stalin's time began, I made sure they dismissed the charges against my mother. I received a sealed document that, posthumously, 'for lack of corpus delicti.' And so on. Well, when I rummaged through her papers, which she managed to pass on to my aunt before her arrest, I found her letters to my father, who was a Jew. One Grigory Zaltsman. It looks like my mother was in love with the man. She'd named me after him . . .

"So, I made sure they corrected my birth certificate. For me, then a young man, it was shameful having merely a dash where my father's name was supposed to be."

Aus grinned gloomily.

"By the time I had to renew my internal passport, they told me at the police station that, based on my updated birth certificate, I could choose what to put down under 'item five—ethnicity'—that of my mother, an Estonian, or that of my father, a Jew. I need not tell you, having such a choice, only a total nutcase would want to be identified as a Jew in his passport. It's like hanging yourself by your private parts.

"Of course, I told the passport clerk to write in 'Estonian,' and include my patronymic—Grigorievich. That's how I've been all my Soviet life, in the army and after it—an Estonian.

"After the army, I finished our Odessa Institute of Engineers of the Marine Sea Fleet. I wanted to get a job on some overseas trade ship. To be approved for job-related foreign travel, you need to have the state security clearance. My uncle, the brother of my stepmother's husband (should I say step-uncle?) was a big shot. He was in charge of one of the Black Sea Shipping Management's departments. So, I paid him a visit and asked him to take up my case. And he told me point blank, 'You'll go overseas only over my dead body!' He knew my mother had been persecuted as an 'enemy of the people,' but I reasoned with him that they had acquitted her. My profile was clean now. I even showed him the sealed government notification. And he turned his head away from the papers like a puppy from mothballs. 'A certificate, my foot!' he said. 'You don't understand a thing in our life. It doesn't matter much whether she's been acquitted or not.'

"I was flabbergasted. Didn't he trust the Soviet authorities, who would think nothing to clear her name, but still harbor suspicion? Was he afraid they'd dig into his documents and find out his distant relative was once considered an 'enemy of the people'? Or that, not even a relative, a lawful husband, but a lover of a sister of his sister-in-law was a Jew?

"'Only over my dead body!' the man told me. Well, he didn't know he had foretold his own destiny. In time, it turned out the way he pronounced it."

Aus shook his head in grief and looked out the window again. It continued to drizzle.

"Well, then . . . when he turned me down, I worked as a mechanical engineer in the project office the Steamship Line. I worked like a mule hunched over the drawing board for several years in a row, getting the meager salary of a young specialist. They shoved you one hundred and twenty rubles per month. It's enough to make you scream.

"Then a huge accident happened. A large Soviet cargo ship crashed when trying to moor at the port of Sydney. The captain forgot to remove the stabilizer near the keel which prevents the boat from rolling over during a big wave."

Aus showed with his hands how small wings were supposed to straighten out under the water.

"The stabilizer hit the mooring pile and crashed into the bilge sheathing. Water poured into the engine room, and soon the whole ship sank. A huge scandal ensued. They put the captain on trial, together with his assistant and the boatswain. Then they lifted the vessel from the sea bottom and put it in for repairs there, at the port of Sydney."

Aus sighed and continued somberly.

"Well, seven months down the road, when they raised the sunken cargo ship and repaired it, my uncle flew to Australia for the official vessel repair approval and acceptance. It went over with great pomp. The crew took part in the celebration. My uncle flew the next day to Moscow with his report to the Minister of the Maritime Fleet . . . Well, what my uncle didn't know was that, after he left, the ship's crew continued to celebrate their 'victory on the labor front.' They did it the Russian way. When they ran out of all their hard currency for buying alcohol, they switched to brake fluid. They got hold of it in a local car repair shop.

"Well, now my uncle reported to the minister about the glorious achievement of the ship's collective, which had restored one of the best Soviet cargo ships. But the minister was unimpressed. 'You tell me everything is wonderful,' he said, looking my uncle in the eye, 'Wow, I wasn't aware that, in our maritime fleet, we have our own, domestic Cicero. I can't hear enough of it . . . While in reality, it is far from it. Why did you keep this news from me?'

"And with these words, he slapped a telegram on his desk for my uncle to read. The telegram stated that, after filling themselves to the eyeballs with brake fluid, three crew members dropped dead right there and then, two others were close to joining them, and three more lost their sight and were taken to the local hospital.

"After reading the telegram, my uncle returned to his hotel, where he had a heart attack. He died a few days later."

Aus sighed, went silent for a while, then continued sullenly.

"They buried the man . . . Well, over time, things settled down, and I resumed my quest for an overseas job. I talked to my uncle's secretary, who had a new boss now. Perhaps in memory of my late uncle, she wanted to help me. Through an acquaintance of hers, another secretary, she placed a call to the First Secretary of the Regional Committee and explained everything. That my personal case is whistle clean because my mother's name was officially cleared. And so on. She told me, 'Now wait.'

"Man, I waited *nine long* months. They needed nine damned months to decide on my case. During this time, one could both conceive a baby and give birth to it . . . I had a friend who worked in the local KGB office. We grew up together as young boys. He was reporting on the progress of my case . . .

"At last, I received my clearance. I sailed as a mechanic. First, on a freighter. When I crossed the Bosporus Strait for the first time, I cried.

It took so many years for that to happen. I worked first on a few short lines—from two to four weeks. We sailed around the Mediterranean Sea region. Visited Greece . . . Italy . . . Egypt . . . Later on, they transferred me to one of the Soviet cruisers."

"So, how was Egypt?" Boris said. "Have you seen the pyramids of Cheops?"

"The pyramids?" Aus stared at Boris, his eyes wide as if he had asked him an idiotic question. "What are you talking about? Heavens no! What the hell pyramids are you talking about? They gave us just enough time to get to the local shops in Alexandria. For nineteen exchange rubles, I could buy a few T-shirts, folding umbrellas, and a package or two of women's underwear called a 'weekly set,' *nedel'ka*. My salary was enough to make a cat laugh, but now I brought stuff back to Odessa from my trips and sold it."

"Oh, yes, yes," Boris remembered. "The Odessa consignment shops . . ."

"Yes, there," Aus nodded sadly. "And on the flea market . . . Wherever I could . . ."

He waved his hand as if to say it goes without saying.

"Yes, I stood with my stuff on the market for hours. I felt humiliated. I wrapped myself in a scarf. Turned my head away when I saw my Odessa neighbors in the crowd."

And Aus showed Boris how he raised the collar of his coat, so they wouldn't recognize him.

"What else could I do! How else could I make a living? Every year the same thing over and over . . . It made me sick. I thought of defecting during the forthcoming trip to Istanbul. I even began learning how to pronounce *Kusurlu olmak istiyorum*, which means 'I want to defect' in Turkish."

Aus smiled faintly. "Thank God, soon after the opportunity to emigrate opened. Now I could try to leave the country legally."

"Well," Boris said, "aren't you an Estonian according to your Soviet passport? Nowadays, it isn't easy to emigrate from the USSR if you aren't Jewish."

"You're right," Aus said. "I'm not a Jew by Halakha, the Jewish law. That is, I'm not considered a Jew on my mother's side. But, by Soviet law, I'm one because of my father. Once I thought of emigration, I began to do my papers over again. I started, so to speak, to *Jewify myself*. My passport and other matters . . . Luckily, my birth certificate shows my father was Grigory Zaltsman."

And, for the first time, a warm smile lighted up Aus's face.

"At the end of the day," he said, "by stepping over prejudice, by following her heart, my mother had given me the best gift I've ever gotten: freedom."

"*Stazione Termini*," a man's voice came over the train intercom, "*Tutti escono.*"

33
IT DOESN'T COUNT HERE!

Used to living on the run as a journalist, Boris led a sedentary life now. Soon after he settled on the second floor of the building on Vasco da Gama Street in Ostia, populated by the Russian emigrants, he dreamt of his longtime friend, Alexei Lesnoy, who was a Soviet celebrity.

They had met on a train; Boris was returning from his trip to the Siberian city of Tyumen and Lesnoy from his tour in Alma-Ata, the capital of Kazakhstan. They befriended each other in the Russian "railway manner." Having a long trip ahead and plenty of time, you confide all the simple facts of your life to your travel companion. Afterward, they would often meet at the Central House of Arts. Lesnoy invited Boris to attend the concerts, which were closed to the general public. Alexei had been over six feet tall, handsome, and gray-haired, though hardly over fifty years old. He loved women, and they returned his affection. "Had been," because a year before Boris left the country, Lesnoy died. According to those familiar with the matter, he died of a heart attack during his romantic advances. He was in a train car going seventy, holding in his arms a charming actress, who giggled like a gopher. She had adored him from afar for a long time and, by chance, got on the same train.

That night, in Ostia, Boris dreamt he was coming out of the marbled lobby of his new dwelling, and, as soon as he stepped outside, he saw Alexei.

In that dream, arms outstretched, Alexei exclaimed, "Long time no see!" and rushed over to embrace him.

"Alyosha?" Boris replied, frozen in fear. "What are you doing in Ostia, aren't you dead? I saw you lying in a coffin at the Central House of the

Arts. Why! Your friends, the actors, came to say farewell to you. And your lover, that little actress you were making love to when you died, cried and cried. They could not tear her away from your coffin. You seemed just sleeping after a long day of work, handsome and spectacular, the makeup still on your face. As if, at any moment, you were ready to throw aside the funeral wreaths, shake yourself off, and declare the whole thing a joke, an April Fool's prank. You gallantly showed off that famous charm of yours. Alyosha, you're dead!"

Lesnoy grabbed Boris's ears, in a gesture of affection, and shook Boris's head.

"Oh, little Boris, dear! You don't understand a thing! It's *over there*." Nodding off somewhere to the side, he whispers emphatically, "over there, I died. *Here, it does not count!*"

He assumed his famous pose as master of ceremonies and smiled:

"Here we can still . . . oho-ho!" He glanced down the street. Young Italian women strolled there, enjoying their ice cream. "Here we can still show what we're capable of!"

The dream touched Boris. So much so that, in the morning, he stayed in bed, eyes closed, thinking, *Why, why did I wake up?*

This dream awoke him from the virtual coma he seemed to have been immersed in since he left the Soviet Union. It made him see his life afresh. Whether it was the blazing sun, deep in the enamel-blue skies, or the noise and smell of the sea wafting in through the window that reminded him of Odessa, or something else, Boris felt freed from his numbness. The whole wide world opened to him now, springing to life like cutouts in a children's pop-up book. Flat, two-dimensional images became voluminous, three-dimensional ones. Standing before him were breathtaking spectacles of Roman cathedrals and the Colosseum. The ancient capital's squares and fountains appeared in all their grandeur and beauty. His heart beat with joy at the thought of recovery. He felt ashamed of himself. "God, why was I sour? I am living next to one of the most glorious cities in the world. A year ago, I could only dream about it."

Along with this spiritual transformation came something else, something even more critical, which gave him a second wind. One day, the new impressions flooding into him from all sides compelled him to recover a barely used notebook from his suitcase and record everything that happened to him on his way to Rome.

Soon the islets of his records drifted together, forming little archipelagos. Rereading these passages strengthened Boris's spirit. A lost feeling of joy in life returned to him. He noticed beautiful Italian women on the streets, and sometimes caught their curious glances as well.

Although these notes lifted his spirits, they were notes only. As he became accustomed to life in Ostia, Boris found fate had provided him with tons of writing material—enough to weave a story, a novel, or even an epic. As in ancient times, all roads led to Rome. Here intersected all routes bound for America, Canada, Australia, New Zealand, and a whole slew of other countries. Many aspects of life he would not have encountered had he not chosen this path. The material fell into his lap. He already saw the characters as if he were among them, one more colorful than the next.

One day, the strange circumstances of the Bumshteins' emigration arrangement, which he had culled from their quarrels in the kitchen, started brewing in his imagination. He pictured Yurik's friend, Zhora Koshtinsky, a lad of the entrepreneurial breed which made Odessa famous. People of this kind didn't avoid the dangers of life. On the contrary, they sought them out, whistling joyfully. Eugene Pozniak, Lyubka's relative who struggled with the question of where to settle outside the Soviet border, wasn't much of a mystery to Boris either. Nor was the underground millionaire, the Baklava man, Yefim Butko, who subsidized the impoverished Jewish émigrés in Odessa.

It wasn't too hard to re-create all of this in detail. These people were from the city where Boris himself was born and raised, a city whose life, in all its exuberance, was always out in the open, whose inhabitants rarely hid anything from strangers. And not only that, but these images—saying farewell to his loved ones, the "meat-grinder" in Chop, the émigré troubles and scrapes in Vienna and Rome—burned in his memory.

The day came when he went to the supermarket, bought a thick notebook, and drafted a novel. The title came to him at once. It was the thought he and all of his fellow travelers had on their minds every single day. The title was an honest answer to the question they all had been asking themselves: Where would they end up after forever abandoning the land where they were born and raised? With his felt pen, he inscribed it on the cover of the notebook, *Farewell, Mama Odessa*.

His work on the novel went well. Boris took breaks only to walk with Kisa along the street near his building and to prepare their meals. He was so taken aback by the heat of his work he didn't even notice how he had filled the first notebook and had to run to the store to get another one.

Only once did he allow himself to stop and attend a showing at the movie theater; his curiosity was too high. On the way to the supermarket, he stumbled upon an advertisement for a new American film titled *Deep Throat*. On the yellow background of the poster, a full-bosomed girl in a bathing suit stretched her hands toward the sky. Had it been a Soviet motion picture, one could assume it was about the benefits of hygienic gymnastics; every day, they broadcast these lessons all over the country from Radio Moscow. The vigorous instruction began with "Put your feet shoulder-width apart," and ended with "Now you may begin your water procedures." (The last instruction had been vague. They couldn't tell you to take a shower because there were plenty of places in the vast country without running water.) However, the movie poster bore the sign: "For adults only." It wasn't clear whether the movie was from the category of Western films that, in the Soviet Union, children under sixteen were forbidden to see, or if it was something a little more potent.

Getting into the movie theater turned out to be not so easy; all tickets were sold out. At the last minute, though, the designer of the Soviet chicken incubators, whom Boris had met at the post office, came running into the theater, excited and sweaty. He sold Boris his own ticket and hurried off to the airport.

Boris found the movie disappointing. For a Hollywood movie, it was poorly made. The acting was crude, as if they used amateurs from some provincial town. The sound quality was equally awful, as if the actors spoke through a hollow barrel. A film school freshman could have cooked up such an unimpressive little film.

Most importantly though, the plot was so primitive that, about ten minutes into it, when everyone supposed to take part in the action got undressed, and there was nothing more to hide—the movie became boring. Boris could hardly wait for it to end. He expected a film on a playful topic to have at least a drop of wit and gaiety. In the movie, the girl from the poster visits a doctor with complaints about her inferior love life, and he discovers the reason for her sexual frustrations. He says that, by some bizarre whim of nature, the most sensitive erogenous zone had been misplaced in her body. Instead of being on the bottom floor, where it should be, her clitoris was at the mezzanine, where ordinary people have tonsils. The tonsils are the same glands that, when you're sick with scarlet fever, hurt when you swallow, and your mom promises you as much ice cream as you want after they are removed. The doctor and other volunteers proved to the damsel the uniqueness of her physiology. And that was all there was to it.

Boris had made his way to his seat after the lights in the hall went down. Now that the film was over, he discovered that the theater was crammed with Soviet émigrés. Some came there with their entire families. The women were leaving the theater, their heads down, and their faces burning with shame. Some of a more aggressive nature spat out their indignation and gave their husbands scornful looks as if they were the ones responsible for the movie production. The men turned away from them, exchanging merry looks with other men. Here's what freedom means, and this isn't even all of it; it seems there is much more to come!

Dr. Blomberg and his wife were among the moviegoers. Boris ran into Mrs. Blomberg in their communal kitchen from time to time. She was a frail little woman, her face always lowered. The woman was forever angry and dissatisfied with life—not in the existential sense, but in its everyday manifestations. Everything irritated her: the Ostia sun, which, for a former Leningrad dweller such as herself, was too hot; the rare rain, which, when it came, drenched the linens she hung outside her window; and the hubbub of the neighboring emigrant children. Now the object of her anger was her husband, who felt the glare of her silent reproach. How dare he bring her to see such an obscenity!

The initial chords of her tantrum were restrained, muffled by the presence of the public, only a prelude to that grand concert that awaited the doctor at home. Her concert would make Wagner sound like a child tapping "Mary Had a Little Lamb" on an out-of-tune piano.

Realizing this, the doctor tried his best to save face in public. With the seriousness of a scientist, he cracked an apologetic smile. The film, he said, fell short of his professional interest. By specialty, he was an otolaryngologist which, in common parlance, means "a specialist of ear, nose, and throat diseases," and this movie was an instructional film that helped him sharpen his skills. Soviet medicine lagged behind the West. No matter how much you study the human body, it still holds many secrets and never ceases to surprise with new discoveries.

Finally, feeling he couldn't reread his writing anymore and needed a fresh perspective on his work, Boris pulled his Olympia typewriter from out of its case and retyped his novel anew.

However, no one he knew in Ostia would be a good test reader for his work. Everyone he knew either didn't care much about literature or had more important things to do than read rough drafts of someone else's novel. Boris phoned Rome to talk to his former schoolmate, Leonid Mak. However, Leonid posed the same problem Boris did—he was too close to the material. Besides, the concierge of the house where Leonid stayed picked up the phone and told Boris that Signore Mak departed for Israel last week.

Since Kisa would have to have some more vaccinations before entering America, Boris knew he'd stay in Italy for a while longer. He put this manuscript aside for some time. Eventually, he'd bring it to Ilya to read in America.

34
POOR WILLIE

Staying in Italy began weighing down upon the Soviet émigrés. The dramatic changes in their lives took a toll on their state of mind. They wanted to believe what lay ahead of them was their final hurdle. The anticipation revived their old anxieties. What should they expect? How would their lives change in the new land? With each day, the conversations at the post office resembled those of Soviet college graduates heading to their government-assigned workplaces.

"Where are they sending you?"

"To Cleveland. What do I know about Cleveland? Zilch. And you?"

"We're going to this, uh, Wisconsia . . ."

"Milwaukee? Yes, I've heard there's such a state."

"They told me the town where they have agreed to send me, but I forgot its name . . . It is somewhere between New York and San Francisco."

Lyubka arrived at the post office, out of breath from making the rounds of the local shops. She chimed in to the discussion of American geography, laughing out loud.

"Yesterday, at HIAS, at my social worker's office, I refused to fly to New York. Told them the only way I'll go is by train. They brought me a map of the world and poked their fingers into the Atlantic Ocean. But still, I told them no. I told them I'm a free person finally, and I'll only travel my way. They had a hard time explaining it was impossible. When they finally broke through, I couldn't stop laughing. I realized what happened. In high school, I always got A's in geography. That's because of that damn Semen Petrovich, a young teacher we had then. The bastard feasted his eyes upon my chest—I developed early and, no matter what crap I uttered, he always gave me an 'A.'"

Among the people who lounged in the corners of the postal lobby, Boris met his old peer from Odessa. He recognized him by his nose; it was so large, it was as if it was its own being. He had lived in a neighboring yard on their street. Boris couldn't remember his name; it was something like Buchbinder or Garfunkel . . . He only knew he became a geography teacher.

"Wow, long time no see!" Boris said, coming up to him.

"Oh, hey," the man replied in a guarded tone. He asked Boris the standard emigrant question with little interest, "Where are you going?"

"New York," Boris said.

"Well, I can tell you what you can expect there."

"What can I expect?" Boris said, tightening up. Really, what could he expect for himself in that mysterious place?

"You can expect fairly hot and humid summers. The best season is fall. September and October. Clear skies and warm weather—an Indian summer. The wintertime is not as bad as in Moscow, but I'd advise you not to sell your warm clothes. It won't be like Southern California winter. There you could do with just a light jacket year round."

"Where are *you* going?" Boris asked.

"To New Zealand."

"Why there?"

"The least number of Jews per square mile," he said. "Nine. That's only among those countries that accept Soviet refugees. According to UNESCO, the smallest number of Jews is in the Coral Islands. One and a half per square mile. But they don't take our émigrés over there," he sighed.

Trying to suppress a laugh, looking at the strong Jewish nose of his former classmate, Boris said: "Tell me, is there a place where there aren't any of us?"

"Maybe there is," said Buchbinder-Garfunkel. "But UNESCO doesn't know about it."

Boris laughed. He bitterly thought, it's no wonder Jews are disliked—they don't even like themselves.

"Gentlemen, former comrades," a voice addressed the crowd, "could any of you inform me what is worth bringing to America? For Italy, it was clear: the wooden Khokhloma souvenirs and Gzhel ceramics. What about America?"

"Who the hell knows!" someone said. "The Braslavsky family, our former neighbors, wrote to us from the States, 'Take everything you can.

When you arrive, you must buy everything with dollars, which you won't have for a while.' Believe it or not, we took their word for it. I shipped not only our bookshelves but also a hammer and nails to mount them to the wall. But my former coworkers who'd settled in Minneapolis write: 'Schlep nothing with you, other than your English.' It's easy for them to say 'bring your English.' You can't buy it from the deli at the big grocery store on Deribasovskaya Street, wrap it in foil, and bring it in your suitcase. How can you learn any language outside its natural habitat? Besides, they say American English differs from British English, which they had taught us in high school. They're as different as Russian and Belarusian."

"That's right, language!" exclaimed a plump brunette wearing a hooded raincoat, though it was a sunny day. The raincoat was all the outerwear she had packed in the frantic hurry of leaving the Soviet Union. "Language! Here's what my girlfriend writes from Boston: 'When I was on my way to this country, I knew in America, they speak English, but not to this extent!'"

"If you go to Brighton Beach," another voice tried to calm everybody down, "you can do well without English—at least in the beginning. My cousin wrote he stopped by a deli run by Russians in Brighton, and he overheard one customer, one of us, saying to the Russian salesgirl there, 'Na-slice-it *mne pliz pol-pounda* that *chiz* . . . is it all right I speak to you in English?' And, if an American customer walks into the store, that's not a problem. The salesgirl shouts to the manager, sitting in his office: 'Dodik, a foreigner's come in.' And Dodik comes out to her rescue."

"Yes, language is perhaps the most difficult part," somebody sighed nearby. "My dear friend, Olga Osipovna, writes to me from Phoenix, Arizona, 'Just think of it, little Sonia, I've been in America for eight years already, but they still haven't learned to speak Russian.'"

"Language is nothing," a solid male voice spoke up in the crowd. "It's a question of finding the time to learn it. Now, if only somebody could explain what all that commotion about Nixon was? Why were they mad at him? For something called Watergate, or something like that? They broadcasted on Voice of America that he allegedly had sent his men to some office to take some documents, and the door was locked. So, they had to break in. Big deal! Nixon was the president of the country. And, mind you, not of some banana republic, but of the United States of America. All the cards are in his hands! Or take, for instance, those Pentagon Papers that the *Washington Post* published. I know freedom of the press and all that! In our country, they would shoot those journalists without a trial for such a thing. And rightly so! Why undermine the defense of your own country? . . . Here's another question, maybe there is some smart aleck here who could explain something I still can't comprehend. Tell me, why did they give Kissinger the Nobel Peace Prize? For giving away South Vietnam to the North Vietnamese Communists? For that shameful act, you give an award to someone?"

"Wouldn't you know it!" said a middle-aged woman in an old-fashioned coat, fidgeting with her handkerchief in confusion and leafing through pages from an opened envelope. "My brother in America is depressed. He even had to see a therapist. In America," she shrugged. "as soon as they feel someone's mood goes south, they turn to a social worker or even a doctor. So, he writes his depression began the moment he stepped into his local supermarket. He lives not in some metropolitan area, like New York or Chicago, but in some smaller town. I can't even pronounce its name. Las Cru . . . Las Cruces, New Mexico. But, seeing the abundance of goods when he peeked into a local supermarket, right there and then he realized he has no future in America. That is," she produced a strained smile, "if you're still alive, there is a future for you by definition . . . But there's no way in the world he'll get back the social status he enjoyed in his native land.

"'Back in my days in Riga, I was a notable, appreciable man,' he writes here. 'And here, who the hell needs me? I wasn't an expert in splitting the atom; I was a managing director of the biggest grocery store in the city. But in Riga, the most prominent people—writers, artists, even nuclear scientists, came to my office. They'd say, their son or daughter has a wedding coming up. Where could they get caviar for the guests, be it black caviar or red? What about a cured fillet of sturgeon or any other scarce delicacy? They asked me to get it for them, no matter what it cost . . . they presented me with their books . . . they offered tickets for their sold-out performances . . . And here in America, once you have the dough, it's not a problem . . .'"

The woman glanced around, as if seeking any suggestion how she could console her brother.

"Language barriers . . . strange politics . . . loss of social status . . ." a middle-aged man with the grim, sallow face of a kidney patient said, chewing the tip of his cigarette, "I wish I had your worries . . . language is nothing! Just a means of communication. But what do you do if you're like me and you aren't all that disposed to your America? I'd go anywhere you wish me to go with no hesitation, but not to those soulless Yankees."

The crowd turned toward this strange fellow—he was using the language of Soviet newspapers. Seeing the emigrants had given him their attention, he confirmed:

"I understand it's a personal thing. But I have a special account to settle with those Yankees. I endured mental trauma dealing with them. So many years passed, but my wound still hasn't healed. Yes, yes, don't look at me like that. I repeat I'd go to any other place, with my eyes closed. To Australia, to New Zealand . . . even to Africa, to the Zambians. Even to the devil himself, the one with horns! I'm heading for these vaunted United States unwillingly. I'm going there because I have no choice. My daughter, along with her husband and my grandson, is moving there. That's why I have to bite the bullet. Yes, everyone wants to go to America, the Promised Land, so to speak. But I have a special account to settle with those Yankees. A long-term account that's still not settled."

The man frowned and paused, looking into the space in front of him, as if remembering something he's never forgotten. He sighed again.

"I understand that, thinking rationally, I may be wrong. But war turns all your values upside down. You exist at the point of death, and if you're lucky enough to survive, you'd never forget the lessons learned."

His journalistic instinct telling him he was about to hear an exciting story, Boris turned his body toward the speaker. Noticing this, the man came to life, realizing he could get what'd been bothering him for so long off his chest.

"During the war, I'd been a car driver. I drove all the way to Berlin from Makhachkala where I'd lived before the war broke out and where they drafted me to the army. Since I was a taxi driver, they put me behind the wheel right away. First, I drove our old truck GAZ-MM. I dragged myself along in that old truck for the first year and a half. Then, in the spring of 1943, under the Lend-Lease Act they gave our division Studebaker trucks and several Jeeps named Willys.

"So, they gave me one of those Willyses. I was lucky. As soon as I sat inside the car, the Willys took me in as its driver. It turned out to be a remarkable creature. In our combat conditions, it was a precious thing. It ran over our dirt roads without a single hiccup. It climbed any hill. You could say I became attached to my Willys with my whole being. Don't be surprised. Those who spent the whole wartime behind the wheel know that has happened more often than you think. We both survived the war; I came out my arms and legs still with me, and my Willys withstood all calamities as well.

"He was my talisman. They bombed us more than once. Occasionally, we took on artillery fire. One day, we were both under heavy machine-gun fire—yet, we both survived. They kept me at the headquarters of the Second Ukrainian Front. Throughout the war, I drove every kind of passenger you can imagine. Three colonels, two lieutenant colonels . . . Once, for about two weeks, I even drove an army general! It was war, after all. My passengers changed often. Some were transferred to another front, others were wounded or killed. Once, a shell exploded next to me. I wasn't wounded, thank God, but I was shell-shocked. To this day, I still hear noises sometimes, as if the needle reached the end of a record, and the gramophone hadn't turned off; it's still hissing and hissing . . . but my Willie, as I nicknamed my car, didn't even know a war was going on; he remained pristine, surviving whatever the Nazis could throw at him.

"Willie took his share of beatings. Once, a blast flipped us over, but we both survived. In fact, he landed on his wheels, as if nothing happened! I took great care of my Willie. You don't even care so much for your own son. For all those years of war, I became attached to him. Sometimes, we'd be driving into a liberated town, transporting my staff officer, and I would scan everything around me, looking for a damaged Willys. Once I'd find it, I'd request a five-minute break from my superior. And he already knew the reason for my request had nothing to do with answering nature's call. I asked for the few minutes I needed to strip the ruined Willys of everything I could use as a spare part. This way, if there was any issue or mechanical failure, I wouldn't have to wait too long to have my beloved Willie repaired.

"So, you know, riding through war-torn roads, I became attached to my Willie with my entire being. Once, some jerk from the commander's office put his eyes on my Willys and handed over my car to the higher-ups. I fell ill out of grief. I begged my boss, Lieutenant Colonel Ivan Andreev-ich Parkhomenko, to let me keep my car.

"Well, the Great Patriotic War ends, everyone is joyous, but I was upset. I had to part with my Willie. By the Lend-Lease stipulations, we were sup-posed to return the borrowed equipment we'd used. They essentially said, *You used our American equipment for a while, but now the war's over, so return it to its rightful owners.*

"Well, in appreciation for his service, I prepared my Willie for his return home. Believe me, you don't dress your son for his wedding day the way I did my Willie. As luck would have it, a few days before the Germans surrendered, some Hitler-Jugend boy fired at my car from a rooftop while

I was driving my general over the streets of Leipzig. The shrimp missed, thank God, but the bullet punctured the radiator. I prowled around the city to plug it until I came upon some auto repair shop. It was closed. The rolling shutters were pulled down and locked up, so I sprayed the lock with my sub-machine gun. The shutters rattled and curled up. I pulled the owner out of the shop basement. He thought I would shoot him. With my sub-machine gun, I waved him toward my Willie. It was like telling him I want to spit on him and his shop twenty times, but I needed him to seal the radiator. It's been leaking from under my Willie, and I was acting like he was my newborn baby.

"After they fixed it, as ordered, I drove to Hamburg where the Americans moored their aircraft carrier. It came to pick up whatever equipment from the Lend-Lease survived. The entire day before that, I'd cleaned my Willie. I made him shine. I cleaned the carburetor and all its little metal crannies with aviation gasoline. I got that gasoline through a technician of one of our airplane workshops. I filled up the tank to the brim, I changed both the oil and the oil filter. I filled the radiator with antifreeze, the best I could get. So, though it was a war veteran, the rest of my Willie was in the best shape, except for the right side of its body, which was a bit dented.

"And there it is, the carrier that will take my Willie is right in front of me. I drive up to the port, onto the pier next to their aircraft carrier. They mounted a wide ramp to the shore so that you could drive aboard, straight from the dock. At the entrance to the ramp, a tall, thin, red-haired Yankee greets me. The devil gives me such a wide smile; I could see all sixty-four of his teeth. I know a human being has only thirty-two of them if they didn't lose at least a couple of them during the war, which is not rare. But, believe me, this dude flashed all sixty-four of the teeth in his mouth. He pats me on the shoulder, as if to say, *Well done, Russia! Hitler's kaput* . . .

"I assumed he'd examine my Willie and thank me because, despite the war, I kept it in presentable shape. But, before he stuck his long legs inside the cabin, he didn't even glance at Willie. I'm standing nearby, in tears, saying farewell to him, my dear friend. Meanwhile, the redheaded Yankee drives my Willie up aboard and then up some wooden boards. He runs a hose into the gas tank. I get it, he wanted to drain the fuel for the journey. You never know. It's the Atlantic Ocean, not your washtub; there could be storms and other tribulations.

"Then, as I'm getting into our company's car," the narrator swallowed air, "I hear behind me: Bang! I turn around—and I don't understand what's happened. Just a minute ago, my Willie was standing on the platform, and he's no longer there, it was as if he evaporated. In his place was only a large metal pancake. That Yankee had put my car under a compactor, and—whop!

"I was later told the Americans didn't repair old cars like mine but used them for scrap. I can understand this logic. But I still can't forgive that blow to my psyche. Don't laugh," the man said, though no one laughed, "but it's still an open wound . . . and I repeat, I'd go anywhere, Canada, Australia—any country where they take our people, but not to this heartless America."

35
ARRIVEDERCI, ROMA

It came time for the Bumshteins to leave. Lyubka arranged a farewell party in her room. She was a sociable person, and people clung to her like burrs on a fur coat. Like all good-hearted people, she found pleasure in bringing joy to others. She went to the Rotondo Market near the Termini Railway Station in Rome and, with the proceeds from selling her Palekh lacquer boxes, bought the cheapest chicken parts—just thighs and wings. These inexpensive poultry parts became popular with the emigrants and gained the nickname "The Wings of the Soviets." Lyubka was a true culinary master, and even the chicken gizzards and other entrails turned out tasty. She also filled large basins (the kind her Odessan girlfriends used to bathe their children) with tiny fish from the same market. Pickled, the fish made for an excellent appetizer.

Wine in Italy was inexpensive. From her suitcases, Luybka retrieved a few bottles of Stolichnaya she kept for this occasion. She also bought several bottles of carbonated orangeade. The soft drink especially impressed the guests who quickly packed Luybka's small room. They gulped the drink down exclaiming, "Stupendous! No chemicals!"

Yurik inhabited the adjacent room, where Lyubka had exiled him after the scandal with the shirt she'd sent to Arkady. Dr. Bromberg's family had left before the end of their lease, and Lyubka made use of her charm to persuade the elderly Italian owner to let her husband stay there. She told him that, due to her husband's nervous condition, the doctors ordered him to be on bed rest until their upcoming departure to America. Since moving in, Yurik paced around his room like an unfed tiger in a cage. Could this be the end? Would he never get her back? Why couldn't he keep his cool? All this because of that damn shirt! Big deal, it was just a shirt, after all . . .

Hope and despair alternated in his heart as fast as cards in the hands of a casino dealer. After learning about Lyubka's "Farewell to Italy" party, Yurik cleaned up, made a trip to the supermarket for a bottle of wine, and appeared on the doorstep of Lyubka's room. Out of kindness, knowing he wouldn't make a scene with strangers present, Lyubka allowed him to join the other guests.

They came in flocks from all over Ostia, and some from Rome. Soon, the party was in full swing. "Ah, Odessa," they sang for the whole wide world to know it, "you're the pearl of the sea!"

> Ah, Odessa, you have known a lot of grief . . .
> Ah, Odessa, my favorite place on earth!
> May you flourish, Odessa, blossom and thrive! . . .

"We love singing and laughing like children, as the popular song about us Odessans goes," the partying crowd told each other. "C'mon, show us people who know how to have a better time than us! Look at us! We're cheerful and plump, like our children. Our pants and dresses are too tight for us. No matter how much we enlarge our armholes, they remain too tight, and all because we love the best in life—be it our Fontan tomatoes, still warm and smelling of the steppe sun, or Duchess pears, or jolly young fish called flounder, flat like a pancake. From the fishing line, all the way to the frying pan, they dance the twist and cha-cha-cha . . ."

"Don't worry, our stomachs don't get in our way. Our butts don't reach our heels, they can't stop us from dancing. Odessa's dancing! Dancing and singing. *You've known a lot of grief!* This line from the song about our city is right. But nobody will scare us. A-ah, Oh-oh-dessa-a-a-a! Tell me, what other city's name makes you gasp in delight! Whose name makes you explode with joy and lust for life! Ah, Kherson? Oh, Nikolaev? Is it even possible to have such feelings about Rostov-on-Don? Our city's name is no accident; the double 's' mimics the sound of one's foot sliding over the polished parquet floor of our Count Vorontsov Palace.

The vowels o(h!) and a(h!) express your surprise and your delight, while the "e" sings. Oh! Odessa. Ah! Odessa. We'll never forget our Mama Odessa, as we call her among ourselves, and wherever we go, we bring her with us. Just give us the warm sea and at least enough sun to make our eyes squint, and we'll be able to live again, playing, dancing, singing with our booming voices, and flooding the world with our jokes. We have so much talent we give it out left and right, and it does not deplete us. You, Moscow, you may have our chansonnier Lyonya Utyosov, but don't worry, we didn't give away the last of our talents. We bring them into the world all the time. So don't feel guilty, we have a bunch of such Lyonyas in every courtyard of ours, and none of us make a big deal out of it. There, in New York, they need a world-class violinist? Here, take our Yasha Heifetz! We can't let New York turn into a musical province. We don't mind, our famous music professor Stolarsky will produce another Yasha. Do you need some poets or writers? Don't be shy, we have more talent than we know what to do with. Don't you worry, we'll lend them to you . . .

"For you, dwellers of bleak St. Petersburg, who suffer from facial muscle paralysis, America is an alien country. We, in Odessa, have lived in it for a long time. From time immemorial, we have called our flea market "Americana," and there, you could buy everything labeled *Made in the USA*. We chewed the scented American gum while you could only eat your own tongues. If you ever came to one of our weddings, you won't be scared to enter an American supermarket. You won't plop to the ground, fainting at the sight of its abundance—you have seen it already! Ask any Odessan, and you'll find he has either an uncle in America or an aunt in Canada. If you dig deeper, we are all Americans ourselves. Who built a civilization in New York? We did! We were the ones who boarded the first trains to America, and now we're jumping onto the last ones:

> Ah, Odessa, we've always been dancing,
> Ah, Odessa, we have never lost heart,
> Ah, Odessa, my dear piece of land,
> Odessa, may you flourish! Flourish and blossom.

"Simon, move the chair. Otherwise, you might knock down that marble lady . . . we paid a *deposito* for it."

> Sima, Sima
> From Jerusalem,
> From Jerusalem,
> We're talking to you,
> Come closer, don't be shy,
> You aren't in an embassy,
> For God's sake . . .

Lyubka laughed along with everyone, singing with them:

There are cities everywhere
And every one of them is known for something.
But you won't find such a city anywhere,
Like my beautiful Odessa!

That night, not only on Vasco da Gama Street but also in the surrounding lanes, their Italian neighbors couldn't fall asleep. They couldn't believe the Russian refugees were capable of such carnival-like gaiety. They marveled at how such a cold country as Russia could produce such human boilers who are able to out-argue, out-yell, out-dance, and out-eat any Sicilian.

A day later, repacking their suitcases, the emigrants flocked to the airport. The stress of being on the road returned. What lies ahead? Clutching their bags and some packages with food for the road in their hands, they dragged along their children, who tried to dash for the vending machine with chewing gum. Holding on to each other like blind men in a Bruegel painting, the departing émigrés passed through a guillotine-like exit gate and climbed the ladder of the Alitalia plane.

Suddenly came the rasping, metallic crackle of the signal. A fit Italian customs officer separated a thirty-five-year-old dental technician from Moscow from the throng of émigrés and asked him to empty his pockets. To everyone's amazement, a small pistol appeared. The police took the dentist away.

After everyone had already been seated in the airplane, they were still processing what they had just seen (you don't meet a man with a gun in his pocket every day). The dentist's wife shook like a beaver, and she was explaining what her life in the Soviet Union was like, when her husband, sweaty-faced and donning a five o'clock shadow, appeared in the cabin. He sat down next to his wife and whispered loudly enough for everybody to hear:

"You know, it's a gas pistol. I got it back in Moscow for self-defense. You know you work all day long and some money for the day piles up. You leave late at night, and, if anyone tries to rob you, puff!—and for half an hour, the robber has a light fainting fit. When he comes to his senses, he doesn't remember a thing. It's a Western-made piece. I got it from a guy who could travel abroad for work."

"So, they took your gun?" Boris asked.

"No way," the dentist said. "They'll mail it to me. They put it in a parcel right in front of my eyes."

Unable to resist, he added:

"That's what I call freedom!"

When everybody settled down in the cabin, a young stewardess in a blue dress appeared in the aisle with a tray of drinks. She smiled at Yurik, offering him lemon drops, and, for a second, he thought she was the same female stranger who had appeared at the door of his apartment in Odessa to tell him about a dramatic change in his life. The same young woman whose full name was *Promise*, and her domestic one *Maybee* . . .

Now, sitting in the plane next to Lyubka and Faina, Yurik perked up. His rival was on the other side of the planet, in the distant Soviet Union where it's difficult to escape. And it was he, Yurik—not Arkady—who was next to his beloved. And as long as he breathes, he won't give up. There is no woman who wouldn't appreciate loyalty. And he knows he would never betray her. Whatever you might say, for more than two months of their tormenting journey, he held on to her, and he had let no lusty man near her. Ahead of them was America, the country known for making one's dreams come true. The most important thing was to keep morale high.

Boris was tense. The last days before leaving for America had been hectic. It turned out he needed a cage for Kisa. He didn't have enough money, but, despite his wife's grumbling that he had a family to take care of, Dr. Bromberg lent Boris the money. During the time they spent together in Ostia, they had become friends. Although the doctor and his family were heading for Idaho, and Boris for New York, they agreed to keep in touch. And now, on the floor under Boris's seat, was Kisa in a white plastic box with a slatted window. How will she handle her first flight, such a long one, across the Atlantic?

On Boris's knees, there was an oilcloth folder with a rough draft of his novel. Glancing at it, he consoled himself with the thought that he wasn't on his way to America empty-handed. The plane would be in flight for many hours, and he would have time to go over the manuscript again. Before sending it to Ilya, he would retype it.

A day before going to the airport, Boris had visited the post office for the last time. There, they handed him another letter from Ilya. When he opened the envelope, he found Xerox copies of two newspaper clippings, one in Russian, one in English, along with a handwritten letter. The headline of the Russian clipping read: "NO HAPPINESS FOR ME IN AMERICA." *Oh?* Boris said to himself, *that's weird.* Ilya never expressed any regrets about leaving the Soviet Union. Intrigued, Boris read the letter:

Dear Boris, I'm overwhelmed by what has happened and want to share it with you. Hope it will cheer you up.

The other day I got a phone call from Si Frumkin.

"Do you subscribe to the *Los Angeles Times*?" he asked me.

I said: "Well, Si. The language of that paper is way too sophisticated for me. After all, I only know as much English as I did in high school."

"Still," he said, " buy yourself a copy tomorrow."

"Thank you, Si," I said. "I know you mean well, but I've told you my English is not at that level yet."

"Well," he says, "buy it anyway. Your essay is there. Look at the op-ed page."

What can I tell you, Boris! If somebody told me my writing would appear in one of the most prominent papers in the country, I'd feel that person was mocking me. I'd feel painfully aware of the fact that, by leaving Russia, I had committed spiritual suicide, once and for all leaving behind my dream of being a writer. Who needs a budding young Russian scribbler in the Anglo-Saxon world! How could I imagine they would publish me in such a prestigious paper, and so soon! You may not believe it, but it happened without me even submitting my work to the paper myself.

Call it a case of sheer luck or divine intervention, but that's how it happened. I finally felt solid ground under my feet. I sensed I had settled in my new country to some degree and thought of trying to write something about my new life. After a few false starts, I wrote a short personal essay about my first experience here in the U.S. Coming from Odessa, irony is in our DNA. My piece was a way to make fun of the misery of my past Soviet life, where happiness meant being able to survive.

I sent my essay to New York, to the only Russian-language paper in America, *The New Russian Word*. I hope you can get a job there! They published my piece. I was happy about it. At least, I wasn't washed out by my immigrant ordeals. I sent Si a clipping of my article from the paper to show him his efforts at keeping us Russian immigrants hopeful were not for naught.

What happened next, I couldn't foresee, even with a crystal ball. Si read it, picked up the phone, and called the op-ed editor of the *Times*. He knew him because they had published him on those same op-ed pages, drawing on the American public to intervene on behalf of us, Soviet Jews left behind the Iron Curtain. Si translated my essay to the editor as he read it aloud right there and then. Here's what came out of it:

RUSSIAN ÉMIGRÉ PURSUIT OF HAPPINESS

No matter what you say, there is no happiness for me in America, no joy. In the Soviet Union, I was so much happier; it's just I didn't know it.

There were days when I could barely open my eyes in the morning and there they would be, all those golden opportunities for happiness waiting to be plucked. I could, for example, jump out of bed and run, half-asleep, to the milk store. There, I would grab a couple of cartons still too firm to leak. (By ten in the morning, all that was left were the half-empty, leaky cartons. By noon, if someone asked for milk it was to make people laugh.)

But, just like that, I'd have my milk, and I'd be happy.

On my way home people running off to work would stop me and ask, "Hey man, where did you get the milk?"

I would chuckle and, remembering Hemingway, answer:

"Over there, across the river and into the trees."

They would hurry off, mumbling "rotten intellectual," but I didn't care. Jealous people can't help how they feel.

Such happiness.

Once home, I would toss the cartons to my wife, grab the shopping bag (in case I would come across some potatoes to buy) and run to catch my bus. Going to the milk store would have made me late, but even tardiness would present opportunities for happiness.

When the bus arrived at my stop, for example, the crowd would push me to get on, and all that shoving and bumping might propel me into an empty seat by the window. Sitting down, I would find my legs shaking with sheer joy. I could sit there reading my newspaper until I got to work.

At the office, there were never any problems. I worked as much as I wanted. Otherwise, I chilled out. Nobody cared, no one bothered us. We were free souls, like Robin Hood's Merry Men. At my office, we had underground bridge tournaments, unofficial chess contests—something was always happening. Once the girls started a sewing circle, and all learned how to knit and crochet.

True, we didn't make a hell of a lot of money, but even that was nice. It was like being back in college, borrowing from each other until payday, sharing a bottle with friends. You couldn't always get your deposit back on that bottle: the lines were too long. But even then, you got a chance for happiness. If your friends were already there with their bottles, you could give them a couple of your empties and catch them at the door to get your money back.

We felt such togetherness, such a brotherhood. And if there was a little sadness or trouble, what of it when all of us shared? It wasn't trouble, just a tiny gray cloud in a vast blue sky.

Here in America where can I find such happiness? I go to the supermarket in the morning, at noon, or at midnight, but it's always the same. There is still plenty, and everybody takes as much as they want. Those places have more milk cartons than a dog has fleas.

They have started a new thing: they stamp a date on each carton, and if it goes sour before then, you can return it and get your money back. But you know, the bastards won't spoil. I'm getting sour myself sitting around waiting for one to go sour.

I've taken a bus only twice in the last six months—just because the carburetor on my car was being adjusted. As for my job, they want me to work. No fun, no conversation, no little favors from the customers—just work.

No wonder Thomas Jefferson wrote about the "pursuit of happiness." In America, what is there to be happy about?

They published it last Saturday. Come Monday, the owner of the small electronic company where I work, an agile and good-natured man of about my age, came up to my desk and asked:

"Is it true, Ilya, it is *your* piece appeared in the *Times* the other day?"

I nodded, not understanding why he was so inquisitive.

"Well, well." He patted me on the shoulder. "Why haven't you told us you're a celebrity?" he said, laughing in pleasure.

At lunchtime, my coworkers lined up at the Xerox machine to make copies of my piece from the paper, then brought them to my desk, asking for an autograph.

I was overwhelmed. I couldn't fathom why the Americans were making such a big deal out of it. You know I'd published some pieces in the past in our Odessan the *Black Sea Commune*. Some friends congratulated me, my mother showed it to our neighbors, and that's about it. And here they treated me like I'm some Hollywood star; like Fred Astaire and Ginger Rogers combined.

Seeing I was having issues accepting my sudden fame, one employee, George, calmed me down, telling me I shouldn't take it so seriously.

"Well, Ilya," he said, "get used to it. We Americans love celebrities. But don't you worry. Trust me, in a week they all will forget about you. Unless you publish something again."

A few days later, a letter was forwarded to my home address from the paper. A professor of philosophy at Loyola Marymount University informed me that he discussed my piece in his class and the opinions of his students were split. Half of them felt I was miserable in America and another half believed I'm happy here. He wanted to know where I stand on this issue.

What can I tell you, Boris! I love this country.

Hugs, Ilya

Ilya's letter cheered Boris. He was happy for his friend. Of course, it was a matter of luck that Ilya's essay appeared in a big American paper. Interacting with other expats, Boris heard stories about new arrivals confirming that yes, it was difficult to get a job in America, but good things happened to them eventually. Boris figured that, although you need some luck to succeed in America, it looks like it is a country where, if you don't give up, luck will find you.

The plane pulled away from the terminal and took off. The airport buildings flitted by Boris's window faster and faster. His heart ached. He was still young, and he still had his whole life ahead of him. Yet he would not have the things that had stirred his heart before. How would it all come together for him in another, utterly unknown world?

The plane gained altitude, and the Italian pasture beneath him grew into a big yellowish-green rectangle. A buzz from the large turbojets was still audible through the thick windows. Alitalia soared into the air with the latest batch of immigrants from the Soviet Union. This bundle of energy, this mass of elementary particles which have now escaped from the mightiest synchrophasotron in the world, will prove their worth.

The flight attendants carried trays of plastic cups with Seven-Up through the cabin. Up, huh? It sounds like that song from the movie screens of our childhood, "We go up higher and higher and higher!" Look where we are now! We have to go up, up, and only up!

Arrivederci, Roma! Hello, America! Here we come!